THE HIGHLANDERS TOUCH

D.K. COMBS

Printed in the United States of America.
ISBN-13: 978-1500885762
ISBN-10: 1500885762

ACKNOWLEDGMENTS

I just want to say a quick thank you to my mom, my husband, my son, and especially my handsome shepherd, Dusk (Bubba). Thank you to everyone who has been with me since the beginning, and thank you to everyone who I've picked up along the way! Also, thank you to Anna Crosswell from Cover Couture for doing such a great job with the cover!

Table of Contents

Chapter One

There were times when Saeran Sinclair felt the need to wring some throats.

Right now was one of them.

"Perhaps we should rethink this," she said, for the hundredth time that morn. Her frustration was barely veiled behind the mask of patience she was forcing herself to use with her sister.

"Nonsense," Blaine said, for once again, the hundredth time that morn. "We've been over this, Sister. 'Tis for the best. I am doing this to protect you. Can you not be grateful for that? Do you want us to be separated? Is that what you wish?"

Saeran pressed her lips together.

"You know that is not my wish. However, I think there is a better way to go about this. What if someone finds out? I don't have the deepest voice in the Highlands." Blaine had a lower tone of voice than she did, but Saeran wasn't going to add that to the list of reasons why this was a bad idea—she had enough points to make!

"Many lads have squeaky voices. You're my younger brother, Sae, not older. 'Tis not expected of you to look and sound like a brute."

"I have breasts," she said bluntly. Her sister didn't seem to understand this. She had breasts that were barely hidden with binding, and hair too thick and curly to be kept in the tight bun she had decided to make. "He will eventually take notice."

Blaine gave her a patronizing look. The need to wring her throat rose again. Her sister did not understand at all.

6

"If you play your part, and help me like you promised, it won't be a problem. He'll be under my thumb so firmly, that when we reveal who you really are, he won't think of sending you away. You can live with us, and life will be well. You'll see."

Then, just like that, she turned to the window of the carriage, forgetting about Saeran's life-altering problem. As if it felt Saeran's pain, the carriage tipped to the side. Blaine gasped, her head hitting the edge of the window.

Saeran hid her spiteful smirk by following her sister's example, looking out the window. The Highlands were beautiful this time of year. With rolling green hills, thick bursts of forests, and flowing rivers…it felt right—like home. It had been so long since Saeran had been to the Highlands.

When their parents, Lord and Lady Sinclair of Wilkshire, had been alive, they'd lived in the Lowlands. Blaine had flourished in court, opening like a flower to both the possible suitors and the gossip. It was never ending and had quickly turned into a pain for Saeran.

Still, in a way, she should be grateful for their time at court. They were the last peaceful moments they'd had as a family, and while it was the court's influence on Blaine that had gotten her into this situation, she couldn't make herself regret it.

If only they had been going to the Highlands for a more pleasant matter.

Saeran sighed.

"Don't be so woeful," Blaine snapped from across the small area. The forest green walls of the carriage only made it seem smaller. "You sound like a lady."

"I *am* a lady," Saeran muttered, crossing her arms over her chest.

"Yes, but you do not look like one, and you certainly should not act like one." She paused, her lip lifting in a sneer. "Saeran, fix your hair. It is starting to fall out of the bun." The only reason Saeran listened to Blaine was because she was older. Otherwise, she would have reached across the carriage and acted on her mental urge to strangle her sister. "We should have sheared it clean off. Then it wouldn't be a problem."

Saeran started to sigh again—then cut herself short. No reason to give her sister more to complain about.

She undid the pins holding the cap to her head and gathered the soft waves in a fist, reaching farther up to re-tie the bun. When her hair wasn't piled on top of her head, it was shoulder length—half of what it had been before this whole fiasco. Her throat was tight as she threaded her fingers through the short curls.

Her hair had been the single redeeming thing about her.

While her sister took every ounce of beauty from their mother, Saeran had been stuck with only one thing to enhance her soft features. Her hair. Once, it had been long, golden, and falling in loose ringlets that curled as naturally as the sun shone. Being cut had taken the wave out. Now she only had intense curls.

"Yes, we definitely should have sheared it off. When we get to Laird Shaw's territory, I will ask a maid for a pair of shears." Blaine reached over, patting Saeran on the hand comfortingly.

It didn't comfort her at all. In fact, it made her stomach drop. She'd definitely drawn the short end of the stick, but Blaine was the oldest...and the bravest. Only her sister would be courageous enough to take on The Lion of the Highlands—and as a prospective groom, no less.

"Did you hear me, Saeran?" Blaine snapped her fingers in Saeran's face, drawing her bitter attention. There was only so much nagging Saeran could take in a day, and she was reaching her limit.

Thank the Lord they were almost to The Lion's territory. In no time at all, she would be settled in a room, and hidden from sight. Mayhap then she could take a relaxing bath and unbind her breasts. Her breath was short and painful, and the relief she craved was much needed.

"Of course, sister," she murmured demurely, finishing her bun and pinning the cap back to her head. It took every bit of strength she had not to growl at Blaine. She'd like to see her with bound breasts.

Although, it probably would not have the same effect. Blaine's breasts were much smaller than Saeran's, blending into her sister's wider figure.

"Good. Now, I think we should smudge your face up a bit more with dirt. We will be there soon, and I fear that some of your womanly features are showing."

Of course they are, you ninny. I'm as much a lady as you are. I can't become a boy overnight, even if I do have the name of one. Saeran held back the retort, as much as she wanted to let it fly. Her sister had been nagging, pestering, and picking at her since the plan entered her head.

Saeran watched her sister notify their horseman of her wish to stop, and sighed.

"What?" Blaine asked sharply.

"Nothing. It's lovely out. I'll look forward to a chance to stretch my legs." She couldn't help the shortness in her voice.

Blaine's harsh expression softened. "You must know how sorry I am for all of this, but it is for the best. It must be horrid, being bound and trussed up like that. If any of the ladies at court saw you in those trews, the scandal would be horrendous!"

Tears welled in her sister's brown eyes, and some of the anger washed out of Saeran. She reached over, feeling terrible for her attitude. She knew her sister only meant to protect her.

"No one will find out," she promised, rubbing her sister's back. "Just as you said, we shall stay together, and you will marry The Lion." A tear rolled down her sister's face. "I shouldn't be so ungrateful. You must be terrified of what's to come."

Blaine's distraught face only made Saeran feel worse. "You know what they say about The Lion. We have both heard tales of him."

Saeran nodded.

The man was a brute. He was the fiercest warrior in all of the Highlands. It was said he had the strength of ten men in each arm, and one heave of his claymore could slice a man in two with ease. His land was reported to be filled with hate and distrust from everyone, and the people were only loyal out of fear. She heard that he killed his own sister *and* mother out of anger.

Fear for her sister came over her. Blaine had a rare confidence that The Lion would only break. The sacrifice she was making for Saeran made tears build in her own eyes. She did not want her sister to be married to such a barbarian. Regardless, orders from the king were orders, no matter that they were cousins to King James.

The thought was too daunting for her to dwell on, so she forced it from her mind.

Saeran put an arm around her sister's back. Blaine had the curvaceous figure that Saeran had never been graced with, though her sister had often told Saeran that her weight was perfectly fine, that she looked better with less meat on her bones. Saeran had a thin waist, with her arms and legs as frail as twigs. Basically, as Blaine had pointed out time and time again, she had no figure to distinguish her as anything but the boy she was claiming to be. She even had a boy's name, thanks to her father hoping for one.

Another reason Saeran was better suited for her role as the brother, despite the danger her sister was in.

9

"Aye," Saeran murmured, patting her sister's head awkwardly. She'd never been one for affection, giving or receiving. Unlike Blaine, she hadn't flourished under the influence of the court, and had rarely partaken in any of the events that would make her socially adequate. Their mother had been the only one with the tenacity to show her the error of her ways. Her father, Lord Sinclair of Wilkshire, had been busy recounting battle tales with his friends.

Blaine looked at her sharply. "'Aye? Is that all you can say for what I'm sacrificing?" More tears welled in her eyes, and Saeran flinched. "I'm sacrificing my body for your freedom, and all you can say is 'aye' to me?"

"Blaine, I—"

The carriage jostled, throwing them both to the side.

Blaine's anguish vanished as quickly as it appeared, panic replacing it as she demanded, "What was that?"

"We may have run over a rock—"

The carriage jerked again, this time worse. There was a shout from outside, sounds of pounding hooves, and the clatter of swords being drawn.

"That wasn't a rock," Blaine whispered frightfully, clutching Saeran's arms.

"Aye."

Saeran pushed herself away from the seat as the carriage came to an abrupt stop.

"Again with the 'aye'," Blaine hissed. Well, at least she wasn't crying.

"Hush," Saeran said quietly, reaching under the seat. This was her father's carriage, and he had always been prepared for the worst. They had been accosted by ruffians once before, and though her father's men had taken care of it, that hadn't stopped her father from reaching for protection. Now, she called on those memories to grab the dirk that was strapped underneath the seat she'd been sitting on.

It was cold and heavy in her hands. Holding it made her want to vomit. She had never been a violent person—she much preferred her books and numbers. But she couldn't leave her sister to suffer a fate worse than death, though she was sure their demise would come shortly after the brutes were finished with them.

Blaine was a beauty. No man would hesitate at possessing her. A sour taste climbed her throat as she clutched the dirk tighter.

The false sense of security she felt with it in her hands was cut short. The second the door opened, all the courage she'd felt slid straight to her stomach, her heart joining the journey downward. The harsh spill of light from the door blocked her view of the enormous man.

There was a tense, horrible silence.

Blaine started to cry. Saeran backed farther into the carriage, out of reach from the barbarian that was reaching towards them. Her back hit her sister's drawn knees.

"If you back away, I will not harm you," she threatened weakly. Even with the danger, something told her to keep up her pretense as a boy. Her lowered tone might need some work, but it served in making the man pause.

Then he laughed.

"We mean no harm, lad. Donna fash yerrself. Step out, and we can carry out proper introductions, aye?"

Saeran swallowed thickly. His voice was rough but pleasant, thick with the Highlander brogue.

"How do we know you're not planning to carry out your attack the moment we move out of this carriage?" she demanded boldly. Blaine's fearful hand on her arm gave her strength she did not possess.

"They're Shaw warriors, come to escort you."

The face of the footman they had hired for the journey poked his head into the carriage window. There was not a bit of fear on his face, a sign that he was not being forced to vouch for them.

She relaxed her grip on the knife, but did not back down completely.

"I heard shouts," she said. Blaine rustled behind her, and then her sister was pushing past Saeran in a flurry of rose perfume and skirts.

"Do not be ridiculous," Blaine chided, hands fluttering delicately in the air. She knew it was a sign for her to quiet down before her sister became angry. She had never been an actor, but she was going to pretend she was one until it was safe to reveal her true identity.

"These men are not a threat to us. Put the weapon down before they take offense." She gave the warrior standing in the door a blinding smile. He returned it with little vigor, but it was enough to convince Saeran to slide the dirk into the leather belt around her waist. There wasn't a sheath, but the cross-guard kept it from slipping.

Still, she kept her hand on the hilt, watching them.

11

If push came to shove, she'd probably cry, then attack. But at least she'd be doing something to defend them.

The warrior stepped away from the carriage. Blaine went after him, acting like a damsel in distress and holding onto both his arms as he lowered her to the ground. When the man set her down with ease, Blaine preened. At court, her weight had often made it hard for the softer courtly men to lift her during dances and horse rides.

As a 'lad' now, Saeran had to help herself out of the carriage. No gentlemen to take her hand, no footman to be concerned about her as she exited. She didn't miss it, per se, but stepping out on wobbly legs made her look like a ninny.

Saeran held onto the carriage as she stepped into the small clearing.

A silence fell over the group as she took in the large, looming men. Fear choked her. Even if these weren't enemies, one wrong move, and they could rip her to shreds.

Her *and* her sister.

From what Saeran could see, there were twenty men. All large. All terrifying. All glaring at her and her sister like they were pieces of meat their laird told them they couldn't eat. Their faces were dirty and harsh, just as cruel as their rugged bodies. Their plaids were threaded with yellow, orange, and green. They were Shaws, no doubt about it. Not only did they wear the colors, but they all looked as fearless and barbaric as they were rumored to be.

The one who had found them inside of the carriage frowned. Saeran tensed, grabbing for her sister's arm.

"The king said there were two lasses. No' just one."

Blaine held onto Saeran's hand tightly, just as terrified as she was.

"The king has too large a family to remember them all accurately," Saeran lied, forcing her voice to be deep. It hurt—and she felt utterly ridiculous. But the men seemed to buy it, so she pressed on. "There's only my sister and I."

"How old are ye', lad?"

Saeran grit her teeth at the word 'lad'.

"Two and twenty—"

"Oh, *my*," Blaine exclaimed, voice weak. Saeran slid her arm under her sister's back worriedly, supporting her even though she herself felt weak. "The strain of the events has made me… made me so tired. Saeran, tell them we must hurry, afore I faint dead away.

Please, dear brother."

Saeran thought Blaine was laying it on a little heavy, but it did the trick. The men heard her not-so-quiet whisper. Half of the warriors saddled their horses, the other half going to the carriage. The one that had found them came forward, leading two mares. The leader of the group, Saeran assumed.

"I had thought we would ride in the..." Blaine trailed off, as the man picked her up by the waist, slinging her onto the saddle.

"The ride is too rough for a carriage like that, lass. The men will take yer things. If ye' need assistance, ye' can ask yer brother or m'self."

Just as he said, men came out, each holding a trunk—most of which were Blaine's. Saeran had never been one for clothing and jewelry. Since she was posing as a male, she hadn't brought along any gowns. Her wardrobe consisted of trews, tunics, and a lone plaid that survived the fire that had killed her parents.

Aye, it was definitely a step down from the extravagance of Blaine's attire. Right now, she was dressed in a deep purple gown that accented the stark blackness of her hair. Though it was not proper at all, her hair had been left down and around her face for the journey.

Blaine seemed not to notice, though the other men did. Saeran had to bite her tongue against saying anything to the men as they stared at her sister. Their expressions were stony, cold, and unwelcoming. She had no way of knowing what they were thinking. Blaine was too busy examining the leader of the men.

"Are you The Lion?" her sister asked boldly. Saeran sucked in a breath, shocked. It was improper to ask such a question like that. Normally, a lady would require that the male initiate the introductions.

"Blaine," she hissed, taking the horse's lead from the man. She was so stunned by her sister's frankness, she forgot about the issue of mounting the horse. She had always preferred her books to other things, like learning how to mount and ride a horse. Now, she gravely wished she had taken an interest in horses. The one in front of her, a gorgeous bay, leaned its giant head towards her, and nudged her by the shoulder. She jerked away. Oh, yes. She should have *definitely* taken an interest.

This journey was going to be a pain.

"Quiet, Saeran. I've asked the barbarian a question, and I would very much like an answer."

13

In an instant, the air stilled.

All of the warriors froze.

Even the footman paled.

Saeran felt the world shift under her feet as Blaine's words echoed in the silent forest. She was too shocked to move, too horrified at what her sister had said to react. The horses around them hooved the ground nervously.

Saeran's blood went cold as the leader's lip lifted in a silent sneer.

She reached for the dirk at her hip, staring at the leader, knowing that she would die to protect her sister.

Chapter Two

"If I were 'The Lion'," the leader growled mockingly, "donna think I'd hesitate to cut yer throat for that."

Blaine visibly paled, but her haughty stance stayed the same. Saeran wanted to grab her sister by her throat and shove her face into a puddle of mud. How could her sister be so bold and offensive to men she knew wouldn't think twice about lopping off their heads?

"I—I apologize for my sister's conduct," Saeran said, forcing the words past trembling lips. "The ride has been long and tiresome. She is weary from travel."

The leader continued to stare down at Blaine, until finally, he gave Saeran a gruff look. Her shoulders dropped with the weight of her relief. No blood would be shed tonight. She knew from seeing the look in his eyes. He was offended, but there was also a charm to him that told her he wouldn't kill without being physically provoked.

"Ewen, take the lass ahead. We should reach the village by the morrow."

Saeran watched a burly, red-haired man, grab her sister's reins. Blaine was unusually quiet when he began leading her away, riding at a steady gallop.

"Is the lass always so discourteous?" the leader grunted, swinging himself onto the saddle.

The men stared down at her expectantly, and Saeran came to a realization that made her palms sweat. They were all on their horses. She was the only one who had yet to mount her beast.

"She is weary from travel," she repeated numbly, coming to yet

15

another horrifying realization.

She would have to ride with these men. All nineteen of these dauntingly large men. Not only that, but she was expected to act as one of them. Saeran stared at the mare. Her mouth dried. She would also have to mount the horse—with experience she didn't have.

Oh, if only her mother could see her now.

She would be appalled.

Lady Sinclair had never understood her daughter's fascination with books and numbers, preferring what Blaine did—court, fashion, and dances. To see her daughter going against the grain even more, by riding a horse, and dressed shamelessly in trews... The shock of it would have made her mother faint dead away.

Her father, however, would have been amused. The memory of her father's smile was the only thing that gave her the courage to go through with the most embarrassing situation she had ever been in.

Mounting the horse.

"Hurry up, lad. We have a ways to go. A storm's comin'," Brodrick said, giving her an odd look.

"Aye," she muttered absently, wringing her hands. Saeran shook herself. She couldn't be weak in front of them. With that thought in mind, she began her first attempt at mounting a horse. The men had grabbed...the men had grabbed their horses *here*...and put their foot *here*... As she tried to mimic the mounting process she'd seen, she somehow managed to do it completely wrong. Completely and *utterly* wrong.

Her fingers slipped from around the beast's mane, and she found herself falling to the ground. She landed on her butt with an *umph*. Several of the men snorted, and her face burned with humiliation.

She'd like to see their first try at this! She bet they had fared worse than her! They had probably been skinny lads with not a single bit of control over their bodies, whereas she was a woman, with grace and composure.

Grace and composure that was starting to crumble around her. She was a lad now. She had to act like one, sound like one, and be one. Swallowing down the tears and cursing her sister for this wretched idea of hers, Saeran pulled herself together, and tried again—only to land right on her butt.

Again.

"Och, yer having a time of it, aren't ye'?" A shadow came over her and she looked up, near tears. So much for her plan to be a lad. The leader finally ended her humiliation. With a quick move, he grabbed her by the back of her shirt and threw her onto the saddle. The mare moved uneasily as she tried to right herself. She rubbed her throat inconspicuously. She was grateful that he'd helped her, yet wincing at the way he'd done it. "Have ye' not ridden a horse before?"

Saeran didn't know a single boy her age who hadn't, so not a single excuse came to her mind. She gave him a shaky smile.

"I...ah, I have ailments. In my leg. It breaks—often. Makes a hassle out of...of mounting." *Worst excuse ever, Saeran. Well done.*

The look on his face told her he didn't believe a single word she said.

Saeran had never been a good liar. Fortunately, she pushed it aside, and they began to ride. Ah, gods, this was uncomfortable. Not even two steps in, and her bum was starting to ache. How did these men do it? She cast them all a covert look. And without trews, no less! Their bare legs were rubbing against the girths of the horses. She could only imagine the itching.

"I'm the laird's first man. My name is Brodrick. The king sent for the laird a few days ago, so we came to retrieve ye'." The leader of the group broke her out of her miserable thoughts. "What do we call ye', lad?

"Saeran," she supplied shortly. The less she spoke, the better. There were nineteen men around her. One of them would catch onto the odd pitch in her voice, or the way she was awkwardly sitting on the saddle, or the way she was trying to rub her arms against the sides of her breasts to keep the binding in place.

Brodrick throwing her had loosened it, and she had a feeling these men weren't going to stop for anything. There was no way she would be able to fix the binding.

"I could have sworn the king said there were two sisters, no' a brother and a sister," he said. She called it what it was—an attempt to wheedle things out of her.

"Aye," she said, at a loss for words. She didn't want to say too much for fear of being caught.

"Ye' donna talk much, do ye'?" Brodrick grumbled. She shook her head, mentally sighing when the cap began to slip. Both her binding and the cap were working against her. Was this Fate's way of telling her that this was a rotten idea?

If it was, she was terribly late. These men all thought she was a

17

lad, and it would have to stay that way until Blaine secured her place as Lady Shaw. Hopefully then, their cousin King James would be content to let her stay there. She could avoid being sent away for marriage completely.

Brodrick whistled sharply, and the horse surged forward. Grasping wildly for the reins of the horse, she tried to pull the beast to a stop, but it would not be deterred. The others began galloping as well.

"What's happening?" she shouted, over the thundering hooves.

Brodrick chuckled, but the sound of it was lost in the fray. All she had was the twinkling in his eyes to go by. "Returning to Laird Shaw's keep, lad. Stay with us now—your sister is a ways ahead o' us."

If she thought her bum was numb before, there was nothing to describe the way it felt as she was forced to bump and flail on the beast. She knew several of the men were laughing at her, but she didn't have time to focus on them. Not only was she struggling to keep her cap atop her head, but her breasts were rebelling against the binding. It was slipping at a dangerously fast rate.

Thankfully, they caught up to her sister quickly. She was chattering away to the man as if he weren't a murderous Highlander. Her sister looked at them fleetingly as they arrived. Saeran bit her lip at the tinge of disappointment in her sister's eyes. It was almost as if Blaine didn't want to see her.

"Oh, Saeran!" she said, the look vanishing as if it had never been there. "'Tis so good to see you. Ewen and I were just discussing their crops and dining schedules. Did you know they do not have a cook?" she exclaimed. "'Tis quite ghastly!"

Ignoring all sense of decorum, Blaine reached out and patted the warrior on the arm. His face was less than pleased. "Do not worry, you poor soldiers. The Lion might not have taken care of his daring warriors, but I shall. Yes, you'll have a cook to feed you warm meals and maids to clean for you."

Several of the men grunted. She couldn't tell if they were happy with her ideas or not.

"Lass," Brodrick interrupted, glaring. "Ye' canna just barge in and undo everything the laird has set. We are fine with our work— now leave it at that."

Blaine gave Saeran a blinding smile.

She sighed.

Her sister was going to be killed the second The Lion returned home.

~

Saeran didn't know what she was getting herself into when she agreed to all of this. Not just pretending to be a lad, but by agreeing to the king's wishes that his two cousins earn the favor of his favorite chieftain.

The choice had been entirely up to the sisters, despite the rumors at court that he wanted to rid his court of Blaine. The king loved his cousins immensely, and would do anything to make up for the loss of their parents.

Though the fire had occurred years ago, he had kept them at court, giving them a life of leisure while he sent a governess to manage the Sinclair estate. Saeran had been so destroyed over their parents' deaths that she couldn't make herself return home, and Blaine...well, Blaine had mourned them in her own way, Saeran was sure.

A sennight ago, the king had drawn them aside, to his study, and solemnly sat them down.

"Your mother was a bright, beautiful woman," he had started. The grief in his eyes had touched Saeran. The king might be ruthless, but he was family. "She always wanted the best for her girls—and so do I."

"Of course, Your Majesty," Saeran had murmured, looking down at her hands. The deaths had hit her the hardest. It had destroyed her whole family.

"It is because of your mother and the close relations I had with her that I would like to make an offer to you two, my favorite cousins."

Tears had stung her eyes, but she'd wiped them away before they could fall. Blaine had sat tensely by her side, unusually quiet. Saeran had looked at them right as Blaine and King James shared a look. She had no idea what to make of it, so she wrote it off as nothing.

"Your Majesty, I do not think I could bare to return—"

"I am aware of this, Saeran. The lands will remain in the Sinclair name, and my people will take care of them. Peace will be kept, and anyone who tries to challenge your family's claims will be punished."

He had come around the large oak table slowly. The candles made the room dim and soothing, as if he knew this would be hard for them and wished to make it easier.

"I would love to keep the both of you in my court, but alas,

19

you're growing up to be mature women, and your mother would hate me if I did not let you live to your full potential. Because of that," he had said, pausing in front of them, "you will travel to the Highlands and stay with my most trusted warrior."

Saeran had gasped. Blaine had straightened in her seat.

"You are both lovely women," he had continued. "Because of that, I will not let age determine who will wed Kane Shaw. He is a tough man to like, I will not lie. But should one of you favor him, I will bless the marriage. The sister who does not marry will be betrothed to Lord Grayham."

Saeran's blood had run cold at the name. Lord Grayham was a reputable ogre. His first wife had taken her life, and the second had jumped off a cliff. The rumors surrounding his third wife's death were chilling.

"Your Majesty—"

He'd held up a hand. "I know your concerns, and they are but rumors. I would not subject my dearest cousins to such a fate."

"Who is this Kane Shaw?" Blaine finally spoke. It was a question that Saeran hadn't even thought to ask.

King James had smiled. "You've heard of The Lion, correct?"

"That...*barbarian*?" Saeran burst out, before she could stop herself. Who didn't know of The Lion? He tore his enemies to shreds. He entered every battle he could. He had murdered his own family in cold blood. There was not a single person who did not know of The Lion and his brutality.

The Lion was a fate worse than Lord Grayham.

"He has many spoils from his wars," Blaine insisted, as if she wanted to believe the words she spoke. "He is powerful."

King James nodded.

"He is all of that, and more. I would only send my cousins to a man I knew could provide for them. Grayham and Shaw are two of those men. Of course," he sighed, waving a lazy hand in front of them, "I will give you some time to digest this news. You have this next month to prepare—"

"I wish to go," Blaine burst out. "Right away."

"Blaine! That is quite impulsive of you," Saeran exclaimed admonishingly. She turned to their mighty cousin. "We need time to think on this. My sister is overwhelmed by your offer."

"Why, of course she is," he said proudly, chest puffing up. "It is a most gracious offer. I will allow you two some time to decide. But that is for later. Tonight, there is a ball." He brought them to their feet.

On their way out, Blaine had given her a glare so fierce, Saeran had actually taken a step away from her sister. "We are going to The Lion's territory, and that is that."

Then she had stormed off, leaving Saeran to stare after her in stony silence.

The whole ordeal had struck her as odd. It had almost been as if Blaine and the King had discussed this beforehand. Her sister hadn't been surprised in the least, and the look the two of them had shared... The more she thought about it, the more uneasy she became.

"I'm just being foolish," she whispered to herself, as their party continued their travel. Blaine would never do anything that wouldn't benefit the both of them. Later, when her sister had come to her with her proposal of turning Saeran into a boy, she'd been reluctant to agree.

Her sister had been quick to point out that Grayham was a known murderer. Saeran couldn't possibly marry him, nor could she marry The Lion.

"Grayham will not have a reason to keep you around," Blaine had told her sadly. "I overheard mother speaking with father once, that you were presumed barren, and—"

"How could they have known that?!" she had gasped. Her hand had flown to her mouth. "I don't believe you—they couldn't have known that, Blaine—"

Her sister had sat down beside her, tears welling in her soft brown eyes. Saeran had fallen against her sister's body, seeking comfort. "When you were a babe, you had the fever," Blaine said quietly, regretfully. "You almost lost your sight, but it came back. A priest prayed for you. Several days later, he came back with a message from God."

"Nay," Saeran had moaned, covering her face. She hadn't considered children an option until she was married, naturally, but the thought of never holding her own babe in her arms, of hearing her own child's laughter, tore at her heart.

"Yes," her sister had whispered, rubbing her back. "I'm so sorry, Saeran. I thought you had known—"

"I didn't," she'd cried. "Why wouldn't they have told me this? Is that why they never pushed suitors at me? Because they knew?"

"Yes," Blaine had murmured. "They were too ashamed of you to—"

"They were *ashamed* of me?" she had exclaimed, fresh tears welling in her eyes. "No, Blaine—Don't tell me that—"

"I only want to protect you. I love you, Saeran. This is why you cannot marry Grayham—He will kill you the second he finds out you're barren, and King James will not be swayed in his decision."

Saeran had grabbed her sister by the hands. Even though the pain had settled in her heart like a rock, she felt a glimmer of hope. "If we tell our cousin about my...my ailment, surely he will reconsider Grayham. Surely he will understand."

Blaine had smiled sadly. "James is but a man—he does not understand the shame a woman feels for being *barren*, my sister. He would not change his mind, not for you."

"Blaine," she had moaned, hope sliding out of her hands. "I don't want to be married to Grayham—I don't know what to do. If you're correct, and he kills me for being—being barren..." she'd whispered, horrified. "I... Blaine, whatever will I do?"

She'd broken down into sobs. Terrified, lonely sobs.

"You will listen to me, my love," Blaine had whispered, lifting Saeran's face up with a finger. "You'll listen to me and you will live—with The Lion and I."

As she stared into her sister's eyes, a thought occurred to her. "Blaine," she'd said slowly. "I've heard rumors at court that Grayham fancies you. Why could I not marry The Lion, while you took Grayham?" The idea took hold. "Then I would not have to hide who I am!" She smiled widely, clasping her sister's hands. "It's a wonderful idea! It's perfect—Oh, Blaine, it's absolutely *perfect.*"

Blaine had shaken her head. "The Lion is just as dangerous as Grayham, if not more. It does not matter which man you are married to, you will still be barren."

"Blaine..."

"No, sister." She'd held Saeran's distraught face between her hands. "All will be well. I have the perfect plan."

Saeran had sucked in a trembling breath, and nodded numbly. So, so numb. "Aye... The perfect plan..."

She hadn't seen the look of malicious intent in her sister's eyes when she collapsed into Blaine's arms. If she had, mayhap she would have been prepared...

Chapter Three

"You arrived much quicker than I expected!" King James said, coming forward to embrace Kane. He reluctantly returned it. Kane had never been one for affection, no matter how brotherly it was. A hug could quickly become a knife in the back.

Luckily, this was the king.

"Yer missive said to ride with haste, so I did."

"As reliable as ever," the king commented. "How have the MacLeods been? I haven't heard them complain about you in a while."

Kane grunted. "Donna care to answer that."

The MacLeods were always searching for compensation for something. Missing cattle, a runaway maid, stolen sheep. It was always the same problem with them, and it was always Kane having the blame foisted on him.

"I'm guessing that means I'll be hearing from them soon, then," the king sighed, though there was a hint of humor to it. "That is fine with me. I always take joy out of watching Connor MacLeod walk in here with the arrogance of a peacock, only to leave with lost hopes. How you haven't gone to war with them amazes me."

"I have too much on my hands to deal with those bastards."

"That is true." The king gave him an odd look, one that instantly set Kane on guard. "Whisky? Bread and cheese? Grapes?"

"Nay." Kane leaned his forearms on the back of the chair, facing the king. "What is it you called me here for? I rode for a fortnight to make it in time."

"Yes. Well." The king sat in his great purple chair. He looked at Kane, consideration lighting his eyes. "I do not feel the need to justify my decisions, as I am your king. However, I will tell you because of your years of loyalty and our friendship."

His stomach dropped. The king never tried to spring things on him—in fact, the only time the king called him aside to speak to him personally for matters of business was...never. If something needed to be done, a missive was sent, and the matter was taken care of.

Now, as Kane stood before King James, he wished he hadn't come with such haste. He wished he hadn't come at all, actually.

"What is it?"

"I have sent you two women. They should have arrived by now."

"Aye?" He knew very well that they had arrived. He'd told his men to escort them as soon as they were a night away from his estate. He hadn't thought anything of it when the king had sent a missive concerning it. Many a traveler stayed on Shaw territory. He was a known friend of the king, and trusted more than any laird in the Highlands. He might have an unsavory battle reputation, but that only added to his credibility with like-minded men. Not that Kane cared. As long as the visitors left him alone and didn't bother his people, he couldn't be bothered.

"They are very dear to me. Their parents passed some time ago, my aunt and uncle-in-law. Very kind, sweet, gentle-hearted people. I've sent their daughters to stay with you."

"Aye?"

The king sighed. "I am relying on your judgement to make the right decision in this." *In what?* "My cousins are very kind-hearted women. They are not ones for games. Although one does cater to her sister's every need. I feel that she needs…." He paused. "A reprieve from her sister."

"Aye?"

The more King James talked, the more Kane felt like a lead weight was pressing on his shoulders.

"It is time you marry."

The lead weight could not have gotten heavier.

"Your Majesty—"

"I will take no ifs, ands, or buts on this matter. You will, of course, have time to become acquainted with both of my cousins."

"I canna marry right now, Your Majesty. The MacIntires are

24

ready for war, and my men and I will be gone for months. It's—"

"You can go to war after you woo one of my cousins," the king snapped. "I told them that they could decide who would marry you. You will do your best to remember that despite our friendship, I am your king, and you are my subject."

Kane ground his teeth together. "How long do I have to 'woo' one of yer cousins?" He was so furious, that he couldn't ask it as the question it should have been.

"As long as is needed. You are to make sure they are content, and have everything they need. For your compliance, there will be a reward as well—besides the happy marriage you will have."

"Aye…"

"The Sinclairs come with lands to their names that are right on the border of the Lowlands."

"You've sent me *Lowlanders?*" he hissed. Lowlanders—especially females—were weak, frivolous. They only lived for court and gossip. There wasn't time for either of those in the Highlands. It was about survival, plain and simple. Lowlanders held no concept of that.

"Do not sound so disgusted," the king ordered. "Blaine is very strong in her will of things. She would make a fine wife for a Highlander. As would her sister, though her ways are more subtle. Do not generalize them."

"Aye," he growled.

The king stared at him.

"My cousin does that same exact thing," he commented fondly, reaching into one of his drawers.

"I donna know what yer talkin' about."

"That 'aye' thing you do. Although she does it when she's distracted. I fear you do it when you're not pleased about things, as you are now. Really, Kane, I've known you for years. Have I ever led you astray?"

"Nay," he bit out.

King James put a piece of parchment on the table, unrolling it.

"The girls are aware of the conditions of this arrangement. They had the choice to stay at court for a little while longer, or go to you and win your favor immediately. It must mean good things are to come that they were so eager to see you. Am I right?"

What kind of women would choose to stay with the fiercest man in the Highlands, when they could have stayed safe and happy at court? His lip lifted in a sneer. The women were going to have a *great* time with him.

"The woman that you do not choose? She will be sent to Lord Grayham."

King James's words chilled him to his very soul.

"No."

The king frowned. "You cannot 'no' me, Kane. What I say is the law—"

"No," he snarled again. He didn't care that he was talking to the king. He didn't care that if King James wanted, he could have Kane's head on a pike. "I will not go through with this, if that sick bastard is involved."

"Yes, you will," the king said stonily.

"I *refuse.*"

His snarl, the word, and the message it carried was not lost on King James. The silence was tense. Kane was too furious to back down. Aye, this could get him killed. But he would not stand back and watch a woman go through what his sister did.

"You seem to have forgotten to whom you are speaking," the king said. "These are my cousins. My dearest family. They went through a terrible loss. If you think I'm some sort of monster to send one of them to Grayham, you're mistaken. He has changed his ways, Kane. He has *learned his lesson.*"

"Aye, because I was the one who taught it to him! With my blood, fists, and weapons. Do these girls know of Grayham?" Surely they couldn't. No woman would ever go through with this if they did.

"They do," King James said. Kane gripped the chair tightly, shaking from the disgust he felt.

"Any woman foolish enough to go through with this is not worthy to be my wife."

"You have not even met the girls." He waved his heavily jeweled hand, and Kane saw red.

"Is there anything else?" he growled, forcing himself to stay where he was. One move, and he'd have his hands around the king's throat. Even mentioning that bastard's name in front of him...

Then, to make him decide which woman was going to die because of his choice? Fury flooded him, robbing him of breath. What kind of sick, disgusting man did that to his cousins? Cousins he claimed to love?

"But of course," King James said, grinning as if he hadn't just infuriated the second most dangerous man in the lands. "Payment for your troubles, and the dowry of each girl."

"I donna want yer payment."

"It has been sent with the girls, so you haven't a choice." The king held up the parchment he'd spread out on the table. "This is the list of the things you will receive for each girl, depending on whom you decide."

Kane barely cast a glance at it.

"Take a look, Kane. It will not kill you."

He held the king's eyes, and saw the challenge in them. He'd already pushed his luck by blatantly refusing a direct order. Keeping the infuriated sound of disgust to himself, he glanced at the parchment—then frowned. Though the second name was written in a way that was hard to read, he caught the gist that there were two separate dowries.

"Why is Blaine's dowry thrice the size of her sister's?"

The king sighed.

"Let me be frank. The girls have a decision on who will go for your hand, but you also have an advantage. Time management. If by any chance Blaine does not want you, I hope that her dowry will encourage you to sway her decision."

"Ye' want me to pick Blaine." Not a question. A statement.

"Yes. I feel that she needs an unwavering man to bring her to heel."

"But ye' said they're both kind. Ye'd have me send a gentle soul to the murderous hands of Grayham?" he snarled. "If ye' think anyone needs a hand to heel them, ye' send them to Grayham. These lasses donna need to be heeled—not in that way." You'd send unruly boys, not women. At least a man could handle the pain and possibly fight back.

He couldn't keep the bitterness out of his voice. The guilt. The regret.

"Do not fight me on this, Kane. The decision is essentially up to the three of you. I'm just here to supply the dowry and payment."

"And to send one of the lasses to their death."

"Grayham," the king snapped, finally letting some of his frustration show, "would not harm a cousin of mine. He knows full well the consequences, should one of them be hurt."

"Oh, aye. Because that stopped him when my sister was involved. Ye'd think that being related to The Lion would scare him into listening—and we both know how that turned out."

"My cousins are not Annalise," the king said softly. "I know the loss of your sister has been hard on you, but he has learned his lesson."

"Aye," he said, voice flat. He rubbed at the tightness forming in his chest, the fury that was burning inside him.

"If I should win the other sister's hand, will ye' rebuke her?" Kane demanded. He didn't know the lass, had never heard her name before. But something about her, the situation she was being put into, made him want to protect her. The king was practically throwing her to the dogs, while taking a favoritism to Blaine.

"No. I would not rebuke her. You understand that she has a small dowry, though, correct?"

Kane peered at the parchment. Aye, it was indeed small. Little gold, a few sheep, a bull. Nothing that he needed. He gazed at the larger list, the one that filled up most of the parchment.

Thrice of everything the other sister had, but the one at the bottom, the last piece to her dowry, made his heart drop to his stomach.

"I see you caught onto what I added at the end," the king said, sounding like a cat who had caught the mouse. Aye, Kane was caught.

"You canna mean it. That canna be real," Kane said, reaching out to touch the finely written words. His finger trailed over the ink, disbelief surging through him.

"Oh, it is real, and I do mean it." The king took the parchment away from his hand and rolled it up quickly, until just the bottom of it was showing. There were two lines there, both marked with a large, black X. "The dowries will, in no way, shape, or form, be modified, lessened, or added to. Payment for their care until they have decided will be sent to you monthly. The dowry of the chosen bride will be yours once they agree to the betrothal. Do you understand and agree to what I've just told you?"

He pulled back, staring at the king.

Shame. He felt so much shame, but he nodded. Blaine would be his chosen bride. He had no choice. The one thing he had been fighting for his whole life could be returned to him, but only with Blaine's dowry. But the other sister... The other sister, this nameless face, would be sent to her death.

He knew it without a doubt in his mind that his decision would get her killed, and there was nothing he could do to stop it.

Not without losing what was promised in Blaine's dowry.

Kane took the feathered pen from the king.
He'd just signed a lass's life away.

Chapter Four

"Saeran!" Her sister's shrill voice echoed through the stone-walled room, causing her to jerk awake. "Saeran! You overslept, and Brodrick is asking after you! Can you be any more irresponsible? Do you wish for Brodrick to complain about you to The Lion? You shall be sent away, if they are as displeased with you as I am!"

"I'm sorry," she muttered. Her voice laden with sleep, she rubbed a hand over her face. "The men... They do not turn in till late."

"That is no excuse! Now get up." Blaine tossed things at Saeran. One by one, they hit her in the face, falling in her lap. She looked down with a heavy heart. Trews. The damn trews. She fisted them in her lap and looked at her sister beseechingly.

"Do I have to?"

Blaine froze, then slowly turned around, her eyes glaring daggers. "Are you being ungrateful?" Her voice had Saeran cringing. Every time Saeran objected to something, that was her retort. She reminded Saeran of her duty, and Blaine's own sacrifice, with those four words nearly every day.

Saeran shook her head, staring down at the bits of clothing.

"No, Blaine," she answered heavily.

"Good," she hissed. "Now get up. The men wish to do more training, or whatever it is you do with them during the day. I must speak with the new cook about the meal for tonight. Oh, and when you're done, find me. Midday I should be tending to the gardens with Gwen. Make sure you're clean," she said, grimacing. "The scent of you is appalling when you're done with those men."

She left the room in a flurry of skirts. Saeran groaned, falling back into the bed.

Aye, well, maybe if you spent all of your day sparring with men thrice your size, you'd know the pain of it all. Alas, her sister had no care for Saeran's pain. Blaine was steadily ignoring all of the hardships that were put on Saeran's shoulders.

Shortly after arriving, people had begun questioning her presence there. Blaine had the most ingenious idea of claiming that Saeran was there to be the laird's squire.

At first, Saeran hadn't known what to make of it, so she'd ignored it—until Brodrick grabbed her in the middle of cleaning dishes with the cook, and threw her into the training field.

The shock, and horror, of what Blaine had done, hit her with the full force of a hundred men bearing down on her—which they had been! Every day, for the past fortnight, she had been forced to get up in the early hours of dawn, bathe in the cool creek that was a horse ride away, and then prepare for a day of what the men felt was mock battle.

It was definitely not mock. She felt every strike and impact, and she had yet to recover from the first day's bout. The wounds, bruises, and aches were piling on top of each other as the days went by.

Tears of frustration stung her eyes as she sat up, throwing the trews on the ground angrily. She hated this. She hated her role as a boy. She hated listening to her sister remind her of her place. She hated being reminded of how brave Blaine was for doing this for Saeran.

Blaine wasn't brave! She was a lady, damn it! Fixing and weeding flowers, and bossing other people around to do her work. No one was here to stop her, and no one had the courage to tell her otherwise. So she was, quite frankly, running wild. It was still better than what Saeran suspected would happen when the laird returned. He had yet to come back, and Saeran was beginning to think that he never would, although it was a foolish hope at best.

She sniffed back her tears and slid out of bed. She shivered when the cool Highland air breezed into the room, through the open window. It helped the pains. Like yesterday, she couldn't escape to the creek to soothe her aching muscles. She scrubbed a hand over her face, pushing back her golden waves, and took a moment to just...relax.

With her shift and a blanket draped around her shoulders, she sat on the sill of the window, leaning against the edge.

The place was not in ruins, as her sister and she had expected. None of the buildings were crumbling, and every shack, building, and stall, were in the utmost of shape.

It was a remarkable sight.

She'd held the thought since she first saw the place, and with her time here, it hadn't changed.

The entire estate was glorious. The keep was large and sprawling, well-kept, despite the lack of maids. Three separate pastures let sheep, cattle, and chickens graze. Chickens were cooped up in the stables with the horses. How the men here had managed to get the two animals to co-exist, she wouldn't know; but to her, it attested to the stability of the estate.

The vibrant, green hills seemed to roll on forever, and hiding within the forestation was her precious creek. It wasn't too far away from the keep, but enough that she had to take a horse to take her baths if she wanted her absence to go unnoticed. She didn't mind the distance—not only was the creek a small safe haven for her, but it gave her time to practice her riding skills.

Another chilly breeze wafted into the room, pulling at her curly hair, as if to tell her to get away from the window. She sighed, casting one last glance over the vibrant land, and sulked her way to her clothes.

She hadn't had a chance to bathe the night before, so she was as dirty and gritty as ever. The only consolation was the fresh-smelling clothes. At least Blaine had enough thought to provide a clean outfit for her every day.

Lord, but binding her breasts was becoming a chore. Not only was it hard to keep them pressed when she was "training", but it only added to the aches and pains of what she went through every day. As she finished binding, she began putting her hair in a bun. It took everything she had not to cry when she raised her arms to pin the cap in place.

"I can't go through this for another day," she moaned, even though she knew she didn't have a choice. She sucked back her frustration and squared her shoulders—then winced.

Today was going to be painful.

~

There wasn't a single person in the training area. Not there, not the stables, not even in the kitchen. For a moment, fear slid down her back. Oh, Brodrick was going to skin her a new one for being this late. She'd been good about getting up and making it to training at the right time.

She stopped a maid running past her.

"Have you seen any of the men? Brodrick? I can't seem to find them."

The girl, no older than Saeran herself, gave her an once-over. She smiled coyly.

"No, but I could entertain ye', if that's what yer lookin' for?" She whispered the heated words. The exact opposite of what Saeran wanted to hear. Her face flamed, and she jerked away from the maid.

"Ah—I think I'll—" She shut her mouth, unable to believe the words that had come out of the maid's mouth, and turned around. She could find the men on her own.

"Aw, the wee lad is a shy one!" the maid exclaimed from behind her. The hand on her arm stopped her from escaping. She swallowed nervously, pulling out of the maid's grip.

"I'm in quite a hurry—"

"Saeran!" a booming voice shouted. She didn't know whether to cower or be relieved. The maid backed away from her before the fear could settle in. Relief it was. "We've been searching for ye' everywhere, lad. Ye' didn't make it to training."

Brodrick's growl washed away the relief. Cowardice it was. He came upon them, the maid with her head down, and Saeran still blushing like a fool. A knowing look came over his face, and he grinned.

"That explains it then." He clapped Saeran on the back, like they had something to celebrate. She didn't understand in the least. The maid scurried away, kicking up dirt as she went. Saeran watched her go, mouth drawn tight, the blush only getting worse. "She's a bonny one, that Denise."

"She is?" Saeran asked blankly. He was talking like they had shared a secret.

"Oh, aye, and ye' found that out right quick I bet." Saeran didn't even want to know what he meant by that. Thankfully, his features became serious. "Ye' should have been to training today, lad."

Her shoulders slumped.

"Aye, I know." There wasn't an excuse that she could give that this large, hulking man would believe. He was strict, rough, and terrifying. No doubt he was going to make her do something strenuous to make up for her irresponsibility. She'd prefer that to anything else—like him doing as Blaine said he would and complain to the laird.

"Lucky for you," he said, a rare smile coming over his face, "we did not train. We went on a ride to secure the fencing in the north pasture."

"There's fencing?" She'd thought the animals roamed free. She hadn't seen any fences on her way in, nor could she see any from her room.

"The MacLeods throw a bloody tantrum if our lands aren't separated. Without the fence, they'd try to claim our land and livestock. They're a bunch of fools," he grunted, beginning to walk to the stables.

Several of the men were there, tending to their stallions. The second she took a step inside, she felt small, like she'd be crushed with one movement. The men *and* the horses were frighteningly huge, and Saeran was...pathetically tiny.

"Ye' missed today's work, so ye'll have to clean out the stalls."

It wasn't much of a punishment, since she did it every day anyway. She gave Brodrick a tight smile, and watched as the warriors began to file out of the stables. Lord, but they were imposing. They towered over her with an incomprehensible height. When they glared at her, she nearly wet herself.

"Blaine wants me to accompany her to the village at midday," Saeran told him. She shouldn't have to, but something about him made her want to report everything she did. He had a hard, honest face. No wonder the laird had chosen Brodrick as his second. He commanded respect.

"Verra well." He nodded his head to her. "Oh, and lad?"

She paused, hand wrapped around the handle. "Aye?"

"Stay away from the maids. They're a greedy bunch, ye' ken."

Her face flamed. He burst into deep, thunderous laughter while striding out of the stables. She slumped against the wall. Cleaning out the stalls might be a pain, but she'd choose that over being near Brodrick any day.

He was too keen, too sharp. He always knew when something was wrong—Saeran just prayed he didn't realize something was wrong with her.

Saeran made sure there was no one left in the stall and began her work, giving each horse an apple as she went. They'd become the only *pleasant* constant in her day. Getting pummeled to a pulp, dealing with her sister's attitudes, and fighting off the aches and pains of the pummels weren't things she looked forward to every day. The horses made it worth it, though.

The one she'd ridden a fortnight ago nuzzled her shoulder as she passed. Saeran smiled.

"Don't tell the other horses," she whispered, feeding it an apple and sliding another one in its feeder. "They get awfully jealous."

The mare chuffed the ground, and she smiled, continuing. She cleaned out the old hay, replaced it with a fresh layer, then brushed down every horse. It wasn't required of her, but she knew they were often worked all through the day. A little relaxation never killed any of them.

When she got to the last horse, a stallion as black as night, she paused. There was a shifty look to his eyes and his breathing was forced, heavy. His barrel chest was heaving. She bit her lip.

"I'm sorry," she whispered, slowly holding her hand out to the stallion. His eyes zeroed in on her hand. "I can't brush you unless you're calm."

He neighed roughly and she jerked away. It only heightened his panic. He reared back, violently kicking his hooves out. They connected with the latch that held the stall door closed and it broke. Saeran didn't have time to react.

The beast came charging out, a shrill sound ripping from his lips.

She flung herself out of the way, but not before his hoof caught her in the thigh. Saeran screamed from the pain and fell back against the stall of another restless horse. The stallion charged out of the stables. Pain wracked her, centering at her thigh. It spread outwards like a wildfire. Despite that, she managed to get to her feet. She could hear the men shouting.

Saeran blinked back her tears, breathing shallowly. Aye, moving was a lot harder than it had seemed. Nevertheless, she had to let them know it wasn't her fault the horse escaped. She'd already made a mess of things today with Brodrick—she didn't need to add more to the list.

Her sister would hear about this, she knew.

She wanted to crawl into a hole and perish. It sounded much easier than dragging herself out of stables and into the chaos of the training grounds. She grabbed a rope from the stables.

Three men were trying to calm the horse, Brodrick was nowhere to be found, and the insane horse was creating a stir. She ran forward—or wobbled. It was hard to run on a leg that felt only of searing pain.

"Here," she called, tossing the rope. The sound of her voice caused everything to still—or rather, the horse. As the horse froze, so did everyone else. Its eyes, black, wide, and crazed, stared at her.

Then it charged. Her leg made it impossible to move out of the way fast enough. Adrenaline rushed through her blood and she pitched to the side—right into waiting arms. She froze.

"I donna know what happened, and I fear I donna want to," the familiar voice said. She sagged against Brodrick in relief—and realized immediately she wasn't a simpering girl, but a lad who had to take care of himself. She yanked herself out of his arms, but not before she saw the speculative look in his eyes.

"It wasn't my fault," she said the second she gathered her wits. The ache in her leg was growing worse. Lord, but the creek sounded nice right then. "He hit the door with his hooves and broke the hatch. I—I'll fix it if I can get the tools."

She put a hand over her chest to still the beating of her heart, though it did no good.

The binding began to loosen. Her eyes widened. Brodrick gave her a narrow look, then focused on the leg she was favoring. She instantly straightened herself, then regretted her decision immediately. A startled gasp of pain left her lips.

"I believe ye'." He gestured toward the keep. "Go on. Have yer sister tend to ye'. We can take care of everything here."

She gave him a grateful smile. That must not have been the thing to do because his eyes narrowed, and then he turned away sharply. She watched him go with pressed lips. Had he noticed her lapse? The way she'd been leaning against him would have made it easy for Brodrick to feel her curves. The clothes hid them well, yes, but even Saeran knew they couldn't hide them when she was being touched.

Her face paled.

Don't think about it, she chided herself. She wrapped her arms around her stomach as she retreated to the keep. *It was one slip. He would not notice.*

The walk to the kitchens was painful. Her leg throbbed so

strongly that tears stung her eyes, but she kept going. Her sister was not going to be pleased about this, not at all. Especially if she found out about Saeran's slip. She chewed on her lower lip as she entered the kitchen. Blaine didn't *have* to find out. She didn't need to know everything that Saeran did during the day.

She glanced at her throbbing leg. There would be no hiding that, though. She could hardly walk on it.

The cook, Sabia, spotted her immediately. The petite woman had come to them recently, just a sennight after the sisters arrived. Her house had caught fire after her youngest boy had tried to play in the hearth. She was a widow with two children, her husband having died in battle. The thought made her lips tighten. Sabia's husband wouldn't have died if her laird weren't as bloodthirsty as he was.

Sabia was holding up well. Not only with the loss of her husband and losing her house, but with her duties as a cook. She made excellent mutton and kept the kitchens cleaner than when the sisters settled in. Her two children, Sorcha and Nial, helped her do the dishes. They weren't even ten years, but they knew their duties to the keep, and did them without complaint. Saeran didn't mind letting them run around when they were done, but Blaine always had something to say about it.

Sabia's face drew tight with concern. "Och, lad, what happened to ye'?" She rushed over and helped Saeran into a chair. Grey speckled her hair, and the harsh lines bracketing her mouth were more pronounced with her concern.

"A stallion and I came to a disagreement," Saeran muttered, finally taking a breath. It felt good to sit down—no, *amazing*. What would be even better, though, was a trip to the creek. She imagined the cool water would soothe most of her aches.

The injury was too high up on her thigh for her to reveal to the cook. She smiled gratefully when Sabia brought her a cool rag.

Saeran reached out to take it, but Sabia waved her hands away. "I can do this. Ye' just relax. I saw them bring in that giant beast a wee bit ago. It's quite an impressive animal, isn't it?"

"Aye, with quite an impressive kick, too!" Saeran laughed ruefully, even though it made every muscle in her body ache. The motherly ministrations of Sabia was the only thing that kept her from bursting into tears. "I just hope Blaine doesn't come in—"

Her mumble was cut short when the object of her misery came striding into the room. Blaine stopped short when she saw Saeran sitting there, Sabia gently dabbing the sweat off her face.

"What in all that is holy is going on here?" she demanded, striding forward with her hands on her ample hips. Saeran sighed. "And *what* have I told you about sighing like that?" Saeran felt Sabia tense from behind her.

Blaine, like a predator sensing fear, snapped her gaze to Sabia. "Is that part of your duties as a cook? Tending to him?"

"No, my lady," Sabia murmured. Saeran sat up, scowling at her sister.

"Blaine, she was just helping me—"

"You're a *man*," her sister hissed. "You can help yourself!" She paused, nose in the air. "You smell. Bathe and then find me in the gardens—as I said to earlier." Back stiff, she stormed out of the kitchen doors. Saeran stared after her sister, mouth open.

"I apologize for taking liberties I should not have," Sabia said quietly from behind her. Saeran closed her eyes, cursing her sister. How could she be so cruel to Sabia like that? After everything the woman had set to order for them?

"No," Saeran said, turning around in her seat. She took Sabia's hand, and patted it gently, sighing. "I apologize for my sister's behavior. She is having a hard time becoming accustomed to the order of the clan."

Sabia's lips tightened, but she nodded demurely. There was something on the tip of her tongue. Saeran could see it in her eyes, in the way she held herself.

"What is it?"

"It's not my place to say, my lord. Excuse me. I have duties to attend to—" Saeran stopped her with a hand on her arm.

"Whatever it is, you can tell me. I am not like my sister. What is wrong?"

"Aye, lad. I ken ye' aren't like yer sister." A small smile lifted her thin lips. "Yer much nicer, even though ye' let the men take a beating at ye'."

Saeran blushed.

"Ah, my lord…" Sabia wrung the damp cloth in her hands, indecisive. "May I speak out of turn?"

"Aye, please." Saeran knew servants had their places. However, she felt that though there were lords and servants, all were equal. Everyone was human and deserved a chance to speak their mind. Especially if it concerned her sister. Saeran had realized that her sister's attitude was becoming worse of late. She wondered if others shared her thoughts—it would certainly clear some of the guilt.

Sabia looked to the floor, then met her eyes. "Lady Blaine plans to become Lady of Shaw lands." She paused. "Correct?"

Saeran nodded slowly, watching the emotions flicker in the cook's eyes. "Aye, she does. Is that a problem?" She was genuinely curious. Saeran had started to notice the control her sister was taking and thought that, yes. It might just be a problem—but she would never admit that to anyone

Sabia stared at Saeran for the longest time, then shook her head. "Nay. Excuse me, my lord. I have duties to attend to."

She watched the woman run out of the room and felt a tightening in her chest. It was becoming clear to her how the people of the keep felt about Blaine and what she was doing.

Grimacing, she walked toward the doors. Her sister was correct; Saeran needed a bath. The thought of going near a horse again made the hair at the back of her neck rise, but her leg hurt too much to walk all the way to the creek.

She made sure no one was near, mounted her mare, and tucked her drying cloth in her lap. No one cast her a glance as she pounded out of the training area. She took the long way around the keep so that if anyone did follow her, they would quickly become bored and leave her.

Saeran had never taken a bath in broad daylight, but she was in so much pain that she didn't care to hurry herself up. As her mare bounded over brush and fallen logs, the fresh scent of the creek overwhelmed her senses.

She was smiling when she slid off the mare. Quickly tying the reins to a fallen log with one hand, she pulled the pins out of the cap and tossed them into the flimsy piece of cloth when it was off.

A thrill went through her. Lord, but this couldn't have happened sooner! She slid off the shirt, shoes and trews, letting them pile by the hat. Even with her aching leg, she managed to hobble her way over the green, prickly grass, and dip her foot into the water.

It was cool to the touch.

She laughed happily, wading into the clear blue stream.

Chapter Five

"Canna wait for a proper meal," one of his men said from behind him.

"Canna wait to get off this horse," another grunted.

"Canna wait for my bonny wife to warm my bed!"

There were several grunts for that one, and even Kane joined in—except it wasn't because he was looking forward to it. Nay, it was the exact opposite. He did not want to return to his keep and face the two lasses pining for his hand. He did not want to go back and face the fact that one of those lasses, a reportedly kind, gentle girl, would be sent to her death because of him.

He reached for the skin, putting it to his lips. The whisky was tasteless by now.

Kane didn't know what to do. Either way, the lass was going to die. Should he put off the courting, and let her have more time to live? Or should he find a way for her to get out of her marriage to Grayham?

If it were any other man, he wouldn't care. It was common for a lass to be sent off to marriage with a man she didn't know. It was the way of things. It had happened to his sister.

But this was different.

He'd learned his mistake with Annalise. Subjecting another innocent to that...it was making him go insane. Several times they had to stop for more whisky, and while Kane wasn't a drunk, he thought the spirits would help alleviate some of the guilt.

They hadn't.

They'd done the exact opposite.

"My wife will no' be so happy," he overheard one of his men say. His eyes narrowed on the space ahead of him. "Our bairn has probably kept her up night and day."

"Aye," one of the men chuckled knowingly. "I feel yer pain. When we went to war with the MacDonalls, my woman was left alone. I had the cold shoulder for a fortnight…" Kane didn't pay attention to the rest of their conversation because an idea so brilliant, so amazing and simple, came to him. It might be the whisky thinking for him, but he didn't care. His idea was perfect.

Neither of the lasses would take his hand.

Nay, he'd make them both hate him so much they couldn't bear the sight of him. He'd be every terrible thing he was accused of. The king's contract hadn't said a single thing about his betrothal being broken. All it had said was for her to accept the betrothal, and the dowry would be his.

Triumph surged through him, and he took another swig of the whisky, this time in celebration. It was a flawless plan. The lasses had no clue what kind of man he was—no one except his clan did. He was the merciless Lion to these girls, and it was that way he would stay.

"Laird Shaw," his squire said from beside him. Kane looked down at him. "You're looking in higher spirits."

"Aye," he said, grinning, taking another swig of whisky.

"Are you excited to meet your betrothal?" No one except Connor knew there were two lasses he had to choose from—well, none, now. His grin only widened.

"Aye."

His squire gave him an uneasy look. "Well, that is good. Might I ask what put you into higher spirits? The whole ride, you've been…brooding."

Kane held up the skin. "The spirits put me in higher spirits, Connor. All of my problems have been solved—though I think I'll be needin' yer assistance in a matter."

Connor eyed him suspiciously, but nodded. The lad was only seven and ten, but he was showing promise as a knight. His father had been a good friend of Kane's, so even though the lad was English, Connor was training under his hand.

"Whatever it is, laird."

Kane knelt down, quietly telling his squire of his plans. When

41

the lad stared up at him in shock, he nodded.

"Are you not concerned with the king's opinion of your treatment of the girls?" Connor asked, stunned.

"Nay. It will no' be me calling off the engagement, but the girl. Even then, the King only says he adores the girls for the sake of appearances. He would turn on his own daughter if he had to," he said, knowing it was true. The king did not know the meaning of love. He knew the meaning of gains and power, but love? Kane could have laughed. "Either way, everything will be over."

"Everything?" Connor asked dubiously.

"Aye. Everything." Then he could get back on his merry way. Kane absently swirled the skin around. The leather was smooth and sturdy, old. The initials on the side were his father's.

"Even the feuds?"

"Even the feuds. Lady Blaine's dowry will cure everything—and then her and her sister will return to the king, unharmed. After that, the fate of the lasses is not my concern."

"That's quite a plan you have, my lord." He didn't meet Kane's eyes, instead choosing to rummage around in his pack. He pulled out an apple and buffed it against his shirt.

"Aye. It is." This time, when the whisky went down his throat, it stung with life. "Blaine will call it off as soon as she sees what a brute her laird is."

"But you're not a—"

"To ye', aye. To these lasses...well, I canna wait to see their terrified hides running back to the Lowlands."

"As you wish. Would you have me notify your clan?" Connor asked, eyeing the apple.

Kane nodded. "I donna want them to hate me."

"They would never—"

"After the next couple of weeks, even knowing this is a farce, they verra well might."

Connor sighed, then took a bite out of the apple and walked off. Kane went back to staring at the skin of whisky. The spirits were guiding him at this point, and he was gladly going to take their advice.

~

After the men were made aware of Kane's plans, and instructed to act as the barbarians they were known as, the ride to his territory was silent. He knew the men did not approve of his decision on the matter. He understood why. They did not know of the terms, or that

42

one of the lasses would be sent to Grayham. Something about the whole situation, and the fact that King James had pulled him aside to speak of this, told him that he should keep some of the details to himself.

His squire was the only one who knew of everything, and so would Brodrick, soon. The Sinclairs had been at his keep for a fortnight now, enough for Brodrick to come up with an in-depth analysis of them.

Several hours later, they were going through the village. Men jumped off their horses to embrace their wives when they came running around, and his squire wandered off to do what Kane had instructed him to.

Kane continued on towards the keep. Just when he was coming up the large hill, at the end of the creek, a sound carried through the air.

He stayed his horse with a sharp movement, listening.

It came again, from up river. He slid off the giant black beast and left him there. If Kane needed his warhorse, a sharp whistle would draw his attention.

He palmed his claymore, following the sound. The closer he got to the source, the less he felt he needed the protection. Splashing water, contented sighs. A giggle.

Kane frowned, walking up the creek.

It was then that he saw it.

Her.

His mouth went dry and every ounce of blood shot straight to his hips. His claymore almost clattered to the ground.

There, bathing in his creek, as nude as the day she was born, was a nymph. She was waist-deep in the water, arms above her head, face tilted toward the sun. She'd just emerged from the water, and droplets were sliding down her slender body.

Kane stumbled backwards, grabbing a tree for support. Her skin was kissed by the sun, and the damp, golden locks falling to her shoulders were shimmering in the broad daylight. She was turned toward him, just enough that he could see her neck, her elegant jaw, and pink, plump lips. He couldn't see the color of her eyes, but he imagined them to be as crystalline as the water she was playing in.

Only when she ducked under the water again did Kane breathe. Who in all that was Holy was that? And why was she in his creek? Naked? For all to see?

For all to...*crave.*

Her golden head broke the surface of the water and she faced him for a second, giving him a view of her breasts and trimmed waist.

She didn't notice him. With a sigh loud and content enough for him to hear, she spread her arms out and floated on the surface of the water. Her breasts were full and tipped with tight, pink nipples. The apex of her thighs was dipped in the water, but that didn't hide the curly mons peeking through the gentle current.

His mouth watered. His fingers itched to touch the breasts that were heaving with her gentle breaths, and his mouth held the same desire. She'd taste of the sweetest honey, he knew it just by looking at her. Her skin was dewy and lightly tanned, so odd from all of the women he had seen.

He realized she was used to bathing in the open. That's where her faint tan had come from. His hands balled into fists, when all they wanted to do was touch her, to see if she was real.

She didn't look real—he could easily blame this hallucination on the whisky. A water nymph, playing in his creek? He had walked into a fairy tale, and he didn't want it to end.

He bit back a groan.

Aye, he'd love to see if she was as magical as she looked.

Nay. What he wanted to do was stride into the creek, take her into his arms, and show her just how much he could pleasure a nymph.

He started forward, mind overtaken by images of her body wrapped around his, fully intent on claiming the mythical creature he'd found. It had been a long time since he'd had a woman, a full two moons, and right now, his body was definitely feeling the pent-up need for release.

As he started to make his descent to her, something stopped him. Her leg had kicked into the air. He might not have thought anything of it, but he saw the wince of pain on her innocent features and the large, blood-red bruise.

He froze.

And stared.

He stared until her leg lowered.

His lips pressed...and then he turned away. He'd find out who the lass was, who her family was, and how she'd gotten the bruise. Aye, that's what he'd do.

Kane did not allow violence of any sort on his lands. Animals, women, or children—if anyone appeared with a mark on them, the abuser would have to face Kane.

His sister had taught him a valuable lesson.

With his hard-on ruined, he stormed to his horse and mounted, riding furiously to his keep. Brodrick would know who the lass was. He knew who everyone was.

As he rode to the training grounds, where Brodrick normally was, his thoughts were a mess.

They all centered around the same thing.

The woman, the water nymph, who'd nearly brought him to his knees with one glance at her body. He knew it was unreasonable to be so attracted to a woman with just a look, but he didn't care. It was because he'd been away for so long and hadn't had a woman to warm his bed.

He was positive that the second he saw his leman, Gwen, he'd have that same rush of hunger. Gwen was a bonny lass, and very eager in bed. He was willing to bet she had thrice more experience than the nymph swimming in his creek, who held the look of sensual innocence, despite her incomparable beauty.

Kane had to turn his thoughts from the woman, and focus on Gwen's face. Aye, he'd take Gwen for a night, and by the morrow, the golden haired lass would be out of his thoughts completely.

After he figured out who'd harmed the wench, that is.

Chapter Six

"There you are!" Blaine hissed the second Saeran walked into the kitchen. Saeran paused, looking at her sister uneasily.

"I didn't take too long, did I?" she asked, adjusting her cap. In truth, she'd taken much less time than she would have preferred. Half-way through her bath, she'd felt the oddest sensation of eyes gazing upon her. Though she hadn't seen anyone who would have been watching, the thought had her leaving the creek.

The cool water had done its job. Her aching muscles were soothed, and it was easier to walk on her leg. She'd nearly cried when she saw how red and angry it looked, but she had held back the tears. No one would have to see it, and it would heal on its own. The trews had created a barrier between the hoof and her body, so no skin had torn. Thankfully, there was no a chance for infection. It would only create more problems with Blaine if she suddenly took ill.

"Yes," Blaine snapped. "You did! The laird has arrived, and you were not here to greet him. Because of the embarrassment you caused, I could not make myself face him."

Saeran grimaced. "I'm sorry, Blaine. I didn't mean to take so long, I swear it. I was kicked by a horse today—"

"I don't care about *that!*" her sister said, incredulous. "I care that my own darling, little sister wasn't here to support me in my time of need! How would you feel if we switched places and I was not there for you, eh?"

Saeran stared at her sister, silent.

46

"Exactly. Now that I see you've cleaned yourself up, accompany me to the dining hall. We will have to make up for your lapse in responsibility—once again—and greet the laird. Do not act so selfish in the future," her sister chastised. Shaking her head in disappointment, she bustled out of the kitchen. Saeran followed at a slower place. She felt like she had just been slapped in the face.

She'd gotten hurt, and her sister hadn't cared. The horse could have killed her had she been but a space forward. Luckily, it had only clipped her thigh, but the fact that her sister didn't care...

Her throat tightened.

No, she chided herself. *My sister is under a lot of pressure. She is justified in feeling that way, and I shouldn't complain. She's making a huge sacrifice to keep us together.*

Still, it didn't stop the hurt from assailing her as they came into the great hall. Unprepared for her sister's abrupt stop, she almost ran into her.

"*What* has happened to my hall?" a thunderous voice shouted. Saeran flinched.

She expected Blaine to simper, but she strode forward with a confidence that was purely Blaine. Her sister's wide body swayed with her movements, and fearful for her life, Saeran followed after her.

"Laird Shaw!" Blaine greeted warmly. "I'm so glad to see you have returned." Saeran peered in front of her sister—or at least tried to. Men were filing into the hall, all wearing equal expressions of disgust.

"What happened to my hall?" the dark voice demanded again, this time his voice deadly soft. It was so chilling that Saeran shivered.

"I would like to introduce myself. Blaine Sinclair," she said, curtseying. He only gave Saeran a fleeting glance. "And my dear younger brother, Saeran Sinclair."

"I demand an answer, *Blaine Sinclair*. What happened to my hall?" he roared. Saeran grabbed her sister by the arm, reacting purely on instinct, and pulled her behind her back.

There was a silence, deathly enough to make Saeran pale. She didn't want to look at the barbarian who was going to marry her sister, but it was the proper thing to do, so she lifted terrified eyes to his—

And stilled.

Her breath stuck in her throat.

The Lion was not a handsome man—but he had a raw, brutal

presence that commanded all attention to be centered on him. He was the largest out of all the men in the hall. Brodrick's head reached his neck, and she could imagine that being placed next to him, she would appear half as tall as he.

His shoulders were bare and thick, wide enough to fill the doorway. The light from the hall slashed across his face, giving her a perfect view of bright, furious green eyes.

His hair was dark and wavy, reaching just past his jaw and setting off the hard, rugged lines of his face. His eyes were a blazing green. Whether the blazing part was from the fury in them, or the vibrancy of his eyes, she didn't know—and didn't care.

He was the kind of man one heard about in legends, whether he was the foe or the hero. He had a body that was built for strength and dominance, and the stance of his shoulders showed clearly that he knew who had the control.

He was...masculine. Not handsome—no, he didn't need to be handsome. The strength that exuded from him spoke for itself. Even though his face was brutal, there was a look in his eyes as he stared down at her.

She didn't know how to describe it, how to describe him, with words. Danger and power oozed out of him in waves, yet the masculinity he possessed robbed her of breath.

He also held...*passion*. As he stared down at her, his body vibrated with the strength of his anger. She felt the passion within him rise and lash out, like a strike of lightning to her gut.

"Saeran," Blaine hissed from behind her. "What are you doing? Get out of my way!" Saeran was snapped out of her stupor as her sister pushed her out of the way, coming forward to graciously bow in front of the laird again.

Saeran thought he'd lop her head off with his claymore, but he surprised her. All he did was sneer at the two of them.

"We've opened the hall, aired it, replaced the rushes, and ordered new tables, my lord. Does it not look lovely?" she asked serenely, holding her hands to her round face.

Her happiness didn't do anything to soften his furious features.

"Who's paying for all of this?" he growled.

His questions served in making Blaine stutter. "I... I had assumed that you would want to return to a clean home."

"It was perfectly fine beforehand, Brodrick," he snapped. "Find someone to get all of this back to the way it was. Now."

"Aye, my laird." Saeran watched her tormenter exit the room...just as Sabia came rushing out of the back, her two children close behind her. When they were standing in front of the laird, beside Saeran, she tensed.

He didn't look happy to see that he had more guests.

"Who are they?" he snapped, jerking his head toward them. The children began to tremble next to her, and she frowned.

"Your new cook and her children. They prepare, serve, and clean up the meals now," Saeran said before her sister could say anything. She didn't like the way this brute of a man was eyeing them. He stared at them as if they were the lowest, most disgusting thing he'd ever seen in his life.

The children subtly moved behind their terrified mother's skirts.

"I don't need a cook," he said harshly. "Send them home."

"Laird Shaw—" she started, hating the paleness on Sabia's face. She'd been through enough, and all of her problems were centered on the man in front of her.

"I want them gone," he snarled, slashing a hand out in front of him. "I want everything that was changed in my absence to be returned to its original state. Every speck of dust, every servant, every rush. All of it."

Saeran felt a burst of anger well inside of her. Sabia didn't have a home or a man to provide for her.

"Sabia's husband died in your service, and she has no home," Saeran snapped. She was too angry to care that she was acting completely out of character. She was supposed to be quiet and unassuming.

Blaine stiffened beside her, and she knew she was going to catch hell for this. She didn't care. Saeran couldn't let Sabia be homeless with two children.

When the laird didn't say anything, she continued. Softer this time, but with just as much force.

"She is an excellent cook. This keep is in need of one, and she has two growing children that do what is asked. Throwing her out would be a travesty—"

"Quiet, Saeran," Blaine finally snapped, rounding on her. Her eyes blazed. "If the laird wants the woman gone, then she'll be gone. You," she said, pointing at Sabia. "Pack your belongings and—"

"Nay," the laird said suddenly.

Blaine paused. "No, my lord?"

49

"Nay." That was all that needed to be said. Sabia gave her a tearfully grateful nod, and then hurried from the room. Saeran felt a moment of relief, then realized the laird was staring at her. Dread settled in her gut, but nevertheless, she met his eyes.

"Who are ye?" he asked, squinting at her.

She swallowed thickly. Mayhap stepping into this man's line of fire hadn't been a wise idea. Regardless, she did not regret her decision. She had saved three lives by it.

"Saeran Sinclair," she said, the pride in her voice clear. If only she were introducing herself as the woman she was.

"And this is yer sister?" he asked, gesturing to Blaine with a nod of his head. Blaine started to open her mouth, but he gave her a quelling look.

"Aye," Saeran said uncertainly. She wasn't supposed to be doing the talking. Blaine should be doing this—Saeran was a terrible liar—always had been.

"Where is the other sister?" he asked, narrowing his eyes on the two of them. The look on his face made her blood turn to ice in her veins.

"Other sister?" she echoed hollowly, heart starting to race. He was staring at them as if he knew she wasn't who she claimed to be.

"Aye, the other sister. I ken there were two lasses, no' one and a brother."

Blaine once again tried to open her mouth, but the laird held up a hand. "I'm no' speaking to ye', lass."

"I am the king's cousin!" she burst out, offended. Saeran wanted to wring her throat. Couldn't her sister, just this once, take the hint that she shouldn't speak? "I am a guest in your home! I can speak for myself, my lord."

"In my home, a lady knows her place. Ye' clearly do not. Come, lad. We'll discuss this elsewhere." With one last look at Blaine, he walked from the room. Saeran gave her sister a pleading look. The only thing she got in return was a face that said, "If you go, you're in big trouble."

For some reason, she was more terrified of the laird than her sister.

With heavy feet, she went after the laird. Men began to restore the hall to its former infamy.

~

Kane was not a pleased laird.

He'd seen Gwen on the way to the keep and hadn't felt a stir of desire for her. Her kisses, naughty whispers, and touches had not done anything to ignite the same hunger he'd felt for the lass at the creek—that was the first part of his problems.

His second had introduced itself right after. The stallion, a gift from the king, had gone berserk. Not even Brodrick, the proclaimed horse whisperer, could get the beast to calm down. The animal had harmed a stable boy, as well. He would work with the beast for a fortnight, but if there was no improvement, he'd get rid of it. He had too much to work to be concerned with such a minimal task.

The third problem was the hall. What woman in her right mind would barge into his home and change his hall without his permission? And to top it off, he'd been guilted by a lad half his size into keeping a woman and her two children at his keep! Then that Blaine chit was just the last straw...

He sighed heavily, pushing open the door to his study. The room was dark and cold, having been vacant for over a month.

"Close the door behind ye'," he commanded the boy, going to the fireplace and setting a flame. Then he went to the window and yanked the curtains aside. Light flooded the room, revealing the interior. The sight of the wee lad cowering against the door like he was a meal being served to a lion almost made him laugh. Almost.

"Blaine does no' have a sister?" he asked, getting right to the point.

The lad shook his head. The cap moved to the side, but it stayed atop his head. Hair darkened by shadow peaked out of the hat, and intelligent blue eyes stared at him from beneath a mask of grime.

He narrowed his eyes on him.

"Aye, just me, her brother," the boy said quickly, looking at the ground. Kane lost his train of thought at the abrupt answer.

"The king said there were two sisters. Yer not a lass."

Small shoulders shrugged. "Aye."

A memory pricked him, something the king had said. If only the king had given him the name of the other sister. Now that he thought about it, he realized he didn't know the other sister's name. Despite the brief mention of the other one, he'd obviously favored Blaine more when he spoke of her.

Mayhap the king had been confused, and there really was one woman.

"Then what is yer purpose here?"

Kane watched as the boy struggled to get words out. He crossed his arms over his chest, waiting.

"Squire—I'm here as a squire. I believe the king might have gotten his subjects mixed up," he said, laughing. It was forced. He's lying.

"I already have a squire," Kane said, waving a hand. He turned to the fire, facing the flames and watching them dance. There was something wrong with the lad, something...strange. He was lying, aye, but what about? Blaine was no doubt the cousin of a king—she had the conduct of one for sure. The king often mixed his subjects around, but these were his "dear cousins".

Kane grunted. The king had many "dear cousins". Mayhap he was confusing Blaine's brother as someone else from his extended family tree. That had to be it.

"The king sent me here to be a squire," the boy insisted. Kane looked over his shoulder to see that he'd finally stepped away from the door, hands clenched at his sides. There was a determination to his eyes. Kane noted the surprise there, as if the boy couldn't believe he was being so bold.

"I can send you to be the squire of another laird. There are plenty in need of one. So many Lowlanders are taking to court rather than battle," he said, disgusted.

"You can have more than one squire, my lord." Kane faced the boy fully. His lips were pressed together. The glance at his lips led Kane's eyes to his jaw. His eye twitched.

Why was he noticing that the lad had a surprisingly elegant jaw?

Kane shook his head mentally, clearing away the thoughts.

"I have enough with Connor on my hands—"

"Talk to Brodrick. He'll vouch for me." The boy crossed the space between them, staring up at him with a fire he hadn't expected from such a small body. It was small, but slender. Very slender.

He had to shake the thoughts out of his head again. "I have no need of another squire—"

"I—"

"Enough," he snapped, slashing a hand through the air. The lad flinched, as if Kane was going to strike him. Kane sighed. "I'm tired of yer interrupting' me, lad. I'm laird here, not ye'. Remember who yer speaking to. If I say I donna need another squire, I donna need another squire."

"My sister needs me," he said quickly. "If I left her,

she'd...she'd..."

"What, run around throwing flowers all over the place? Ye' ain't verra good at controlling her, lad. Ye' saw the state of my hall—what kind of man wants to return to a bonny hall like that?"

"I was busy with training when she took over the hall, my lord," he whispered.

Kane grunted.

"Yer askin' me to let ye' stay here so ye' can babysit yer sister," he said bluntly.

"Aye. She needs me. She has...problems and—" He cut himself off.

At least the lad didn't deny that he was staying to watch his sister. That showed the amount of loyalty he had. Hell, he'd even dragged the chit behind him when Kane saw the state of his hall.

"I donna ken a single brother who would stay behind for his sister," Kane said, shaking his head. A hint of amusement entered his voice. Even when Annalise and he had been close, he preferred training with the men to playing childish games with her.

"She's special," Saeran said, nodding. "Very special." Then his face paled. "She'll make a perfect bride, though—she's very good at...at—"

"I get ye', lad. Fine. Ye' can stay to watch yer sister." As silly as it sounded.

A hopeful look entered his eyes. "Does that mean no more training?"

Kane narrowed his eyes on him.

"Nay. More training. Yer too thin and..." He searched for a word that would properly describe the boy and found none. He shrugged. "Slim. Yer too slim. If yer going to be staying in the Highlands, ye'll need to toughen up a wee bit. Mayhap ye' should get some meat on yer bones, then return to training."

His small shoulders slumped. The boy could definitely use some toughening up, Kane thought, leaning on the edge of the table.

"Find yer sister and watch her. Try to keep her out of my way."

"My lord?"

Kane sighed, swiping a hand over his face. "I'd like some time to myself before I have to face her again."

The boy wore a knowing look on his face while he nodded. He turned to leave.

"Saeran," he called out, a thought coming to him. He watched the boy's back tense.

"My lord."

"Have ye' seen a lass around? Blonde, verra small, about yer size, but thinner?"

"There are many women around who look like that," the boy said easily, not turning around to meet Kane's eyes. His hand was still on the door.

Kane sighed. Mayhap it was just his imagination, a conjuring created by the spirits. That sounded more likely, he thought, rubbing his temples. "Thank ye', lad. Send Brodrick to me if ye' see him."

"Aye, my lord." With a short bow of his head, the boy left him in silence, with only the sound of the crackling fire heating up the spring-cooled room.

Now that the Sinclairs were somewhat taken care of, he took the time to go through the accounts, reading all of the missives that Brodrick had made for him. They had a lot to discuss.

First and foremost being the figment of his imagination...

Chapter Seven

"Oh, Saeran," Blaine wailed the second she saw her sister. She didn't have time to close the door to her sister's room before the curvaceous woman was throwing herself at Saeran, giant tears welling in her eyes. "He is terrible! What kind of man talks to his future wife like that?"

Saeran patted her back uneasily, kicking the door closed. Her sister was hugging her so hard that it was hard to breathe. Not only that, but she was leaning into Saeran so much, her leg began to throb.

"Blaine," she gasped, pushing at her sister's shoulder. "Blaine, sit on the bed."

"Do not boss me around like that!" her sister said, distraught. Still, Blaine pulled away from Saeran and threw herself onto the extravagant bed. She, of course, had taken the room most suited for her lady-like sensibilities. Saeran had thought this was the previous Lady Shaw's room. It was beautifully furnished, and everything was in the best of shape, though there hadn't been a woman in this keep since Annalise Shaw. At least, that's what she'd heard from the maids. "Oh, he is absolutely dreadful! And large! Did you see the width of his shoulders? He is the size of an elephant, all large and clunky in the way he walked."

Saeran hadn't thought he was clunky. Aye, he was large, but he was definitely not 'clunky'. He moved with the grace of a lion. Soundless. Deadly. Everything about him was terrifying—especially the way he looked at her. It was as if he could see straight into her soul. As if he could see straight past all of the lies she was telling him.

55

She sat beside Blaine, letting her complain, whine, and cry over Laird Shaw, while her own mind raced like a horse.

He knew something was wrong. There was no doubt about it, for she knew she was a terrible liar. Everyone who knew Saeran also knew she couldn't even lie over whether she ate a meal or not! Her sister knew this better than most, and that had been one of the reasons why she'd let her sister take care of the talking.

She knew how to work her words so that anyone could believe them. She'd seen it happen with priests, with her parents, and with the men at court, but it had all seemed like fun and games. Saeran had never taken part, or commented for that matter, on her sister's sneaky habits. But now? She sorely wished she'd taken an interest in learning the art behind dishonesty.

Didn't that sound terrible of her?

"—and I have to be married to him, for the sake of your survival," her sister said sharply, jerking Saeran out of her thoughts. She looked at Blaine, shocked.

"Do not give me that look," Blaine said, pushing herself into a sitting position. If it weren't for your barrenness, this would not be a problem. All your fault—this is all your fault! Yes, I know that now. I should go down there right now and reveal—"

But it wasn't her fault. It was the king's, for even suggesting that they both be married. Lord, even her sister shared the blame—she had been the one to accept the deal! But still, she was now apart of the ruse, and if she was found out? Even though she was growing more and more distrustful of her sister, she couldn't let her secret be revealed.

She didn't want to think of what could happen to her if the laird found out she was lying.

Saeran grabbed her sister by the arm. "Blaine, whatever I did to upset you, I'm sorry—please, *please* do not go down there. Mayhap he is sore from his journey, or stunned by the king's announcement for him to be married."

Blaine's lip trembled, and she fell into the bed. "I'm sorry, Saeran. I don't know what came over me—I'm just so scared. The rumors surrounding him are true. I can feel it just by looking at him," she whispered.

Saeran's heart broke at the sight of her sister's distress. She scooted toward her, slipping her arm around Blaine's wide shoulders.

"Blaine, listen to me." Saeran took her sister by the chin and forced their eyes to meet. "Every heart of ice eventually melts. Everyone loves you, Blaine. Even the cats at court love you, why should a lion do any less?" she said, smiling when the confidence returned to her sister's eyes. "Soon enough, he'll be crawling on his bare knees to take your hand."

Blaine rested her dark head against Saeran's shoulder. "Thank you, Sae. You always manage to make me happy."

"We're sisters," Saeran murmured. "It's my job to make you happy."

"Yes, that it is." Blaine looked up with a frown. "Why do you favor your leg like such?"

She took her hand away from under her knee, the only place she felt comfortable nursing it, and shrugged.

"It's nothing." Nay, it wasn't nothing. But she'd tried to tell her sister about the injury earlier, and had gotten shut down. She didn't want to deal with the ache in her chest when it happened again. Too often, her sister was putting Saeran's needs and concerns aside. Their time here, and the muttered comments from the servants, had finally opened her eyes to the selfishness of her sister.

Saeran looked at her lap, feeling horrible for thinking such things. Her sister was justified in being selfish. She was saving Saeran's life while risking her own by marrying The Lion. With the added duties to keeping the estate running properly, Saeran could only imagine the stress her sister felt.

"No, let me see," Blaine said, uncharacteristically concerned. She reached out, probing Saeran's leg before she could stop her. A pained breath hissed from between her teeth. Her sister blanched. "Oh, no. Let me see it this instant."

Saeran shook her head, moving away from her sister. "It's on my upper thigh. Really, Blaine, it's nothing for you to fret over."

"Of course it is," she snapped, pointing at her thigh. "Take off the trews. Let me see what's happened."

"But...it's broad daylight and...Blaine," she said pleadingly.

"No, off with the trews!"

Saeran shook her head. Blaine had always been the curvaceous sister with the flawless skin, whereas Saeran was too scrawny and dotted with bruises from her training. Knowing that her sister knew she was the better-looking one made it that much harder for Saeran to reveal her body.

Blaine sighed. "I am your sister. Lord, I gave you baths all of the time when you'd get into mud, or some other ungodly substance. I know what you look like unclothed. Not being as curvy as I, does not mean you are not beautiful."

The way she said that, made Saeran feel the exact opposite.

"Come now, off with the trews. We still have duties to attend to, you know. I can't wait all day for you."

There was the Blaine she knew.

Sighing, she stood up. She hid her flaming face as she unwound the belt and let the trews fall to the ground.

"Oh, my. Saeran, what did you do to yourself?" Blaine reached out to lightly brush her fingers over the blood-red bruise. It was so gentle that she didn't feel it—until Blaine pressed a little harder.

She jerked away from her sister's hand.

"Did that hurt?" she asked, staring at the bruise with fascination. It was like she'd never seen one before—which she very well might not have. Blaine had lived the majority of her life at court, and nothing daring or dangerous happened there. If Saeran were honest with herself, coming to this keep was the first time she'd ever been exposed to fighting and bruising—and it was only the latter that she excelled at.

Thinking of the training made her stomach flip. She shouldn't have mentioned anything to the laird—he might have forgotten about it completely. Nay, wait. Brodrick would have hunted her down. She sighed to herself, and then began pulling up her trews.

"That's...quite atrocious," Blaine said, wringing her hands together. "Have you done anything to lessen the pain of it? I can imagine it feels as if someone had cut you in two!"

"Sabia was trying to help me when you walked in. It doesn't hurt so much that I can't walk, though. The horse didn't do as much damage as it could have.

A look crossed over her face, but it was gone quickly enough that Saeran didn't have a chance to decipher it.

Blaine stood. "Yes, well. I still need someone to come to the village with me."

"I'll go saddle your horse for you," she offered. She might be a terrible rider, but at least she could do that much. Saeran took guilty pleasure in knowing she could saddle a horse while her perfect sister could not.

Blaine looked at her as if she'd grown two heads. "Horses? No, we will walk."

The thought of walking made her leg throb. "Walk? Blaine, my leg..."

"You said yourself you can walk on it," she said, waving a hand through the air. She crossed to her door, opening it. "Now that I have regained my composure, I can show my face in the hall. How barbaric of him," Blaine snapped to Saeran, as if it was her fault. "The hall looked lovely and he did not like it. It is a blatant insult to his betrothed!"

She stormed out of the room. For a second, all Saeran could do was stare after her sister.

Now that she thought about it, the cats at court had actually hated her.

She's just stressed, Saeran, she chided herself. *She must marry an ogre of a man so that you can live. An ogre of a man with startling green eyes...*

Eyes that suspected too much.

She'd have to stay away from The Lion if she wanted to keep the two of them safe. In a way, she was grateful that he already had a squire. That way, she wouldn't have to cater to his needs, and there would be less chance of her slipping up.

"Saeran!" her sister yelled from out in the hall. Saeran tied her belt and ran out of the door, closing it behind her.

"Coming, sister—"

Her words were cut short by a slender body colliding with hers. "I'm so—"

"Excuse you!" a male voice said sharply, grabbing her by the arms. She would have fallen if not for the surprisingly strong boy who'd grabbed her.

"I'm so sorry," she finished quickly, pulling out of his arms. If she didn't catch up to her sister soon, there'd be hell to pay. Blaine had already yelled at her about being irresponsible.

When she turned to leave, she was stopped once again. The boy ran in front of her. She paused, looking at him.

The boy she'd run into wasn't slender, but lithe. Mayhap she'd been around too many brawny men to recognize anything except sheer strength and domination. The boy standing in front of her wasn't quite a boy, yet he wasn't quite a man, either. He was at that awkward in-between phase. Unfortunately, the interest in his eyes as he stared down at her wasn't purely boy.

"What are you running for?" he asked, cocking his head.

"My sister is waiting for me."

He nodded slowly, still looking her over. She backed away from him, thinking that putting some space between them would act as a barrier. It looked as if he was undressing her with his eyes—and not in the way that the laird had.

She didn't much like that, even if the boy thought she was a completely different gender—which made it that much more strange. A strange feeling settled in her gut.

"Why don't you come with me?" he said, more of a demand than anything.

She frowned. "I just said that my sister was—"

"Who is your sister?"

"Blaine Sinclair, future Lady Shaw."

Realization dawned on his face. "I was not aware she had a brother. I'd been told she had a sister."

Saeran smiled uneasily. He didn't give her a bad feeling—as in, he wasn't coming off as lecherous. The boy was simply curious. That, she could understand.

"The king has many family members. It's easy for him to get confused," she said, feeding him the lie the two sisters had agreed on.

"Yes, well. That's interesting enough." He leaned against the wall, gazing at her still. Saeran heard her sister vaguely call her name, and he raised a brow. "Don't tell me you'll go running after her like a pup."

Saeran frowned.

"She is my sister. I have to escort her."

"There are plenty of people here that could take her to the village. She needs another woman to do the shopping with her." He frowned. "Although, the laird won't like her going to the village at all right now."

"Why is that?"

"I am not sure if I should tell you," he said ruefully. The charming, boyish smile drew her back.

Saeran, ever curious, leaned forward. "You can tell me. I'm an excellent keeper of secrets." She might be an excellent keeper, but lying...not her specialty.

"No, I think it best that I keep it to myself for now. The laird wouldn't be so pleased to have his fun spoiled."

She couldn't stop her derisive snort and spoke before she could stop herself. "The laird would not know how to have fun if a jester were dancing in front of him."

He frowned sharply. "You cannot say such things about him, especially in the open. It's highly offensive."

"Well, I apologize. May I be frank?"

"Yes, of course," he said, leaning forward conspiratorially. If it hadn't been for the gleam of humor in his eyes, she would have walked away. His interest in her was intense, but not enough that she couldn't overlook it and see a future friend.

She had never had a real friend. Besides Blaine and a boy she'd known when she was younger. Her sister liked to keep Saeran to herself, and she didn't mind. Books and her sister were all she had needed after their parent's death.

"I am worried for my sister's safety," she said quietly, glancing down the hall. She hadn't heard or seen her sister in a couple of moments, and with Blaine's fickle mind, she might get off the hook just this once.

The boy burst into laughter. Just like his smile, it was charming, though there was a tone to it she'd never heard. It wasn't unpleasant, but it made her curious.

"Trust me when I say that your sister does not need to fear the laird."

"What about myself?" she asked. "Should I fear being sent away? He would not let me be his squire. I'm merely a chaperone for my sister. The second they are married, he'll send me away."

His laughter returned with full force. "Oh, you're killing me here! Listen," he said, choking down his amusement. "I swear to you, you do not have to worry about being sent away because of a marriage."

She frowned. "You say that strangely. Why?"

"For private reasons," he said, chuckling. He covered his hand with his mouth, an oddly feminine gesture. "Soon enough, you'll know everything."

"Aye? How soon? What is there to know?" she asked, crossing her arms over her chest. "I ought to be like my sister and demand answers."

His eyes rolled. Again, a very...feminine gesture. At least, the way he did it was. She looked closer. Was that...was that blush, upon his cheeks?

"I've heard much about your sister and her demands. I do not think I could handle them from her brother as well."

Saeran laughed, despite herself.

"For some reason, I agree with you."

Their laughter fell into an odd silence.

Finally, when it became too much for Saeran, she bowed her head. "It was nice to—"

"My name is Connor," he blurted, sticking out his hand. She stared at it. "Laird Shaw's squire."

Tentatively, she held out her hand. As a lady, she never "shook hands". It was bowing, nodding, and curtseying. He didn't comment on how utterly foolish she looked as she worked the dynamics of the manly handshake. If anything, his smile widened.

"Would you walk with me?" he asked, gesturing down the hall, in the direction her sister had went. Now that Blaine had forgotten about her, she didn't want to put herself in Blaine's vision. But she nodded, knowing that if her mother saw her refuse a gentleman's offer, she'd be horrified.

"How long have you been a squire?" she asked. Saeran had no clue how small talk was done, especially between two men.

"For as long as I can remember."

"Is that...bad?"

He gave her a look. "In some eyes, yes. The laird has been very generous and understanding. My father and he were friends. Once my father realized I had no intention of becoming a knight, he made it his goal for me to become one."

"Why would you not wish to become a knight?"

He gave her a small smile. "I've proven to these Highlanders that Lowlanders are just as lazy as we appear."

Despite the barb at her own people, Saeran snickered. "Your humor is most dry. I'll have you know, my sister and I come from the Lowlands. It was not all that bad."

Connor ran his eyes over Saeran, then turned a raised brow to her. She flushed. "If you'd have grown up here, you would not have the stature of a leaf."

She scowled. "You're not much better yourself!"

"Yes, well, I'm a squire in partial-name-only. I am not required to be buff and masculine. For you, on the other hand...You're out here chaperoning your sister. One should have some skill in combat for that sort of thing. The men out here are like rabid dogs. If one of them so desired Blaine, they'd take her without a second thought, and bully you for being a leaf."

"I am not a leaf, sir," she said, though she was trying her best not to laugh. "I am but a las—lad who has taken the slender side of the family. 'Tis not a crime where I come from."

"That is true. However, in the Highlands, it's kill or be killed. And you, my lord, are of the size to be killed."

"What if I were smart? Would I be more likely to survive then?" His words were no longer amusing her. Images of being run through with a sword played in her mind, and she shuddered. Blaine was a rare find. Men would come for her left and right. And Saeran! Saeran was expected to protect her sister's honor by defending her.

Connor laughed. "Half the men in these parts have more muscle than brain, my lord."

So basically, she was not in luck's favor. Saeran's shoulders slumped.

"Do not worry. I happen to like men who are more slender than burly. It's refreshing."

"You like..." She stopped before she could finish the sentence. Not only was it ridiculous, but it made her feel like a fool for beginning to suspect something that couldn't be possible.

But he blushed. Sweetly. Adorably. She moved away from him so quickly that she bumped into the wall. Saeran stared at him with wide eyes.

"'Tis not a secret around here that I do not prefer women."

"What—"

He came close to her, bracing his hands on either side of her head. Suddenly, all of those odd gestures made sense. The look in his eyes when he'd first seen her. The way he'd gazed at her as if she was a piece of meat to be devoured.

Saeran was so stunned that she couldn't move as his head dipped to her neck.

"Sir, this is—"

"The laird has always been tolerant of my ways," he murmured soothingly. "He will not care if we share something like this."

"This is—too fast—I'm not like that—"

He chuckled, reaching up to rub a thumb over her cheek. "There's no need to lie about it. Your flirting was enough for me."

"What—" He puckered like a fish, and moved in for the kill. Quicker than she'd ever moved in her life, Saeran ducked under his arms and backed away from him. He whirled around, face full of confusion, and reached for her arm. She expected a wall to catch her.

There wasn't. All there was to save her was a banister—that her

63

fingers missed.

Fear locked in her throat. But before she could tumble to her death, Connor grabbed her by her shirt, right in the center. His fingers curled not only around her shirt, but the binding that spread over her breasts. The shirt tore under his fingers, revealing the binding.

His quick grab was enough to give her time to grab the banister. Thank the Lord, because a second later he was swiping his hands on his thighs as if he'd touched fire.

The look he gave her told her everything she needed to know. She quickly gathered the edges of her shirt together, cursing herself. She hadn't put on the shift after her bath because of the way it clung to her body, and now, she might just pay for her lapse.

"Why," he hissed, "do you have *breasts*?"

Chapter Eight

"Did ye' talk to the king about the MacLeods?"

He looked up at Brodrick, a man he'd known since they were but bairns. The darkness in the hall cast shadows over his face, and it was just how it should have been. The windows were covered and the only source of light came from the candles and the fire in the hearth. Though it was spring, the Highlands became chilly. With the two children that were now running around his keep, he didn't want his keep to be an ice block.

Kane grunted. "Every time I come in contact with the king, we talk of those bastards."

"Ye' didn't tell him about the latest attack?" The two of them were in the hall, watching the maids return it to its original glory, and drinking some ale. He didn't normally turn to the spirits, and after his brilliant plan on his way home, he'd thought he was done with them. But now things were different.

Very, very different.

"The king will no' understand these matters," he said, knowing it was the truth. The king never understood. Just like the rest of the Lowlanders, he had no notion of what it took to be a chieftain, thinking it only fun and games. That opinion coming from a man who ruled far more lands than Kane was irritating, and also one of the contributing reasons why he didn't bother the king with the MacLeods.

The MacLeods, however, didn't think twice about running to the higher power.

Like right now.

"They're trying to gain the other clans' favor," Brodrick said. "The Blacks haven't sided with them, but the Campbells have."

Kane set down the chalice.

"Why the hell would they be finding allies? Everything is over. As far as I'm concerned, the wars are done."

"They donna think it's over," Brodrick said. "Black sent his son here with the warning."

"Ye' can't be serious."

"Unfortunately, I am. The McGregors are coming to talk to you about the feud within a sennight, as well. I do not think the clans are taking well to being petitioned like this." The McGregors were long-time allies of Shaw. Laird McGregor had been the one to pick-up the pieces for Kane after his father's death. Kane knew without a doubt in his mind who the McGregors were siding with.

"I donna even want this," Kane growled, swiping a hand over his face. "The Campbells are the second largest clan in the Highlands. To go to war with them would be... God damnit. The MacLeod men need to realize that this is over."

Brodrick gave him an arched look. "I had expected ye' to be happy about this. They've been asking for it since the day your sister was betrothed to Hans Grayham, and ye've not been so chaste about battle lately."

"I had planned to be done with it all. Marrying Blaine was to be a cure-all for the clans." He didn't elaborate. Brodrick stared at him. The story of how the Shaws had almost become extinct by the king's decree was well-known.

"Why would the Campbells side with MacLeod, is what I'm wondering," Brodrick mused. "If it hadn't been for the Campbell's hot-headedness, Helen would be here today. The Campbell's are the last people I'd expect the MacLeods to ally themselves with."

"The MacLeods are weak. They haven't been to a proper battle since my parent's marriage. The only clan strong enough to have a fighting chance against us is the Campbells."

"Aye, but we have the McGregors on our side. The fight has already been won."

"Something tells me that MacLeod does no' think everything is settled. He's desperate if he's going to Campbell. He's the reason my mother was sent away in the first place."

"I feel like there's something more to this than MacLeod craving blood," Brodrick bit out. They shared a look. Kane couldn't help but to agree with him. MacLeod knew who the greater force was.

Could the king be siding with them again? Though Kane and King James were 'friends'—he used the term lightly, especially after the recent events—the king was always a lover of drama.

"I say we cut them down before they can attack. I donna want my family being put in danger because Alasdair has grown soft in the head."

"Aye," Kane agreed. "But what of the Campbells? Ye' said the McGregors were coming within a sennight. Campbell might have the patience it requires to start an effective battle, but the MacLeods do no'."

"Mayhap less than a sennight. His squire arrived a couple of days ago with news that McGregor was approaching fast." Brodrick paused. "Ye donna think the McGregors are concerned about this, do ye'?" His question held a subtle meaning that was not lost to Kane.

"This battle will not be as bloody as you fear. I can send to the king—"

"I suspect the MacLeods have already done so, and I know ye' do too, my laird. Though he's your friend, he has always catered to the MacLeods."

"Like anyone would for whiny dirt mongers," Kane grunted.

"Aye, well, the MacLeods are a bunch of wee, undeveloped lassies. They wave their swords around with the vigor of a bairn with a feather. It does just as much damage."

Kane laughed. "You're correct. Truly, if we were to leave now, just the two of us, we would reach MacLeod land in less than a night."

"I donna see the point of us walking out of the lion's den when there are plenty a lass to be found. Ye' haven't taken a moment to yourself in the whole last moon. What could we be leavin' here for if the McGregors are coming?"

Kane grinned. "A little bloody foreplay never hurt anyone."

"Were ye' no' just saying ye' didn't want this?" Brodrick said, shaking his auburn head. "Now yer wantin' to play with the girls across the creek? Och, poor Kane. Yer starting to contradict yourself, my friend. Mayhap I should try for lairdship. That way it would be women galore, instead of all this bloodshed."

Kane snorted, then pushed the ale away from him with a rueful shake of his head. "It takes a certain kind of man to be put in my position and not lose his head."

"You've already succumbed to the madness. It's my turn now," Brodrick said, laughing.

If it had been any other man speaking to him like this, Kane could guarantee that they wouldn't make it away from the table without a black eye. Fortunately for Brodrick, they'd been friends since they were wee lads. Kane knew that Brodrick did not envy him his responsibilities. As far as Kane knew, no one in the clan would dare try him. The feud with the MacLeods was too much of a threat.

The MacLeods were a bunch of cowards looking for handouts. Besides their feeble attempts at attacks and riling Kane to retaliate, they were not a threat. A bee held more promise of danger than that sorry lot.

A sharp, feminine voice jerked him out of his thoughts. The look on Brodrick's face made him raise a brow.

"Saeran!" the voice snapped. He recognized it as Blaine Sinclair's voice. The irritation in her voice made him frown. One of the maids, one he'd never seen before, came rushing by him. "I swear, he gets on my nerves so much that I feel as if my head will explode."

"Aye, my lady," the servant murmured. Bowing her head, she held Lady Blaine's hand to help her with the final steps.

"She does that," Brodrick said, almost bitterly. "Has the servants help her with every little thing. The last steps of the stairs, lifting a pot. 'Tis like the lady canna support herself." Kane grunted, watching the woman. He finally got a good look at her.

She was quite...thick. Not lean like her brother or small, either. She had black hair that was nearly white with powder. The only reason he could tell that it was black was because there was a spot on her head that had been missed. He wondered if she knew it was there.

Her gown was a deep red, and jewelry lined her neck. Even her fingers wore jewels. He imagined it was hard for her to bend them. She stopped chattering about Saeran the moment she saw him studying her. A splotchy blush rose up her chest to her cheeks.

"My lord!" she said, walking towards him. His lips pressed, and he looked down at his ale.

"Ye' get the same feeling from her that I do, don't ye?" Brodrick muttered. He nodded his head to Kane, then stood. "I'll leave ye' to it, then."

Kane watched his long-time friend, a man he'd been to battle with countless times, run away from the large, red-faced lady who was striding towards him as if she owned the place. If he were honest with himself, this wasn't how he wanted his day to go.

Talk about the clans, find out who the golden nymph swimming in his creek was, and avoid talking to Blaine at all costs. That had been his plan. Now that there was only one sister to deal with, his plan felt foolish—but he was not ready to marry, especially with this lady. She wasn't the bonny girl the king had claimed her to be.

She was a viper with a poisoned tongue.

Aye, he definitely wasn't going to marry the chit. Alas, he still had to get her to say yes to the betrothal.

"I've been meaning to talk to you!" she exclaimed, sitting next to him.

"Have ye'?" he muttered, grabbing the chalice that he'd just pushed away.

"Oh, yes. My brother and I had planned to go to the market today—"

"For?"

She blinked, her thick eyebrows turning downward. "Excuse me?" It was as though she was shocked that he was questioning her. He didn't care in the slightest. This was his home, and his pocket was paying for whatever she was planning on doing. He was sure the king's payment wouldn't cover the make-over she seemed to want for his estate.

"I asked what ye' were going to the market for. 'Tis not a hard concept to understand, woman."

Her cheeks turned red. "Excuse me, my lord, but I fail to see—"

"My keep. My pocket. My rules. If yer planning to get more maids and rushes, ye' better think otherwise." He took a swig of his ale, then slammed the empty chalice onto the wooden table. She stood at the sound.

"I do not appreciate being spoken to as if I am a simpleton, my lord," she snapped. Now he knew why the king's dowry for this girl was so large—she didn't know her place.

"And I donna appreciate having my home upturned without my wishes. Where is yer brother?" he asked, watching the drawn look come over her face.

"He was supposed to be right behind me..." She looked over her shoulder. Her face turned red when she found he wasn't. Who could blame him? If Kane had to listen to Annalise complain about the way he breathed air, he'd have been fine if someone stole her away, too.

69

He frowned down at the lass. Why would Saeran want to stay here if his sister was only going to berate him? His lips pressed.

"Aye, well, yer brother will be quite busy with me and—"

"No, no," she said quickly, sternly. "That simply won't do. He is my companion while I'm here. He should be by my side every second."

"It was my understanding that he was to be a squire of mine. Do ye' happen to know the duties of a squire, my lady?" he asked mockingly. Her thin, red lips tightened until they disappeared completely. Kane was not often a superficial man, but it appeared to him that Blaine Sinclair was as ugly on the outside as she was on the inside.

He'd heard plenty about her, seen enough of her, and if Brodrick didn't like her? Well, he also knew enough about her from just that. He was glad he'd thought of a plan to get out of the king's ridiculous contract. He wasn't afraid to admit that he didn't want a thing to do with Blaine. His gut never lied, and Blaine Sinclair did not make an exception.

Chapter Nine

"My sister is probably very worried about me—"

"Do not try to get out of this," Connor said sharply. He grabbed her by the arm when she would have run away. Fear slid down her throat. The torn piece of her shirt fell to the side, revealing the binding once again. His face hardened.

"There is not a single thing I'm trying to get out of," she said through tight lips, wrapping the shirt tightly around her. Her face must have looked as pale as snow. "I must be off—" Saeran tried to pull herself out of his grip. Instead of letting her go, he threw open a door and pushed her inside.

"Why are you parading around as if you're a man?" he asked. "If the laird knew you were a woman—" He cut himself off, and his eyes widened. "If he knew you were a woman, he would have to choose."

She swallowed thickly, staring at him. A cool draft was breezing through the unused room, making the skin on the back of her neck raise. Or, mayhap it was the fact that he'd connected everything together so quickly. Or, mayhap it was the fact that she'd failed herself and her sister.

The person standing in front of her was the laird's squire. They talked every day. What were the chances that he would hide this for her, a complete stranger?

Her throat became tight. It was impossible to breathe.

"Please," she said quietly, strangled. "Do not let him know of this. I have to stay with my sister."

He stared at her. For so long, nothing happened. She started to tremble.

"You are lying to a man who is ultimately going to protect you," he said, disbelieving.

"No," she said, shaking her head. "No, he won't have to protect me. I can take care of myself."

He snorted. "Yes, because you can definitely protect yourself. What happened moments ago was a clear example of that." His sarcasm stung her.

"You caught me off guard!" she said defensively.

Connor stared at her again. "You're lying to the second most powerful man in the Highlands, and about something that's...that's serious. Is your real name even Saeran? Does that not hurt your...your..." He gestured to the torn binding and, she assumed, her chest. She couldn't make herself answer him.

Her face flamed. The rush of blood to her face made her dizzy. This was a mess. Not even a fortnight after her arrival, someone knew—and someone who was nearly as dangerous to her safety as the laird himself was.

"Please—"

"Saeran—or whatever your name is. Do not ask me to lie to the laird about this. He might not seem like a barbarian to some, but he has the power to be the most ruthless person ever known. To lie to him...not only would I be punished, but so would you."

"I know I would be," she said quickly. Fear made her desperate—bolder than she'd ever been. To have her secret found out... Blaine would kill her before Grayham could get to her.

"Then why risk it?" he asked, astounded. "Being a woman is much easier than being a man."

"I—"

He held up a hand quickly, horror lighting his eyes. "You've been training as a squire, haven't you?"

She nodded, not understanding what was so wrong about it.

"You've been training with swords and fists."

Again, she nodded. She'd been doing it for the past fortnight. It wasn't a big deal anymore. All she suffered from were bruises.

Her lips pressed.

Blaine.

This was all Blaine's fault.

Nay, she thought. *Blaine is only trying to keep us together.*

For some reason, the thought didn't feel as comforting as it used to. It only made her angry, as completely unjustified as it was. She wanted to be a lady. She wanted to be safe with a strong husband. She wanted to have her family. She wanted to have children. She wanted... She wanted everything that Blaine was going to get by being married to The Lion, as dangerous and threatening as he was.

He was a threat to her. Earlier, with the fire crackling and his eyes staring at her as if he were stripping her of all her secrets, he hadn't seemed like The Lion should have.

In the hall he had. His roaring and rudeness, the brute strength he had exuded... It had been terrifying in an enchanting way.

But in his study, he'd been a completely different man—and that had terrified her for reasons she couldn't explain.

"You could have been hurt!" he suddenly burst out. Horror washed over his face.

Saeran grimaced.

"We have to tell the laird. A woman—a *lady*—should not be involved in sword play!" He whirled around, pale as a ghost. Panic climbed up her throat.

"No! No, you can't do that," she burst out, grabbing his arm. He tensed under her, but at least he stopped. "I can't be taken away. He can't choose me, and he definitely can't know who I really am. Please, do not do this to me."

He slowly turned his head. "You are asking me to lie to him."

"I cannot be taken away from my sister."

"Why?"

She blinked. "Why?"

"Yes. Why can't you leave Blaine? Why would you want to stay here with her? Are you a spy? Do you work for the English?" he asked, narrowing his eyes on her.

"No! No—I'm here for her, I'm not a spy at all!"

"But she is wretched!"

Saeran bit her lip. "She is worried about becoming the laird's wife. He's reputed to be a barbarian and—"

"'Reputed'", he echoed. He glared at her, and she took a step back. Only seconds ago this boy had tried to accost her, thinking she was the same gender as he. Now, he was defaming her sister—in front of her! The situation was too odd for her to dwell on. All that mattered was getting him to stay quiet.

"You do not even know the man!" he said, clearly offended on behalf of his laird. "If you just tell him, he will understand."

73

"He will not," she denied, shaking her head. The way he'd yelled about the hall and its changes came back to her. She wrung her trembling hands together. "He will be forced to pick between Blaine and I. She will be picked, and I—I will be sent off to marry." Grayham. Bile rose in her throat.

"Now, now," he said, holding a hand out. "I highly doubt he'd choose Blaine if you came into the picture. He'd be pleased to know your true gender."

"You can't know that," she insisted, taking the hand he held out. She clasped it tightly, trying to make him believe her. "And I cannot risk it."

"It won't be a risk," he denied.

She stared at him. Saeran didn't think he'd be swayed in the matter, as much as she desperately needed him to.

"What do I have to do to convince you that revealing me is a bad idea?"

"Bribery?" He laughed a little.

Her lips tightened. She'd do anything. Forced to Grayham's side, as barren as she was, would result in her death.

"I'd try anything," she said with conviction.

Connor didn't react.

"Anything," she pleaded, tightening her fingers around his. He looked down between them, brows drawn over his eyes.

"You're asking me to lie to the laird," he repeated quietly. "What has you so terrified of marriage to him? He would not hurt a woman."

She didn't know if she could tell him everything. Blaine would flog her if she knew they were having this conversation, if she knew Saeran had gotten into this situation at all.

She needed Connor to trust her. If he thought for a second that she was a threat to the laird, he would expose her. Telling him the truth about why she couldn't marry would eliminate the possible threat he thought she posed.

"I will not be the one to marry him," she finally said. She dropped his hand, instead wrapping her arms around herself. "Blaine will."

"He has a choice in who he marries, though. He should know there's another option."

She looked at the ground. "Tell me. The laird needs an heir, does he not?"

"Well—" He leaned against the door, crossing his arms over his chest. "Before the king brought you two to him, he was not concerned. If anything happens to him, Brodrick will take over. But now that it has been presented to him, yes, he does need an heir. I always believed he did."

Her chest tightened even worse than before. The only one who knew Saeran's problem was Blaine.

"What does this have to do with you?" he asked, coming forward.

"I cannot marry the laird because I am barren," she said, refusing to meet his eyes. All she would see was pity. Connor made a sound, and then swiped a hand over his face. "I'm..."

"He can't know," she insisted softly, unable to look at him.

"The king would give you a husband who will understand." He sounded so sure of himself. She only laughed.

"Have you ever heard of Hans Grayham?"

Stony silence. So bad that it made her shiver. Saeran cast a glance to Connor.

"Yes, I know of him. Everyone does."

"That's who I'm going to marry if the king realizes any of this is going on." She worried her lip, tightening the torn cloth around her chest. Speaking, even thinking about him, gave her shivers. Made it hard for her to breathe. "How do you know of him, all the way in the Highlands?"

"There's much to know," Connor muttered. "He was the laird's sister's husband."

She stared at him.

"Grayham's third wife?"

"Yes." One word. Short. Pained.

"I'd heard rumors...that...that the laird was the one to kill her," she whispered.

Connor's eyes blazed. "Who did you hear that from? Kane would have never done *anything* to hurt Annalise. He worshipped her every breath."

She backed away at his vehemence. "It was only a rumor I heard—"

He laughed sharply. "Oh, so you're one of those ladies. The ones who believe and simper over everything they hear at court." He raked his eyes over her. Disgust that she couldn't understand darkened his eyes.

"I'm sorr—"

"Oh, I just bet," he snapped. This was not going well. Instead of making him favor her, she'd angered him. It rubbed off on her, causing frustration to flare inside of her.

She stepped forward, stabbing a finger at him. "I don't understand what has you so angry! All I did was voice my suspicions."

"Gossiping," he said, shaking his head. "Gossiping to me about the death of a beautiful woman. Thinking that her brother was the one who ended her life. Have you ever watched a lion stalk his prey?" he asked, raising a brow.

She wanted to vomit. A threat. He was threatening her— because she had misspoken.

"I take that as a no," he said. He stalked to the door, his lithe body stiff with anger. "Well, you might want to take note of how Shaw will react when he learns of your...secret, and how you lied to him."

Connor was going to tell him. Her blood ran cold. "Connor, please, I meant no—"

"Offense? 'Tis quite all right," he murmured, smiling at her. "I'll not be the one to worry over it anymore. I'll leave that to The Lion when he finds out that a person he had planned to protect is not only lying to him, but spreading rumors about his sister's death."

Before she could say anything else, he stalked out of the door. She watched him go, trembling.

She'd begun to grow hopeful, but now…

Chapter Ten

"I'm quite thirsty," Blaine said as Saeran passed her sister's room. She'd hoped to just sneak by without her noticing, but luck was not in Saeran's favor, and hadn't been for quite some time. A full moon here, and not a single day had gotten better.

Her sister was slowly growing worse in attitude and actions. Servants had become too terrified to show their faces. Sabia's children no longer ran around the hall. The Lion was home as much as cows flew, and even Brodrick had become scarce of late.

Even Connor, though he was around the keep more than the laird, stayed away from the halls, the kitchens, the gardens, and anywhere else Blaine was.

Saeran couldn't even blame them anymore.

"Aye," she muttered, forcing herself to smile. "I bet—"

"Why," Blaine said with an irritated smile, "must you do that 'aye' thing? It is annoying to the point of distraction, sister. You've been doing it since we were children. I don't even know where you learned that!"

At least Blaine was honest...

"I'm sorry," she said, even though she wasn't. It had become such a habit when she was younger that it had stuck with her and grew. In a way, it was a connection to her childhood.

She smiled a little.

Every year, there had been a fair with all of the clans— Lowlanders and Highlanders alike would come. The Sinclairs had not missed a single year of those fairs, but only because Saeran had forced them to go.

The laughing, the smells, the animals, the events. It had all been a thrill. Even as a girl, she'd known that feuds existed between every clan, born purely from pride and greed. Her mother had made Saeran promise that she wouldn't repeat the muttered words she'd spoken, but they'd stuck with Saeran all through her childhood.

She hadn't been able to understand them. The Lowlanders got along just fine. Since they rarely visited the Highlands, she hadn't known of the brutes that roamed the dangerous land.

That is, up until she got lost at the fair one year. She'd only been the tender age of six, but filled with curiosity and excitement, she'd wandered off. It wasn't until she'd stumbled into an area with large, burly men who all wore swords, that she realized she was lost.

Almost instantly, she'd started to cry. Saeran bit her lip as she remembered her own foolishness. Luckily, a small lad with hair as dark as night had come to her aid. He'd escorted her out of the area with a gentlemanly hand on her elbow.

He'd immediately became her hero. What a brave boy, she had thought with wonder, gazing up at him. He was so stern in the face, and he looked as if he never smiled. His young strength and confidence had given her the courage she needed to stop sniveling.

When he realized she'd calmed down, he began to talk.

The brogue in his voice was thick and heavy, much more so than hers. It had only added to her adoration of her savior.

As a young, silly girl, she hadn't thought to ask his name. Every year during the fair, they would find each other for a day. Talking, laughing, and playing was all they'd do. He'd saved her countless times from wandering off, and had even escorted her to events.

Their fun was always cut short, and so they would part on sad terms, promising to meet each other the next year.

Over the years, she'd become so fascinated with his brogue that when she was home, she'd practice it. "Aye," she'd say, over and over until she got it just right. Eventually it became habit for her to respond with 'aye', and as hard as her mother had tried to make her change her ways, she hadn't.

The year that she'd perfected it, hoping to impress her friend, he hadn't appeared at the fair.

He hadn't come that year, or the year after *that*, or the year after *that*.

"Why are you just standing there?" Blaine asked, leaning out of the cracked door. Saeran sighed, closing her eyes. "I'm thirsty. I demand a drink, sister."

"Yes, Blaine," she said tiredly, rolling her eyes when Blaine slammed the door in Saeran's face. Oh, her sister was such a joy these days. As she continued her way down the hall, past her room, she debated with herself. Her feet were sore, her arms were trembling from working, and her back ached like no other. Mayhap, if she were quiet enough, her sister would forget the demand she could have taken care of herself, and Saeran could just climb into bed.

Of course, if that happened, Blaine would only have words for her in the morning.

She glanced toward the kitchen. An apple for her troubles didn't sound too bad, if she were honest with herself. Saeran rubbed the small of her back, then sighed, slouching her way down the stairs. Aye, her sister needed a swift kick in her lumpy arse if she—

Saeran stopped. Her eyes widened.

Lumpy arse.

She'd said her sister had a *lumpy arse*. She immediately felt guilty. So, so guilty. By today's standards, her sister was gorgeous. She'd said it out of spitefulness, and there was a difference between spite and truth.

Saeran pressed her lips, continuing her way down the hall, becoming angry with herself.

"I've been at this keep for a full moon," she whispered to herself angrily. "I've been here for a full moon, and every single day, it only gets worse. Why do I put up with her attitude?" she asked herself, throwing up her hands.

"She isn't even herself anymore!" She mumbled on about her sister, filling a cup with water. She made her way out of the kitchen. "By all rights, I am her 'brother'. I should be disciplining her! Lord! Even the laird does not favor her attitude."

"Mayhap if he knew there was another option, he would further the process along," a familiar voice said. She froze, hand tightening around the cup. Connor came from around the corner with a raised brow. "Do you talk to yourself often, my lady?"

Her lips tightened. She'd made an enemy out of Connor, and she had no wish to further the reasons why he should report her to the laird. For whatever reason, the day that he'd stormed away from her, he hadn't revealed her secret—nor the day after that.

Every time the laird walked into the hall or singled her out, she began to shake with so much force she had to hold onto something to keep her balance. Ever since Connor had made it clear he wanted nothing more than to reveal who and what she really was, her life had been ruled by paranoia.

She passed him, expecting to just breeze away from him without a care in the world. He took hold of her arm, and the cup flew out of her hands.

Anger burned inside of her as she faced him.

"Not only do you make me fear for my life every day, now you manhandle me?" she hissed, yanking out of his grip. "I've come to the end of my rope with people forcing me to do this and that."

He held up his hands defensively.

"Listen, my lady. I meant no—"

"Do not call me 'my lady' unless you plan on telling the laird. Otherwise, someone could hear you. Or is that your plan?" she asked. Her lower lip trembled with the force of her anger. The days of fear and anxiety had taken their toll on her, and she could hardly face the man who could ruin everything.

"No," he said vehemently, shaking his head. "No, that is not what I plan."

"You want to be the one to tell the laird," she said, nodding. "Oh, aye. I completely understand. Take the glory of sniffing out a rat in your precious laird's defenses for yourself, true?"

He frowned. Guilt flickered in his eyes. "No. My lady—"

The look on her face must have stopped him.

"My lady," he said, this time softly, quietly. His voice barely carried to her, and she almost sighed with relief. "I have been watching you lately. I... I fear I understand where you are coming from now."

Saeran didn't say anything. Her heart was pounding too forcefully.

"Although you are wrong about the laird, I understand your concerns. And..." He sighed, giving her a beseeching look. "And any woman who has the patience to put up with Blaine's demands as you have does not deserve to be treated like this."

"I don't understand what you're talking about," she said thickly. She forgot all about the water that was soaking into her shoes. Her hands started to tremble.

He came closer. "Yes you do, Saeran... I want to help you."

"There's nothing you can do," she said, laughing bitterly.

"Nothing you can do besides keep my secret, and you've made it perfectly clear that your loyalty lies with the laird—and I understand that."

"Which is exactly why I want to help you. Saeran, you understand loyalty. The way you deal with your sister, how you ignore all of her bad habits just so you can make her happy, is what makes you...different."

She blushed. Though his words were not said in the most romantic of ways, she couldn't help herself. Never before had she gotten a compliment like that.

He smiled. She remembered the first time they spoke, before he found out what she was hiding. He was not a bad person—she could see that clear as day. She wanted to think he had an ulterior motive by helping her, but she didn't think that was the case.

"I do not agree that keeping this from the laird is your best option." She opened her mouth to say that he was wrong, but he held up a hand. "However, if it makes you feel safe to parade around as a man and get beat up every day while dealing with your witch of a sister, then I will support you."

She blinked.

"You will?"

"Yes. I will—but only because I know that sooner or later, you're going to want to reveal yourself to the laird."

"Why on earth would I do that?" she asked incredulously. "The man is the devil! Have you not seen the way he yells at everything?"

Connor smiled. A small secret smile that made her frown. "I'll enjoy watching you be proved wrong, my lady."

She returned his smile, though hers was more uneasy. "And I'll enjoy watching myself be proved right. There is not a single redeeming quality about the laird that could make me want to reveal myself. He is my sister's betrothed," she said indignantly. "That is the only thing I see about him."

He laughed. "I just bet. You do realize that he hasn't yet asked for her hand, though, correct? He still has time to decide."

"Decide on what? There's no other choice than for him to marry Blaine."

His eyes rolled. "The other option is standing right in front of me."

"Ha!" she said, laughing and waving a finger in his face. "You're wrong about that. He *has* to marry Blaine. She is the only one that can

81

provide an heir for him."

"Whatever you wish to believe," he said, shrugging. "Oh! I forgot to mention. I have conversed with him about your 'training'. I pointed out that in the past moon, you've managed to break more things than learn, so he has agreed to let you clean the stables instead."

Saeran could have cried. Finally, after so long of aching and being hit by men three times her size, she was free of the nightmare. She nodded stiffly, forcing the tears of relief from her eyes. Then dread began to settle in.

Blaine.

She'd have to deal with more of Blaine. The only redeeming thing from her time in the training grounds was that it gave her time to ignore Blaine and everything she wanted to complain about. Now, she wouldn't have a choice except to put up with Blaine.

"...Though I do believe the laird needs someone to help him with accounts."

Her ears perked up.

"Accounts?" She'd done them plenty of times for the Sinclair estate. Her mother had either been too busy prepping Blaine for another ball, and her father had... Well, he'd never preferred to work with numbers. That was what had started her on books, accounts, and everything not court related. Though it had started out as a bother and a frustration, she'd excelled in her work. She had eventually taken over everything that required running an estate.

"Yes, accounts. The laird does not have time to do them; and when he leaves, I leave. With the MacLeod's waging war, it's becoming a hassle for him."

"Didn't he have someone to do it before?" she asked, wringing her hands.

"Blaine scared him away." Of course she did. Saeran should have been angry over it, but she found her opening.

"I—I can do the accounts. It's only fair, since my sister is the reason they aren't being done now," she said, practically jumping on her feet. Oh, she'd missed doing them! Numbers were numbers. Simple. Practical. Perfect. There was only one way the sums could add up, and she reveled in knowing that she could do it correctly. It was the only thing she could do correctly.

"You?" he asked, raising a brow. "What does a lady know about—"

"I did them for my family. Could you speak to the laird? About me doing the accounts for him? That would be another way to do my part around here. I'm quite efficient." She nodded. She needed to do this. Numbers were the one thing she could do without a problem. And, if she were stuck doing accounts all day, her sister would have no reason to bother her.

He started to frown. "I know he must seem terrifying to you, but if you want the job, you will have to ask him yourself for it."

"But I thought you were going to help me," she whined playfully, knowing he was right. It didn't matter to her if she had to talk to The Lion or not—there was now a light at the end of the tunnel and she could practically feel its warmth.

"After the McGregors leave on the morrow, he'll be free to talk. But only for a moment. After that, he's paying a visit to the MacLeods, and I do not know when we'll be back."

"The MacLeods?" She stilled, meeting his eyes. Trepidation went through her. "Does that mean you're going to…"

"No." He shook his head sternly. "There will not be a battle unless they attack first. I fear the MacLeod is planning more than just taking his revenge for his sister, and if the Campbells are involved…" He swiped a hand over his face. "The laird has been too concerned over this to court your sister."

"It's understandable," she murmured. She still didn't have the best of thoughts toward the laird, but at least this gave her a reason as to why he was so barbaric whenever he came around. Too often he'd been out in the fields, talking with the McGregors—who had been there for a fortnight—and too little time had he spent getting to know Blaine.

She knew her sister was difficult to get along with. She was sure that once the laird spent more time with her, he'd realize they could be happy together. The only reason Blaine had grown irritable with Saeran was because of the laird. The more she thought that, the truer it became. With his lack of ambition in taking Blaine as his wife, Blaine was beginning to feel inferior. Because of that, she was taking her frustrations out on everyone around her.

Saeran knew she'd never felt that a day in her life, and blamed her attitude and selfishness on the laird's negligence. She was terrified of him, but Blaine was stronger than Saeran. Stronger and braver. She could handle him better than Saeran would ever be able to—and luckily, they were avoiding that all together. He'd been too busy dealing with the impending battle to worry about the Sinclairs, who were taking over his keep.

"You are indeed one of a kind," he said quietly, gazing at her. There was a look in his eyes, an appreciation that she'd never seen before, that made her blush and back away. He shook his head, and then that same humorous smile lit his face. "It's late, and I imagine you're tired. Now that we have established I am your ally, and not your enemy, I think it's time you go to bed. You'll have to wake early if you wish to catch him."

She blinked. "What do you—oh! The accounts!" She grinned, unable to help herself from hugging him. The joy inside her was so abundant that it was practically pouring out. "I'm so thankful," she said earnestly, clasping him. He returned the hug, then set her away from him.

"Any woman being put in your situation needs all the help they can get," he said with a sigh. He nodded his head to her, exiting the kitchen before she could ask what he meant by that.

"Saeran?!"

The sound of her sister's ungodly loud shout made her flinch. The water—That's right. She'd spilled the water. She heaved a sigh. There was a tinge of hope now—hope that for once, something good might happen to her.

Chapter Eleven

Quicker than she would have thought possible, she retrieved more water for her sister and told herself that she would return to clean up the mess as soon as she was done. When she handed her sister the cup, though, Blaine didn't let her slip away so easily.

"What has you in such a good mood?" she asked, taking Saeran by the arm and dragging her into the room. The door closed behind her, cutting her off from the outside world, and her newfound happiness. All of the joy she'd just felt came to a painful end.

Her sister didn't sound like she was in a good mood—not that she ever was, anyway.

"Nothing," she said, grateful that the lie sounded natural. "I'm just glad to finally have a chance to rest." If the words weren't a good hint, taking the handle in her hand was. Blaine stared at her with narrowed eyes.

Just as quickly as the suspicious look had appeared, a woeful sigh and a sad look replaced it. "Does my own sister dislike me so much that she cannot spare a moment to talk?"

Saeran forced herself not to roll her eyes. "What has you troubled this time, Sister?"

Blaine jumped into the conversation immediately, as she always did. It had become a ritual for this to happen, and each night, it made her tolerance of Blaine less and less.

Saeran wasn't a violent person by nature.

Right now, however, she wanted to shove a stocking into her sister's mouth and run from the room. It was the same thing, every night.

"If Father were alive, he would have challenged The Lion for his negligence! Do you know," Blaine said, sitting on the edge of her bed, "that he hasn't dined with me at all since we've come here? He hasn't even inquired after my health! I fear that he is going to be the most unreasonable husband." She reached forward, taking Saeran's hands. Her large fingers squeezed impossibly tight. "I'm terrified of him. He has such cold eyes. They're as dead as a corpse! You've seen them, haven't you?"

Aye, Saeran had seen them.

A couple times, in fact. And each time, they hadn't been cold or dead... They'd been vibrant and gorgeous, hot with life. The image of him flashed in her mind and she swallowed, pulling away from her sister's hand.

She nodded, even though she couldn't agree with complete conviction. He appeared to be and act like a barbarian, but... His eyes spoke otherwise. She looked at her lap, feeling guilty.

"He can't be all that bad," she tried. Every night, Blaine spoke of how murderous and beastly the laird was.

"Yes, well—I wouldn't know otherwise! The man cannot spare the time of day for his future wife."

"He hasn't yet asked for your hand," she pointed out, recalling Connor's words from just moments ago.

"What are you trying to say, Sister?" Her eyes narrowed. "Do you harbor thoughts about a man who is to be mine?"

Saeran shook her head, reaching out to appease her sister—even though the lie sat like lead in her stomach. Aye, she'd been thinking about the laird. With horrified fascination, each time he came around. He was aptly named—he moved with the grace of a lion. It was hard not to watch him and speculate.

"Never, Blaine. I just think you should make more of an effort to know him, besides..." She trailed off, realizing what she had almost said.

"Besides what, Saeran?" her sister murmured, dangerously quiet.

"Besides letting him hide from you," she filled in. When Blaine only stared at her, she worried her lip. Her sister stood up in a rage. The movement was so quick that Saeran didn't have time to react, to appease her before she went on a rampage.

"I think you meant to say something else," Blaine snapped, crossing her arms over her chest. "I do not appreciate being lied to, especially by my own blood! What kind of a sister are you, Saeran? If you have something to say, then say it!"

Saeran clenched her hands in her lap. She wouldn't fuel her sister's anger. Blaine was only confused and angry, and Saeran had spoken out of turn.

She wearily stood, giving her sister a demure smile. "I will retire for the night."

Blaine watched her with an open mouth. Saeran had her hand on the door, ready to escape.

"Oh, no you won't." Saeran felt the sharp sting of her sister's hand slapping against her arm, then nails dug into her skin. She gasped, yanking herself out of her sister's grip. "You're only alive because I saved you. You owe it to me to listen to my concerns, Saeran! Or should I go to the laird and tell him who you really are?" Blaine threatened maliciously.

"What is wrong with you?" she burst out, clutching her arm to her chest. It was as if Blaine had known she had a bruise there! Blaine opened her mouth to speak, a sneer on her face, but Saeran was done! The pain in her arm only furthered her anger. "Nay, do not answer that. I don't *care* what is wrong with you. You've been acting like a harpy lately, and I've had enough of it!"

Blaine snapped her mouth closed.

"Instead of making a victim out of yourself where the laird is concerned, maybe you should go to him. You act like *everyone* has to cater to your every need. Do I have to remind you that he is the laird of these lands? Do I have to remind you that he answers to no one, including you? Goodness, Blaine!" she shouted, throwing her hands up. It felt so amazing to get this off her chest. The whole entire month, she'd been dying to say something, dying to let her sister know how she felt. For the first time in her whole life, Saeran was finally doing it.

"The only thing you do is order people around and complain about them behind their backs! I'm tired of it. Until you can act like the kind woman I know you can be, I want nothing to do with you. I'm sorry, and I love you, but I've simply had enough." She whirled around, throwing open the door.

Blaine hissed after her, "I'm of the mind to go to the laird right now and tell him about—"

"Do it," Saeran snapped. "I dare you to. He'll be angry at you for cooking up the lie, and then you'll have to go against me in earning his affections. If you haven't noticed, I've spent more time with him than you have, and Brodrick already likes me." Every single word out of her mouth was a bluff. She knew that if the laird found out she was lying to him, he'd be furious, and definitely not consider her for a wife. Connor's words came back to her. The ones where he'd said the laird would understand. On the off chance that he was correct, she let her words fly free.

Saeran was sick and tired of being her sister's lap dog.

Going by the look on Blaine's face, she believed what Connor did—that the laird wouldn't mind if Saeran was a woman. She gave her sister a tight-lipped smile and stepped out of the room.

"Unless you want competition with a woman who actually knows how to run the lands she lives on, I suggest you leave me alone, and keep your words to yourself." Saeran slammed the door in her sister's face, then raced to her room.

The breath she'd been holding was only released once she leaned against the cool stone wall. At first, she was numb to what had happened. She began to undress, undoing the belt and then sliding up her shirt. Once she had the trews off, she sought out the nightgown she kept hidden under the bed.

That's when the shock began to settle in.

The nightgown slid over her body. Her hair fell around her shoulders as the pins came out. Panic made her heart pound like that of a racehorse. How had the fight escalated so quickly? Saeran had always been good at keeping herself calm and collected. She had always been able to listen to her sister without complaining.

What had made tonight different?

The relief over realizing that Connor wasn't an enemy, but an ally? Her sister's constant demand for everything and anything? How selfish her sister was beginning to appear?

Aye, she'd saved Saeran's life by doing this, and she'd said she'd done it out of love. But if Blaine *had* done it out of love, she wouldn't throw it in Saeran's face every day. Blaine wouldn't point it out to her whenever she wanted something or didn't like something that Saeran did. If she really had done it out of love, the "sacrifice" wouldn't need to be brought up every minute!

Saeran didn't want to seem ungrateful for what her sister was doing for her, but what was there to be grateful for?

Her life was no better than it had been.

She was bruised and beaten on every day. She had to hide who she really was. She couldn't enjoy the comfort of books and numbers because she was so busy cleaning up horse shite. She rarely finished with her duties in time for dinner!

While Saeran was living the life of a boy, Blaine was living the life of luxury. Not just the life of a woman, but the life of real luxury, and all because the laird was too busy to tell her otherwise.

Saeran plopped herself onto the bed, glaring at the door she'd previously leaned against. She wasn't ungrateful in the least—she was just tired of putting up with the injustice of her treatment.

She sighed.

Blaine was going to approach her in the morning, with big fat tears on her plump face, and Saeran was going to melt. All of the anger she was feeling right now? Useless. Blaine would somehow manage to wheedle her way back into Saeran's good graces, and then... Well, then she would have to go back to listening to her sister complain about things.

Things like how the laird is never there, or how the laird always glares, growls, and yells, or how the laird doesn't offer her a plate of food like a real man should, or...

Food.

All thoughts of Blaine fled.

She hadn't eaten since yesterday. Her stomach growled so painfully that she moaned and got to her feet. As she crossed to the door, intent on finding that apple she'd thought about earlier, she vaguely realized that her hair was down.

Even as she passed the tossed clothing she'd been wearing earlier, the need for food was more pressing than dressing. If someone found her and it came down to it, she could say she was a maid. The keep had plenty of them, courtesy of Blaine and her neediness. Her modesty had gone out the window the second she started wearing trews and bathing in the river, and the chances of anyone seeing her this late, coupled with the darkness, was zero.

Still, she paused, looking at the trews. Then her stomach cramped. She shook it off, throwing open the door. Not only did she need to find some food, but she needed to clean up the mess she'd made with Blaine's water.

It was late and dark. She'd be as quiet, quick, and stealthy as a mouse.

Aye, no one would see her.

Chapter Twelve

"They left us a present," Brodrick said, storming into the hall. Kane looked up from his chalice.

"What kind o' present?"

"Daniel Duncan's boy was found dead in town. Daniel is down there now, tending to the body."

Kane closed his eyes. "Are ye' sure it was them?"

"Aye. No doubt. They left a piece of their plaid behind, a clear message. They are gearing for battle faster than yer preparing for it, my laird. This is the second sign in the last fortnight. Surely ye' aren't thinking about letting this go. Daniel is demanding blood."

"They're trying to get my men riled," he murmured, swiping a hand over his face. He pushed the chalice away from him, glaring into the fire.

"It's working. Ye' canna sit back and let this go on as if ye' donna notice it."

"I donna plan on it," he growled, glaring at Brodrick. The man stared at him, his jaw ticking. He understood his friend's concerns and wanted to act on them, but it was not the time. The MacLeods expected him to retaliate immediately. They were impatient, unskilled, and unknowing in the world of battle.

Nay, his clan would wait. They would wait until it would hurt the MacLeods the most to attack—after the next storm. They were downhill, and the creek rose to raging heights when Mother Nature tempered with it. When the next storm came, their lands would be flooded, their village at a loss of supplies, and their men tired from fixing the damages.

Once they were weak, Kane would attack with a fury so strong and swift, it would be over as soon as the fight had begun. By the end of the next storm, the MacLeods would no longer be a threat.

Brodrick stared down at him, then stiffly squared his shoulders. Kane would tell him everything when he had his final meeting with the McGregors.

"Donna worry," Kane said, waving a hand. "I have it taken care of." Brodrick didn't speak, but sat down. Kane grinned.

"Ye' give me that look like ye' ken I'd get over it."

"I did," he said, chuckling. "Yer not the most stubborn of men."

"Tell that to Saeran Sinclair. As far as he's concerned, I'm as hard-headed as Ol' Garry's mule." Brodrick gave him a weary smile.

He raised a brow. "What makes ye' say that?"

"Och, but the lad is a wee wimp. I'm the devil! I see the looks he gives me when I send Cameron after him in the ring. I think he's the only one here who hates me more than everyone hates Blaine."

"Do ye' want me to have a talk with him?" he asked, purposely ignoring the mention of his to-be betrothed. Thinking about her gave him a sour taste in his mouth. "Ye' know he's to be taken off his normal duties. Connor pointed out to me that he's cost me more in damages than he can repay in battle."

Brodrick burst into laughter. "Oh, but he has! Almost took my head off once, too! The lad is a menace with a sword, but no' the kind we are looking for. I should have brought it to yer attention beforehand, but ye've been too busy. I'd rather have him contained to an area where people will keep an eye on him than let him loose amongst the lands."

"Is he that bad?"

"Aye, he's that bad."

"Poor lad. And he wanted to be my squire, too." He started to laugh. Conversation with Brodrick had always gotten him out of the dark moods, though it had been harder of late. At least this Saeran provided something other than battle to talk about.

"Actually, it was his sister that wanted him to be a squire. The lad was quite resistant at first. But I figured he'd rather play with the men than follow after his sister, ye' ken? The woman is a terror, though ye' haven't taken much time to figure that out, from what I've seen."

Kane grunted.

"If the lady is as much of a dragon as I've heard she is, I donna want anything to do with her."

"But what about the dowry? Helen and Alex?"

"Let me correct myself. I donna want anything to do with her yet. Have ye' heard her yell at Saeran? 'Tis the most unpleasant thing. If she can yell at her brother, how far do ye' think she'll go in offending me? I heard she called ye' a barbarian to yer face. I donna need a wife offending every damn person she meets."

"Aye," Brodrick said, nodding with understanding. "Some o' the Highlanders out here will think nothing of it to silence her."

"Out of obligation to my wife," he said, shuddering at the word, "I'd have to wage war with yet another clan. I donna want to be stuck with a dragon for my first wife, ye' ken?"

Brodrick shrugged. "Falling off a cliff the night of the wedding never raised suspicious, my laird. Hell, ye've done such a good job of being a beastly man that she may end her life before ye' have to do anything about it."

Kane chuckled. "Aye, well, the king promised me her dowry once we both agreed to the betrothal. He never said anything about going through with the marriage if she backs out from how ungodly a barbarian I am," he said mockingly.

"I donna think the king will let go of such a prize that easily. He'd have something to say to ye' if she went back to him in tears. Though as The Lion, I bet yer actions are expected from the women."

"That's what Saeran is here for," Kane said, shrugging. He ignored his friend's comment. He'd been acting like a beast without any help of Blaine's. "If she has to complain about something, it's normally to him."

"Kane, that's downright evil." Still, Brodrick continued to laugh.

"I haven't noticed," he lied, taking back his chalice from Brodrick. He tilted it to his mouth, then realized it was empty. "First ye' mock me. Now ye' drink all my ale? What kind of clansmen are ye'," he growled, getting to his feet.

Brodrick followed suit. "The most loyal one ye' can have. After all your lazyin' around, ye' need to get up, if only to get yer own ale."

"I should beat you," he said over his shoulder, on his way to the kitchen.

"Aye, but ye' won't!"

He started to his chamber. He'd had enough for the night, and tomorrow was the last day the McGregors would be there. He didn't need to show up stumbling around like a lad who'd just had ale for the first time. That would give the McGregor something to laugh about.

The stairs loomed in front of him. His head started to pound. He hadn't gotten any sleep lately, and his bed was calling to him. As he took the first step, a sound came from the left of him, from the kitchens. He frowned.

It was probably a servant. He took another step, and then the sound came again. He looked to the heavens and sighed. Servants were normally in bed by this time of night. Kane swiped a hand over his face and retracted his steps, storming into the kitchen. It was probably the cook's children. They were always stealing pastries, and while he didn't mind it, it was late. They should be in bed with their mother, not ransacking his kitchen like thieves in the night.

He entered the kitchen, prepared to deal with two little children.

Except, the person leaning over the counter with an apple in her mouth was not a child.

Recognition slapped him in the face.

The water nymph.

She was standing in his kitchen, eating his apple, and staring at him...as if she'd seen a ghost.

A panicked, high-pitch sound came from around the apple. Faster than he could blink, she was running across the kitchen, away from him.

"Wait!" he growled, furious that she'd run from him. He chased after her, taking her by the arm when she would have climbed the steps. "Donna go."

She refused to look at him, trying to pull her arm from his grip. He loosened his hold so that it wouldn't hurt her, but he refused to let her go. The object of his late-night fascination was standing in front of him—in nothing but a filmy shift.

His mouth went dry. All of the blood in his head rushed to his cock, and the only thing he wanted to do was peel the material away from her smooth flesh and gaze upon it. Her skin would still have that soft tan, her body as perfect for him as if he'd molded it himself. Against his will, he tugged her closer to him. His body demanded a connection to her, demanded that after nights of dreaming about her, he touch her.

She stopped struggling. All she did was stare up at him, eyes wide with terror…and something else. Something like fascination, almost.

"What is yer name, lass?" Lord, he'd been dying to ask that question. A whole month, the only thing he had to think of her by was the brief view he'd seen of her by the creek, and her image had haunted him.

"I—Please, let me go," she whispered, turning her face from him.

"Just tell me yer name, lass," he said softly. He turned her face towards his. God, the clarity of her eyes was overwhelming. As blue as the creek he'd found her in, he knew that if he stared long enough, he could easily drown in them.

"My lord, I—"

"A name. A name is all I ask for." She had to be a servant. Though he'd never seen her, it was the only explanation he could think of as to why she was roaming around his home. He slid his hand from her jaw to her neck, feeling the frantic beat of her heart. The fear in her eyes intensified.

"No. Please. I must go."

"There is no' a single thing ye' could be doing this late at night," he murmured, making her look at him again. She turned her head away as quickly as she looked at him, as if she was terrified of him seeing her face.

"Sleeping," she said quickly, yanking herself out of his arms. They felt cold. Empty. He clenched his teeth against the urge to draw her back into them. She was obviously terrified, though he had no clue why. He would never force a woman, and all he wanted was her name.

"Ye' can spare a moment to tell me yer name, lass. 'Tis all I'm asking for."

"I do not have one." He moved in front of her when she would have ran past him. Kane wasn't letting her out of his sight until he knew his nymph's name.

He chuckled. "Of course ye' do. I'm no' going to punish ye' for being in the kitchens, if that's what yer afraid of. Come, lass. Tell me. Then ye' can go to bed."

She shook her head, blonde locks falling in front of her eyes, and once again tried to move past him. He growled. What was so damn bad about him that she couldn't tell him her name? Especially if she was a servant of his? He knew that most lairds wouldn't think twice about taking a maid, willing or no'. Mayhap she suspected that giving into him on anything would result to that.

His heart softened. The lass was only frightened for her safety. It only endeared her to him that she wouldn't use her body to get out of the situation like other servants. Although he had to wonder why she was running around in nothing but a shift.

She tried to slip under his arm. He sighed and grabbed her by the waist, smiling when she made a sound of frightened frustration and hit at him. At least the lass was not so weak that she couldn't try to escape him.

He tried to ignore how comfortable she felt against him, even though she was struggling like a wild animal to get out of his grip. He brought her to the hall and stood there until he knew she wouldn't run, then sat in his chair.

He had things he wanted to know, and she was not—

Kane lunged for her when she sprung out of the chair, then plopped her right on his lap.

"Yer not going anywhere until ye' tell me yer name," he warned her, making sure to keep his hands on her modest parts.

She gazed at him with wide eyes. God, they were so damn blue. When she wiggled in his lap uncomfortably, he realized he was staring and that she'd just roused exactly what he'd been trying to hide. He lifted her and moved her bottom away from his cock, growling a little.

"Name, lass."

Her head shook. The locks once again fell in front of her face, and he reached up, pushing them away. Kane didn't like her face being hidden like that. He wanted to see the face he'd been dreaming about every night.

She grabbed for his wrist when he pulled away. Her hand was trembling, but her grip was firm. The feel of her fingers on him, of their physical connection, burned him like fire. The sensation ran up his arm, to his chest, then down to his gut.

The woman felt it too. She held his eyes, and a fine shiver wracked her delicate body. His teeth ground together.

"I do not have one," she insisted faintly. His hand felt the leap of her pulse, and he leaned forward.

"Yer lying to me."

"Aye, well, you're holding me in a most improper way," she said, her voice holding more steel. A faint blush came over her cheeks, mixing with the fear that had overcome her features. Her modesty cleared away the panic.

"Aye, well, yer trying to run from me. I just want a name." He tightened his hand around her trim waist. What could be so bad about giving him a damn name? Mayhap she wasn't a servant, but an intruder as he'd thought before. He narrowed his eyes on her.

She drew away from him as much as his hold would allow her.

"Alice," she said abruptly. "Alice is a name. May I go now?"

Alice, he thought, watching emotions flicker over her face. The name was as innocent as the woman sitting on his lap appeared to be. He let his hand slide from her neck, away from the pounding pulse, and to her arm.

"Now that I've given you my name," she said stiffly, drawing her arm away from his touch, though a faint blush spread to her cheeks, "I will retire to my bed."

If only I could join her.

He could let her go and continue his life as if she'd never bitten into the apple. That was exactly what he should do, what with the feuding and the MacLeods' threats. There was simply too much going on to consider keeping the lass in his life, especially since he should be courting Blaine.

Aye, that's exactly what he should do. Let her go and gain Lady Blaine's hand in marriage.

However, he was going to do the exact opposite. Now that he had her on his lap, he wanted to keep her there—at least until he had his fill of her. Gwen had come to his bed nearly every night, offering herself to him, and every night she came, he'd send her away because this woman's face was in his mind.

Once he had her, he was sure she'd fade from his mind.

That was the only reason why he did what he did next, a silent "seal of the deal" to himself. Taking her chin between his thumb and forefinger, he drew her face until it was directly in front of his. Her breath came in short, uneven gasps. Her lips were parted, ready for him to take what he'd been dying to since he first saw her in the creek.

When she made a small sound in the back of her throat, rationality hit him.

He pulled away.

Aye, Kane wanted her. His throbbing cock was proof enough. But he wanted her to want him back, this nymph, this golden angel. He didn't want to kiss her while fear darkened her eyes.

Even though he wasn't going to kiss her just yet, even though every ounce of blood within him was screaming at him to, he set her away from him.

"I have no' seen you around here," he said, holding her hand to keep her from running away. She stood before him in nothing but a filmy shift. His eyes latched onto her peaked nipples. Oh, aye. She'd felt what he had.

"That...that is because I am visiting and—"

"I donna care about that," he said, waving a hand. Despite how much he knew he needed to wait, he drew her close. She stood between his knees. He stared up at her, enthralled by the way the candlelight caught on her golden hair, creating a golden halo around her head. "I want to see more of ye'."

She drew back as if he'd punched her. Alice stared at him with wide, horrified eyes. "That cannot happen, my lord. I'm—you're far too busy. I am only here as a visitor and—"

He growled. She snapped her mouth closed.

"I donna care for excuses. Yer a visitor here, aye?"

She nodded silently. Her hands began to wring in front of her. He wanted to reach out and take them, soothe her fears. But he didn't. She'd only become edgier.

"Well, if yer under my care, then I say ye' can spare some time to visit with me."

"I do not know if that is such a good idea, my lord." She shook her head, adding emphasis to her words. Kane grunted.

"O' course it's a good idea. Yer a visitor. A visitor visits her host. I'm the host, the laird. I want ye' to visit me." He was barely focusing on the conversation at this point. His eyes had focused on an errant curl. It stuck out from the side of her head, making her look adorably flustered.

"Visit...you how?" she asked hesitantly. The second the question was out of her mouth, her eyes widened. She took a frightened step back. "My lord, you are to be betrothed!"

"No' like that." *Yet.* "I want to see ye' more, and that's that. Starting tomorrow, after the McGregors leave."

Her head shook. "My lord, I simply cannot allow this. Bl—Lady Blaine would be furious to know her soon-to-be betrothed is...is...philandering around with another woman."

"But we're no' philandering," he pointed out, drawing her between his legs again. "Company. I want yer company, lass. No more, no less." He ignored the way she spoke against him so boldly. Sure as hell he'd picked the one woman in the house, despite Blaine, that would not agree to everything he said. 'Twas not a bad thing, though. He actually liked it. The only person to deny him anything was Brodrick.

"My...company," she said, dumbfounded.

He nodded, raising a brow when she only stared at him as if he'd grown two heads. "I do no' see why that is such a shock, Alice. A man and a woman canna share company?"

"It's highly uncommon, especially under these...circumstances." Once again, she drew away from him, even pulling her arm against her. She didn't look like she was going to run. Rather, she looked like she was morbidly intrigued. He smiled, leaning into his chair with his elbow propped on the arm rest.

"What circumstances could you possibly be talking about, my lady?" Her face turned pink, but there was a spark of something in her eyes, something he couldn't identify. It wasn't bad, though. Curiosity mixed with longing. Kane's chest tightened. What could the lass be longing for?

A woman liked to feel important, he thought, watching the way she held herself. By the way she stood with her shoulders curled, she must not be used to feeling like such.

"Well," she stuttered, gesturing between the two of them. "You are...and I am...oh, and Lady Blaine," she said, eyes widening. "No, this will not do. I'm sorry, my lord. This is not doable. You haven't even spent time with your betrothal! It is quite unfair to her that you enjoy my company, and not hers."

Kane couldn't stop himself from smiling. If she was concerned about his betrothal, then she sure as hell wasn't here for his title. Alice was honestly concerned. God, but she was quite a little thing. She was concerned for Lady Blaine, and by the formality she was showing, she didn't know her all that well.

Poor lass. If only she knew Lady Sinclair.

"Yer worried about Lady Blaine's part in this?" he asked, raising a brow.

She nodded quickly. "Aye. It's wrong that her betrothed ignore her for another woman."

He waved her censure away. "Lady" Blaine didn't deserve an ounce of his time, but alas! A man must make sacrifices.

"I know of a way to fix this," he said, gesturing for her to come forward. With the same trapped doe look in her eyes, she hesitantly crossed the space to stand in front of him.

"If ye' agree to meet me tomorrow, I shall spend time with Lady Blaine."

She considered his words for a moment, and then her eyes brightened. "Would you really?"

He nodded, even as she abruptly frowned.

"I'll know if you don't," she warned.

"I would never go back on my word to a lady." That was a lie. Most times, a lady was a pompous gossiper from court who knew nothing of his ways. Alice was different. A certain kind of lady, one he'd never encountered.

As if she knew what he was thinking, she blushed. "I am not a lady by any means, my lord. Simply a visitor. It would be best if you'd stop calling me as such."

He smiled a little. "Well, for someone who is 'no' a lady', yer very bonny," he said, telling the complete truth. He'd never seen anyone as beautiful as she, in a shift, no less! Kane almost didn't want to know what she looked like during the day. He feared it would knock him off his feet.

"I believe you may have had too much to drink," she whispered, that becoming blush rising once again. He liked that. Kane liked knowing he could please her just with words.

"I believe that I'm actually quite sober," he murmured. Then he straightened in his chair. "Meet me here tomorrow at midday."

"When will you set time aside for Lady Blaine?" she asked, worrying her hands in front of her. He couldn't stop himself from smiling wider. Her concern for Lady Blaine was too sweet, though the viper didn't deserve it.

"As soon as I've had my time with you."

"Only as...friends, correct?"

He nodded. "As friends."

"Then Blaine will have your attention."

When I'm with her, I'll most likely be thinking of you, so nay. She'll no' have my attention.

Still, he nodded.

She bit her lip, then curtsied. "Tomorrow, midday. Then you shall sit with Lady Blaine to sup." Without waiting for his approval, she gave a short nod, and then turned on her heel.

The grace with which she strode away in her filmy shift made him laugh.

Adorable. The water nymph was simply adorable.

Chapter Thirteen

Saeran forgot all about the food as she raced to her room. Her heart was pounding, her face was burning, and her limbs were trembling.

What was wrong with her? Moreover, what was wrong with him?

She threw open the door and slammed it shut behind her, locking it. Wobbly legs carried her to the bed, and then she was spread-eagle.

When he'd first found her, she hadn't known what to think. Escape. Escape and return to safety. Blaine. Blaine and her betrothal to the laird. Anything but let him manhandle her into his chair, his lap, his arms.

A shiver went through her at the memory of his arms around her. Thick, heavenly arms that were made for holding a woman. More than a tremble went through her—it was a burst of heat between her legs.

She moaned, partly from despair, and partly from her reaction to him.

He was meant for her sister, damnit. Not her! Not Saeran, who was meant to be a boy for all of this. Tears of frustration and fear burned her eyes. She could have been found out. She'd walked right into The Lion's den without even knowing it.

None of the tears fell. She closed her eyes and tried to breathe deeply.

He'd almost kissed her.

He'd taken her by the chin and had been a breath away from pressing his lips to hers.

She nearly fainted at the mere memory. Then the anger set in.

"How dare he!" she raged, slapping the bed with a balled up fist—a fist she should have driven into his face when he'd pulled her onto his lap. It was wrong, scandalous, and unseemly! What kind of man would drag a servant onto his lap and hold her there as if she were a pet?

A barbarian, that's who. And a barbarian was what he should be!

Except for the fact that he hadn't done anything in the "I see, I take, I beast" manner. Aye, he'd forced her to sit on his lap, but if she were honest with herself, she would say that she hadn't given up much of a fight. The shock and fear had kept her still, as well as the interest that had welled inside of her at the hard contact of their bodies meeting.

Never in her life had she experienced something like that. The only man to embrace her had been her father. The last time she sat on his lap was when she had been a toddler.

The way Shaw had held her in his arms had not been paternal. It had held the promise of bliss, as much as he tried to remain chaste with his hold on her.

That should have been Blaine in his arms. Her sister, the one meant for him, should have been the one on his lap with his gentle, commanding teasing. It should have been her sister hearing his chuckles and watching him smile.

Blaine. Not Saeran.

"No," she whispered to herself, scrubbing a hand over her face. She closed her eyes, pushing her head into the bed. "No, I made it okay. He'll dine with Blaine on the morrow's eve. He'll begin to notice my sister, and then Blaine will start to calm down, and then everything will be okay."

Everything.

Except she had to endure more of The Lion tomorrow. Her stomach cramped at the thought, but it wasn't purely from trepidation. It was more of a mixture of dread, excitement, and guilt. Always the guilt. Saeran rolled onto her stomach, groaning.

How had she gotten herself into this situation? How? Why was Saeran always the one thrown into the terrible situations? Why was Saeran making a fool of herself and ruining everything? He was more likely to find out now. After they spent time together, in the daylight, he'd recognize who she was. He had to. He'd note the similarities between the boy he knew as Saeran, and the woman he knew as Alice. The only hope she had at hiding her identity from him was the dirt and soot she spread over her face when she was a boy. The idea had been Blaine's from the beginning, and truly, besides the short appearance of her hair, she wasn't sure if it was a very convincing disguise.

Once he found out, Blaine would know. He'd mention it to her. Saeran knew it.

Bile rose in her throat.

If that were to happen, that would create an even thicker barrier between her and her sister. She'd already threatened her sister. Even though it had been empty, Blaine would take it to heart—it didn't matter if the threats were made up or not.

As much as she disliked her sister right now, the thought of that happening was unbearable. Blaine was all she had left.

She sucked back her tears, maneuvering until she was cuddled under the covers. *I could keep myself in the dark*, she thought, rubbing her arms as a chill stole over her. She could hide her face in the shadows and use more soot as a boy. *Plus*, she thought desperately, *The Lion wouldn't notice right away, would he?* He'd hardly ever seen Saeran as a boy. Definitely not enough to tell if she was one person pretending to be another. Aye, and Connor had already said he'd be too busy with his feuding to bother with anyone except work.

Mayhap that applied to not only Saeran, but Alice as well. If he were gone so much that he didn't notice, and she was hiding and doing the accounts, everything could work out. She would go to him as a woman on the morrow as a favor to Blaine. Then he would realize what he was missing and he'd forget all about 'Alice'.

Problem solved.

She settled into the bed, nodding to herself. The problem was most definitely solved.

Saeran gradually fell asleep, and her dreams were the exact opposite of what she'd concluded.

The problem wasn't solved in her dreams. The only thing she saw behind her closed lids was a large, burly man, with a small, blonde woman cradled in his arms, her face lifted to his...ready for a kiss that most certainly happened.

~

Waking up was painful, to say the least. Her body was sore, her mind was drained, and she was dreading the entire day. To add to that, her body wasn't only sore. It was throbbing with the dreams she'd had of a man she couldn't bring herself to name, not when she was about to face him.

She dressed in her boyish garb and headed downstairs, stealing an apple. Blaine was never up this early, so she hoped she could ask the laird about the accounts before her sister came down. Her face flamed at the first sight of him coming in from the kitchen doors.

His chest was bare, sweat dotting his heavily muscled body. Her mouth went dry.

She hadn't thought of how daunting it would be to approach him as another person. As she came up to him in the kitchen, she had to repeat herself several times to make her voice loud enough for him to hear.

"What was that?" he asked sharply, shoving an apple into his mouth. He grabbed a cloth off the counter, swiping it over his face and neck, then tossed it aside. The apple crunched as he bit into it.

"Connor told me that you needed someone to work the accounts for you," she said loudly.

He gave her an arch look, taking another bite. "Ye' ken numbers?"

She nodded. "Aye. Ever since I was a lad. I know I was taken off the training so—"

"Start on them tomorrow. Brodrick will review your work. If yer proficient enough, I'll let ye' do them." He took one more bite of the apple, then set it on the counter.

"Och, where do ye' think yer going?" a familiar voice called from behind her. She moved out of the way as Brodrick walked in, followed by several redheaded men—the McGregors. Saeran pressed herself so far into the wall that she nearly blended in.

Just like The Lion, the McGregors had an equally renowned name. The McGregor had been the one to train Kane Shaw in battle after his father had died, and together, they'd dominated the Highlands. Besides the Campbells, the Shaws and McGregors were the two most powerful clans in the Highlands, and Saeran was not foolish enough to ignore that.

She'd been lucky so far. Not a single McGregor had spared her a glance.

"Fields," the laird grunted. "Need to work off this...this problem."

Brodrick burst into laughter. The McGregor, the laird of the clan, chuckled. "What kind o' problem are ye' having, lad? Ye' look like someone set fire to yer best plaid."

"She might as well have," he growled, glaring at Brodrick when he tossed the unfinished apple to him.

"'She'?" The McGregor asked, raising a brow. "Have ye' finally spoken to Blaine then?"

Saeran looked between the laird and the redheaded man. He knew of Blaine? She wanted to slap herself at the question. Of course he did. There wasn't a single person at this keep who didn't know of Blaine.

"If it'd been Blaine, I wouldn't be working off a night of no sleep. Nay, it was a bonny lass," he said, shaking his head. He took a chunk out of the apple, biting right to the core. Saeran flinched pressed as far into the wall as she could.

He was talking about her.

Then she frowned.

What had he meant by that? Saeran had half a mind to ask him, but the McGregor was too busy laughing. Brodrick waved his brows suggestively while taking a loaf of bread. He leaned against the counter, tearing off chunks and tossing them to the other McGregors.

They were making themselves comfortable right in the kitchen. She mentally slapped herself. Unless Saeran wanted all attention drawn to her, she wouldn't be able to move from her spot. The men would focus on a rat if it scurried by, and Saeran definitely felt like one.

"Ye' ken ye' got to be focusing on Blaine," Brodrick muttered around a piece of bread. "Although, none of us blame ye'. The woman is a right dragon. Does no' hurt to have a bit o' fun before it's too late."

Kane rolled his eyes.

The McGregor spoke up before he could continue his banter with Brodrick. "We've all discussed yer proposition and found it the most logical. Quick, easy, painful. It'll hit them hard when they are no' prepared for it."

Kane nodded, obviously pleased. He finished off the apple while she frowned. What were they talking about?

"I donna want this bloody. I want it to be a lesson for them."

"Aye. Ye' do realize that by doing this, the Campbells will be drawn into it."

"Do I have yer backing?" Kane asked, sounding like he already knew the answer.

The McGregor grunted. "Ye' ken ye' do, Kane. I'd no' leave my favorite Shaw to go against those sorry bastards, although I'm sure ye' could take them by yerself."

Kane laughed. The sound was low and deadly. Chilling. Not close to the man she'd met the night before. Saeran wrapped her arms around her chest, watching him intently.

"If this gets too out of hand, I may just take it upon myself to show him how a battle is actually fought."

"Aye, well, I want to be there for it," The McGregor said, nodding his head. "Our men are packed, and the ride will take us a sennight. We are heading off now. If anything happens, ye' ken to send for me."

Kane raised a brow. "Are ye' doubting my skills, brother?"

The McGregor chuckled ruefully. "I trained ye', didn't I? To doubt ye' would be to doubt myself, and I'm much too arrogant for that."

"Not so much arrogant as old," Kane said, laughing when The McGregor slapped him on the back with extra force.

"Keep yer jabs to yerself, lad. I'm no' too old that I canna kick yer ass to Sunday and back."

They said their goodbyes, with more jokes from Kane, and then the McGregors were gone.

"Going to miss ye' in the mornings," Brodrick said, jerking her back to reality. She froze, staring at him.

"Me?" she asked, pointing at herself.

He laughed, nodding. "Yer so amusing to watch, lad. The way you throw things about. It's like watching a—"

"Saeran!"

All three of them made a sound of displeasure as Blaine's furious voice echoed through the halls.

"Saeran, where are you!"

"I think yer on yer own," Brodrick said, nodding his head to Kane. "I have men to train." He was out the door before he'd finished his sentence.

"I do not enjoy searching for you, Saeran!" her sister continued loudly. Saeran's lips pressed. Obviously her outburst hadn't done a single thing.

"If she's looking for ye', I think I left my horse on fire," Kane said, completely serious. She stared at him with a dropped jaw.

"You cannot just run away from her," she hissed as her sister's steps came closer.

"If my horse is on fire, I sure as hell can run away. Who else will water it?" he growled, pushing away from the counter. He stalked to the door, just as Blaine stepped into the kitchen.

She stopped, then stared. Kane froze in his tracks, like he knew he'd been caught. Which he had. Saeran felt a small moment of triumph when Blaine's eyes zeroed in on him.

"My lord!" Blaine said brightly, running up to him. The dirty look she cast Saeran only lasted a moment. "How did your morning fare?"

Saeran watched as her sister curtsied. Kane only stared—at the space beside Blaine's head. She frowned. How utterly rude! And he thought that "Alice" was going to show up for a conversation with him when he couldn't carry out on his part of the bargain? No way, no how. She crossed her arms over her chest.

"It fared quite well, my lady." He looked at the door, not a single ounce of interest in his voice for Blaine.

"The cook will be preparing mutton for supper." Blaine was trying to draw his attention back to her, and it obviously wasn't working. Saeran was getting angrier by the second. He'd lied to her! He thought "Alice" wouldn't know he wasn't doing his part of the deal, so he could get away with it. "Would you sit with me tonight?"

Saeran fully expected Kane to either shrug or walk away. But he didn't.

"Well?" Blaine asked, peering up at him. She looked lovely today. The sanguine red of her gown set off the deep, black-as-night color of her hair. Coal lined her eyes, and her lips were as red as her dress.

Saeran waited with baited breath. If he said no, she'd be off the hook. She wouldn't have to see him as Alice. If he said yes, she would, and then Blaine would have her time with the laird. She wanted him to say no—for more reasons than she was willing to admit.

"Aye," he said after a moment. "Tonight."

Without another word, he nodded. He strode out of the door, into the blinding light of the morning sun. Blaine rounded on her with a wide, happy grin.

Saeran didn't return it.

She was still angry over last night and what had happened between the two of them. She'd helped her sister with the laird only because that was what needed to happen, not because Blaine was back in her good graces.

Saeran turned away from Blaine, walking out of the same door the laird had. She only had a little bit of time before midday. The stables needed cleaning, as well as the horses.

"Where do you think you're going?" Blaine asked from behind her. Saeran sighed, ignoring her sister. "I asked you a question, Saeran! Where are you going?"

Blaine ran in front of the doorway. Saeran stared at her, lips pressed.

Her sister frowned. "What is your problem?"

"Are you serious?" Saeran asked quietly, angrily.

"Yes," she said, crossing her arms over her chest. "I am. You didn't even say good morning to me before you came down for breakfast." Her eyes narrowed into slits. "Are you truly still upset from last night?"

Saeran shook her head, laughing ruefully. "I have duties to attend to, Blaine."

"You cannot just walk away from me like this!" Blaine exclaimed.

Saeran did exactly that.

"Aye," she said emotionlessly, striding away from her. The stables were her haven. Blaine was too proper to come to the dirty grounds. When she was close enough to smell the telltale scent that clung to the stables, she knew her sister would leave her alone, at least for a little while.

She set to work, her chest hurting and her head pounding. There was too much for her to worry about, she thought as she brushed down the horses. When her mare moved uneasily under her hands, she realized her movements were angry and rushed. She slowed, leaning her forehead against the mare's neck.

"Why is everything so complicated?" she whispered. "Everything is falling down around me."

The horse neighed as if it felt her pain.

"Did you know," she said softly, "that I have an ally now? Connor, the laird's squire. It is strange, isn't it, after how angry he was with me. It's like God is trying to balance my life. Now that Connor knows, Blaine and I are not getting along at all. Though I fear it's entirely my fault."

"How is that?"

She whirled around at the sound of Connor's voice, putting a hand over her heart.

"You scared me," she whispered fiercely, rubbing her mare's nose before moving to the next one.

He laughed, grabbing a brush. "You scared me, my lady. This is the second time I've walked upon you talking to yourself."

She sniffed indignantly, gesturing to the mare with a wave of her brush. "I was not talking to myself. She happens to be a very good listener, which is more than I can say for my sister."

Connor grimaced sympathetically, taking the horse adjacent to her. "Do you mind if I ask what happened between the two of you? All you've done is serve her every need. I can't imagine what would make her angry with you," he said, the bitterness barely veiled. She wrinkled her nose.

"It wasn't something she did," she admitted. "You see how she is."

"Everyone here does. Did you finally stick up for yourself?"

"What might you mean by that?"

He gave her a point-blank stare. Saeran sighed, dropping her gaze. She knew what he was talking about. Blaine had everyone she knew wrapped around her finger, whether they hated or loved her. She had the kind of personality that wouldn't be denied. As her younger sister, Saeran had simply accepted that.

If Blaine wanted something, she'd take it or use other people to get it. Saeran had been one of her main scapegoats throughout life. She hated herself for only realizing it now. Blaine was her sister, her blood. It wasn't fair that Saeran was always the one put out.

Even now, with what she was doing with the laird, it was for Blaine. So *Blaine* could have the romance. So *Blaine* could have the power. So *Blaine* could have the opportunity Saeran would never have.

A husband. Love. Children.

Blaine was going to get all of it, and even though Saeran realized that and *hated* it out of pure jealousy, she was helping her sister.

She guessed that it made up for her nasty thoughts toward her sister. She shouldn't be jealous of Blaine for something she had no part in. Saeran's barrenness was God's way of telling her that she wasn't suited for married life or children.

"I suppose I finally said 'no'," she murmured. Her anger drained completely. She had no reason to be angry with Blaine. She couldn't help that her sister had led a pampered life, that she was who she was. Blaine couldn't help herself any more than Saeran could make herself hate books. Change in a person wasn't as simple as it appeared.

"You do not sound too happy about that," Connor said, finishing the horse he'd been on and moving to the next. She shrugged, following suit.

"I think I was wrong in—"

Connor came to her stall and grabbed her by the shoulders so quickly, she didn't realize what was happening until it was over.

"Don't you dare say that," he warned, shaking her gently. His voice was fiercer than his hold. "We've all seen the way she treats you. It is good that you took a stand for yourself—so do not think otherwise. She has to get it through her thick, pampered skull that you aren't built for her pleasure. You are a human with feelings, just like the rest of us. How can you justify the way she treats you?"

She pulled back from the vehemence of his conviction.

"She's my sister," Saeran said quietly. "My first loyalty is to her."

"No," he snapped, pulling away from her and pushing a hand through his hair. "Your first loyalty is to yourself. My lady, I am the youngest of seven older brothers and five older sisters. Do you think I survived them because I did everything they asked of me? Listened to them berate me on every single thing I did?"

She stared at him.

"I put them in their place as much as they put me in mine," he told her, point a finger in her face. "I never—not once—let my siblings walk on me as much as you've let Blaine. When was the last time the two of you spoke about you?"

Saeran worried her lip.

"I do not see how that—"

"Answer the question, my lady," he snapped.

She looked at her lap, sighing. "If I must be honest...I cannot remember."

"Exactly. Blaine is not a true sister if she can't get out of her own head long enough to talk about your day, or how much it pains you to be beat on in the training field, or how much it hurts your back to clean out the stalls. You never had to do any of this before, correct?"

She nodded slightly.

Connor sighed and shook his head angrily. "Does she not think this hasn't been hard on you, as well? God, I could take a pitchfork and shove it up her—"

"Connor," she said quickly, putting a comforting hand on his elbow. "It's fine. Truly—"

"How can you say that?!" He pulled away from her angrily. "She has you so brainwashed that you don't even realize how much of a problem this is! Does she ever compliment you? Ever?"

"Now that does not have anything to do with what we are discussing—"

"Tell me, Saeran," he demanded. The hard edge he put to her name made her eyes close with acceptance. Connor was dead set on proving whatever point he felt he had to make.

"There is not much to compliment me about," she said, sighing. "If you did not notice, I am dressed in trews and covered in horse manure."

He gave her a flat glare.

"When you are dressed as a proper lady. What does she say to you?"

"Well…" She frowned, hands wringing. Blaine never complimented her, she realized. Whenever Blaine wanted attention and compliments, she got them.

Saeran could recall the one time she'd been excited about a gown their father had gotten her for her birthday. A beautiful sky-blue piece. It had only enhanced the blue of her eyes and the gold locks of her hair—at least, that's what her mother had told her.

She'd ran to her sister's room, excited to show off the new gown. Instead, she was greeted with a pitiful sneer. "You're too thin for such a dress, dear sister. Mother only said you looked beautiful to make you feel better," she'd said. When Saeran had only stared at her, too stunned to speak, Blaine had smiled. "Gray is a color more suited to you, and it should be baggy. It'll add some girth to you!"

Saeran had run out of the room in tears.

"I'm too thin," she said, frowning at him. "Too thin, too big in the chest, and too…blonde."

"Are you serious?"

She blushed, crossing her arms over her chest. "I can't help the way I—"

"No, Saeran. Do you truly believe what she said to you? That's the biggest load of shite I've ever heard—excuse my language." He continued to watch Saeran, his eyes blazing, and then he turned away sharply, once again shaking his head.

A thought occurred to her.

"Do you think... Do you think the laird will think I'm repulsive if I came to him as a woman and not a man?"

He turned around sharply, eyes wide with hope. "Why do you ask? Are you going to reveal yourself to him?"

"No, no. I was simply...curious."

Connor slumped against the stall, obviously disappointed. "If you aren't going to tell him the truth, why are you thinking on it?" he muttered petulantly. "There isn't any use in it."

Saeran blushed, feeling like a fool. There had to be something about her that the laird liked, or he wouldn't have made such a silly deal with her. What kind of man would go as far as to ask a woman he'd never met to share her company? It was only an exchange for what they both knew would be an unpleasant encounter with Blaine. Aye, there had to be something about her that was likeable. She did, after all, have Connor as a friend.

Connor, who was friends with the laird, and who knew what the man liked.

She gave him a look, then smiled, ignoring the guilt that rose inside of her. She shouldn't try to impress the laird, as he was meant for her sister. But in that moment, she didn't care.

"Connor, I do not want you to get the wrong idea in your head," she warned, already groaning mentally when his face perked up. He straightened from the wall. "But... The laird and I are meeting at midday."

"You're meeting," he repeated. "Didn't you just say that you weren't going to—?"

"He thinks I am someone else," she told him, waving his concern away. "Alice, though I didn't tell him that was my name directly."

"How does that make sense?" he asked. "Actually, how on earth did this come about? Is your sister aware of this? Has she already given you trouble over it?" His eyes widened, and his hands began flapping in the air excitedly. "Oh, you need a beautiful gown for this. He'll fall at your feet, I just know it!"

Saeran blushed.

"Mayhap, but... I do not wish to go overboard on the matter, Connor. This is the only time I'll be meeting with the laird."

"How did this even happen?"

Her blush worsened. "I...last night, I had a bit of a lapse in judgment. He came upon me in the kitchen. To shorten the story, he promised me that if I met with him today, he would eat with my sister tonight. Blaine has been getting awfully angry over his negligence," she explained, wincing when his eyes darkened.

"You agreed to help your sister? Even after everything she's put you through?" He threw up his hands. She ran forward, calmly patting his arm.

"I did not start the night off with that intention," she said wearily. "It just...happened. The laird can be quite adamant when he wants something."

Connor's eyes locked on hers, widening. "He wants you."

Saeran burst into laughter.

"No, my lady. He does! He's had no time for women of late, including Gwen. He wants to spend time with you," Connor said, his voice dropping to a sigh of happiness. She looked at him strangely. "That is so romantic! You're going to look *beautiful*."

"I am?" She backed away from him uneasily, not trusting the determination that had settled over his face.

"Yes. You are. So enchanting that the laird will lose all thoughts of Blaine and ask for your hand."

Her jaw dropped.

"Connor, do not say such things! That cannot happen. Kane Shaw is meant for Blaine, and that's that."

He waggled his brows at her.

"The heart wants what the heart wants, love. Come! We must get you ready for your lover's tryst."

"This is in no way a lover's tryst! Not of any kind," she insisted, resisting when he took her by the hand, dragging her out of the stables. "What about my duties? Brodrick will have my hide if he finds that I didn't complete them."

"You would rather wade through horse shite than turn into a beauty for the laird? My lady, we need to discuss your priorities."

Chapter Fourteen

"I feel ridiculous," she hissed, grabbing a fistful of her skirts and holding them up. "These are blue."

"Yes, and?" Connor walked behind her, taking one of her curls and wrapping it around his finger. He stared at her speculatively, like she was a prized pastry he was presenting to the king. She pulled herself away from him, gesturing to her outfit sharply.

"This is not my color! I told you that gray was the best, and—and this makes me look too…too... I don't know. Highlanders like women who are curvy, like Blaine. Look at me! I'm as thin as a stick, Connor. This a terrible idea. I do not see the point of dressing up. You're acting as though I am going to court!"

Connor rolled his eyes, reaching forward to swipe his thumb under her lip. She stuck her tongue out, licking it. He yanked his hand way from her, wiping his thumb on his sleeve. He frowned at her.

"That is disgusting."

She hmph'ed, crossing her arms over her chest. His eyes dropped to her cleavage, and he grinned.

"That is disgusting," she muttered. Connor only shook his head, reaching out to adjust another curl.

"I have a question, actually."

She raised a brow. "Aye?"

"Does that…" He waved a hand toward her bosom. She started to blush. "Does that not hurt? To have them bound when you pretend to be a boy?"

"I… It is hard to breathe sometimes, but the overly large shirt

114

helps disguise them if I do not tighten the binding as much as I should."

Connor nodded slowly, taking that in with a dubious look.

"Well, in any case, you look wonderful," he said, stepping away from her. He sounded like her mother had whenever Blaine would show off a dress. "He's going to faint at your feet!"

"You keep saying that, but the laird does not seem like one to faint at a woman's feet. He's more likely to impale her with his claymore, or whatever it is he uses in battle."

"What kind of battle are you talking about?" Connor asked, snickering. She didn't understand what he—oh.

"That is disgusting! There will be no impaling of that sort." She closed her eyes, sighing. She wondered what the laird was doing now. Was he as nervous as she was? She could have laughed at her own question if she weren't beginning to feel sick.

Connor pinched her cheeks. She gasped, pulling away from him.

"You look a bit pale," he said, chuckling. Then he started to pull her to the door. "Come, he's waiting."

"What—how do you know? Oh, Lord," she whispered, her face losing the color Connor had tried to force into it. "What if Blaine sees me? I completely forgot!"

He rolled his eyes. "Who cares if she does?"

"I do! I'll never hear the end of it if she sees me cavorting with Lord Shaw like some lady of the night. She will hate me!" She moved away from the door, shaking her head. "I cannot do this, Connor. I simply can't. This feels—"

"Do not say it feels wrong," he warned her, waving a finger in her face. "This is most definitely not wrong. This is right, and this is perfect. Blaine will not see you—she's out in the gardens or in the village, like always. Either way, you're safe. And if you're not, and she sees you? What does it matter?"

"She'll get on me about my cover being blown—"

"Saeran," he said, giving her a flat look. "You are more naive than I thought if you think your cover won't be blown. Now! The laird awaits."

~

The laird was indeed waiting. Connor shoved her into the hall, right in front of the mountain of a man. She realized that he'd thrown her to the lion, like a piece of meat to be devoured. She turned around, desperate to follow him in his escape, but the laird's sharp

115

intake held her back.

Slowly, heart sinking with every movement, she turned around. He knew—he recognized her as Saeran. Her ruse was up, and she was going to die by his sword.

Though the fear was so intense that her heart was climbing up her throat, she managed to meet his eyes... And everything stilled.

He was breathtaking. He'd cleaned up since that morning. His hair was still wild, long, and mussed like he had just woken from a nap. His jaw still held the stubble that had grown overnight, and his eyes were filled with a look she didn't understand.

All she knew was that he made her face turn pink and her body tremble.

"I was beginning to think ye' were no' going to show," he grunted. The look left his eyes, and he came forward, until he was standing in front of her. That was all he did. Stand there. Staring down at her. No bow or any other sort of greeting.

She smiled weakly, forcing her nerves down.

It didn't seem like her cover had been blown. He hadn't noticed, she realized with a start. She didn't know what his gasp had been for, but it wasn't because he'd realized who she was. A rush of relief ran through her.

"I was beginning to hope I wouldn't have to," she replied. His eyes widened. Just barely, but enough for her to know she had spoken out of turn. "I did not mean it like—"

He bowed his head to her, but not before she saw the flash of white when he smiled. "I'm going to take that as ye' didn't want me to agree to eat with Blaine, and no' that yer going to dread my company."

"I'm so sorry for—"

"Nay, lass. Donna fash yerself." He started walking away from her, towards the kitchens. Saeran watched him go, her feet glued to the ground. Blaine could be in there. If her sister saw her— "Are ye' coming?"

She looked between him and the direction he'd been going, biting her lip.

He turned to her fully, raising a brow. "I'll only dine with Blaine if ye' go with me, lass. That is the deal. Do ye' not want me to sup with her?"

I don't know what I want you to do, she thought, worrying her hands in front of her.

"I'll take that as a no," he said, flashing that same smile and coming to take her hand. He twined his fingers through hers, ignoring her shocked gasp, and began pulling her to the doors.

"Where are we going?" she demanded, trying to pull her hand away from him. He held fast, continuing to pull her. She would have fought harder had she not realized how big his hand was around hers, how utterly masculine this beast of a man was compared to her willowy daintiness. She was entranced into silence, simply by his presence, when she should have been anything but.

"Out. I need to check the fences near the MacLeod border to see if they'll hold up for the next storm, and yer coming with me." He held the door open for her, then gestured her inside. Her heart nearly stopped with the relief she felt when she saw that Blaine wasn't near—nor could she hear her voice coming from the open door that lead to the training grounds.

"So far out?" She met his eyes over her shoulder when he stayed close behind her. "It's quite a ride. It would take us several hours to get back. I fear that without a chaperone, I cannot let this happen."

He chuckled. The sound was so deep and silky that it rolled down her back like hot water. A warm feeling settled in her stomach. She picked up her pace, struggling to ignore how affected she was by just a laugh.

"We have all the time in the world, lass, and ye' have no need for a chaperone. I'm the host. I'm guardianship enough. Donna worry, ye'll be well protected from any enemies we may cross."

But who will protect me from you? she thought, shivering when his hand landed on the small of her back. He led her to the stables, seeming to miss her reaction to him. Thank lord for that.

"How well o' a rider are ye'?" He handed her a rein to a horse that wasn't the one she'd claimed as her own. Saeran peaked inside the stables and saw the poor beast looking at her with betrayal in her big brown eyes. She turned back to the laird.

"I'm proficient," she lied, nervously patting the horse on the butt. The laird raised a brow.

"Something tells me yer lying to me, lass."

She started to shake her head to deny him. Before she could speak, his hands were on her waist, her feet off the ground, and her breasts pressed against his chest.

Time stood still.

All she saw was the forest green flecks in his eyes. The animal he hid so well, lurking behind them, waited patiently at the edge of darkness. All she could smell was the woodsy, musky scent of him, and all she could hear was the beating of her own heart.

Saeran wanted to lose herself in the moment, but all too soon, it was over. The spell broke, and he tossed her onto the saddle. She blinked, then cautiously righted herself.

He mounted his horse with an ease that stole her breath—well, what was left of it, anyway.

"You know," she said hesitantly, feeling compelled to talk to him, "I did not expect this when I agreed to your silly request."

"It's silly, is it?" he grunted, giving her a side-look as he took her rein. He brought them to a gallop, cutting off all conversation. They rode over hills, through trees, and past her creek. The ride felt long and gruesome, though she knew only a couple of minutes had passed. She didn't take any joy in the ride until he let go of her reins, giving her horse a slap on its bum.

She went flying.

"How silly is that?" he shouted from behind her. The laughter in his voice only made her own bubble to the forefront, and soon, she was letting herself go. Her hair flew out behind her. Her face tilted to the sun, and the horse became pure power and energy underneath her.

I'd needed this, she thought vaguely, letting the sun warm her face. Fresh Highland air washed over and around her, cleansing her. She'd needed the freedom that came with open lands, with going as fast as one can go. She'd needed a break from the tyranny of her sister. Now that she had it, she was reluctant to let it go.

But she had to. Kane rode in front of her just as they came to a section of the fence, bringing her horse to a gradual stop. She couldn't stop the laughter that was bursting from her lips, especially when she saw the long strands of his hair and how tangled they were.

"What are ye' laughing at? That was meant to be a lesson. Ye' donna insult the great laird," he growled. The playful light in his eyes only made it worse.

"Your hair," she said, pointing to it. He came close to her, close enough that she could fix the mess. "It's...it's quite a mess."

He frowned at her. "Ye' should see yer own hair! 'Tis transformed into a golden mess as well." Saeran knew he was teasing her, but the comment made her sober. This was wrong. This should be Blaine! She should be the one laughing, teasing, and riding with him.

Not Saeran.

"My lady?"

She looked at him and saw the concern in his eyes. He was worried he'd offended her, she thought, unable to stop herself from smiling. Only a few moments in his presence, and he was turning out to be much more than just The Lion. The man didn't seem to be a complete barbarian, she thought. But there was still time for that to change.

"How long are we going to be out here for?" she asked. The fence went on for as long as she could see.

"No' long," he said after a moment. The laird turned away from her, swinging himself to the ground. The horse ambled off, but he paid it no mind. He knelt in front of the fence, checked the wiring and the post, and then straightened. "The MacLeods are always complaining about our lands being separated, and then they come around and ruin the fence when they see fit. I have to check it every once in a while."

"That's ridiculous," she said, frowning. "Why would you put up with that?"

He shrugged, gave her a smirk from over his shoulder, and went to work.

She paused, watching him. He appeared to be teasing, but something told her that he wasn't. Kane Shaw might appear to be a laidback man to Alice, but underneath all of that, she saw him for what he was.

A ruthless man.

She knew it in her gut, could feel it with every sense she possessed. Watching him move, watching his muscles tense at the slightest sound and noticing the way his eyes scanned the area with trained precision, showed her a man she had every right to be terrified of.

Yet she wasn't.

For Blaine, she told herself as she tried to find a way to get off the horse without falling on her face. She was here with this man for Blaine. She was only gauging his personality. Aye, all for Blaine.

She continued to tell herself that when she awkwardly tried to adjust herself on the saddle. She'd never ridden in a skirt before, nor had she ever dismounted with her legs constrained. Saeran muttered a small curse when her leg became caught.

Her head fell back in embarrassed frustration.

"Seems that someone is no' as proficient as she claims to be," the laird said from beside her. She bit her lip.

"You never asked whether I was good at dismounting, only if I could ride," she said smartly, trying to keep an upper hand. Blaine would do that. She'd keep an upper hand. She would know what to say to not embarrass herself, as Saeran now was.

"Oh, aye," he murmured, chuckling. "I'll remember to be more precise with my questions."

The laird reached up, ignoring her hands when she batted at him, and took her by the waist once again. This time, she was prepared—and felt the full force of his hands on her, holding her, supporting all of her weight. His hands were the only thing that kept her from falling to the ground. With her heart in her throat, she grabbed for his shoulders.

Chapter Fifteen

Her breath caught. Warm, thick. Bare. His shoulders were always bare, begging to be touched—and now she was touching them. Her fingers dug into his skin as he held her up, slowly setting her on the ground.

Their bodies didn't have an inch of space between them.

When her feet were on the ground, she backed into the horse. He didn't take his hands from her waist. Instead, he came forward, walking till he was against her so that she had to brace her hands against his chest to feel a semblance of balance.

It didn't help as she'd thought it would. If anything, the sensation of her hands on the hard planes of his body only worsened her disorientation.

She lifted her face to his, and her hands fisted. God, he was so fierce. His body, his face, his eyes. He gazed at her as if he were remembering everything about her and storing it away for later. It was discerning and exciting at the same time.

Blaine, her mind snapped. Just like that, with that one name, the spell broke for her. She cleared her throat and ducked out of his arm, giving him a falsely bright smile.

"My lord, I would appreciate it if—"

"Kane," he said, swiping a hand over his face.

"Pardon?"

"Ye'll call me Kane, no' 'my lord'."

"My lord, I cannot call you—"

He surged forward, taking her jaw in his hand, much like he had when he'd been close to kissing her the night before. Her heart jumped to her throat, but she didn't move. She held his eyes, an odd sense of warmth blanketing her.

"I donna want to be called lord by you, Alice. We'll be on a first-name basis and that is that. Do ye' understand?"

She swallowed. "I do not think you understand. This is improper and only Blaine should—"

"I donna want to hear about that woman," he growled, leaning close to her. "I am with ye' right now, no' her."

"The whole reason we are together right now is because of her! My lord, I do not understand why we cannot remain proper. This is a simple arrangement so that you will form a relationship with Blaine."

"'A simple arrangement'?" he echoed, eyes narrowing. "Nay, my lady. This is no' just a 'simple arrangement'."

"Of course it is," she snapped, starting to get irate. People were too often trying to make decisions for her, and though this man was the laird and her protector, he could not order her about on lessons about being proper.

He was meant for Blaine, and he would stay that way.

That meant no touching, no heated stares, and no demands. She was here to gauge what kind of man he was while urging him closer to Blaine.

"I won't allow it to be anything other than that. You are meant for another woman," she hissed, pulling away from him sharply. "That is all there is to it. You said you would entertain Blaine if I did this. That is the whole reason for everything right now!"

"The deal was only for one evening with Blaine. If ye' want me to have more with her, I'm going to need to see ye' more."

Saeran ground her teeth together. It was so hard not to say something, to curse or to stamp her foot. She would retain the composure of a lady, no matter how hard she wanted to slap his hard, sculpted jaw.

"I have faith that after tonight, you will not require any urging from me."

He made a rough sound. It was part laugh, part groan. "Have ye' not seen the woman? Or heard her? Lass, yer naivety is starting to wear on me. Blaine is the last woman I'd want to have dinner with willingly."

She gasped. How rude of him! He didn't even know her sister! "Oh, really? Then who else? Name one woman you'd having dinner with, with no urging. You avoid them like the plague! Blaine is the opportune woman. She has a dowry, influence, charisma, all of the things you should admire."

"Ye'."

"What?" she asked, drawing away from him. His brows dropped over his eyes and he came forward, stalking her as a lion stalked its prey.

"Ex—excuse me?"

"Ye' asked me to name one woman I'd have dinner with. I choose ye'."

"I never made myself an option," she said thinly. Her eyes widened when her back hit the post. He kept coming, even when she raised her hands to fend him off. They landed on his chest for the second time that day. His heart was pounding as wildly as hers, and she knew it wasn't because he was worked up over their miniature debate.

"Aye, well, I did."

"You cannot just do that!" she exclaimed, pushing at his chest. "What if I'm married? You don't know me from high heaven, my lord. You cannot possibly think this is alright. Especially when Blaine is in the picture."

"I donna see her here, and I know yer not married." He smiled down at her, and it was so sensual that her legs turned to liquid. She caught herself on the fence before she could fall.

"She doesn't have to be here to be in the picture, you brute!" she snapped, furious over this man's stubbornness. He was not as ignorant as he was sounding—she knew it, felt it, but couldn't understand why he was throwing caution out the window. Her hand itched to slap him. Then she stiffened. "How do you know I'm not married?"

One corner of his mouth went up. She wrapped her arms around her chest, keeping her shiver to herself. He had to stop doing that, he really did. His face was too harsh to seem attractive when he smiled, but it was, and it made her feel something she'd never felt, right in the pit of her stomach.

"It's in yer eyes."

She frowned. "It's in my eyes? What does that mean?"

"It means," he growled, catching her chin between his thumb and forefinger, "that I can see the innocence in yer eyes."

Her face flamed. "My 'innocence' is my own business, and I

mean to keep it to myself."

Kane chuckled. "Aye, I'm sure ye' do."

She sighed heavily. "My lord—"

"*Kane.*"

"*Kane,*" she started, hoping that the small appeasement might make him more willing to listen to her. "Blaine is your intended. We must keep it that way, meaning whatever....whatever was happening a moment ago, must not happen again."

"What if it does?" he asked, raising a brow.

"It will not."

"But—"

"It will not," she said firmly, jabbing a finger at his chest. He caught her wrist in his hand, stared down at her, then dropped it. He backed away.

"I have a question for ye', lass."

She nodded, crossing her arms over her chest. At least he wouldn't press the silent issue of their personal space.

"Why is Blaine so important to ye'?"

She froze.

"She..."

Saeran avoided his eyes, unable to finish the sentence. Blaine wasn't important to her—at least, that's how it felt. Blaine was more of an excuse to hide behind than anything. But he couldn't know that—and neither could he know about their relation.

"Do ye' know her?" he asked, raising a brow.

Saeran shook her head. "Nay. I told you before; I am visiting a friend—"

"Blaine?"

"Someone else. I only know Blaine because of the impending nuptials that should be happening. I noticed the way you avoided her," Saeran said uneasily. "It made me feel terrible. If I can help her, I should... Shouldn't I?"

His eyes softened for a fraction of a second, then he scowled. "Who is it that yer visiting, then?"

Her stomach tightened. She was a terrible liar—everyone knew this. The lie stuck in her throat like molasses, thick and unmoving. She shrugged, feigning nonchalance. "My brother. He's...he's been there for some time, and I came from Abernethy to spend time with him."

"Really," he said dubiously. Obviously her lie had not been said with much conviction. "What is yer brother's name then, lass? I donna remember agreeing to any guests staying with me."

Her mind raced. She didn't know a single person that would willingly cover for her. "My brother asked Lady Blaine—she said it was okay." She pressed a hand to her forehead, hating the corset that was choking her just as much as her lies were. "My lord, I am starting to feel faint."

All of the suspicion dropped from his face, concern taking over. He gently took her by the elbow, so at odds with the brute strength he exuded.

"I've brought water. Do ye' need to sit down?"

She nodded tiredly, relieved he didn't notice she was more exhausted with everything, rather than faint because of the weather. Still, she felt bad when he led her to her horse, quickly setting her on top of it.

He retrieved a skin and held it to her. She took it, meeting his eyes.

"I think we're done here for today." He mounted his horse and took her rein. She finished taking her drink, then handed the skin back to him. Their fingers brushed. The sensation made her quickly retract her hand

"Are we done now? Can we go back?"

He sighed, shaking his head. "Nay, I'm going to make this as unpleasant as I can for ye', lass. Yer going to have to stomach my presence awhile more before I let ye' go."

She shivered at his words. Let her go... As if he wanted to hold onto her.

Saeran made herself smile. "Where are we off to, then?" *Please do not say the keep, pleeeease do not say the keep.* She might have gotten lucky by missing Blaine the first time, but her luck could only do so much. It would figure that after the flirtatious way the laird and her had acted, that her sister would catch sight of her.

"There's a creek that runs behind my keep. I'd like to take ye' there."

She knew exactly what he was talking about, and the way he said it... Saeran didn't know what to do. There was a soft gleam in his eyes, like he knew something she didn't.

"A creek? In this weather? What for? It's quite chilly, and there is not much to do at a creek."

"O' course there is, lass. Have ye' never taken a dunk in one?"

He gave her a knowing look, like they shared a secret.

"We'll not be taking one now," she said, relieved to have avoided a lie. She hated to be untruthful.

"Aye," he said, chuckling. "We wouldn't want to hurt yer womanly sensitivities now, would we?"

"What is that supposed to mean?" she asked, frowning at him. She wasn't womanly at all—for the past month, she hadn't been allowed! The only thing she was doing right now was trying to keep the man at a distance, since he was meant for her sister!

"Nothing at all." He smiled in her direction, and then kicked his horse into a gallop. Hers followed suit, forcing her to simmer in silence. He was making fun of her, she realized angrily. He was making fun of her for acting like a lady and keeping her distance! Not only that, but he was avoiding all and any conversation of Blaine. That was the exact opposite of what should be happening!

She should subtly try to reveal traits that he would admire, implanting the idea that she would make a good wife for him. That was the goal of her mission.

So far, she was failing and being teased for it in the process!

The realization forced a blush into her cheeks. He was making it hard for her to stay indifferent, as well. Indifferent and distant was how she needed to be, and it seemed he was doing everything he could to make that impossible!

Just like that, Saeran became furious. So furious that she wanted to reach over and shove him off his horse. How dare he not be as she had thought he was? He was meant to be a barbarian, The Lion of the Highlands. Brutal and merciless, with not a funny bone in his body. Yet...here he was. *Teasing* her. Not beating her to death like she had been prepared for—

He drew them to an abrupt halt. They weren't even near the creek.

She frowned, confused.

"What is—"

"Quiet," he growled, holding up a hand. Saeran didn't need to be told twice.

She watched as he scanned the surroundings, and a chill took over her. Not because she was frightened of what was wrong—but because of the deadly calm that came over his face. The deadly calm that was mixed with the promise of death.

She heard it.

The pounding hooves, the clatter of metal, and war cries.

"Go," he commanded, turning toward the attackers. She couldn't see them, but they were coming up the hill—and fast.

"I cannot just leave—"

"If ye' donna leave, ye'll only be a burden. Do ye' want to die?" he snapped, not even looking at her. She trembled, shaking her head. Her stomach roiled at what he wanted her to do, at the fear that was lacing itself around her heart.

"No," she whispered, taking her reins tightly in her hands. "But I cannot just leave you here."

"I'm no' going to tell ye' again, lass. Go."

He didn't give her a choice over the matter. One second she was staring at him in mute horror, then the next he was slapping her horse's rear, sending her racing to the keep.

Chapter Sixteen

Kane didn't say a word as the five figures rode towards him. As Alice cleared the field, he prayed to God that she stayed away like he'd told her. If she didn't, he was going to punish the disobedience out of her *after* he killed the MacLeod bastards.

There was no a doubt as to who was on his land. The colors and the arrogant smirks on the dirty men in front of him told him all he needed to know.

He could have waited and asked them questions. Like why they were killing his clansmen? Or why they were on his land to begin with? He could have—it's what any laird with a lick of sense would have done.

But all he could think about was the fear that had entered Alice's eyes when she'd realized something was wrong. MacLeods were entitled sons of bitches. If they saw Alice, they'd take her—and not pleasantly.

"Kane," one of the men said stonily. His eyes flickered around the area, most likely searching for the rest of the Shaw clansmen who guarded the lands. None of them were out today because he'd specifically told them to stay at the keep.

Kane had planned to take Alice on a tour of the lands. They were his pride and joy, the most precious thing he possessed. Sharing them with her had been the only thing he could think of that she might find interesting. He'd wanted their time together to be private, with no one bothering them.

He knew without a doubt he could kill these men by himself—if he didn't have a woman to worry about.

"The MacLeod sends his greetings," another one said, a redhead. He was pudgier than the rest of them.

"Does he?" Kane gave them each an assessing glance. God, the MacLeods have really fallen. The men were not in shape. They looked like lads with a stick as they held their swords, and they were as cocky as a damn rooster. He'd take too much pleasure out of ridding his lands of these pathetic men.

"Aye, he—"

There was a scream. A scream that was all too feminine, all too close, and all too Alice. Heat surged through him as the men's attention snapped in the direction. They all grinned.

"Looks like Robert found something—" The redhead didn't have a chance to finish his sentence. Kane urged his horse a few steps forward and slammed his arm out. He caught the redhead on the arm with his sword, elbow connecting with a blonde man's face simultaneously. The two went toppling to the ground, leaving one on the saddle.

The battle was short-lived. The one on the saddle, a dark-haired lad, surged into a gallop toward Alice. Kane knew that if he didn't do something about the two men groaning on the ground, they'd show up in the middle of the battle, and it'd only make the odds worse for Alice. But Alice was in immediate danger. The men on the ground could be taken care of later, after he got his woman to safety.

The scene that met him had him seeing red.

Alice had just fallen off her horse, a blonde man he hadn't noticed standing over her. His knife was crusted with old blood, and parts of it glinted like a warning to Kane. Alice was trying to get to her feet, but every time she stood, he'd just shove her back down, laughing. The fury in her eyes was blatant, and he felt a brief moment of pride—until the man knelt down, pressing the blade to her throat.

Bloodlust surged through him.

With a roar, he leapt off his beast, swinging his claymore over his head and striking at the man closest to Alice. The man stumbled back, bone crunching, and the blonde from earlier came at him. Kane rolled forward, placing himself between Alice and the men. He ducked under the attacker and swung again. His claymore caught flesh.

The two men he'd previously struck down came charging over the hill. He groaned, especially when he felt Alice's tiny body stir

129

behind his. When her slender hand touched his arm, he wanted to murder someone. She was too innocent to see this, to see death.

"Alice," he hissed, "I'm going to distract them. I want you to take my horse and get to the keep. Find Brodrick and tell him what's happening. Do ye' understand?"

Her short, gasping breath fell on his shoulder. He could feel her tremors from behind him, and his heart clenched.

"If I take the horse, you'll be alone. I will not leave you to your death!" she said fiercely. One of the men came at him, and Kane growled, bracing himself for the impact. He couldn't swing with his body guarding Alice so closely, especially since the two of them were on the ground. Kane knocked the man's sword out of his hands, then quickly dragged Alice to her feet, shoving her farther behind him.

"Do no' fight me on this, lass. Go, damn you," he snarled. He didn't give her a second glance. Two of them came for him at once.

The battle had begun in earnest.

~

Saeran watched in horror as two men came at Kane with the speed and strength of a bull. He dodged them, moving with a grace that couldn't be real. He grabbed one of them by the hair, throwing him into the ground. The rest of them came, and he took care of them with ease, not even breaking a sweat.

She couldn't make herself get to the horse. That's what he was waiting for—she knew it. He wouldn't kill a man in front of her. Instead, he was going to wait until she was gone, tiring them out, and make them weak.

The ferocity of his movements, the precise dictation of his claymore and the way it sliced through the air held her still. Fear climbed in her throat, even though she knew that Kane would be victorious in this fight.

She also knew why he was called The Lion of the Highlands.

His grace. The menacing aura that came from his every pore. Even the men he was fighting began to realize this, backing away from him. Their eyes widened with the realization that they would die by his hand.

Saeran wasn't going to leave him. It was a coward's way out, even if everyone here knew he was going to win. He was still in front of her, his huge, thick shoulders flexing with every move. With a quick prayer, she reached forward and deftly slid one of his daggers from around his waist. It was large in her hands, but the training she'd been forced to endure for the past month prepared her for it.

Too bad for her, her thievery drew the attention of the man who'd first came upon her. His eyes raked over her with a lust-filled sneer. Her blood ran cold. Kane became a vague figure in her peripheral as she backed away from him, drawing the man towards her.

She was scared, so scared that her heart was climbing up her throat. But she would not become weak. Being weak had gotten her into this situation. If she'd fought him off as she knew how the first time he came for her, this wouldn't be happening right now, and Kane would have one less thing to worry about.

As it was, the fight managed to draw enough of Kane's attention that he didn't notice the blonde man giving him a wide berth as he ran around the fight, to Saeran. She held the knife in front of her, forcing herself to look weak, terrified.

She was terrified, but she wasn't as weak as she appeared to be. She might feel like it in front of the large man, but she wasn't. Brodrick had shown her enough that she could do this.

He leered.

"The MacLeod would like a piece of ye', I bet. Especially if yer the laird's betrothed, the lass everyone has been talking about," he mused, flashing a yellow smile at her. Her blood could have turned to ice. She met his eyes, holding the knife tightly. She didn't say a word. The smile dropped from his face. "Mayhap I'd like a taste of ye' myself."

Then he moved. It was quicker than she'd expected, but Brodrick hadn't held back with her in the ring. She moved out of his way, letting her body roll into the ground. She slashed outward with the dirk, catching him on the back of his calf. He made a rough sound of pain, and then turned around, sword falling onto the ground.

He planned to have his way with her the second he grabbed her, she realized.

Shaking and more terrified than she'd ever been in her life, she did the only thing she could think to.

Pushing herself to her feet, she waited until he was just in front of her. She met his eyes, then raised her leg.

Her foot connected with his bollocks. He lurched forward, face turning red.

"Bitch," he hissed. She wasn't prepared for the hand that came for her throat, or how tight his fingers were when they wrapped around her neck. Her breath cut off as he dragged her to the ground with him, one of his hands pressed between his legs. She couldn't make a sound, not even to cry out for Kane.

Kane's dagger clattered to the ground when the man grabbed her by the arms, holding her down by her wrists with one hand. She gasped for air, only finding...nothing. Blackness began to dot her vision, pain slamming behind her eyes.

"Going to pay for that," he snarled, pulling her head back by her neck, only to slam her back into the ground. The sound that wrenched from her throat was stuck by his hand, and she would have screamed from the pain of it, if she could.

The battle warred on behind her. She vaguely heard Kane's roar of fury in the background, but the clatter of swords striking against each other did not lessen. Blindly, terror beginning to take over her mind, she used the last of her strength to break free of his hold. She slapped out with her hands, raking him across the face with her nails. Her hand jabbed into his throat. Her other hand reached for the fallen dirk, and when her fingers wrapped around the hilt, tears of relief stung her eyes.

The hope of escape gave her the strength to bring the dagger up and thrust it into the arm that was cutting off her breath. He reared back, howling, and air rushed into her lungs with such force that she became lightheaded.

She didn't have time to adjust. He came for her, bleeding, and she rolled out of his way. She slammed the blade into his back when he crumpled into the ground. She gasped for breath, the tears finally falling down her cheeks.

He wasn't dead, but he was stunned.

"Fuck," a familiar voice snarled. Kane came into her vision. She couldn't make herself look at him. All she could see was the blood that was pooling out of the man's back, sliding down the side of his ribs. She swallowed, vomit rising in her throat.

"If I ever see any of ye' again, ye'll no' make it out alive," Kane snarled.

Thick arms wrapped around her body, drawing her close against Kane's warm chest. The shock of everything that had just happened kept her still, shocked. Terrified. She met Kane's eyes, her lower lip trembling as her panting turned into full gasps for air.

She vaguely realized that the fight was over, that Kane was carrying her away from the men who were scrambling away from the scene. The scene where she'd almost died, where Kane hadn't been there to save her, and she'd had to do it herself.

"Let's go," Kane bit out. He mounted, then dragged her up with him, setting her on his lap. One of his arms wrapped around her waist. As they took off, she let the rush of emotion she'd been holding back wash over her.

The pounding of hooves and the wind in her face gave her the cover she needed to let it go.

Chapter Seventeen

"When I told ye' to go, ye' were supposed to listen. What is so hard to understand about that?" He dismounted, dragging her with him. When he stood in front of her, the water from the creek trickling beside them, he finally had a clear look at her. He was livid. Furious. The rush of emotion from the battle was slowly fading away.

Kane wanted to wring her fragile neck. The urge to wrap his hands around her throat and shake sense into her was nearly overwhelming, but he managed to restrain himself.

Barely. Just barely.

Large, blue eyes looked up at his. They weren't filled with tears like he'd expected.

What he saw was so much worse.

Shame. She was ashamed. Not terrified and weeping like weak, tiny women should, but ashamed.

Kane had a feeling that it wasn't because of her failing to follow orders. It was because he had snapped at her. He knew it as surely as he knew the blade of his claymore. His chest tightened.

"I'm sorry," she said quietly, lowering her head. Her shoulders curled into a defensive slouch. He wanted to roar. She had to be traumatized by the event in some way, and he was only making it worse.

He came toward her, holding out his hand. "Lass," he said lowly, hating his burst of anger. He'd failed to protect her. She had been vulnerable, and he hadn't been there to save her. She should be the furious one, not he.

Though, if she had listened to him...

The fury returned with a vengeance. It nearly robbed him of breath. A simple order, and the lass couldn't have listened to him. It would have saved her, and none of this would have happened. She could have left. He could have killed the MacLeods, and she wouldn't have had to harm a man.

A man who she'd left alive.

A man who would, most likely, seek revenge.

"I couldn't leave you," she said. Her eyes raised to his, and the fire there only fueled his own. "How could you ask me to do that? They would have killed you! I could have helped!"

He roared with laughter. "Ye'? Ye' could have helped me? Lass, yer a waif. Ye' couldn't lift a dagger if it would save yer life."

Her eyes snapped with fire. "I remember quite clearly taking your own dagger from you. I also remember *quite clearly* when I had to use it against that man. Do not say that I couldn't have helped you." She threw the said dagger on the ground.

"If ye'd have listened to me, this wouldn't be a problem. Ye' should have ran when I said to."

"I did!" she said furiously, slapping her hands onto her hips.

"But no' the second time," he growled, taking an involuntary step forward. She met him step for step, hands fisted at her sides. He wanted to be confused and shocked by the outburst. But one: he was too angry with the unreasonable lass, and two: he should have expected it. She'd already shown him how high her flames could jump when he tested them.

To think that she'd remain docile under a chastising would be absurd. Still, something felt wrong. Her reaction, the immediate shame she'd seemed to feel... It felt wrong. Like it was an automatic reaction, imbedded into her being. What could make a woman like that?

There was more to Alice than a pretty face, and he wanted to know what it was.

"I was trying to help you. Ye'd just turn away an extra hand?"

"Alice, yer a lady. Ye' donna fight, and I sure as hell willna let you. If ye'd have just left when I told you to, both times, without hesitating or disobeying me, I could have taken care o' the threat—instead, I let it get right to ye'. Alice, that bastard, he almost..."

Her gaze softened.

"But he didn't."

"And that made ye' have to stab him. Yer a lady," he repeated, dragging a hand through his hair. "A lady does no' fight with a man, Alice. I'm to protect ye'. That is how it is. I say jump, and ye' jump. I say run, and ye' run. If ye'd listened, it wouldn't have escalated so far."

She rolled her eyes. "Please—you saw perfectly well that I can protect myself."

"Aye, with a wee dagger, after he had ye' on the ground and was choking ye'." The words were like acid coming out of his mouth. He pressed his lips, shaking his head. "We'll no' be discussing this. 'Tis over and yer safe."

"Because I saved myself," she said proudly, crossing her arms over her chest. He growled, taking another step towards her. She didn't move an inch. The only thing that happened was a quirk to her full, pink lips, and her thin brow rose.

He growled, acting before he could think about it. She wasn't ready. They were both fighting for control of the situation, but damn her, she was beautiful. One moment, they were squaring off. The next, his arm was wrapping around her waist, his hand sliding into the back of her hair, and her lips were against his.

~

Saeran froze.

Her breath, her heart, her body. All of her concentration centered on the pair of lips that were moving over hers with smooth strokes.

She'd never been kissed.

She'd never seen anyone kiss, either. Her parents had kept it away from her, and while at court, she'd hid in the library and studied. She'd avoided it religiously.

There was no way for her to avoid this, though. It was happening to her. His hand was at the back of her head, his thumb holding her jaw, urging it open. She wanted to hate what was happening, but she couldn't. The longer he held her there, his mouth on hers, the more she started to relax. Gradually, kiss by kiss, her body began to melt against his.

As if he was asking permission, he slid his tongue along her lower lip.

"Kiss me, lass," he grated against her mouth. The deep desire she heard in his commanding words was enough to melt the rest of her resistance. With a little sigh, she opened fully for him. Moving her hands from his chest to his shoulders, she clutched his large body to hers.

He groaned and the sound sent a shiver through her. His hands slid around her back and down, until he could hold her hips tightly against his, letting her feel the hard length of his body. Stars swam in her vision, lungs seizing.

His tongue probed her mouth. Confusion and desire rose at the same time. She didn't know what to do, but that was fine. He dominated her with his kiss, robbed her of control, sense, and propriety. He was attacking her mouth with the ferocity he'd used against the MacLeods, but the underlying tenderness, the passion, made it all the more delicious.

"There ye' go," he growled, pulling away from her slightly. A sound left her lips, one of desperation. How could he pull away from her like—

Saeran didn't have to continue her anguished mental rant. Kane slid an arm under her knees and one around her back. She didn't have time to protest before he was setting her on a section of wooden fencing. He moved between her legs, dipping his head to her neck. Her eyes shot wide as his mouth opened against her neck. Heat pooled in her stomach.

"What...what are you doing to me?" she asked, voice airy, shocked.

"Kissing ye'. Do ye' no' like it, lass?" he asked, chuckling against her neck. Her pulse pounded, and she was sure he could feel it. When he brushed his lips against it, she knew her suspicion had been confirmed. A shudder went through her.

"I...my lord, this is wrong..." She forgot why, but she knew it was. He kissed her again, lightly nipping the flesh above her racing pulse. He grunted, sliding his hand from around her back to her waist, traveling dangerously close to her breasts. She instinctively pulled away from him.

Saeran forgot that she was balanced on a fence, of course, and began to fall backwards. She grabbed for his shoulders as his arms came around her. She clung to him, then lifted her eyes to his.

His lips came over hers with a vengeance, as if making up for the time they hadn't been there. She moaned, forgetting everything except him. When one of his hands closed over her breasts, she didn't pull away from him. She should have, but her body was screaming at her to let him touch her, to touch him back, and to take as much as he was willing to give her.

When his lips once again left her neck, she gave reign to her instincts, determined to let her passions run free. She'd spent so long keeping them hidden, keeping everything hidden. Now, with Kane, she was slowly losing control of herself—and she loved it.

She didn't know the man who was wringing such passionate feelings from her, but it didn't feel like that. His lips roamed over her neck, down to her collarbone. Her hands threaded into his hair, holding his head against her. It felt natural, like this was how it should be, how she should feel.

Wild. Free. Desired.

Kane was doing this to her, making her feel like this.

Heat ran through her body, striking her right in the gut. Her legs tightened around him, pulling him even closer. The only thing separating them was her clothing, and not even the thin layers of clothing could block the heat that was emitting from him. The heat that was affecting her in the worst of passionate ways.

"Are ye' alright, my lady?" His voice sent shivers over her skin. She pressed her hands into his shoulders, urging him on with a silent "yes". She felt intoxicated. That was the only reason she was letting this happen, she thought vaguely, gasping when he reached behind her, undoing some of the top laces of her dress. His fingers were deft and warm, every brush of his skin against hers had tendrils of desire curl in her gut.

Soon enough, her bodice wasn't as tight, and the small bit of control she had was gone. His lips caressed her collarbone, up until the top of her dress was loose. She froze at the first draft of wind across her breasts. Saeran started to pull away, heart thundering with a mixture of confusion and desire. Her face heated when she saw the hunger in his eyes. As he stared at her, at a place no one but her mother and sister had seen, embarrassment had her arms lifting. She started to cover herself, but his growl of disapproval stopped her.

She stared at him like a rabbit about to be shot with an arrow.

"Why...why did you do that?" she asked shakily. Saeran wanted to draw the dress to her chest, to shield herself from him. But there was also a part of her that...didn't. She wanted him to see her as she was. She wanted him to see a part of her that she'd kept hidden from him when she pretended to be a boy.

"Because," he said lowly, the thickness of his desire-laden brogue enough to make her eyes close, "I wanted to see ye'. Donna cover yerself, lass. I'll be taking my fill of ye'." Then, without another word, he wrapped an arm around her waist and pulled her flush against him—except this time, her breasts were eye level with his face. Saeran was still, afraid to move lest he stop himself from whatever he had planned for her.

"What do you mean by that?" she asked before she could stop herself. When one corner of his mouth lifted into a smirk, she wanted to weep at the wave of lust that shot through her.

"This," he said, bending his head and closing his mouth right over her breast. Her eyes widened, and shock held her still—along with pleasure. His mouth was warm and wet, biting at first, then sucking on her with great pulls. The feeling blinded her, made a strangled sound rip from her throat.

"What are you doing to me?" she whimpered, threading her fingers into his hair. She didn't know whether to pull him close or push him away. The emotions she felt terrified her and intrigued her—and she knew he could tell she had wavered.

He abruptly pulled away. All of the sensations, all of the passion, drained out of her like a plug had been pulled. Out went the fantasy, and in came the reality. It was so sudden that she was left trembling.

"Alice, I can no' do this. No' right now," he said, regret and something deeper tinging his voice.

She stared up at him, panting, the reality of what had happened leaving her bereft. She had just done something unimaginable, unforgivable.

"I know…" Her whisper caused a flash of pain to cross his face. Now was not the time—there would never be a time. He was not hers to have. She kept the words to herself, shame nearly choking her.

"Good. That's…good, lass." Then, even though his voice was strained and his eyes were piercing, he helped her down from the fence and turned her around, nimbly tying her laces and straightening her dress. When he came into her view again, she stared up at him, lips pressed, feeling...empty. Aye, without him, she felt lonely. Even though he was standing in front of her, she felt as if he were half way across the world.

His lips quirked at the corners and he reached up, gently threading his fingers through her hair. She lowered her eyes, body still high from the pleasure. She was wet, hot, and burning for him. She was willing to bet that he was in no better condition.

"'Tis too soon for you," he murmured. "Ye'd hate me for taking more advantage of ye' than I already have, Alice."

"Nay, I—"

He pressed a finger to her lips. "Donna deny it, lass. Ye' ken ye' would." Kane took his finger from her lips, letting it slide down her cheek, to her jaw. He tilted her face towards his, then smiled. "Soon."

"Soon?" she repeated. This couldn't happen again! He was her sister's betrothed! And yet, even as she thought that, her heart thundered in her chest.

"Aye. When I ken ye' better, and when ye' get off my arse about Lady Blaine. I donna want ye' to be plagued by guilt when I finally take what we both want."

Chapter Eighteen

"Sae, I have been hearing the most distressing rumors!"

She almost didn't hear her sister as she flew into the laird's study, where Saeran was between working and daydreaming. She was too distracted to pay attention to anything. Her hands and mind were doing their own thing while she thought of what had happened only an hour ago.

She'd had her first kiss. Even now, thinking about it, her lips tingled at the remembered sensation of the laird's mouth moving over hers with enough skill to take her breath away. She shivered delicately, reaching up to touch her lips with wonder.

A blush came over her face.

"Sae, listen to me!" A chubby hand grabbed her by the shoulder, and Saeran nearly fell out of the chair. She braced her hands on the desk, causing some of her good mood to deplete. Not even thoughts of Kane could distract her from her sister's fury.

"*What?*" she snapped, harsher than she'd intended.

Blaine's lips pressed, but only for a second.

"I heard something!"

Saeran sighed, barely holding down her annoyance. Blaine was always "hearing things".

"You mentioned that already," Saeran said, turning back to her books. If she could, she'd order her sister to leave her to her work. Saeran doubted that would go well.

Kane hadn't given her time to react to his claim on her before throwing her onto the saddle. The two of them had rode in silence.

141

Saeran with her body filled with heat and panic, and Kane with...whatever he was feeling beneath his stony exterior.

"Sae, don't be like that," Blaine admonished, resting her bum on the table, far back enough to sit on the papers Saeran had just been reaching for. She crossed her arms over her chest, staring at the wall, jaw working. It was hard not to shove her off the desk. So. Hard.

"What did you hear?" She didn't care what her sister had heard. It was always the same thing. Gwen did this, Sabia did that, one of her children did something. Someone from town was the new trollop. Same thing every day. Saeran hoped that by getting her sister's need to gossip over with, she could get back to work.

She could have laughed at herself. Who was she kidding—she wasn't working; she was daydreaming about Kane.

Saeran looked up in time to see her sister's face flush with fury. "There is some...some whore!" she burst out, throwing her hands in the air. "Gwen saw my husband with some blonde tramp. They were riding into the fields together," she said furiously, moving away from the edge of the desk.

I should move those papers, she thought numbly, feeling a sense of dread coil in her stomach. Kane wasn't married to Blaine—not yet. But the reality of her words slapped Saeran in the face. Her sister's betrothed had kissed her. She had encouraged it. He had even seen parts of her—kissed parts of her!—that were forbidden to any man except her own husband.

Bile rose in her throat. She would never have a husband.

Kane was Blaine's. Saeran should never have known the pleasure one could find in a man's arms—more specifically, Kane's arms. Guilt and shame coursed through her like acid. Even though she knew lusting after her sister's betrothed was wrong, she was still doing it. Still craving him. Still taking her anger over not having him out on Blaine.

One kiss hadn't squelched the flames—the only thing it had done was make the flame hotter, brighter...and showed her just how badly she wanted Kane. If she could forget her duties as a sister, as a maiden, for the touch of one man, Saeran knew without a doubt that she would be in trouble. Deep, horrible trouble—because she also knew that if Kane wanted to see her again, she wouldn't fight him.

Her mind would rebel against everything she did with him, but even a fraction of that one rational part of her wanted to surrender.

"Are you sure Gwen saw that? Maybe it was Brodrick. He often goes riding in the fields," she lied, her throat thick. Never before would she have considered lying to her sister—and carrying out with it, no less! She put a hand to her throat, trying to calm her heart. The guilt felt like it was burning her from the inside out, starting with the destruction of her heart.

"No," Blaine denied, shaking her head sternly. "Gwen knows what she saw. The woman was blonde and small—a horror to look upon, I'll bet. Anyone who's blonde and waif-like is—"

Saeran's gaze snapped to her sister's. Blaine kept going, as if she hadn't just told Saeran she was basically a horror. Waif-like was Blaine's go-to expression to insult women who were of a smaller, thinner figure. Being thin was revolting to Blaine.

"—disgusting. Lord!" Blaine finished, putting a hand to her forehead. "I cannot help but wonder why the laird would ask me to dine with him this night after he was cavorting around with some blonde hussy!"

"What if he wasn't cavorting with her?" Saeran asked, even though she knew better than anyone that he *had* been "cavorting" with the "blonde hussy".

Blaine gave her a flat look.

"Men do not simply 'take a woman out for a ride' without cavorting, my simpleton sister." She collapsed onto the desk again, appearing not to have heard Saeran's breath hiss between her teeth. She wanted to hate how she wasn't sympathetic to her sister's plight anymore, or how she was rapidly losing patience with the one person who had always *demanded* it, but she was torn.

Something inside of her was beginning to click together, and Saeran didn't know if she could ignore it—even if the guilt of what she'd done with Kane was eating at her.

"Blaine," she said tiredly, "I am quite busy. We can discuss more of this tonight—"

"You're acting strange," Blaine accused. Her eyes narrowed. "Do you know that I have only seen two blonde women here since we arrived? Neither of them were slender. Everyone is so burly and dark. Gwen also said that she heard the two of them talking, and the girl didn't have a brogue."

Saeran felt her heart skip a beat. Her hands started to shake. She shoved them in her lap, clenching her fingers together. She could feel Blaine watching her closely.

"What were you doing today?" Blaine asked sharply. Saeran

barely stopped herself from jumping at the harshness of her voice.

"Numbers. Stables. Speaking with the men about training. Blaine," she said softly, trying to use a reasonable tone to cover the shakiness of her voice. "Are you trying to accuse me of something?"

God, the conflict inside of her was horrendous, but she knew that if Blaine found out about her time with Kane, the emotional flaying would be much worse than what she was feeling now. At least without Blaine's knowledge, Saeran had the advantage of choosing how she got Kane to spend time with Blaine.

Blaine knowing of her arrangement with Kane could either be good or bad. Good, because she could be glad of Saeran's help and let her off easy; or bad, because Blaine would demand more and more time with Kane, and that would mean Saeran wouldn't have a choice in how much she wanted to be in Kane's presence.

Which would also mean that there was more of a chance of Saeran losing any sense of modesty with him. She clenched her fingers tighter, hating that she felt she had to lie to her sister. If she didn't lie, so many bad things would happen—like Blaine realizing that *Saeran* had been the one cavorting with Kane!

Some of the anger died out of Blaine's gaze.

"No, Sae. I know you would never betray me like that. Plus, Gwen had said the blonde appeared to be beautiful—at least to her. I've never liked blondes," she reminded Saeran, something that she'd heard her whole entire life. The sting of Blaine's implied words, where she basically called Saeran hideous and unappealing, was not lost on her.

As horrible of a person as it made her feel, some of the guilt began to lessen. Her sister was making sacrifices for Saeran's safety, but Blaine wasn't the only one who had more problems than she could handle now.

"Oh!" Blaine suddenly piped, clapping her hands. "What color gown do you think he would like to see me in? Mayhap tonight he is going to ask me to marry him. Yes," she said, nodding her head. "That is what has him so shy with me. He is worried about asking for my hand."

"I don't thi—"

"Mayhap I can save him that trouble," Blaine continued, raising her voice to be louder than Saeran. She sighed, slumping into the chair—until she heard what Blaine had said.

"What do you mean, save him the trouble?"

"Why, I can ask him to marry me! It should not matter that I've taken control of the situation, of course, because we all know he plans to ask me this night. By eliminating this problem of his, I will be one step closer to—"

She cut off abruptly. Saeran frowned.

"One step closer to what?"

"Saeran! The laird wants to speak to—oh." She looked up at Connor's entrance, unsure whether to be happy to see him or not. Going by the displeased look in his eyes as he stopped at the door, he wasn't happy to see Blaine. She couldn't help her little smile.

"What are you doing in here?" he asked Blaine sharply. When she sputtered, Saeran rose a brow. "Women are not permitted to be in this room."

"Excuse me," Blaine said sharply, rising to her feet. Her hands planted on her hips, and Saeran felt sorry for Connor. Luckily, he didn't back down. She could have applauded him. "Do you know who I am?"

He rolled his eyes. "You're a woman. Get out, before I am forced to bring the laird into this."

"He'll have you flogged for speaking to me in such a manner!" Blaine spat.

"You think a man who would kill his own flesh and blood would care what a woman like you has to say?"

Saeran almost gasped with her sister. The insult did the trick, and she stormed out of the room, but not before hissing, "The second I am Lady of this household, you are done for, squire."

"The second you're lady of this household, you'll be dead."

"Was that a threat?" She honestly looked shocked. Saeran could imagine—her sister had never been confronted with such obvious dislike. The whole encounter made her appreciate Connor all the more.

"No. 'Tis but a warning. A man who kills his mother will gladly kill his wife. Don't you agree? Now, leave us. I have important business with Lord Saeran, and fortunately, you are not allowed to be in here."

Blaine rounded on Saeran, obviously expecting her to say something. Saeran fought down the tightness in her throat and nodded toward the door. Blaine's face went red. With a furious sound, she stormed through the dimly lit room and out of the door.

"She is a terror. His mother is not truly dead—but watching

how horrified she became was worth the lie," Connor said with a content sigh, sitting on the edge of the desk. "What was she complaining about this time?"

Saeran winced, dropping her eyes to her lap. She heard his quick intake of breath, then the sound of him moving across the room. The door whooshed closed, and then he was grabbing her by the hand.

"What is it? Do I need to bring out some oil for the stairs? A slip down the stairs never hurt anyone—if they end up dead."

Unused to the concern, Saeran blushed.

"I think I've done something terrible," she said quietly, finally letting the kernel of guilt pop inside of her. She realized that she was not feeling guilty because of her time with Kane, or the lying—but because the old meek Saeran would have felt that way. It was the principle behind her actions that made her feel so terrible.

"What?"

She looked at Connor beseechingly. "You cannot repeat a word of this, to anyone. Or think badly of me—I feel terrible enough for the both of us. I promise, though... I didn't know what was happening and when I did, it was too late and I didn't want it to—"

"My lady!" Connor said sharply, excitement tinging his voice. "What are you talking about? What did you do?" He wiggled on the desk almost like a happy puppy, like he knew what she'd done before she told him.

"The laird...he... I was so foolish, Connor," she said, distraught. "So incredibly foolish. I thought this would be a one-time thing!"

He nodded, encouraging her to continue. She bit her lip. This was her friend. Not her sister, the woman who judged everything she did. Connor was nice. Good. Helpful. He wanted her to trust him as a confidant, and if she were honest with herself, she would admit that he was the only one she felt she could trust.

He was so refreshingly flamboyant once you got to know him. Not like the callous and distanced man she'd met before. It was like she'd opened a closet and a new and happy Connor had stepped out of it.

"Instead, I do believe this will be happening even more..."

"Tell me what happened!" he gasped. His eyes were as wide as her own, and she nodded, continuing her tale. She told him of their "deal", the ride in the field, the attack, and the kiss. The scorching-hot kiss that had stolen all of her control. By the time she finished recounting the events of the day, she was trembling.

Just then she realized she had been attacked. Honestly and truly attacked. It hadn't been a mere nightmare—it had actually happened.

"The two of you kissed," he repeated, completely ignoring the mention of ruffians.

"Aye, Connor, but there was more—the laird, Kane. He did not seem surprised over the attack," she recalled, finally letting the effects of the attack come over her. The kiss had been a distraction, taking precedence over the real matter at hand—a matter that could have gotten her killed.

Chills stole over her.

"He wouldn't have been," he said, staring at her with the same wide brown eyes. "But my lady, the two of you kissed?"

"After the attack—"

He waved it away. "I do not want to hear about that. Tell me about the kiss! My god, did he enjoy it?"

"Enjoy it?" Her mouth dropped. "How on earth would I know?! One second I was considering slapping him, and the next he was kissing me!" She frowned, then leaned forward, whispering, "How would one know if their kissing partner enjoyed said kiss?"

He pursed his lips.

"You know, I've never taken note of such things. It is just a feeling you have, in your gut. He started the kiss, correct?"

She nodded, wringing her hands together. Why it was important to her that he enjoyed the kiss, she didn't know. But already she was dreading the results. Blaine had never approved of anything she did— why should Kane approve of her kissing skills? She was a novice, never having even seen a couple kiss! Reading and seeing it were two different things, right?

"How long would you say it lasted?" He peered at her, the look of a very determined man on his face.

"I would say that it lasted...more than a couple of seconds." She nodded. "Yes, much more. Then he began to..." She trailed off, flushing. She hadn't told him *that* part.

"What, my lady? What did he begin to do? Gah, why do you not tell me these things?"

"If I tell you what happened, you would think me a harlot— which I am most definitely not!" she insisted, grabbing his hands when he began to wave them around excitedly. Saeran swore, once again, he was happier than a pup. He could barely contain his excitement.

Excitement for what, she didn't know.

The matter at hand was most distressing.

"Oh my God. My lady. Saeran. Just tell me."

She shook her head, face beginning to flame worse than it had before. She couldn't possibly tell him. To tell Connor, a male, what Saeran had experienced at the hands and mouth of the laird would be scandalous—and make it all the more real. A shiver went through her.

"If you do not tell me," he said, waving his fingers at her as he stood gracefully to his feet, "I shall have to ask the laird what happened myself."

She lunged for him, grabbing his arm. He raised an expectant brow.

Saeran pressed her lips.

"I remember seeing him in the courtyard with Brodrick..."

"Oh, fine!" she snapped, yanking him to the desk. She flopped into her seat with a sigh of frustration, and Connor followed suit, his butt on the edge of the desk. "The kissing became heated. There. I told you. Now, how do I know if he enjoyed it or not?"

His brow went so high it could have reached his hairline.

"Heated? Really, my lady? I am a poor lonely squire to the laird. I finally have some excitement in my life, and you want to feed me the 'heated kissing' line? My dear, if you want to lie to me, you should do a better job of it. I have many older brothers. I know how to tell when someone isn't being completely honest."

She raised her hands in frustration. "Why is it such a big deal?!"

"Why do you want to know if he liked it?" he replied, giving her a sly smile.

She grunted, crossing her arms over her chest.

"It became a lot more than heated—and that's all I'm going to say on the matter! The excitement from the attack, and the anger, was probably the only reason it happened at all. I doubt he enjoyed it," she said, looking at her lap. If it weren't Blaine's betrothed, and Blaine would speak to her about things like this, Saeran was willing to bet her sister would say the same thing.

She sighed.

"Did he further the kissing?" Connor asked.

Saeran nodded. "But he also ended it."

He slapped his hands on his lap, standing. "Well, there is your answer."

"What do you mean?" she asked, standing with him. She

frowned when he began walking to the door.

"The laird wants to see you in the stables," he said, completely ignoring her question. She followed after him. Connor stepped out of the room, fixing his clothing. When he looked at her, his gaze was composed, with just a hint of mischief in his eyes. She didn't think that boded well for herself.

"You didn't answer me—!"

"The stables, my lady," he said loudly over his shoulder before darting down the hall, laughing happily as he went. Saeran stared after him, completely confused about what had just happened. Had the laird enjoyed it or not? Had Connor randomly gone insane, or did he have his own little secret agenda? That smile on his face had been anything but malicious, more like... More like he was excited about something.

But *what*? As Saeran closed up the ledgers on the desk and blew out the few candles that scattered the room, she worried. Not that he would reveal her secret, since he had promised not to, but that—

Oh god.

The laird. Kane. He wanted to see her in the stables. Her heart dropped to her stomach, and she swayed. After the conversation she'd just had with Connor, and their "cavorting" in the fields, she didn't know if she could face him as Saeran. Alice was too close to the surface when it came to him.

All thoughts of Connor, of his smiles and excitement, died.

She had to face Kane.

Chapter Nineteen

Kane cursed as he came out of the stables, rubbing his arm. The damn beast was just as unruly as a wild horse, which he very well could be. The king had sent him the horse a full moon ago, and just now, Kane was getting around to taming the monster.

Or he would be, if the beast could stay still for a second. Kane should have done it ages ago, but the brewing feud with the bordering clans was too pressing for him to put off. The only reason he was dealing with the beast now was because he had to take his mind off of Alice.

It had been several hours since he'd seen her, and even without her crystalline eyes gazing into his, he couldn't get her out of his head. The softness of her body against his, her golden hair, the fire in her eyes. He'd be damned if a monk could resist her!

His hands physically ached to touch her. But since their return, he hadn't seen her—though he forced himself not to look for her. He knew the second he saw her, he'd be in trouble. Not only that, but he wouldn't let her escape from him again.

Pulling away from her had been the hardest thing he'd ever had to do. He was the laird. He was *Kane*. He should be able to take what he wanted—hell, he could. Alice hadn't put up an ounce of fight with him! But he knew that if he took what she so willingly offered to him so soon, she would regret it immediately after—and he'd feel like the worst ass in the world.

Nay, he had to prepare her for him. She had to trust him and know him—as much as he was willing to let her know, that is. Aye,

Alice had to be comfortable with him.

Kane leaned against the side of the stables, taking a moment for himself for the first time in... Hell, he couldn't remember the last time he wasn't running somewhere or fighting someone. For this one moment, though, he had a chance to look at what was his. Pride swelled inside of him at the sight of his keep.

The area was not as busy as it normally was this time of day, but he'd sent several of his men out to finish fixing the broken fence. He'd sent them back up in case the MacLeod men came back for another attack.

A growl slipped through his lips as he thought of what had happened. The damn MacLeods were going to pay for their attack. In a sennights time, he was going to end the threat—with the rain, or without. So long as they paid for what they tried to do to Alice, Kane would be pleased.

The poor lass had been terrified, and Kane felt like punching himself for that. He'd probably worsened her fear by the force of his kiss, and how far he'd taken it. Her nerves had been rattled enough, and he hadn't helped.

He should have soothed her—not ravaged her. Yet he couldn't regret his actions. Not after the way she blossomed like a flower under him.

His body tensed with desire, and he wanted to curse. Aye, Alice was a distraction that had consumed too much of his day—and he couldn't bring himself to be worried about it. Not when he would see her soon. The thought made him smile.

"It's time," Brodrick said from beside him. He cast a glance at his friend. Maybe Alice distracting him was not such a good thing. He hadn't even noticed Brodrick there.

"For?" he asked, pushing away from the stables. Where was Saeran? He'd told Connor to fetch him a while ago. You'd think they were gossiping like girls for the amount of time it took for Saeran to join him. He grunted, crossing his arms over his chest.

"To retaliate." He didn't miss the fury in his friend's voice.

Brodrick was furious. Kane knew it; everyone knew it. An attack on his laird was an attack on his clan, and Kane knew more than anyone that Brodrick wanted to put the MacLeods in their place. He felt the same burning need. To attack while he was with a woman...inexcusable. Especially since they'd planned to rape her. Disgust rolled through him. Disgust and fury.

"Aye. It is. In a sennight, we'll leave."

"So long?" Brodrick demanded, hands fisting at his side. "My laird, I have a wife and son. In a sennight's time, they could attack again—this time the village."

"They would no' be so stupid as to attack the clan as a whole," Kane said, shaking his head.

"They attacked ye', did they no'? What makes ye' think they'd show any caution before coming after my wife? My son?"

Kane growled. "Are ye' doubting my judgment?"

"Ye' lapsed today," Brodrick pointed out furiously. "Ye' gave them the perfect chance to attack ye', all because of a woman. Mayhap yer judgment is starting to falter."

"Mayhap yer overstepping yer boundaries," Kane warned darkly, chest tightening. It was true. He had failed in judgment today—but he was not going to be so foolish in the future. Before he left, though, he had to make Blaine agree to marry him. The second a messenger was on his way to the king with news of the betrothal, he would leave—but only then.

He couldn't take the risk of not returning—unless he proposed to Blaine before he left. At least if he died in battle on the off-chance that the Campbells interfered, he would still have Blaine's dowry for his clan.

Brodrick narrowed his eyes at Kane. Kane took a threatening step forward. They stayed like that, tense. Silent. The warning from both of them clear.

From Kane, the promise that if Brodrick didn't back down, he wouldn't hesitate to put him in his place.

From Brodrick, the threat that if Kane didn't protect his clan like he should, Brodrick wouldn't give two shits about status. That was the only reason Kane lessened his tense muscles. That was the only reason Kane didn't show him who was the laird. Brodrick was a man with a family, and he would do anything to protect them—a trait that Kane not only admired, but envied.

"I want to do this soon," Brodrick said. His words were nothing but an angry growl. Kane watched him storm off, shoving a hand through his hair. He wanted to do it soon, as well. Letting the MacLeods think they could overpower him, control him with fear, and attack his woman?

Not acceptable.

~

"Lad," Brodrick said stiffly as he passed Saeran. His shoulders were hunched and his face was lined with fury. Saeran started to take a skittish step away from him, then remembered that she was a boy. She couldn't just dance away from him. She forced her gate to be more stiff, and kept an eye on how much her hips swayed.

"Brodrick." Lord, she sounded like she was walking to her death. What if she really was? What if Connor's slyness had been because he knew the laird had found out about her deception? Oh, God. He was going to lop her head off, and that would be the end of her.

Brodrick paused. "Are ye' okay, lad? Ye' sound sick."

She shook her head, giving him a small smile. It would have been bigger, had she not been trembling. "Aye, my lord. I am completely fine." *Liar.*

"Are ye' sure? Ye' look like yer walking to yer death there." He raised a brow. The irony was not lost on her. Some of his dark mood seemed to slip. Brodrick had never been a man that stayed angry for long. He liked to *appear* threatening, but when he got down to it, he was a man who took many joys in life.

One of those joys was watching her shuck horse shite out of a stall all day. If some of it splattered him, it was a complete accident, no matter how much he tried to insist otherwise. Seeing him now, this man who'd grown into an almost uncle-like figure for her, was enough to help her relax.

At least, only a tad. Her knees didn't shake as much when she saw the concern on his face.

"I'm fine," she insisted. God, she hated how hard it was to change the tone of her voice. Lately, she had been receiving odd looks from everyone whenever she spoke. She realized this wasn't as easy as she originally thought. If anything, it got a little harder every day.

She constantly reminded herself to lower her voice, hold her shoulders a different way, keep the sway of her hips to a minimum… Connor had started giving her tips whenever he could, and she had started taking them to heart. He had even mentioned cutting her hair a little shorter, but she couldn't bring herself to do it.

"Why do I feel as if yer lying to me, lad?" He chuckled, but it was tinged with worry. She understood what he was thinking as surely as if she'd been reading his mind.

Saeran wasn't one to balk at the things she had to go through on a daily basis. When she'd been beat up by men every day, she'd taken it like the lad she had to pretend to be. When she woke up in the early hours of morning to take a bath in the creek, she didn't squeal about the cold water. When she didn't have a meal, she didn't ask for one.

She normally hid her weakness pretty well. Living with Blaine had taught her that the only option she had when she was uncomfortable with something was to bear through it. That's just how it was, and how it had always been.

Right now, the sun was hot, beating down on her like a branding poker—an exaggeration caused by her nerves. She tugged at her shirt, trying to breathe some fresh air, and attempted to give him a more convincing smile.

"Lady Blaine had me help her with...bunions," she lied weakly. God, the amount of lying she was doing today would have her mother rolling in her grave, God bless her soul.

"Bunions," he repeated dubiously, raising his brow yet another time. He didn't believe her, and she couldn't blame him.

"Aye, bunions. It was a terror, really. "

"I can only imagine," he said, scratching his jaw. "Are ye' positive it isn't something else, lad? Ye' ken ye' can talk to me about it. Is it Connor? Has the lad been pestering ye'? I ken he can be overbearing, but ye've no reason to be worried about him."

She wanted to laugh. Brodrick obviously knew of Connor's preferences when it came to the pleasures of oneself, but he didn't know about Connor and Saeran's alliance. She didn't know whether it was good or bad that he was inferring Connor pined after her.

"Nay, he's not bothering me." She worried her lip. Brodrick had always been a trustworthy man. Though Kane and he were obviously friends, she felt safe in confessing some of her worries. It was expected of her anyway—when the second man to the laird spoke to you, you were bound to reply. "It...it is the laird."

He snorted. She glanced up, confused.

"The laird has had a stick up his arse ever since this bonny lass came about," he said, rolling his eyes. The action was so odd in comparison to his barbaric stature. She smiled a little—then her eyes widened.

"Bonny lass?" she echoed.

"Aye. Alice, I believe he said. Are ye' sure yer okay, lad? Ye' really do look pale."

She was too busy trying to catch her breath to pay attention to him, or notice the calculative way he was watching her.

"Nay, I—how long has he been speaking of this Alice?" she asked, dazedly meeting his eyes. It hadn't occurred to her that Kane would speak about her—or rather, the fake her. The realization that Kane would, and did, talk of Alice made her mouth go dry.

What if Blaine found out? Her heart dropped to her stomach.

"Oh, I'd say about a good month, ever since he returned."

"A month?" *He's only known of me for a day!* Panic assailed her. How could he possibly have known of her that long?

"Aye, a month. Says he happened across a water nym—"

"Saeran!"

She almost vomited all over Brodrick. The voice of the laird made everything in her body go numb. She didn't notice the pounding of her heart or the way her hands shook when she turned around. She forgot about Brodrick completely.

The man of her moral destruction stood in front of her, his face as dark as his mood appeared to be. His lips were pressed, eyes glaring daggers. She swore, if she were a MacLeod, he wouldn't hesitate to rip her to shreds.

He knew. That's all she could think as she stared up at him. He knew, and he was going to kill her.

"Stables. Now."

He gave the harsh command, then turned away. She watched him go, mouth dry and hands shaking, with death hanging over her head. She was definitely going to die today. By a pitchfork, most likely. Aye, she could see it. He'd use a pitchfork to end her life.

"Good luck, lad," Brodrick grunted. Then he, too, turned and continued on his way.

With no other choice, she followed the imposing man who was going to kill her with a pitchfork. Still, even with the threat of death imminent, she felt her body react to the sight of him.

Her earlier opinion about his handsomeness remained the same—he was not handsome by any means. He was imposing and commanding, and mayhap that was all that was needed for her to want him. He did not remind her of the frilly boys at court, or the men who tried to pretend they were tough and brawl. He actually *was* tough and brawl, and every step in his gait showed that.

"Hurry up," he said sharply over his shoulder. She hurried. And waited. Waited to die. By a pitchfork. It was going to fly through the air and pierce her heart, and she wasn't even surprised anymore. It seemed that anything that could go wrong, would go wrong.

Chapter Twenty

Why was the lad acting so skittish? Over the course of the month, he'd become less scared of Kane, and now, he was shaking like a leaf. Brodrick must have said something to shake him up, he thought while throwing the stable door open. He caught it before it could slam into the stall, then stood back as Saeran walked passed him.

Aye, the lad was shaking and pale. Very pale. Kane frowned at him.

"Brodrick told me ye' were good with horses," he started. The lad flinched back with every word. Kane stared. "Aye, well…Yer good with horses, though I understand ye' had a problem with this one a while back."

Blue eyes—he paused. Scowled. Where had he seen those blue eyes before? The face staring up at him was pale beneath the grunge covering his face, making any chance of recognition impossible. The same hat he wore everyday dipped as his gaze focused on the beast.

"I'm afraid I'm too busy to be training him. Since yer doing the numbers and stables, I figured ye' wouldn't mind spending some extra time with the beast."

"What?" the lad asked thinly. Something about his voice made Kane's eyes narrow, but he couldn't place what it was that bothered him. The lad's face lifted for a second, then he looked at the ground. Kane shook himself out of it, glowering. "I thought…"

"Whatever ye' thought, forget it. Ye'll be taming the beast. He's a gift from the king. Do ye' think ye' can do it?" An odd look passed over Saeran's face, then he moved.

Kane stepped back as the lad skittered around him, keeping closer to the stalls than Kane, until he came to the stall that held the black beast. His hooves batted at the ground, body shifting restlessly. Mayhap it wasn't a good idea to have such a small lad handling a giant animal, but Brodrick had said the boy had skills, and Kane trusted his judgment.

"Ye'll start tomorrow, after working the accounts."

The lad's face briefly lifted, and Kane saw a flash of blue eyes. "My laird, I do not know how to train a…"

Kane scrubbed a hand over his face. "Brodrick will assist ye' until ye' learn the ropes. I donna have the time, and he does no' have much to spare either. Good?"

The pale, dirty face nodded quickly. Why did the lad always look so dirty, while his sister looked like she was going to a ball every day? Did the boy not know how to clean himself up a bit? Aye, the Highlanders liked to stay a bit dirty, but the lad's face was…extremely so.

Kane nodded, then turned to leave. From the corner of his eye, he saw the lad's shoulders droop. He paused before stepping out of the stables.

"I have a mission for ye'."

The same shoulders that had dropped, immediately tensed.

"Yes, my lord?" Och, where did he remember that voice from? He couldn't remember *hearing* it, but he knew it from somewhere, except…maybe the tone was different? He shook it off, focusing on the matter at hand. Kane worked on what he wanted to say, apprehensive. Alice was a beautiful woman. Anything with a prick would want her upon sight, and he knew to be wary of randy lads around a woman, having been one himself.

"There's a lass," he said slowly, gauging Saeran's reaction. Nothing so far besides the clenching of fists. He found it odd that the lad always kept his face angled to the ground. His posture was also a little…off. "Blonde, blue-eyed. If ye' see her around, pass the word to her that I'd like to speak to her."

"What…what is her name?" he choked out. Kane narrowed his eyes on Saeran. His eyes were still staring at the ground, and the big hat covered most of his face like that. Now that he thought about it, he really hadn't had a good look at the lad's face. Right when Kane started to speculate on something, the boy lowered his gaze.

"Alice. Find her and tell her." Kane started to turn away, saying over his shoulder, "If ye' offend her, donna think I will no' cut yer heart out."

He strode out of the stables, but not before he heard the sharp intake of breath.

~

"My lord, I wish to speak with you."

Kane slowly put down the chalice.

Maids were cleaning up the remains of sup, and this was normally the time he took to relax.

Brodrick and the rest of the men sitting around him lowered their pity-filled gazes, as if keeping out of Blaine's view meant they'd avoid a lashing. Kane almost did the same thing, but it was unavoidable. He'd made a deal with Alice, and if he wanted to see her again, he would have to see it through.

"What is it, Lady Blaine?" He glanced at her, keeping his distaste to himself. It wasn't that he didn't appreciate a plump lass—hell, Gwen had been his leman for as long as he could remember, and she was just about the same size as Blaine. Nay, it was more than that.

Her body was too large for her skirts. Instead of her cleavage being emphasized, it looked lumpy and squished at the same time. Her hair was, once again, powdered to the point of being a dull, unattractive white, and her face was drowned in whatever women used to "pretty" themselves.

Though with this woman, it had done the exact opposite.

She cocked an eyebrow at him.

"If you would rise and follow me, we could take this conversation to a private setting."

"Lady Blaine," he said tiredly. "I've already ate with ye'. Dinner is over. Whatever ye' had to say should have been said earlier." Kane picked up the chalice, putting the edge to his lips. The ale was just beginning to burn his throat, when Blaine made a sound.

He looked at her over the rim.

"Now, my lord," she said sharply.

His eyes narrowed on her. If there was one thing he disliked about her, it was her demand for respect, when she did nothing to earn it. She wanted him to obey her like her brother did. It was laughable, but he was in too much of a mood to care much.

Saeran had never returned, and he'd seen nothing of Alice.

Kane had sat beside Blaine like a dutiful suitor, listening to her complaints with a deaf ear, grunting when she paused for him. All in all, he hadn't said a word to her—which was perfectly fine, as Alice hadn't made that part of the deal. He'd much rather have *Alice* sit with him, and have *Alice* talk with him.

"It should have been said earlier," he growled. "Is it no' time for ye' to retire?" He'd seen Alice late at night. Mayhap, if the rest of the keep were asleep, she'd appear again.

"My lord, I am not a simpleton you can boss about," Blaine said sternly, taking a step toward the table. One of his men inched away from her on the bench. Kane sighed, set down the chalice once again, and lifted his eyes to her.

She paused, a flicker of fear flashing in her eyes. Then she squared her shoulders and raised an imperial brow.

"Now, my lord," she repeated, using that same imperious tone. His lip lifted in a sneer. Unfortunately, rationality won over his urge to throttle her. Silently cursing his men as they began to snicker, he got to his feet, taking the chalice with him. No sane man could listen to this woman without being deep in the cups.

Sadly for him, he wasn't an easy drunk.

Kane stood and glanced around the hall. No sign of a bonny blonde lass, or Saeran. He mentally scowled, wondering if Saeran had done anything to hurt Alice. His threat hadn't been empty—if Alice came to him perturbed in any way, he wouldn't hesitate to teach Saeran how to treat a lady—at least, Kane's lady. Temporary lady. Something. She was something to him, a fascination. His fascination.

He shook his head. Point of the matter was, Saeran better keep his hands to himself.

Lady Blaine raked her gaze over him, then turned on her heel, leading him out of the hall. Once they were outside the entrance, he leaned against the wall, arms crossed over his chest, scowl on his face.

"What."

"That is no way to speak to me—"

"Lady Blaine," he growled, "ye've interrupted the only time o' night that I get to relax. Tell me what ye' want, so I can get back to it."

She raised a brow. Part of her attitude dropped, replaced by a flirtatious gaze that only made him grimace with distaste. That was not the look of an innocent woman who was ready for marriage— that was the look of a woman who knew what it took to please a man.

"Do you not feel relaxed with me, my lord?" she purred. Her

dark lashes, clumpy and thick, batted at him. He stared for a moment, wondering how her eyes had the strength to lift those things. They were a mess, he thought.

Then he realized what she'd said.

He burst out laughing. So hard that he couldn't stop himself from catching the wall support.

"Och, lass, ye' may be many things, but yer definitely humorous," he said between guffaws.

"What do you mean by that?" she demanded, all pretenses of being coy fleeing. Kane couldn't stop the laughter. Gods, but the lass was horrible! Thank God he didn't have to marry her. The thought sobered him.

He still had to ask for her hand and send the king a missive. He had a sennight to get the messenger on his way, and he would have to talk to a priest about the banns. The king would demand proof of the proposal. By the time he got back from the battle, the king would have received the missive, and he could carry out his plan to ruin himself in Blaine's eyes.

Aye. He just had to gather the courage. It was not that he was frightened of the lass, but there was something about her that he couldn't stand. Being tied to her in any way, even if it was temporary, made him feel constrained, like someone was shackling him.

A warrior never wanted to be shackled or chained to anything, especially a woman.

"My lord," Blaine snapped, putting her hands on her hips. "I do not find this amusing in the least. I brought you aside to offer you a proposition."

"Aye." Truthfully, he didn't want to know what this proposition of hers was.

She smiled, taking his grunted word as a signal to continue. "Now, I've been here for quite some time, and we have yet to discuss the reason for my arrival." She frowned. "It seems that every time I approach you, you find some reason to leave."

"Aye," he said absently, reaching up to scratch his jaw. What would happen to Alice and him, if he proposed to Blaine now? Would she be put off? Angry? Hurt? He frowned. He may not know her well yet, but he knew that after the kiss, she'd crave more of him—and guilt over craving a betrothed man would not sit well with her.

"I finally have your attention," Blaine continued, "and I plan to take advantage of our time together. You are aware of why I was sent here, correct?"

"Aye." He frowned, vaguely realizing that she was talking. Of course he knew why she was there—to ruin his life!

"It's high time that we progress with our relationship—"

Kane froze.

"—and to do that—I know I'm going against the grain with this, my lord, so bear with me—I would like to ask for your—"

"One moment, please," he said quickly, pushing away from the wall. So quickly that she didn't have time to continue, he strode away from her, brows lowered, heart racing. God, but she was forward. Kane liked his women with a will, but hers was…overbearing and strange.

He much preferred Alice. She was gentle, yet fiery. Beautiful. Strong. Blaine appeared to be strong, but he knew that if she'd been put in the same situation as Alice in the field, she would have wilted like a flower.

Another reason why he would not marry Blaine. The wife of a Highlander had to be strong. Brave. Willing to do what it took to survive. He wondered if Alice… Kane shook his head. There was no use thinking about things like that. He was never going to marry.

When he was a good distance away from the fuming Blaine, he rounded a corner, intending to go to his study. The last thing he needed was Brodrick laughing at his reluctance, his cowardice. Blaine was the solution to ending his clan's misery. The fighting would stop, his family would be together, and he would finally be *happy* with something.

He should not be putting off his proposal. He should be sucking up his misery, and asking Blaine to marry him. It was the cure-all. It was the Holy Grail. It was what his people needed—what he needed. Kane would not marry her, anyway, so what was the problem?

"*Umph!*" The soft grunt would have gone unnoticed if, right before it, he hadn't ran into someone. He reached out to catch the person before they stumbled back—then grinned. All of his worries over Blaine fled in the presence of the one person he'd been wanting to see.

Alice. His bonny lass had stumbled right into him! He gently caught her by the arms, tugging her flush against him. She made a sound of defiance and struggled against him, keeping her face averted.

"Unhand—"

"Lass, I've been waiting for ye'."

Shocked eyes met his, and his grin widened. She hadn't known who had caught her. He had the pleasure of watching her eyes darken as she adjusted to his hold on her. Aye, she liked his hands on her as much as he liked them.

"My lord, someone could see us," she whispered, pulling away from him. He only let her go so he could get a good look at her. He'd seen her earlier that day, but she had fled from him immediately after they'd returned. He hadn't known whether she was okay or not.

"They would no' care," he said easily, taking her hand. He had only one thought in mind, and that was getting her away from the viewing eyes of others. Aye, they might not care, but he certainly did. Even dressed as dourly as she was, she held his attention like a moth to a flame.

He grunted with pleasure when she didn't pull her hand out of his. She even went with him willingly, though she would cast glances over her shoulder that gave him the sense she was worried. About what? Another attack? Kane's chest tightened. Aye, of course she would be scared. He'd failed to protect her in the face of danger.

But not again.

Never again.

"Where are we going?" she asked, keeping her voice so quiet it was barely a whisper. He tightened his fingers around hers, smiling.

"To my study. Ye' wanted privacy, no?" He also wanted to check Saeran's work with the accounts. The previous man that had done them had never been good at keeping track of the numbers. Saeran seemed too weak of a lad to have a sharp mind, but mayhap there was some hope for him.

Her eyes widened. "My lord, this is highly improper." Kane couldn't help but notice the way she kept following him, though. She wanted to resist him, but it seemed her attraction to him was just as fierce as his was for her. That pleased him.

Kane didn't respond to her.

When they were finally in his study, he was burning for her. Mayhap it was the ale that made his control snap, coupled with the heat he saw in her eyes. The second the door closed, he pushed her gently into the wall, took her jaw in his hands, and closed his mouth over hers.

He could have died and gone to heaven, and he wouldn't have known it. She tasted like freshly fallen rain, and when her lips began to move against his…there was no doubt about it. He was dead. He had drowned in her sweetness, and gone to heaven.

Hungry little hands slipped up his chest, to his neck. He groaned against her lips, loving the feel of her hands on him. Soon. Soon, they would touch more than just his chest—and his hands wouldn't be caging her against the wall. Nay, they'd be touching her breasts, her hips, her thighs. They'd be touching everywhere they could reach.

He swiped his tongue over her lower lip. A surprised gasp left her, and he took advantage of it, kissing her deeper and harder. He could have laughed when her tongue began to battle for dominance with his, but the only thing he could manage was a groan…And he drew her closer against him, letting her feel his hardness.

Kane growled against her mouth. Her nails pricked his shoulder, her breath ragged and erratic. He could feel her body thrumming with a desire that matched the ferocity of his own—and then common sense kicked in.

He could not take her as he wanted. Not yet, not while he knew she would only hate him in the end. Kane pulled away from her drugging kiss, hating himself.

"Kane?" she asked, dazed. Just like she had at the creek, she tried to pull him closer.

"I'm sorry, lass," he said roughly, reluctantly letting his hands drop. She stared at him, confusion and desire mixing in her eyes. It pained him to see it. So easily, he could relieve both of them of the wait, the anticipation. But he would not take an innocent lass—a lady, for God's sake—without knowing she would not regret it.

Any other woman, he would forget about. He had Gwen for pleasures of the body. There was no use for him to play with a lady when he could not give her what she deserved—marriage to a fine, wealthy husband.

Kane planned to take her, despite how much of a bastard it would make him. There was no way he could deny her. Not when everything inside of him was fighting for another taste of her. Nay, he wasn't going to let her leave him, even though he could never offer her marriage. He had a feeling that after he had her, Gwen would become a thing of the past—and Kane didn't care. Alice was his; he could feel it.

Chapter Twenty-One

Saeran wanted to weep as he once again pulled away from their kiss. It was so wrong for it to feel so right. He was meant for her sister. He was meant to marry Blaine. He was meant...to not even know she existed.

Her heart clenched. She shouldn't have sought him out. Really, she would have been smarter to stay away from sup altogether. Her sister had planned to propose to Kane. The thought made her sick. Her stomach roiled, and her hands shook.

After her sister had departed and Connor had left, she'd had a moment to face the reality. Her sister *was* going to propose to Kane.

"Why were ye' looking for me?" Kane asked, breaking into her morbid thoughts. His eyes were blank when he looked at her. Thankfully, he turned his attention to the pieces of parchment on the desk.

"I...I was told you wanted to see me," she said, crossing her arms over her chest. She came forward, watching as he sifted through the accounts she'd previously corrected. When he'd agreed to let her do them, he had forgotten to mention that there were several months of mistakes in the accounts. She was only now correcting them. Otherwise, the desk would have been cleaner.

"Aye, a while ago."

Saeran didn't say anything. It had taken her hours of careful thought and brow beating for her to gain the courage to see him again. After her near-death experience in the stables and spending every waking moment reliving their kiss, she'd almost convinced herself that seeing him was a terrible idea.

Of course, her body and mind had completely opposing opinions on what she should do. In the end, her interest in seeing Kane had won.

"What is that?" she asked, hoping to get him to talk. The silence was terrifying. He raised a brow at her, and she gestured toward his hands. He was sifting through the papers with quick, calculative eyes.

"Nothing," he said shortly, putting papers on the desk and picking up another stack. She knew what they were, but if she hadn't…He did not want to discuss important things with her. *That is expected*, she told herself in reassurance. Not many women knew numbers, so why would he expect her to?

An idea occurred to her. She knew how to stop the silence and learn more of her sister's soon-to-be husband! She ignored the roiling of her stomach the thought gave her and sat in one of the chairs in front of his desk.

He watched her. She smiled with forced pleasantness.

"What do ye' think yer doing?" he asked wearily, slowly setting down the papers. She gave him an innocent brow.

"What do you mean?" she asked. The look in his eye, the suspicion there, should have worried her. All she wanted to do was learn a little about him. Instead of being terrified, she was quite pleased with his reaction.

Despite his rudeness to Blaine, he was cautious of women. He had the right to be, she thought with another pleased smile. She was going to dissect and learn everything she could about him. For the sake of Blaine, of course. Saeran had no real interest in him. None at all.

She started with her most prominent concern. Whispers of coming war have been running around the keep like cockroaches. She couldn't have Blaine married to a senseless, warring man.

"I've heard rumors that you fight many battles."

He nodded slowly.

"Aye."

"Why?"

"What do ye' mean, 'why'? Lass, that's my duty." He grunted like he couldn't believe she wouldn't know better and went to sort through another stack. Saeran frowned at him.

"Your duty is to protect your clan. I do not think that fighting as many battles as you have, have benefitted your people."

He narrowed his eyes on her.

"I'm the laird here. Do ye' understand that?"

"Of course I do. As laird, you shouldn't be waging war. Especially if you are going to be taking a wife!" she said, cross. Did he care so little for his people? Would he care so little for her sister?

"My lady," he said lowly, coming forward. She clenched her hands together, not knowing what to expect. She had insulted him, but she didn't much care.

"No," she said sharply. He paused.

"No, what?"

"No, to whatever you're about to say to defend yourself. My father was once a Highlander, and he led many a battle—but not as much as you have, my lord. He did it to defend his home and honor. You're allies with The McGregor—you have no reason to war with anyone! They're all too terrified of you."

"Was? Yer father was a Highlander?" He raised a brow.

She stilled. Saeran could have slapped herself for her stupidity.

"Aye, he was. Before I was born. Then he became betrothed to my mother, and moved to the Lowlands with her. She had a fancy for court."

"I donna know a single Highlander that would lower himself by going to court."

"Aye, well, he was getting older. He was done with warring, and took to my mother's estate that he obtained through her dowry. He was never far from the Highlands," she said, smiling a little at the memory. Blaine never spoke of their parents, and since they'd arrived here, she had been alone with her thoughts. It felt nice to share them with someone, with Kane. "We lived right near the border. They had the Highlander games every summer."

"Aye, I know of them. My family and I used to go to them every year." A flash of tenderness crossed his face, but it disappeared as soon as it came.

"Same with ours. Oh, my," she said, laughing. By that point, she had completely forgotten her earlier anger. "One year—oh, one year, my older sister was meant to be watching me. My parents were speaking with an old friend of theirs, and we got tired of waiting for them to finish. We walked off, and she became distracted by the merchants. I was too young to know how to get around, but I still went off to do my own thing—without telling her. She was quite furious," she recalled.

"Go on," he urged, sitting on the edge of the desk. His legs crossed at his ankles and he watched her intently as she spoke. She blushed, but continued. Blaine had never encouraged her tales. Lord, she was lucky if she could get her sister to listen to her for a minute!

"I wandered off to the games. The big tents were all intriguing and lovely. There were so many horses and beautiful ladies," she said wistfully. "Without my sister, I did not know where to go—I became afraid and—well, I became a scared little girl. I could not find my parents nor my sister, and the people were too busy to help an errant girl. I don't know how it happened exactly, but I ran into this boy.

"He turned into my hero that day. I didn't know it, but my parents and sister were searching for me. When they found me, I was sitting behind one of the tents with the boy, our hands and face covered in paint and pastries." She laughed at the memory of her father's stunned fury.

"How long ago was this?" he asked. He was watching her with lowered brows.

"Quite some time. I was only a girl, six or seven years."

"The boy. Was there anything about him that you remembered?"

She frowned. "Well...no—oh! Yes! His mother was pregnant. I remember comparing a large cow to my sister." Kane's eyes darkened. She waved a hand at him. "Just her stomach, my lord. She was quite beautiful."

"Aye, she was," he said. "The pastries that day were the best I'd ever had."

She nodded in agreement, then stilled.

"No," she said, hand covering her mouth. There was no way he could possibly be the same boy from the fair!

"Aye," he responded, chuckling. "The jester we took the paints from chased us half around the tournament. Do ye' remember that?"

She nodded, too stunned to comprehend. "But that would mean you were the boy that—"

"Aye. How strange that we were friends when we were young, and know each other now."

Saeran nodded again. The strangeness of this was too much for her to handle. She stared at him.

"We never learned each other's names. I cannot fathom...this is so strange for me, my lord."

"I think we were too busy to learn our names. We had to make the most of our day together. I remember always rushing off to find you the second my family arrived there. When I talked about ye' Brodrick always called ye' the wee mystery girl."

"You'd talk about me?" she asked. For some reason, her cheeks heated. It was silly of her to blush over it. He talked about her all of the time, apparently. Not only to other people now, but back then as well!

"Couldn't keep my mouth shut about ye', lass. Mayhap it was fate that we met again, aye?" he said, smiling at her coyly. She blushed.

"Mayhap," she said softly. Saeran lifted her eyes to his. "My lord, why did you stop coming to the fair?"

He shrugged, and like a candle had been blown out, all tender emotion fled his face. The change in emotion was so abrupt that she frowned. Deep in his eyes, behind the thick veil of lashes, there was pain. Pain…and anger.

"My lord?" she asked quietly, rising to her feet. Something compelled her to touch him, to take his hand in her own. "You can tell me."

"Tis not something I wish to share," he said. There was a catch in his voice, one she'd never heard. She smiled, almost tenderly, and threaded their fingers. He looked away from her but didn't move. After a lengthy pause, where she began to think he really wouldn't tell her, he looked her straight in the eyes.

"My father was killed."

The abruptness, the flat emotion in his voice, seared her. She reared away from him, eyes widening.

"Kane…"

His lips lifted, bitterness etched into every line of his face.

"By the king. He commanded the Lowlander bastards to attack, and took my father from us."

"That…that doesn't make sense," she said quietly, staring at him. She knew the agony of losing a parent—she had lost both of hers to a fire. She couldn't imagine knowing her beloved father had been murdered, though. "The Lowlanders are no match for Highlanders…"

"They are if they come in the dead of night, with none of us prepared," he snarled, pulling away from her. She stayed in her place, watching him, heart aching. Bitter. So bitter and angry—and she understood.

168

"Why did the king do that?" she asked before she could stop herself. Saeran cursed. God, she was insensitive. How could she ask something like that? Saeran wrapped her arms around herself, biting her lip. If he didn't answer, she wouldn't blame him. Saeran wouldn't be surprised if he sent her away.

"Why?" he echoed. Kane lifted tormented eyes to hers. She shivered, hating herself for putting him through this. She should have left it alone. She should have let him be, not pushed him into a corner filled with demons of the past. "My father was a foolish bastard."

His answer shocked her. Heart melting, she stood, reaching for him. He didn't move.

"Kane," she said softly, putting her hand on his arm. Vaguely, she realized she was too forward with him. "If you do not wish to talk of this, then you do not have to. Please, forgive me for being insensitive."

He stared at her. Slowly, gradually, his chest began to heave, like he was fighting for breath. There was so much fury laying in his eyes that she wanted to back away from him, to put a safe distance between them. She didn't.

When her parents had died, Blaine hadn't been there for her. She had wanted the contact and comfort of someone else—and something told her that Kane had been in the same position she had been. Alone. Scared. No one to comfort him, who knew what he was going through.

So she stayed. Even though she knew he could kill her in the blink of an eye, she stayed with him through the storm, watching him as his eyes began to blaze. The fury burning so brightly that she could feel the heat of it against her skin as he stared at her.

Through the fiery storm, a bond began to form. She felt it in her gut, in every movement he made. He wanted her to stay—the realization grew in his eyes, replacing some of the fire. She didn't think her actions were bold when she moved closer to him, close enough that their hips were touching, their breath fanning each other. His hands clenched at his sides. She took one of them within her own.

"I lost my family to a fire," she murmured. He tensed. "They were not murdered. They did not die a worthy death in battle. A simple house fire took their lives from me." She lifted her eyes to his. "I may not know exactly what you are going through, Kane, but I do know the pain of having your family ripped from you—and, like

169

myself, being alone when the realization that they are really gone hits you."

Despite the fact that she was saying this to comfort him, to make him realize he had an ally, tears stung her eyes. She had lost more than her parents that day. She had lost her life, her happiness. Blaine had been cold. Emotionless. Unaffected by the death of her parents. With her new clarity toward Blaine, she knew that—and was infuriated by it. But this was for Kane.

She couldn't dwell on her sister's cruelty, or her growing hatred for her.

Thick, heavy arms came around her body. She stilled before realizing that he only wanted to hold her. He pulled her against his chest, securing her tightly against him. Then he leaned against the wall, still clutching her smaller body to his large one.

It wasn't sexual. It was the complete opposite.

He was silently begging her to comfort him.

Saeran did the only thing she could. She rested her cheek against his warm chest, closed her eyes, and held him back.

"Helen MacLeod was engaged to the Campbell's son," he said quietly. He sounded strained, like his throat was too tight to talk. She turned her face into his chest, hearing the pounding of his heart.

"My father wanted her for himself. Had ever since they were children. They were betrothed to be married, until the MacLeods accused my grandfather of stealing a chicken."

"A chicken?"

"Aye. The MacLeods have always been possessive—even of things that are no' theirs. The chicken was actually ours. When the MacLeod accused us, my grandfather broke the engagement. MacLeod gave Helen to the Campbells, in hopes of creating a stronger force, one that he could fight with against the Shaws."

"The MacLeod sounds like a right arse," she said quietly, wishing she could find all of the MacLeods and teach them a lesson.

"They are the clan that attacked us earlier," he growled. Saeran stilled, lifting her eyes to his. She smoothed her hand over his pounding heart, feeling the anger rise inside of him once again. She would rather have him be angry than agonizing. The thought of this big, strong man in pain…broke her. "Duncan Shaw, my father, did no' take well to being told he could no' marry Helen. Before her marriage, he took her from her keep, and they were married in less than a sennight."

She gasped. "But that—"

"Aye. It created a war between the Campbells, MacLeods, and the Shaws. If the marriage had no' been consummated, and she was not found to be pregnant several moons later, MacLeod would have taken her back. The Campbells were willing to forgive her transgressions, until it was learned she was with child."

"You."

"Me. The strain of it all was too much for the MacLeod. He died a natural death. Alasdair MacLeod, Helen's brother, took his place as laird. Unlike his father, Alasdair was actually considerate of his sister's happiness. When he finally had a chance to see her, he realized how happy she was, and left her alone, so long as she promised to give her first daughter to the Campbells, as appeasement.

"The three clans were finally at peace. I was training with Connor Campbell, who was betrothed to my sister, and Alasdair's son, Robert. My mother had twins—Annalise and Alex. Annalise was of marriageable age." He made a rough sound, body stiffening under hers. She inhaled slowly, feeling that she knew where this would go.

"We were out riding. Rogue Englishmen found us. We fought, but we were just lads. We had no chance against seasoned rogues. Two of us survived—Robert and myself. Connor, my sister's betrothed, was lost. His father found out and sent word to the king. He was furious over his son's death and wanted retribution for it.

"When the king took too long to respond, he came after me. He hunted me, and almost killed me. His sword was pressed to my neck when my father arrived and put the Campbell in his place. It only infuriated him further."

He stopped, chest heaving. Saeran wanted to weep. For a laird to attack a boy for the death of his son, when Kane hadn't had the skill to protect him… It was terrible, and showed just how bad of a man the Campbell was.

"My mother was so distraught," he recalled roughly. "She wanted to go after the Campbell herself for what he tried to do with me. The night before the Shaw men planned on retaliating for what he did to me, the king finally responded to Campbell's call for retribution—when no one was ready. We were all asleep. The attack came in the dead of night.

"My father ran into battle, unprepared. My mother hid us away and then left us to help fight. By the time my father's warriors came to his aid, it was too late. My mother was taken, and Duncan was dead."

Chapter Twenty-Two

"Kane…" He shook his head, silencing her. Saeran stared up at him, horrified by his tale. Feuds in the Highlands were common—but this was tragic. Simply tragic. Duncan Shaw had done nothing wrong except love a forbidden woman and his children—and Campbell, the selfish, arrogant son of a bitch, had taken it too far.

"I saw it. Through the crack in the wardrobe she pushed us into. She was running to join my father when he stumbled into the room—with a sword embedded into his stomach. He fell into her. She caught him. The English man knocked her unconscious and threw her over his shoulder, laughing. It was like he wiped his hands clean of the fight the second his sword was in my father's heart."

Kane laughed bitterly. The bitterness wasn't the only thing she saw when she looked up at him. It was the horror of a child who'd seen his father killed in front of him. It was the horror of realizing he had lost the one man he never should have lost, and that his mother had been taken. In that instant, she could see the image of him as a child—confused and frightened. Saeran fought back her tears.

She wanted to ask after his mother, if he had ever found her again. But the anguish in his eyes was too great.

In a horrible way, she had been lucky. She hadn't seen her parents die—instead, she had been at court with her sister, hiding in the library.

"My father's second in command went after my mother. They found her and brought her home, but…Mother went insane," he said quietly. She didn't think he was all the way there. His voice was distant, eyes glazed over. "The McGregor was training me for leadership of the Shaw clan, and my mother lost her mind. She became obsessed with having her revenge. When I refused to help her, too busy training to take over as Laird, she went to Alex.

"I think, even if I had known what she was up to, I couldn't have stopped her. Annalise was sent to marry Hans Grayham—a measure she took for his loyalty and Anna's safety—and went after the king. Alex and my mother didn't come back to the keep."

"You mean...he killed them?" Saeran was stunned—and disbelieving. Her cousin would never do such a thing, not ever! He was one of the most fair and considerate people she knew. Surely he would not condemn a woman tormented by the loss of her husband to death.

"He didn't kill her. He banished her—and would have done so to the whole Shaw clan, had McGregor not been there. He saved the clan," Kane murmured, head falling back against the wall.

"Kane, the king would not—"

"He did. I was there. I heard the order."

"Nay—"

Hard, cold eyes snapped to hers. "Donna tell me what I did and did no' see and hear, lass. Yer a Lowlander. Of course ye' care about the good king's name—but I donna, and I never will."

"How did McGregor save the clan?" she asked thinly. She couldn't believe him—King James, her dear cousin, would never do something so terrible as to banish a whole clan for the grieving actions of one woman. *He was honorable*, she thought dazedly.

"The McGregor made me fight for the king."

She stared at him.

"If I did no', the king would have exiled the whole clan. Me fighting for him, wars with my men that should have been fought with his, ensured my loyalty."

"How could you stay loyal to a man who threatened you like that?" she whispered, still unable to believe that her own cousin had done that to Kane.

He stared at her for a tense moment.

"I think I am done with this conversation," he growled, stiffly pulling away from her. There was something he wasn't telling her. Saeran watched him turn away from her, heart crashing in her chest.

The conversation had turned into one she hadn't anticipated. Not only did he have a deeper side to him than she'd originally thought, but she had revealed things about herself that she never should have. He wasn't supposed to know that "Alice's" family had died in a fire. He wasn't supposed to know that she had gone to the fairs. He wasn't supposed to know anything about her except the fake name she had given him…and yet, there was something about him that made it easy for her to talk to him.

Blaine.

It was all Blaine, she thought, digging her nails into her palm as sudden anger surged through her. Blaine was the reason she felt so alone, so deprived of human contact. Blaine was the reason that Saeran felt comfortable talking to the one man she shouldn't be.

For that alone, she wanted to hate her sister.

"Lass," Kane said, drawing her attention. His back was to hers, tense, and forbidding. She unclenched her hands, fighting for composure. He couldn't see her, but that didn't mean he wasn't as attuned to her as she was to him.

"Aye, my lord."

"Kane," he corrected her, looking at her over his shoulder. "When does yer stay here end?"

She paused.

"I…I am not entirely sure." Yes she was. So long as Blaine and Kane married, she would be here for as long as they permitted her presence. Blaine had said she would reveal who Saeran really was after the wedding, but she doubted that would happen now. The more her sister demanded, the more she began to realize that Blaine was…selfish. Selfish and greedy. If she could bribe Saeran with the truth of her condition for eternity, Blaine would.

Saeran still loved her sister, deep down, but she was incredibly angry with her. No longer would she idly sit by as she controlled everyone around her unjustly—nor would she let Blaine control Saeran. No more. It ended today.

"Where are ye' staying? What wing?"

She went pale.

"It does not matter, does it?" she asked, fighting for composure in earnest. Saeran felt her hands begin to sweat. She slept in the east wing, where Blaine's, Saeran's, and Kane's rooms were. It was the family wing, whereas the other wings were meant for servants or simply empty.

"O' course it does," he growled, turning around. Thick arms crossed over an even thicker chest. Lord, but he was large. Her mouth somehow managed to water with desire and dry with fear at the same time. *How did that even happen?* she thought dazedly.

Kane. Kane did that to her.

"My lord—"

His low growl of disapproval shushed her.

"I never see ye' during the day."

She smiled uneasily. "You've only known me for a night. You must not have noticed me—"

"No," he said bluntly, giving her a hard stare. "Ye've been here for a full moon, and I only saw ye' last night and today. What do ye' even do during the day?"

She stared at him. Oh, why did he have to be so nosy? Actually, no. Why had she been so foolish as to go into the kitchens not dressed as a boy? If she had taken that precaution, like she should have, she would not be in this position. She would be in her room, safe and sound, without him nitpicking every fake detail she'd given.

"I am feeling…quite tired," she said weakly. It was not entirely feigned. The toll of her fears, and of his pestering, was making her dizzy. He could never find out who she was, not truly. Him asking all of these questions, with all of her slip-ups, was leading right to that!

Almost instantly, his eyes changed. Softening around the edges, the hard lines of his face no longer appeared terrifyingly tense—he was concerned. Before she could make an excuse to leave, he came forward, taking her in his arms.

His body was hot. Overwhelming. The confidence she had felt with him earlier fled, replaced by a sense of shy security. She felt safe in his arms, but she could not be as forward as she had been. Not in this way. Trembling hands cautiously landed on his chest.

"Yer secretive, nymph."

"Nay, I—" He cut off her denial with a kiss to her temple. She quieted, cheeks heating.

"Aye, ye' are. One second, ye'll tell me about yer family, then the next, yer retreating into a defense position, avoiding my questions. It makes me curious, but I will no' push you."

She lifted her eyes to his. They were soft, but determined. He may not push her, but that would not deter him from learning all he could about her. She saw the knowledge in his eyes as clearly as the sun shone during the day. She shivered—not from fear, but from anticipation. *A game*, she thought. *He was thinking of this as a game.*

She would not lose.

"I do not understand what you mean," she said lightly. She did, though, and to quickly change the subject, she asked, "I heard that you are once again going to war."

He sighed.

"Back to that, are we?"

"It's a colossal matter, Kane!" she said, offended by the exasperation in his voice. "Whenever you go to war, men die."

"My men donna."

"But they do—"

"No. They donna. The weak bastards we fight against do."

She pulled out of his arms, putting her hands on her hips. "Either way, men die. People die. The war takes a toll on your own clan—"

"No it doesna."

"Kane!"

"Alice!" he said in falsetto, rolling his eyes at her. "Yer lack of faith in me is quite offensive. My men donna die, my clan does no' feel the toll of war, and yer best to mind yer own business."

She stared at him.

He stared right back.

Then he smiled. It was a terrible smile, one that she knew he gave just to rile her. Still, the sight of it sent butterflies fluttering in her stomach.

"If ye' must know, my men and I are leaving within the sennight."

"What?"

He burst into laughter. "Donna fash yerself, lass. Ye'll be safe and sound here. Although," he said with a sigh. "I do have a new lad to look after. You know him—he's the one who found ye'. Saeran Sinclair."

"What?"

That's all she could manage. Her thoughts were going wild, panic was beginning to build, and confusion was right on her heels. Saeran. Herself. War. Within a week. A battle—that she would be going to. *What.*

She couldn't ride a horse properly, let alone wield a sword! What was he thinking, taking her out to battle? Hadn't he withdrawn her from the training? Shouldn't that mean she should stay behind, at the keep?

"My lord—"

"Kane."

"Kane, I…Do not you think Saeran is too…I don't know how to put this. Feminine? He's small, not…"

"Not what?" He frowned at her.

"…large."

"Saeran canna help that he is a late bloomer. I was once a small lad like him," he said, scowling at her. "It was no' until I was seven and ten until I started to grow. Donna doubt the lad's strength even though he is small. If he heard ye'…Lass, I donna want to hear negative things like that in my keep."

Even though he was defending her other identity, she blushed.

"I was just pointing it out… Wasn't he taken out of training?"

"Aye, but what does that have to does with anything?"

"Kane. He obviously won't be prepared—"

"In the heat of battle, I am sure he will rise to the occasion. That's what it took for myself. Saeran is very similar to myself as a lad," he said, almost proudly. Her heart softened, even though she disagreed with him completely.

She had always thought he hated her. Every time she was forced to be in his presence, he would either ignore her or snap at her. Rarely would he praise her, as he was doing now. That just showed the kind of man he was.

He would not admit to feeling soft towards anyone, but he did. He was not as hateful as she had assumed. Aye, he was rough around the edges, and strict and insistent, with determination that should terrify her, but he was not as bad a man as The Lion was reputed to be.

"Why are ye' looking at me like that, lass?"

She blinked. "Pardon?"

A slow smile came over his face.

"Are ye' worried about me now?" *I'm worried about that look on your face!* she thought. Instead of saying that, she backed away. He was slowly coming forward, his body moving as gracefully as she'd ever seen it, muscles rippling in the dim light of the room. How could she speak, when her mouth was so dry?

The only thing she could manage was a choked gasp when his body pressed against the length of hers.

"Donna worry, lass. I'll come back for ye'."

The words were spoken in a near growl, sending a shiver down her back, washing away the fear of what was to come. He wouldn't have to come back for her, since she would be there the whole time. But she did not say that.

His head lowered. Her breath left her mouth on a gasp. He took advantage of it, taking her lips with his own, and masterfully clearing away any thoughts of everything else. Except, that is, for the hands that were now on her waist, the hardness that was pressing into her hip, and the feel of his hot, dominant mouth against her own.

Then, just as quickly as he had kissed her, he left. She watched him go with her hand over her mouth, cheeks flushed.

Chapter Twenty-Three

Saeran knew that Blaine knew about the battle. It was all she talked about to anyone but Saeran. Lately, she'd been avoiding Saeran, and she honestly couldn't blame her sister. Saeran's outbursts and complete disregard for her sister's "problems" were causing a rift between them.

In the past week, the rift became worse.

Being with Kane gave her hope—hope for the future. That maybe, just maybe, she wouldn't have to hide from him. That she could show him who she really was. Alice was only a name. Everything else he knew about her was true.

They were…perfect together. Aye, perfect. Even though she had only spent time with her father, the only other male she had known, she felt like she connected with Kane on a level that she could never achieve with another man. He was hard, yet soft. He was stoic, yet sweet. He was smart, yet naïve—at least when it came to her. He was all she could think about now—him, and how they might have a future together. Connor might have been correct when he assumed that he would accept her. The only thing that held her back from exposing herself was the fear of the unknown, and…Blaine.

Saeran couldn't stand the sight of her sister. Thinking of Kane proposing to her, taking Blaine into his arms and kissing her with the passion he gave her, created a sensation in her heart that robbed her of breath. She should be *happy* that Blaine was closer to achieving her goal, but Saeran couldn't make herself be happy for them. If anything, she wanted to keep the two of them apart.

It didn't even bother her anymore. Before, the thought of angering her sister into silence was terrifying. Now, Saeran was actually relieved. Her sister's unreasonable attitude made it easier for her to see Kane. Though with him preparing for battle, and her working herself into a fit to organize the accounts before they left, they hadn't seen much of each other.

For that, she was both grateful and upset. She missed him. Aye, she was able to see him as Saeran the boy, but it was purely business. He didn't take her into his arms, didn't hold her or kiss her. He didn't even know who she was! The good thing about this, however, was that she could learn more about him.

He was a completely different man around Saeran and her counterpart, Alice. She had expected it to be a drastic, terrible change. It was anything but. With both personalities, he was kind, considerate, and he had a good sense of humor.

After their steamy kiss in his study, they had only seen each other twice that week. Her body craved him more than before every time she saw him, and she knew it would only become worse in the coming weeks.

Saeran set down the sealed parchment and stood, stretching her arms. She had been sitting in the same chair for the past two hours and she was sure it was dark outside. Her whole day had been spent correcting the accounts. Luckily, they were done, and she could finally relax. The only thing she had to worry about when she returned was training the beast with Brodrick, and cleaning the stables. The accounts were in order and could practically take care of themselves until she returned.

Happy and feeling like the world had been lifted from her shoulders, she practically ran to the door. She could hear the ruckus in the hall and knew it was time to sup. Finally, she could have a *real* meal with a moment to herself.

At least, she thought that until a plump figure ran into her while she was coming around the corner. She cursed before she could stop herself.

"Why are you running in my halls?" Blaine snapped, grabbing Saeran by the wrist when she would have fallen into the ground. Saeran could have gaped at her from the shock of her sister's help, but then Blaine shoved her away, sending Saeran crashing into the wall.

She could barely keep her temper to under control.

"The cook has set the table, has she not?" Saeran snapped. She pushed passed Blaine, angry. These were not her halls—they were Kane's. He had yet to propose to the woman who she used to adore.

"I am getting tired of your attitude," her sister snapped from behind her. "It is like all of your responsibilities are getting to your head, sister."

Saeran froze. Her hands clenched at her sides. Of course her sister would pick now to confront her on something that was not even her fault. Blaine had been the one to cause this. If not for coercing Saeran into pretending to be a boy, she would not have all the time she had with Kane and all of the responsibilities that came with managing the accounts. All the years she had insulted Saeran, making her think it was for the good of her health and beauty, came back to her.

"Are you so important that you cannot speak to me anymore? What, do you think that because you were assigned to do my duties, that you're better than me?" Blaine laughed, but the sound was anything but joyful.

Saeran stared at the wall, fighting. Fighting so hard not to turn around and show her sister how much she had learned in the dusty training area. She couldn't stop the flow of anger and betrayal—*frustration*—that coursed through her. Even when Saeran had made it a point to avoid her sister, Blaine found something to complain about.

"What are you talking about?" she asked, clenching her teeth. Saeran had done nothing but dirty work. Cleaning the stalls and training an insane horse that was bent on killing her was not part of "Blaine's duties". Lord, the only duty she had was walking around and looking pretty, and she couldn't even do that properly.

The pinch of guilt she should have felt at her cruel thoughts were absent. She wasn't even concerned by the lack of them.

"The accounts. Spending all your time with that beast of a man. Who do you think you are?" A hand grabbed her by the elbow, jerking her around. Saeran yanked herself away from her sister's hard grip and ground her teeth.

"Do you even know how to do the accounts, Blaine?" She met her sister's eyes for the first time since being stopped. What she saw there made it all the more impossible not to do something she wouldn't regret later.

Jealousy. Fury. Greed. It was all there, and for the first time since Saeran and Blaine had reached their womanhood, she saw it for what it was. There was not a single ounce of love in her sister's face—and there never had been. The realization was not shocking, but it was painful.

The look Blaine was giving her now was everything she had seen in her eyes since the day their parents had died. Her sister had stopped loving her somewhere along the line, and Saeran was no longer fooled.

She bit back the hurt at the realization.

"I do not have to know yet! The fact of the matter is, you are trying to take my place, and I do not appreciate it."

Lord, Blaine sounded ridiculous. Saeran smiled a little. It was more sarcastic than adoring, and her sister took note of it. Blaine watched her narrowly.

"I fail to see how I am 'taking your place' when I am a boy in the man's eyes. And he is not a beast," she hissed. He was the exact opposite, and the fact that Blaine refused to understand that infuriated Saeran. Kane was good. He was rough, but good.

More than good.

Amazing. Stunning. His strength, both mental and physical…entrancing.

"I should be the one doing the accounts and spending time with him. The whole of this week, it seems the two of you are sneaking off! He is my husband, Saeran. Not yours," she hissed. Her pudgy hands clenched at her sides, and she looked ready to strike Saeran.

She wanted to be hit. She wanted to be hit so hard that Blaine drew blood, so that she could return the strike tenfold.

"He is not your husband." He had yet to propose, and she hoped it stayed that way. The more she thought about the two of them, the angrier she became. It had been a constant threat the entire week. To think of them together…as man and wife…when Kane and Saeran created fire with their passion…it was inconceivable. Her chest tightened.

Suspicion glistened in her sister's eyes.

"Jealous? Saeran, are you *jealous*?" Sick pleasure gleamed in her eyes. It was so shocking that she couldn't respond. Her sister *wanted* her to feel like this. Choked up, sick to her stomach. She was baiting Saeran for it. Then the suspicion worsened into pure fury. "He knows who you are. He knows that you're a woman, doesn't he?"

Saeran hated herself for it, but she smiled. Not wide enough to be a yes, and not small enough to be a no. Just enough to make her sister think.

"We spend so much time together…"

"You whore." Blaine reached out. Her hand moved fast enough that Saeran almost didn't stop it in time, but she did. She caught her sister's hand in a tight grip. The urge to twist was so strong that it took all of her willpower to simply shove her sister aside.

"I cannot believe you," Saeran said, staring at her sister. "What did I ever do to you?"

Blaine's body stilled, as if time stopped. Saeran felt the shift in the air, and suddenly, this turned into more than jealousy over Kane. This turned into something darker, deeper, and dangerous. This was not normal.

Saeran should be able to look past this. She should be able look past Blaine's greed. They were sisters and Saeran loved Blaine…to a point. Lately, the point had become more and more dull, until it was so blunt, it was like a gleaming flat surface. The surface was flat enough for the love she held for her sister to slide right into hatred.

Time did still. Saeran and Blaine were frozen in time as they stared at each other. A feather could have dropped, and it would have sounded like the screams of battle. Saeran's aching heart dropped to her stomach, and the shaking in her hands became too much.

She clenched them together. Her sister, like she always had, would latch onto the weakness like an animal, and she wouldn't stop until Saeran was bleeding.

"You've changed," Blaine whispered, holding Saeran's eyes. They were wide, muddy brown, and the realization seemed to shock her. "What happened to the girl that would follow me around like a lost puppy? What happened to that Saeran?"

Saeran felt sick. Aye, she had followed her sister around like a lost puppy—up until their arrival on Shaw lands. Mayhap hiding at court had kept her sister's greed and selfishness at a low point, but now, when she saw and heard her sister everyday…

In a way, she was grateful for coming here. She feared that, had she not come, Saeran would never have noticed the way her sister used her weak feelings to manipulate her. Court had allowed her to be soft—in the Highlands, you became strong whether you wanted to or not. Now her feelings were stronger, deeper, and clearer than ever.

Blaine hated her to the point of destroying her with Saeran's own kindness.

And Saeran didn't know what she had done to deserve it.

"Blaine, what did I do to you? Why do you hate me?" Saeran's thoughts were running wild. Never had she back-talked her sister. Never had she intentionally offended her. Whatever she had done to make Blaine hate her must have happened a long time ago because Saeran, for the life of her, couldn't recall a time when Blaine wasn't belittling her.

Blaine laughed.

"What would you do," she murmured, raking disgusted eyes over Saeran, "if I said *we weren't actually sisters?*"

Blaine stormed away without another word.

Chapter Twenty-Four

"Yer really going to do it," Brodrick said from beside Kane. The disbelief was clear in his voice, and Kane understood it perfectly. Even he couldn't believe what he was going to do, the night before he left for battle. His hand tightened around the chalice.

"I have no choice," he murmured, lowering his eyes into the cup. "If I donna make it back from this…"

The unspoken message was clear between them. "Aye," Brodrick said. As simple as that, he understood. "Though I donna doubt ye'll make it back. Ye've never lost a battle before."

"I've never gone against the Campbells," Kane said into his cup before he took a quick swig. The warriors were gathered around their tables, talking, laughing, and grunting as they always did. Blaine was nowhere to be seen, and he didn't know whether to be grateful or concerned. He had to do it tonight—there was no question about it.

"The Campbells are just as bad as the MacLeods. They're only a slightly larger clan full of idiots. Donna worry, Kane." Brodrick slapped him on the back, earning a grunt from Kane. He wasn't worried about the battle—he was worried about proposing to Blaine.

It wasn't like he was going to *stay* betrothed to her. Hell, the second he returned and had the one thing from her dowry that he wanted, he would send her packing. If Saeran wanted to stay on his land, he would grant it. But Blaine was not to stay here any longer than was necessary.

"How does yer lass feel about this?"

His lass. His woman. A smile curled Kane's lips despite himself.

186

Aye, she was his. He had yet to claim her, but she was his.

"I donna ken. At first, she spent time with me as a way for Blaine and I to spend time together, but this week…I donna ken. She seems to avoid all talk of Blaine now."

"Is she jealous?" Brodrick asked, raising a brow.

"Mayhap." Kane liked the thought of Alice as his lass because by now, she practically was.

He frowned, realizing that she wasn't coming for him. The last three days, she wouldn't seek him outright, instead choosing to hide behind a pillar until he noticed her. It was a cute game she played, but he wished for once, she would make herself known. All of his men knew of her—she was the mysterious blonde beauty that their laird was giving all of his time to. How could they not know of her?

Kane began to stand. He'd check her pillar. If she was not there, he would drop it. He understood that a woman needed her space as much as a man needed his. Lately, he had been pushing her harder and harder, testing the limits with which she would resist him. Their desire was almost strong enough to make her forget about her reservations. But alas, her will was strong, despite her innocence.

He wanted to take her. Before he left for battle, before he proposed to Blaine—he wanted to take her as his own, just that once. Mayhap that was all it would take for him to forget about her. One night with her. He strode to the pillar, knowing he was only lying to himself. One night with Alice would only make him need more, and more, and more—which was reason enough for him to break the betrothal to Blaine as soon as possible.

Kane fully expected to see her leaning against the pillar, soft blue eyes luring him with their passionate innocence, but she wasn't there. His shoulders dropped and disappointment crashed through him. Aye, he'd have liked to at least see her before proposing to Blaine.

"My lord!" He grinned. Alice *had*—

"My lord, I have a request!" The voice became clear. He turned slowly, his mood crashing. All of the happiness he'd felt slid out of him. Blaine. It was Blaine, the woman he had to propose to.

He didn't know what the problem was. All it would take was a couple words, a missive would be sent to the king, and then he would have what he'd been fighting for his whole life. Then he could make Blaine break the engagement, and it would be over.

It sounded so simple, but he knew there was much more. He sighed, leaning against the pillar that Alice normally hid behind. It was set in the shadows, with only a lone candle to light the entrance to a hallway. It was also close enough to his table that, if she stood on a certain side, he was the only one who could see her.

"As do I," he said tiredly.

"I fear mine is far more impromptu. My lord," she said faintly, a hand fluttering to her mouth. Tears welled in her eyes. He stiffened.

"What?" Kane didn't know what to do. Women never cried in front of him, and if they did, it was normally because he'd given them the best orgasm of their life. Blaine hadn't yet received his passions, and she never would; he could only assume the worst of what she was fretting over.

"My brother! He has…he has shamed our family."

Kane frowned. Saeran was a soft-spoken lad, but he had a heart of gold. There was no way he could shame the Sinclair family. Kane simply did not believe it, not for a second. He sighed once again, deciding it was best to humor her.

"How has the lad shamed his name?"

"He…oh, my lord. I do not know if I can say this to you." She burst into fresh tears. They rolled down her powdered face, creating unattractive streaks. He squinted down at her, then grunted. He awkwardly pat her shoulder. What else was there to do?

"Ye' can tell me," he said, already knowing that Blaine was over reacting. She had a need for drama that was incredibly frustrating. Never had he met a more theatrical woman as her.

"Truly? My lord, I do not want him hurt because of this—not too harshly. He…he…oh, my lord!" she wailed, throwing herself at him. He rocked back by the force of her large body, his back hitting the pillar behind him. "I came upon them in the hall. It was horrid. The sounds were disgusting, and the scandal…the scandal it will create! How could he?"

He pushed her away from him, frowning. "Came upon who? What sounds?"

"Saeran….he…he was defiling a maid in the middle of the hall for all to see!" Furious, watery eyes glared into his. "I demand that he be punished!"

His frown worsened. From what he'd heard from Connor, the lad had no interest in females, or sex at all. He had always seemed like such a straight-laced boy.

"…and the maid. The poor, blonde woman. She was….The devil is inside of her," Blaine whispered in horror. "Only a woman possessed could enjoy it so much."

"Lady Blaine, I know this is a foreign concept to ye', but when lads reach a certain age, they become interested in…things." Lord, how awkward was this. He couldn't stand her crying, wailing, and over exaggerating. Kane shouldn't be the one to explain that it was common for a man and a woman to join with each other. Especially if a young lord like Saeran was walking around as many servants as he is.

Though, with his dirty face, Kane wondered how any of the servants could even consider it. Skill, he thought with a nod, proud of the lad. He must have skill.

"It's…My lord, what if she were a lady, though? I've never seen her before! She…I do not think she's a servant," she said fearfully. This made Kane pause. There wasn't a single person in his keep that he did not know about. Of course, Blaine was too busy ordering others around, so she would not take notice of people like he did. The only woman to have gone unnoticed, even by Brodrick except for Kane's mentions of her, had remained hidden…

"Ye' said she was blonde?" Kane growled. Blondes were rare in his land. He only knew of two others besides Alice.

"Oh, yes," she said emphatically. "With bright blue eyes. She was small, my lord. Definitely a lady."

Definitely Alice.

He stood there, staring down at Blaine, as the thought ran through his mind. No. No, it couldn't be Alice. There was no way— she was too pure, too virginal to be fornicating with another man in the hall—hell, she was too much his to be with another man.

Pure, unadulterated rage flowed through him.

He wanted to believe it was someone else with Saeran, but he couldn't. Highlanders were thick, buff. Even the women—and Alice was the only woman he knew that would match Blaine's explanation of her.

He snarled. *Saeran.* He'd warned that bastard what would happen to him if he touched Alice. He had *warned* him, a *clear* threat, and he had gone against Kane's wishes.

Saeran was going to die. The second he saw that bastard, he was going to die—by eating Kane's sword. Furious, he started to push past Blaine.

"Where are they?" he bit out, fury pumping through his blood. Murder. That's all he wanted to do—he wanted to kill Saeran. Alice

189

was not at fault—she couldn't be. He refused to believe that she held a part in the betrayal. Mayhap Blaine had mistaken her pain for pleasure...

He saw red.

Saeran had *raped* his woman. Roaring, he surged forward, forgetting all about Blaine. He was going to castrate the bastard.

He ran into the hall, from the direction Blaine had come from, when something wrapped around his neck. He fought against it, roaring with his fury and betrayal.

"Kane."

Brodrick. Brodrick was holding him back by his neck.

"Kill," he grated, driving his elbow backwards. Brodrick grunted, but managed to hold on. "Going to kill him."

"Kane, damnit. Stop—*stop*," he snapped, wrenching Kane's head back. "Calm the bloody hell down, and think. Yer going to kill a lad in yer own home. The men are going to become bloodthirsty. There are *children* in here. Do ye' really want to do this? Right now?"

"Yes."

Brodrick shoved him away, and his body hit the wall. Before he could react, Brodrick's fist came flying at his face. It struck him with the force of a hammer, knocking his head into the wall. The pain managed to subdue him, but the urge to kill Saeran was still there. He was nearly mindless with his need to avenge Alice's stolen innocence. Innocence that should have been his. Innocence that shouldn't have been ripped from her in the first place!

He growled, ready to fight Brodrick to the death.

The second the sound left his throat, Brodrick's fist connected with his jaw.

"What yer going to do," his longest friend snarled, leaning forward, "is go into the hall and claim Blaine as yers. Do ye' understand me?"

He balled his fist, ready to strike—Brodrick slammed him back into the wall.

"*Do ye' understand me?*" he shouted. "I donna care if ye' want to kill Saeran. Blaine is who ye' need to propose to. Or do ye' no' care about her dowry at all? Do ye' no' care about yer family at all? Ye' have two seconds to stand up and go out there before I force ye' myself, ye' ken?"

Kane stared into his eyes. Furious. He was so furious, so enraged...but a thread of sanity managed to sneak through the film of his bloodlust.

Saeran didn't have the strength to rape a woman—nor did he have the drive. Kane knew that above all else. He had known Saeran longer than Alice, and while he felt a deep, sexual, and emotional connection to her, he knew that Saeran was not that kind of boy. He had balked at the thought of flogging a horse into action—he would never rape a woman…which meant that Alice had been willing.

Pain, unlike anything he had ever felt before, seared him to his core. Pain and betrayal. The past week, they had gotten closer. Closer than he had with anyone. He grabbed his chest, hating the ragged knife of treachery that was digging itself deeper and deeper.

But with the agony of Alice's betrayal came the renewed fury.

"Aye," he said roughly, locking eyes with Brodrick. "Aye. Blaine. Proposal."

Brodrick smiled grimly. There was no real pleasure in his eyes. He helped Kane to his feet. When he made to help him walk, Kane shot him a glare so hot, he took a step away. He pushed away from the wall, storming into the hall and grabbing Blaine by the wrist as they went. She was oddly silent, but he didn't care.

He hoped that Alice appeared in time for his claim on Blaine. He hoped to God that she felt the same betrayal that he did in this moment, but he doubted it. A whore did not feel betrayal. The whole of the time she had spent with him had probably been an attempt to gain his favor so that he would take her as a mistress. If he had done that, she would have been set for life.

Mentally, he laughed. Alice was a fool, but even worse than that, so was he. He had fallen for her tricks, her kindness, her false purity—as had Saeran, but he could not blame the lad. He was young, and if Alice could fool Kane, she could fool anyone.

But why, he asked himself as he dragged Blaine to the center of his hall, would she give herself to Saeran? When she wouldn't give herself to him? The betrayal cut a fresh wound in his heart. He was not the monster he was reputed to be. He was not the mindless killer everyone thought he was. If he had felt mindless rage at the destroyed innocence of a woman, he couldn't stop it. Having his sister die by the hands of Grayham and his cruelty, he couldn't stand harm to befall a woman.

He might make an exception for Alice, though.

The thought made his stomach clench—with shame. No woman, not even Alice, deserved cruelty. Nay, not cruelty, but certainly punishment.

The hall began to quiet. Feeling the treachery pump through his blood, he stared into the crowd, waiting for the flash of blonde to appear. His eyes strayed to the pillar. Nothing. To hell with her, then. She was too busy spreading her legs for another man.

"Lady Blaine has been here for over a full moon. It is time that I reveal her reasons for being here." Jaw clenched, he looked down at Blaine, who was staring up at him with a look he couldn't decipher. He passed it off, listening to the silence, waiting for the stir in the air he felt whenever Alice entered the room. When the hall began to stir with unease, he growled lowly. It was not Alice's presence who caused the unrest, but his hesitancy in finishing the announcements. Blaine grabbed his hand, twining her fingers with his own.

In a way, he should be thanking Alice. Without his fury over her actions, he would not have had the drive to do what he was going to do now.

"Lady Blaine Sinclair—" There. By the pillar was his blonde seductress. He would have missed it had he not physically felt it like a slap to his face, and the flash of gold that came from her hair. With a sick, disgusting sneer in Alice's direction, he said, loud enough to ensure she heard it, "Lady Blaine of Sinclair is to be my wife. From this day forth we are betrothed for marriage."

As his words echoed into the hall, the blonde head of the woman he had craved and begun to care for slowly came around the pillar. Her body followed until she was staring at him. Her eyes dropped to the hand that held Blaine's. Even from his place in the center of the room, he could see the confusion, the hurt, in her eyes.

Even when she had been found out, she continued to play the game.

Still, the sight of the hurt on her face wrenched his gut. Her angelic face retreated into the shadows, while Kane dropped his new betrothed's hand. The hall was still silent, not a single word spoken. Not one of congratulations, not one of good tiding. Nothing. It was as if the hall had emptied of life, except everyone was there—and staring at him as if he were crazy.

He took a step away from Blaine, planning to retreat to his table, to where his precious ale was. No doubt Alice had run back to Saeran, and he felt no need to entertain Blaine. One of his men, a black haired man with sharp green eyes, caught Kane's attention.

A short nod was all it took for the man to stride out of the room. Within a moon, he would have all that he had fought for his entire life, and within a moon, Blaine would be off his land. Both Blaine *and* Saeran. He would not let the boy stay here when Kane had specifically told him to stay from Alice.

He heard Blaine's outraged gasp before he knew why she was drawing attention to herself. Rather than look at her, his eyes darted to the pillar as if they had known something his mind hadn't.

What he saw made him freeze.

Alice, for the first time since he'd known her, was walking in view of others. Towards him. Hands clenched. Eyes blazing. Body tense. Her whole person…beautiful. He tried to stay angry at her. The betrayal of what she had done was there, but in the face of her beautiful fury, he choked on words.

Brodrick made a move to stop her, but she held up her hand, not taking her determined eyes off him. The entire hall was staring at her, and she…didn't even notice. Her sole attention seemed to be locked on him.

"I want ye' out of my home," he growled when she was close enough to hear. From behind him, Blaine made a sound of appreciation, as if she thought he was saying that for her sake. He cast her a glance, long enough to see the fury there, and knew that this was, in fact, the woman Blaine had seen with Saeran.

Alice stared back at Blaine with a hard, cold look. There wasn't an ounce of the soft, innocent woman he knew in those blue depths, and he was glad. It would have made it that much harder to hate her.

"We must speak in private," she said, her voice quiet, commanding. He laughed. The sound was wrought with resentment. The people in the hall shifted, all of them gasping at the sight of the blonde beauty who had certainly dressed for the occasion. He'd never seen her dressed so elegantly, and he had to admit it—she looked beautiful. So beautiful that even through his anger, she took his breath away.

"I have nothing to say to you."

Blaine came beside him, slipping her hand through his. He held back a shudder of disgust, but the way Alice's eyes flickered to their hands made him go through with it, until Blaine leaned her head against his shoulder.

She wasn't soft and sweet like Alice. Hating himself for that thought, he couldn't stop himself from pulling away from her. He took Alice by the arm.

"Kane," she snapped, wrapping her hand around the wrist that held her arm. She stared up at him with wide eyes. Some of her strength seemed to deteriorate. He understood completely. Her arm was warm and delicate under his palm, calling to his primal senses and ripping away his rationality.

He tightened his grip on her…then grunted. Blaine gasped with outrage from behind him, but he paid no mind to her. The hall parted like the Red Sea for them as he dragged her away.

Chapter Twenty-Five

Saeran was shaking. Trembling. Ready to explode. The hurt and betrayal, the small, unrealistic ounce of hope she had begun to feel...it was eating her alive.

She didn't know whether to cry, punch, or kiss him. Most likely all three, at the same time. How dare he claim Blaine in that way? How *dare* he do it, while staring at her as if he took pleasure in her pain? How dare he?

The second the door was closed, she went after him, crying out at the pain in her chest. She couldn't feel her hits as her balled fists connected with his chest. He stood there, letting her hit him, as her rage became so high—that it crashed and burned.

In the end, she was left standing there, staring at the floor. Tears streamed down her cheeks. She was confused and lost. She didn't know what to do with herself. She wanted to stay strong in front of him, but without the pressure of Blaine and the visitors in the hall, she felt her willpower to remain strong crumbling.

The silence was deafening. The only thing she could recognize was the heat of his chest under her balled fists. The pounding of her heart. The wetness of her face.

"How?" she whispered, lifting her eyes to his. "How...could you have done that?"

He stared down at her, gaze guarded. There wasn't an ounce of warmth to it. It only made her emotions run more wild. Only hours ago, they had been so happy and content to spend their time talking, flirting, touching, and kissing. Only hours ago, she had thought...she had thought there was a chance that she could reveal herself to Kane as who she really was. She still wanted to—but the cruelty in his eyes was enough to make her silent. He didn't seem to care for a word she would say to him.

"Me?" He took her by the shoulders and moved her away. Saeran stared at him, shocked to her core. He had never pushed her away from him. He had always been the one to draw her to him, to win a hug with one of his smiles. "Lass, ye' must be delusional. I ken yer secret. I ken what ye' did behind my back."

She paled. How had he…Blaine. Blaine had told him her true identity. Her stomach roiled.

He was livid. She should have known Connor was wrong—she should have known.

"Kane, I—"

"Ye' donna get to call me that anymore, *my lady*. I want yer shite gone. Out of my keep and away from my land."

Her chest constricted. He could have broken her arm and it would have hurt less than the pain she felt.

"Ka—My lord. I…I swear, it wasn't my idea. I never planned for it to happen. I thought that—I thought that the whole affair would end as soon as we arrived!" She reared away from him when his eyes began to blaze.

"It's been going on since before ye' arrived?" he roared.

"My lord…"

He raked his eyes over her, then looked into hers. They weren't the eyes of the man who she had come to feel for. They weren't the eyes of the man she had grown to know, to trust. They were they were the eyes of The Lion. Cold. Cruel. Disgusted. He was…He was disgusted with her.

Tears stung her eyes.

Blaine…had won.

She didn't know when it had turned into a competition, but it had, and her sister—nay, Blaine, for Saeran was not sure what to believe anymore—had won. She had won The Lion over, when Saeran had started to fall in love with him.

How? How could this have happened? He should have understood. He should have understood that Blaine had manipulated her, used Saeran's fear as a leash. He should have known that she had only done what she did to be safe. And her sister—or whoever Blaine was—had betrayed her.

Pain clenched her heart. Blaine…

What she had said couldn't be true. It had to have been said in a moment of anger. Even though Saeran wanted to hate Blaine, they were still sisters—they had to be. Blaine had always been there, even when her parents weren't. She had been the one constant in Saeran's life—her presence, and her put-downs.

Tears stung her eyes. God, she prayed that Blaine had spoken out of anger…yet, at the same time, she didn't. Saeran would feel like a fool for her bold move in taking Kane away in front of Blaine. It was sad of her to hide behind an excuse, but…she didn't know what to think or do anymore.

It didn't matter now, though, did it? Blaine had gotten her wish. The Lion hated Saeran now, and all because she had been manipulated. He was going to kick her out, put her into the wilderness, where she would starve and die.

He made a rough sound, drawing her attention. Her eyes landed on him, and tears stung her eyes with renewed pain.

"I should no' be surprised," he said bitingly. "I did no' have a clue of what ye' were. It was my foolish infatuation with ye' that kept me from preparing for this." He raked a hand through his dark hair, laughing. The sound of it sent a shiver down her back.

With the shiver came a whimper. Of fear. She had never feared him before, but now she did. She felt helpless—as she rightfully should, for lying to him and continuing to see him when he was practically forbidden to her.

"I should never have trusted him," he growled, turning away from me. "There was something too good about him. That damn boy…"

Saeran wiped at her tears—then frowned. *That damn boy…?*

He faced her, body tense. His hands were clenched at his side. "I want to know why," he snarled, storming forward. "I want to know why ye' lied to me? Why ye' hid it from me? Did ye' think you could get away with being the lairds little whore and have a nice, paid for life?"

She took a step back, eyes wide. What was he talking about?

When she only stared at him, mouth gaping open, he barked out another laugh. Every time he spoke, his voice became more and more cruel.

"The one thing that I canna believe," he said, sneering, "Is that Blaine turned out to be better than ye'. Now *that* I did no' expect."

She froze.

"What?"

"Oh, ye' heard me, lass." He looked at her with cold eyes. "I want ye' gone. Now."

Her throat tightened. She clutched her throat, the pain in her chest unimaginable. Aye, she'd lied to him, but how could she deserve this? All of the times she trained with grown men. All of the times she took a beating for Blaine's sake in the arena. All of the times she fell off a horse. Even nearly having her leg bashed in by the black beast in the stables...hadn't that been penance enough?

"Do not you think that after...after everything I did, I could have some leniency?" Mayhap she did not. It was her own fault for being so foolish. To believe a word out of Blaine's mouth, when everything she did was for her own self-gain.

Kane stared at her. He didn't say anything, didn't laugh, didn't move. He just stared. Feeling like her heart had been ripped out of her chest and trampled on, she slowly bowed her head, backing away from him.

"I am sorry for any inconvenience I have caused you," she murmured. If her head were not bowed and her voice not so quiet, she wouldn't have been able to hold back the trembling that would have shown in her voice. She crossed her arms over her gut, trying to hold back the onslaught of emotion. Once she was out in the hall, she didn't think she would be able to hold herself back.

He watched her leave. She did not dare lift her eyes to his, but she knew. She felt it. Just like she always had.

The door closed softly in front of her when she was over the threshold. The last look she had of him tore her apart. He did not care. Of course he didn't. He had no need for her—Saeran had done her job perfectly. Blaine and Kane were now engaged, and she...was leaving.

The realization struck her like a slap in the face. A sob tearing out of her throat, she whirled around, blind—only to smack right into another person.

"Saeran?"

Connor's voice made her pause. Why. Why now, of all times?

She pulled herself away from him, keeping her head down, but unable to stifle the sounds of her pain.

"Saeran, oh my Lord." He took her by the shoulder, dragging her into an open room. "What happened? Why are you crying?

Why—oh, no, look at you!" He dragged her into his arms and she let it all out, hating herself for her need of comfort, yet unable to stem her sobs.

"Look at me," he said sternly when she had cried herself out. She refused, covering her face with her hands. Blaine had always told her she was an ugly crier. "My lady, look at me." Connor took her chin between his thumb and forefinger, tilting her head up. Despite what she wanted, she was forced to look at him.

The tears began to well again.

"Connor, I'm so confused…" She pressed a hand to her trembling lips. The words tumbled out of her anyway, until they were rushing together. "Kane and I were becoming closer, and I thought that if I revealed myself to him, he would forgive my lies and—and be *happy* about it! Like you said, Connor. But—but he knows." Her shoulders curled, stomach heaving. "Kane is—the laird is not…happy. He…Connor, he proposed to Blaine."

Her only ally stared down at her, his face a mask.

"Is that what has you crying so much?" he asked softly, reaching up to swipe at her cheeks with his thumbs. She nodded, choking up.

He was treating her as if he were an older brother, and it made her strength crumble that much more. Blaine could have been the one comforting her. If she had acted as a true sister would, she would be…

What would you do if I said we weren't actually sisters? The words came back to haunt her.

"Blaine…she said something to me…after we fought. Do you think she would lie? About the two of us not being sisters?"

His face darkened. "She said you are not sisters?"

Saeran nodded, wrapping her arms around herself. "Do you think she would lie about something like that?"

"My lady, I believe that Blaine would do anything if it contributed to her own goals—and as of late, I do not think they are very savory." Complete and utter hate stained his voice. It was so forceful that Saeran had to step away from him.

"What makes you say that?" she asked quietly. Before, she would have tried to deny his words, however truthful they were. Now, they were sitting on her shoulders like a rock, weighing her into silence.

"A maid of hers has been running around here, asking questions. She came up to me the other day, asking about you. Her name was

Gwen. I sent her away of course, so she had no information on you, but...it worried me."

"Why would she be asking about *me*?"

"Blaine must think that you haven't been completely honest with everything," he said, pressing his lips.

Saeran looked at her hands. She hadn't been completely honest with everything, yet...

"I don't care."

"You don't care? About the fact that your sister is sending a maid around to ask questions about you? My lady..."

"No," she said, shaking her head. "She's only doing it to scare me. She knows everything about me. Kane knows who I am, and will soon know every terrible thing there is about me. Mayhap it's not Blaine asking, but truly Gwen for her own reasons, because Blaine...she's already won." The words caused her chest to tighten. She'd been too late to reveal herself to Kane, and now...he hated her.

"What do you mean, already won? My lady, just because he proposed to her does not mean that she has his heart. It's obvious he cares for you, or he wouldn't feel so betrayed at finding out your secret! There has to be something wrong here," he said, taking her hand. Saeran shook her head, throat tight. "No. I know Kane. He wouldn't treat you like this if something else hadn't happened."

"It doesn't matter anymore," she whispered, lowering her eyes. "He's already commanded me to leave here. He's the laird—and he hates me so much he would not hesitate to kill me."

"Now you're being juvenile," he spat angrily. Connor grabbed her shoulders, shaking her. "What happened to you? Why are you being so weak? Nothing is set in stone. His supposed 'hatred' of you is a reaction out of betrayal. If you want Kane, go get him. I don't understand how one second, you can be a strong, enduring lass, then the next...this. It's painful to watch, my lady, and you need to snap out of it."

Saeran stared at him, lips pressed. She wanted to. She had tried to.

But he had rejected her, cast her out of his land. There was nothing to get from him anymore. He had all he wanted with Blaine.

Connor was right about one thing, though. She needed to get over her petty emotions. Heartbreak was painful, but it was surely easy to get over. If she could fall so easily for a man she did not know, then she must be able to fall out with just as much ease! Even though he had chosen Blaine, when Saeran had gone through so much because of her...

She shook her head, steeling herself against those thoughts.

"You're right," she said, meeting his eyes. Approval gleamed in them. "I will—"

A resounding, heavy thump from behind cut off her words. She tensed, a sinking feeling going through her at Connor's suddenly pale expression.

"What are ye' doing with her?" a familiar voice demanded. Connor dropped his hands, his face wiped clean of emotion now. It was cool, collected, and she was reminded that he was a squire. It was so easy to forget. When he was with her, he was open, the boy he kept hidden. When he was in front of other men, he was reserved. Calm. The future lord of a great estate.

"Lass," Kane said sharply. She slowly turned, clenching her trembling hands together. Her resolve to be strong crumbled like stale bread. "Come."

"Laird, I think it best that she begin packing," Connor said. She looked at him, as shocked as Kane was at his subtle defiance. "Since you so kindly exiled her from your lands."

The shock dissipated under the force of his disgust. "Oh, so she came to complain to ye' about me. Has she won ye' over, too?" He sneered at Saeran. "It would appear ye' have. Figures." The way he said that...it hurt her. It was as if he thought it was common for her to woo men, like he thought she was some leper of a woman.

Connor took a step in front of her, hands clenched. A flush climbed up the back of his neck. She didn't know what to do. Saeran was sure he had never gone against Kane like he was now, and the way Kane was thinking about her...she was terrified that they would take it too far.

Her worry over Connor was the only reason she found the strength to step beside him. She couldn't let him be hurt because of her own weakness. Swallowing down her fear, she squared her shoulders and met Kane straight in the eye.

"I will take my leave now," she said quietly.

"My lady—" She cut Connor off with a raised hand. Kane reached out, wrapping a large hand around her wrist. She was too shocked to pull away.

Then the fear set in.

Without another word, he yanked her closer to him, slid an arm around her knees, then hoisted her over his shoulder. "If ye' say anything, I'll spank ye'."

Her eyes widened. As he started to carry her out of the room, she met Connor's eyes and saw a glimmer of…of satisfaction?

Chapter Twenty-Six

"Someone could see us," she hissed, slapping at his back. He continued walking, ignoring all of her attempts at freedom. Fear was sitting in her chest, not only of being discovered, but of what he was going to do to her.

A sharp slap echoed in the hall, and she squealed, her bum stinging.

"Why did you hit me?!" she asked furiously, hitting him back.

"I told ye', if ye' speak, yer getting spanked. Now quiet, lass. Unless ye' want more…"

She instantly quieted, but that didn't stop her from pinching and hitting him in an attempt to be let go. He gave no indication that he noticed.

The corridor was dark, with only a couple candles lit. Even if someone saw them, they wouldn't recognize anything but two dark figures—mayhap not even that. She pounded at his back, tears of frustration stinging her eyes. She had just come to the realization that she would actually be leaving Shaw lands, and he…He was destroying her resolution with no more than a command.

They came to a stop, then the door was thrown open. Her eyes didn't have time to adjust to the dark before he was tossing her into the air. A scream built in her throat, and she braced herself for the pain of crashing into the wall or ground.

There wasn't any pain. Her body landed on a downy surface, and she dug her nails into it, heart racing.

"Where did you bring me?" she asked, hating how thin her voice was. If the room hadn't been silent, she doubt he would have heard her. Saeran lifted terrified eyes to Kane. He came to the edge of what she now knew was a bed. With a harsh movement that she could barely make out through the darkness, he unwound his plaid.

Saeran watched in complete silence as he became naked, with nothing but the shadows to cover him. Her mouth went dry. The panic that she should have felt was absent. All she could focus on was the hard planes of his body, the thick arms and chest, the trimmed hips. Her face flamed, and she looked up at him.

She could have melted from the need that was in his eyes. It was mixed with fury so intense that she felt it in her soul, but the desire in his eyes... It scorched her with its heat. She had dreamed about this happening. He might not be saying out loud what he had planned for her, but she knew without a doubt that he wanted to take her—and he was going to.

"My lord, please...I...you're betrothed to Blaine now and you've cast me—"

"I donna want to talk about Blaine," he snarled. He knelt on the bed. She scooted away, staring at him. She tried not to gaze at his length as he crawled toward her, his body as lithe and silent as a cat's. Saeran had never seen anything like it. Perhaps her shock was the only reason she was still until he had her back pressed into the bed. His hands locked her wrists above her head.

Her breath caught when he leaned his head down to her neck. Why wasn't she fighting this? Hadn't he just commanded her to leave? Didn't he hate her? Wasn't he engaged to her own sister? Why was she letting this happen, when it was so clearly wrong? Tears stung her eyes—not from fear, but shame. Shame because she wanted this to happen. She wanted to be as close to him as she could be, before he banished her for good. This was her farewell to him...And she wasn't going to fight her body's response to him.

This was the one and only time she would ever get to experience this, whatever this was. But she knew that once she felt him, her body would accept no one else. Her heart began to race as pain welled inside of her.

"I canna let ye' go," he whispered against her neck, "until I've had ye'. I donna care if ye've shared yerself with another. I want ye'." He pulled back, and she stared at him, confusion mingling with the pain.

"I have had no other, my lord," she whispered, twisting her

hands in his grip. He was unrelenting, pressing his body onto hers. Saeran stared at him through the dark, wishing he would look at her…

~

Kane wanted so badly to believe her lie, but he knew better. A woman would lie about anything, and Alice had proven herself to be just like every other woman with an agenda. Lying and conniving to meet her own goals.

The thought sat ill with him, so he pushed it aside. He was going to have her, and then she was leaving. Once she was out of his system, all of his problems would be over, and his conscience would be cleared.

Wouldn't you kill your men for doing this to a woman? When have you ever gone this far with one, out of anger? Is Alice really as vindictive as you've made yourself think?

He shoved the thoughts into the back of his mind. He wanted her. It was that simple. He didn't want or need anything else from her, except her body. She had betrayed him, lied to him. Had given herself to another male while working herself into his mind. Day and night, she was all he could think of, and she had gone to another man.

"Do no' lie to me," he bit out.

"But I am not—" Knowing she would only continue to deceive him, he leaned down, taking her mouth with his own. If she could not speak, she would not anger him anymore than she already had. As he stole the words out of her mouth with his kiss, it turned into more. Into what he had taken her here for in the first place.

With a growl of approval when her lips began to move against him, he wasted no time in reaching behind her, fumbling with the strings. When they resisted, he pulled away from the kiss just long enough to grip her dress by the bodice. He held her eyes.

The fabric tore under his hands. The aroused fear in her eyes made him grunt. Shoving aside the torn bodice, he finished the skirt off and cleared the bed of her clothing, taking satisfaction in the becoming blush that spread over her face, neck, and breasts. Seeing her like that, it was almost easy to believe that she was a virgin, that she had saved herself for him, for this moment.

"Gods, yer breasts are perfection," he said quietly, reverently. He palmed one, ignoring her surprised gasp, and bit back a groan. Aye, perfection. They were round, full, and tipped with pink nipples. He took it between his thumb and forefinger, enjoying the way she squirmed under him. He remembered their first kiss in the field, the way she had blossomed like a flower under his touch.

Feeling his cock swell, he bent down, taking the nipple he'd been pinching into his mouth. She made another sound, this one keen, shocked. Always so shocked, like she didn't expect the pleasure. He laved the soft flesh with his tongue, hardening it. He rolled it between his teeth and tongue, dying to touch her, to hear more of her, to taste more of her.

He let go of her wrists, using his now free hand to fondle her other breast, as his other slid down her stomach. He sucked hard, reveling in her moan, and gently brushed his fingers over the soft blonde curls.

Kane had planned to be rough. Angry, fast, and quick. He had planned to take her, get her out of his head, and then send her on her way. This was not angry, nor was it fast. His body was taking his time with her, no matter how much he wanted to take her. He wanted to give her pleasure, no matter how much she didn't deserve it. He wanted to enjoy this, no matter how much he felt betrayed by her. He wanted her to enjoy this, no matter how much he hated his weakness.

"Kane…what—what are you doing to me?" she gasped. Tiny, greedy hands grabbed his shoulders. Her hands were hot enough to burn him. He felt her desire, her desperation. The fear she had felt earlier was gone, replaced by pleasure. He saw it in her crystalline eyes, in the flushed cheeks. Her lips were full and pink, begging to be kissed.

He gave one last tug to her nipple, then kissed his way up her chest. His finger brushed against her clit. She jerked against his body, wide eyes meeting his. He smiled despite himself.

"Do ye' like that, lass?"

Her blonde curls moved as she nodded her head frantically. She broke his gaze by closing her eyes, head tilting backward. He pressed his thumb harder against her clit. Her nails dug into his shoulders so sharply, he swore they broke skin.

The biting pain only urged him to kiss her—so he did. He bent down, took her lips with his own, and dominated her with his mouth and hand. His loving of her body was gentle and slow, exactly how he hadn't pictured this—and he was fine with that. Alice was acting like the virgin she claimed to be, and even if he knew it was a farce, he didn't mind being fooled for this one instance.

"I want ye' to touch me." He couldn't believe he said that—but he had. He felt her body stiffen under his, and his chest tightened, until she spoke.

"H…how do I…" She ran her hands over his shoulders and back, as if she were unsure of what to do with him. The uncertainty in her voice shook him. Mayhap she was not as experienced as he had suspected. Aye, she had given herself to another, but that did not mean she was an experienced harlot.

The realization both put him at ease and fired his desires.

"Like this." He stole her lips for another kiss, simultaneously taking her hand and leading it to his cock. The first gentle touch of her fingers made him groan, all of the blood in his head dropping to his hips. God, the pleasure was instantaneous. Her movements were tentative, but gradually, she took the hint.

Her small hand wrapped around him, gently tugging. His whole body convulsed and he gasped, lungs robbed of breath. The pleasure of that one movement had…not killed him, but revived him in a way he couldn't explain. Alice took her hand away, making him curse.

"I am sorry," she whispered, face turning an even brighter red. Though he could tell she felt sorry, there was a spark of desire in her eyes that made him curse again. Without conscious thought, he took her hand and led it to his cock. Her thumb gently brushed his head. Alice met his eyes, a silent request for permission.

When he guided her fingers around his length and she swiped her finger over the dot of pre-cum, he could have wept from the pleasure of it. Taking another kiss from her, he dominated her mouth, letting his tongue sweep inside to taste the sweetness that was Alice. As he did that, reveling in her kiss and the innocence it held, he parted her nether lips with his thumb and forefinger. She tensed under him, but barely.

Her hips moved against his hand, begging him to carry out with what he was teasing her with. He held himself back, needing so badly to touch her, but even more so wanting to torture her, to bring her to the brink of pleasure, just to let her fall back down. That way, when she came for him, he would be the only one she remembered in the future…

~

Saeran was dying. Aye, it was true. As virginal and clueless as she was about what men and women did behind closed doors, Saeran was dying—to let him take her. As instinctual as breathing was, she wanted Kane to pleasure her, to let her pleasure him. She wanted to feel like the woman she was. She wanted to feel *Kane*.

And right now, she definitely was. She had never held a man's member in her hands before, but now that she was… It was daunting and exhilarating at the same time. He was large and full in her hand. She didn't want to look down at him for fear of shying away and ruining the moment, but her eyes strayed nonetheless as he pulled back from their kiss.

If she had been struggling for breath before, she was completely robbed of it now. The angry red skin was pulled tight. As she tentatively ran her thumb over the plump head, the tip of it wept. She met his eyes, desire coursing through her so painfully that it turned into a burning need to explore him further.

"Do ye' want to touch me, lass?" He meant more than what she was now. Touch him—as in actually explore a man's body, Kane's body. She didn't know whether it was a trick of his or not, but she took a leap of faith, nodding. There wasn't an ounce of hate or anger in his gaze as he watched her. His gaze was intense, studying her, gauging her reaction.

When she began to fear that it was indeed a trick, he nodded, a smile curling his lips. He removed himself from her, laying back on the bed. She rolled onto her side, her breasts touching his ribs. He had lain right in the streak of moonlight that was cascading into the room, truly giving her a full view of him.

The sight of his body was shocking, terrifying, and thrilling. Saeran sat up, running her hands over his arm, wonder filling her—wonder and horror. God, how many wars must he have fought.

His body was covered with all shapes of scars. There were several of them that truly made her tremble. Though, she had known he was scarred because of the bare skin he revealed on a daily basis. What was hidden under the plaid was just as soul-shattering, and made him all the more real to her.

With trembling fingers, she softly ran her fingertips up his arm, to his chest. Another scar…and another, and another… She closed her eyes briefly, sending a prayer for him. How had he managed to survive for so long? Surely all of them had hurt…She opened her eyes, staring right into his, and put her hand over his heart.

It was pounding just as fiercely as hers was. It urged her on, gave her courage. At least she wasn't the only one reacting to this passion… Of course, she knew that by the hardness that was resting between his legs. Her fingers itched to touch him again, to wrap around his thickness. She wanted to see him wither. She wanted to watch him lose himself because of her.

The longer she held his gaze, the more it felt that she was losing herself in him, and not the other way around. The flecks of green in his eyes were dark with his desire. It was entrancing, addictive. Heart in her throat, she followed what her body was telling her to do.

Saeran leaned down, her hands on either side of his head, and tentatively put her lips to his. Though he had accepted her moments before, she was terrified of being rejected, discarded. His moods were so fluctuant that she didn't know what to expect from him—

Oh. Faster than she could blink, he tangled one hand in her hair, wrapped an arm around her waist, then dragged her on top of him. She spread her thighs over his hips as he swiftly opened her mouth with his own, his tongue brushing against her. The taste of him burned her senses, and all she could think about was him. About having him, taking him as her own.

There was no Blaine. There were no lies. There was no betrayal. All there was right now was Kane, Saeran, and their need for each other. The hand that had tangled in her hair slid out of it, going down her back, pressing her body harder against his. Her nipples brushed against his chest, and she shivered into the kiss.

He made a rough, almost laughing sound against her lips, then took her breast in his palm. Saeran could have cried when he broke the kiss. He was hot, masculine. Seeing him below her, knowing that she could make him forget himself with just a touch, empowered her. It also made her crave him. She reached between them, taking him into her palm as punishment.

His face went rigid.

"Fighting fire with fire only creates a greater flame," he warned, right before a devilish look flashed in his eyes. Saeran didn't know what to make of it until he was rolling her onto her back, his mouth around her nipple, and a soft pressure was beginning to form at her entrance.

They were right back where they had been in the beginning. She grabbed for his shoulders, forgetting all about their small game. Later. Later, she would take her revenge and give him the pleasure that she wanted to, without his interference. For now, however…

Saeran moaned, tendrils of fire curling along her skin. Tendrils of fire that he had created in an instant. He nipped, sucked, and laved her nipple, making her cry out at the shocking sensation. He had done

209

it earlier, aye, but it was still different, still wonderful. His mouth was making love to her breast, and all she could do was try to keep herself together, even though she was falling apart at the seams.

Then she realized something. The pressure at her core was his fingers.

Saeran froze, fear welling inside of her.

Chapter Twenty-Seven

"K...Kane, what are you—oh, God, what are you doing to me?" She started to pull away, fear overwhelming her pleasure, but he stopped her with a hand to her shoulder. Cool air wafted over her damp nipple, making her shudder, a soft reminder of the need that was racing through her.

"What are ye' afraid of, lass? I ken ye've done—"

She shook her head frantically, grabbing his wrist. She didn't push him away for her. His fingers stayed inside of her, and he held her eyes. The forest green depths swirled with sensuality. It caught and held her attention, and gradually, her heaving pants lessened.

"I...I don't know what to do," she said, dazed that she would admit to it. In the midst of heat and passion, she was admitting her shortcomings to a man who would just as soon send her away, as take her in his arms.

"O' course ye' do." His voice dropped to a near growl, making her shiver. How could he do that, with just his voice? The sound washed over her, and she felt her body react. Her gut clenched, her core wept for more, and her hands began to grab for him, fingers curling around his skin. Still, even as she curled up to him like a kitten, she shook her head.

Kane slid a finger under her chin, tilting her head back. The dark smile on his face told her that he knew he'd made her wet with just his voice.

"Do ye' need me to tell ye' what I'm going to do to ye'?" he murmured, raising a brow. Heat flamed her cheeks.

211

"I—Kane, I—"

His soft, hot kiss cut her off. When he pulled back, she was gasping for breath and trembling in his arms. "I think ye' do, lass."

When she opened her mouth to speak, he silenced her with another kiss, taking his fingers out of her. It wasn't until he ended it that she noticed he'd laid her back into the bed with his body between her legs. He sat up, pulling her legs up so that her feet reached his shoulders. He kissed her bare calf, and she swallowed thickly.

With her body like this, he could see every part of her—even the part that no other man had before. She covered herself, blushing, and turned her face into the downy bed. How was she supposed to act when she was presented like this?

Large hands moved her own aside.

"Ye'll no' be hiding yerself from me, lass." He placed another kiss to her calf.

"But I—"

"Nay." He put a hand on her stomach, sliding it downward. She watched him with wide eyes, breath still. She wanted to pull away, but at the same time, she was curious. What was he going to do to her? When was he going to tell her? When would the torture end? Was this normal for a married couple? Aye, they weren't married, but…But this was what a man and a woman did with each other, correct? Surely a man was not allowed to torture his woman thusly. Surely there was some sort of rule about it.

"Watch me," he said quietly, nipping her calf. She jerked to attention just as his hand disappeared into the juncture of her thighs. His thumb once again played with her, but this time, there was purpose to it, a skill that she hadn't noticed. Saeran's body denied her mental command and pressed toward him. A soft sound came from her throat before she could silence herself.

"Ye' like that? Me touching ye' like that?"

She gave a mixture between a nod and a shake, unable to form a word. Even if she did, she suspected he wouldn't let it past her lips.

"I'm going to touch ye' some more, lass. Donna tense. Just relax." The instant one of his fingers found her core, she did the exact opposite of what he said. His thumb stayed on her clit, a little warning. "Shh," he soothed, reaching for her face with one hand. She leaned into his caress, fighting her fear.

She didn't want to be scared of Kane. She knew he could give her pleasure she'd never felt before, and understood that him

212

touching her in a forbidden place was…was necessary. She couldn't help the fear, though. Her mother had never talked about what happened between a man and woman with her—that conversation was meant to be saved for the night of her marriage ceremony. Saeran had never witnessed it, either, unlike her sister when they were at court. The rumors had flown around, with excited talks between women, but Saeran had never participated, nor paid attention—and now she sorely regretted her ignorance.

His fingers tenderly brushed over her cheek, and then he slid a finger inside of her. Her breath came in short gasps, mind blanking out. There was going to be pain—she knew it. Right now it might not hurt, but soon…Soon it would hurt her. Tears welled in her eyes and she trembled, wrapping her arms around herself.

After what seemed like forever, the trembling subsided, and she realized that Kane was waiting for her. He hadn't moved. The only thing he was doing was staring down at her, a troubled look in his eyes. Saeran swallowed thickly. This was it. She couldn't get past her own fears long enough to enjoy what he was giving her, to give him the same pleasure that he had given her.

This…was it.

Except, instead of shoving her out of his bed, he moved her legs so that they were bent and spread. She dug her toes into the bed, torn between…everything. She didn't want him to stop. She wanted to take him as her own. The thought of him touching her down there was enough to make her pant, but when he actually went through with it…Fear overwhelmed her, and she couldn't stop it. When he touched her clit, kissed her, and caressed her, it was like heaven parted, and she could finally see light in the darkness.

What was wrong with her?

Without a word, Kane lowered himself between her legs so that he was resting on his forearms, his head right above her blonde curls.

"I want ye' to be honest with me, lass. Do ye' want this?"

She stared into his eyes. They were so dark, so troubled. He seemed to be avoiding looking at her body, only looking into her eyes. That gave her the courage to nod. The memory of how he'd pulled back in the field, the memory of their conversations, all came back to her. Saeran had absolutely no reason to fear this man. He had been hurt by her betrayal—she understood that now. If he had really meant to banish her, she wouldn't be here now. She knew that as surely as she could breathe.

"Aye," she whispered. He took her hand, threading her fingers. Warmth spread through her, clearing out the fear and trepidation. He wouldn't hurt her—not physically. Kane would never harm her. "Aye, I want this."

He studied her for a moment, then nodded as if he had come to a decision.

Then a wicked smile came over his face. "I'm going to kiss ye' now."

She smiled, reaching for his shoulders. Aye, she would very much like to be kissed by him.

He put a hand on her stomach, holding her still. The smile dropped from her face.

"What are you—oh, *Kane*."

His mouth attacked her core like a man starved. Her hands slammed into the bed, and she expected to feel fear, hesitation, disgust—but she didn't. All she felt was mind-numbing sensations, and Kane was giving that to her.

"Ye' taste so good," he growled against her body. "Like freshly fallen rain."

Saeran shuddered, threading her hands in his hair. She wanted to drag him away from her, but her body had different ideas. She began tugging him closer to her, and her legs wrapped around his shoulders, locking him to her.

He kissed her clit. Fire shot through her body, so intense that a moan ripped from her throat. Then…Then he did something else, something that had the power to sear her. His tongue swirled around her clit, then he sucked. Hard. While he did that, the familiar pressure of his fingers tested her entrance—and this time, there was no fear. Only pleasure. Only pleasure so strong that she was left gasping for breath.

"Shite, yer wet," he groaned around her core. "So damn wet."

Saeran didn't know whether that was good or bad. When one of his hands lowered to his hips, she guessed it was good. Biting back another moan, she grabbed for his shoulders, realizing that he was just as hot as she was—and like her, he must need something besides this as well.

When she grabbed for him, however, he didn't stop his attack on her body. Another finger joined the first, and then he was pumping his hand against her. His fingers gave her a pleasure she had never known. Saeran gasped, and that was the last of her breath for a while.

"Aye, ye' like that, lass. Ye' like that quite a bit…" The growled approval ended, and then he returned to her body. Holding one of her legs back, his tongue played with her clit and simultaneously drank at her like a cat drank milk. Sensually, slowly. He took his time with her, fingers slowly pumping, moving inside of her.

Then he added a third.

She was full. So full that she wanted to cry—because it wasn't enough. She wanted more. She wanted him. She wanted the part of him that had wept at her touch, and she wanted it inside of her now. Still, as he suckled her clit and wrung pleasure from a well that should have been dry by then, the sensation built inside of her until it was a raging fire. Her body began to convulse in waves that she couldn't stop. It was exquisite, overpowering.

When the wave finally crashed, she felt as if she had been drowned with the sensations Kane caused within her. Her body thrummed, and it took forever to come down from the cloud he'd put her on.

"Och, there ye' go, lass," he whispered. His voice was right next to her ear. Making a small sound and unable to stop the smile that came over her face, she wrapped her arms around his neck and held him to her. "However, I'm no' done with ye'."

She stilled, excitement rushing through her.

He grinned, burying his lips in her throat and rolling her under him once again. The teasing and provocative man that was before her now was the complete opposite of the man he'd been before their love making. There was a tenderness to him that shook her, that made her forget about everything except Kane.

She squealed at the hot lick to her neck, then moaned. He'd bitten down.

Just like that, the mood changed.

He reached between them, pushing her leg open.

"I've been dying for this," he whispered, keeping his face in her neck. He laved the spot he'd bitten with his tongue. The hand he'd used to move her leg came up, covering her breast. His fingers pinched her nipple, rolling it. He kissed her collar bone.

"For…for what?" she gasped, wrapping her arms around his neck. God, that felt good. Everything he was doing felt good. Nay, better than good. Amazing. It felt…amazing. Saeran held him tighter, her legs going around his waist.

He groaned against her neck.

"To be inside of ye'. To feel yer heat. To feel ye' milking me. I've been dying for ye', lass." Then, with another open-mouth kiss to her neck, he braced himself above her on his forearms. She felt the beat of his heart increase and then…then it happened.

The head of his length pressed against her core. She stilled, feeling like her heart had stopped.

"Shh, lass," he murmured against her neck. He gently played with her clit, making her back arch as pleasure ran through her. His breath wafted over her neck. Saeran shivered. "Ye' want more?" He pressed harder, going deeper. The first inch of him was inside. She whimpered, nodding her head.

She should be terrified. She had no clue what was happening to her, or what he was doing, but she loved it—and wanted more. So much more.

"Are ye' sure?" he asked. He was holding back. Saeran growled, grabbing him by the hips and trying to pull on him. Kane resisted her tugging. Instinct drove her to clench around him, and he made a rough sound.

Kane pulled back, making her gasp with sexual frustration, then thrust inside of her.

The gasp turned into a pained cry. The shock of his entry was enough to make tears spring to her eyes, and suddenly, the pleasure began to ebb, replaced by an uncomfortable sensation.

She wasn't the only one who noticed it.

Kane was frozen above her, as hard and cold as ice.

"Nay," he whispered, staring down at her. His eyes fixed on the salty tear that trailed down her cheek. He didn't move—didn't pull out, or go farther in. He stayed there, still. "Nay, lass, ye' canna be—"

"Kane," she whimpered, grabbing him by the shoulders. She curled her arms around his neck, her mind needing comfort just as much as her body. "Why—why did that hurt? I did not—no one told me it was going to hurt…" Then a thought came to her, one that made her stomach drop. "Did it hurt you as well? Kane? Are you hurt? Is that why you're not moving?"

Saeran started to push herself onto her elbows. He didn't roll off of her. He stayed there, staring down at her with horror in his eyes.

"Kane?" she asked worriedly, touching his face. Her body had adjusted to his hardness, and it was even beginning to feel almost…nice. The only thing wrong was his unwillingness to respond to her. She'd hurt him. Aye, Saeran had hurt him. She put her arms around his neck, drawing her to him. His face buried in her neck, but still, he did not speak. "I'm sorry. I'm so, so sorry. I didn't know it would hurt you…"

"Lass," he said raggedly, his voice muffled. He pushed himself up so that he was braced above her body once again. It caused him to move, and she gasped, surprised by the soft tendril of pleasure. How could something so amazing for her, hurt him? Even as she bit back another airy moan, she saw the pain in his eyes. "It does no' hurt me."

She swiped a hand over her face, feeling the heat there. Lord, she was burning.

"It doesn't?" Saeran asked, frowning. She clenched around him involuntarily, and they both moaned. "It…If it doesn't, then why did you stop?"

Kane looked at her, tormented for reasons she couldn't understand. If it didn't hurt, he should continue. Aye, it had pained her, but only for a moment. Now that it was over, and she was adjusting to him, she wanted more.

Every inch of her skin that he was touching was on fire. Before, she hadn't noticed it, but now she did. It was eating at her senses, destroying thoughts that didn't revolve around Kane and how amazing he felt inside of her. He wanted to be—he said so!

So why wasn't he continuing? Saeran leaned forward, enjoying his hiss when she pressed her lips to his shoulder.

"Lass…yer a virgin. This—this has to stop." Though he said the words, he made no move to leave her. She smiled with womanly triumph, tightening her walls around him, milking him, drawing him farther into her body. She spread her legs, bracing them against the bed, and pushed upwards.

They growled together—Saeran's one of sexual victory, and Kane's one of sexual frustration. The roles were reversed, she thought, sliding her hands up his shoulders. That was fine. As long as he stayed inside of her, everything was fine.

"I do not want it to stop," she whispered, opening her mouth on his shoulder. He groaned, head falling forward. His hips moved with a jerk, and she knew he was trying to hold himself back. She pushed against the bed and drew him inside of her once again.

"Lass, *please*," he hissed, desperation in his voice. She felt him swell inside of her, felt her juices coat him. He had started this, so he would stay till the end—and she was not done with him, not until she knew he'd felt the same earth-shattering experience she had.

"If it doesn't hurt you, I want to keep going," she said forcefully, digging her nails into him. God, but he was thick. The way he filled her was exquisite and deliciously painful. Saeran was definitely not letting him go until they had found completion together.

"But lass—"

"No, Kane." She lightly smacked him on the face. Her body was dying of heat for him, and he was trying to tell her no. "I want this. You want it. I can feel it."

To show him that she did, she let body tighten around his. He groaned, still shaking his head.

"Why?" she demanded, becoming frustrated in earnest now. Why wasn't he doing as she commanded? Why wasn't he doing what he wanted to with her? Saeran nipped his shoulder when he didn't answer her. Sweat dropped down his temples, and the strain was evident. If he just continued, it wouldn't be an issue!

"God, lass. Yer a damn virgin. I canna—I hurt ye'. I saw it and heard it. I canna—"

"Yes," she said, grabbing him by the jaw. "Yes, you can. And you will."

Tormented eyes met hers, but she paid no heed. She had been frightened at one point, and he had kissed and caressed her through it. Now was her time to make sure he felt the same pleasure she had. She took advantage of his weakness, and pushed at his shoulder.

He instantly rolled to the side, his body slipping out of hers. "Lass, I am so—"

"Quiet," she snapped. Honestly, men were exasperating.

Chapter Twenty-Eight

How could he have done this to her? How could Kane, a man who would kill anyone for doing what he had done to the innocent Alice, go through with what she wanted him to do? After he had defiled her? This whole ordeal had started off as a means to an end to his desire for her…and his drive had been completely misplaced.

Guilt and shame ate at him like a parasite, but at the same time, his need for her was nearly overwhelming. She didn't care that this had started out as angry—it was obvious by the way her slick walls were clenching, the way her hips were moving.

She put her hand on his shoulder. He expected her to curse at him, to slap him. How she hadn't done so already was a mystery. He rolled onto his side, nearly weeping when he slid free of her warmth. Still, the shame over what he had done made him ache.

"Lass, I am so—"

"Quiet," she snapped, an adorably annoyed look passing over her face. He listened, feeling like he had been kicked in the gut. Of course she was angry with him—

The thought cut off when she sat on top of him. Her legs spread over his waist, one hand on his chest. The other reached between them. He jerked into a near sitting position when she wrapped her hand around his cock.

"What are ye' doing to me?" he groaned. She pushed at his chest, and he effortless fell back into the bed. He could have easily pushed her aside and left, but something was holding him back—and it wasn't her hand on him.

"I'm going to finish what you started," she murmured. There was a look in her eyes that he'd never seen before. It was sultry and hot, the look of a woman who knew what she wanted—and Kane was exactly it.

He swiped a hand over his face when he realized how badly he was sweating. "Do ye' no' hurt? I…lass, I know I hurt ye'…nay, stop. We canna do this."

Even though he wanted to stop what she was doing, Kane's body was stronger than his mind. He reached up, palming her breast. God, she was a vision atop him like that. Her waist was trim, breasts large enough to fill his hands, and her eyes…Lord, but those eyes had the power to destroy his control with a simple, searing look.

When she rose above him, her hand guiding him into her with an innocence that killed him, he could have died. The pleasure over rode the shame, and before he could stop himself, he thrust upward, filling her wet, tight sheath completely.

Her eyes widened and a small sound left her lips. He froze—until he saw the ecstasy in her eyes. His bonny lass liked him inside of her—even when he'd brutally broken her maidenhead. She had to be hurting, but she didn't say anything, and if Kane were honest with himself…he wanted her to continue.

She began to ride him. The innocence in her movements was prominent, and that she'd gained the courage to do this with him, on her first time, was enough to wipe the rest of his resistance away. She wanted this, and he was going to give it to her.

Her body milked him with greedy pulls. When he'd had enough of her slow, leisurely pace as she got the hang of it, he rolled them over, putting her on her back. She hadn't fully settled into the bed before he was pumping inside of her.

Cries of pleasure rang through the room, both his and hers. She was so tight, so wet. It was so good that it was nearly painful. That only drove him further, harder…And Alice didn't seem to mind at all.

~

The sounds of their slapping flesh should have alarmed her, worried her, embarrassed her. It didn't do any of the above. If anything, it made her more desperate for him. She wrapped her arms around his neck, thanking the higher power that he had listened to her.

Tears welled in her eyes, her mind and body overwhelmed with Kane.

"Kane," she moaned, pressing her face against his neck. "God, Kane, I want you to go faster—oh, *aye, like that*—" He cut off her scream of pleasure with a kiss so hot it drove her insane. His hand roamed over her body, burning a trail of fire as he continued to thrust inside of her.

"Lass, I want—I want this to be gentle for ye'," he grunted, pumping his length inside of her. She wrapped her legs around his waist, locking him to her.

"Nay," she whimpered, arching under him. The action brought him even deeper. She felt her body begin to heat, flaming even higher than before. "Hard. Oh, Kane—so good."

A devilish smile curled his lips, and then it was gone. He pulled out of her arms, their bodies still connected, and grabbed her by the knees.

"What are you—" She found her calves once again on his chest, and then he was hauling her up by her buttocks. Then he pushed forward, slowly, his hand reaching between them. He began to rub her clit, softly plucking at it, and she gasped, slamming her hands into the bed. "Again. Kane, *again*."

"Anything for my woman," he growled against her calf. He bit down, and her body tensed. The pleasure began to singe her from the inside out. Her breath stilled, the world falling away. He continued to thrust his hips against her. Sending his length into her tightness over and over again, until she was screaming his name, grabbing for his shoulders.

He took her hand, connecting them in an even deeper way. Then it all ended when she felt as if their souls had bonded together in the midst of their passion. A rush of ecstasy swept through her, and Saeran wept from the sheer intensity of her orgasm, and shortly after, she felt his body buckle as he joined her.

He set her legs down onto the bed and fell forward. After a moment of catching his breath, he dragged her against his chest. Their hearts raced together, and Saeran thought she had died and gone to heaven.

That had brought them together on a level she had never felt—and she never wanted it to end. Saeran pressed her face against his neck, breathing a sigh of content as she gradually came down from the europhic sensations still coursing in her body.

Kane drew her closer to his body. When he slid out of her, she had to fight to keep back a sound of disappointment. His hands began to trail down her back, making her shiver.

"Are ye' cold, my love?" he asked quietly. He reached for a nearby plaid before she could object and slid it around her. It smelled like him—masculine, musky. Perfect. She snuggled into the cloth and kissed his neck, sighing again.

Perfect.

Everything was perfect.

Saeran had never felt more relaxed and safe in her life. The cat was out of the bag with Blaine, and she knew that her sister knew what Saeran had done with Kane. She should feel guilt, but she didn't. She felt content, relaxed, and…loved. She felt loved by the man who was holding her so tenderly against his chest. With a patience she wouldn't have expected from her, he had walked her through her fears and given her the best experience of her life.

Her eyes closed, sleep starting to take over. Aye, sleep. Sleep was what she needed.

"Alice." She was so close to falling into the darkness that she almost didn't realize he hadn't said her name. "Alice, why did ye' no tell me you were a virgin?"

If his words hadn't gotten her attention before, they sure did now. Her eyes popped open, and she stared at him, confused.

"I…Why wouldn't I be a virgin, Kane? I tried to tell you…"

He stared at her, realization dawning in his eyes. He cursed. Her breath was cut off when he crushed her against his chest, a ragged apology breaking through his lips. It was probably the first he had ever uttered. Saeran frowned against his chest, confused.

Why wouldn't she be a virgin, really? Had he thought her some whore?

She asked him as much. He stiffened against her.

"I was foolish," he bit out, kissing her temple. He sounded furious, yet the tenderness of his embrace told her something else. "I was so damn foolish—I should have known she would lie about it. Ye've always seemed so pure, Alice. So innocent. Precious." He buried his face in her hair, but she couldn't register it.

"What…What are you talking about?"

Hadn't he figured out her secret? Hadn't Blaine told him that Alice was actually Saeran? What he was saying now didn't make sense. Blaine had revealed her secret to him, but that didn't mean she wasn't a virgin. Also, if he knew her real name, why did he continue to call her Alice?

He shook his head, pressing an open-mouth kiss against her neck. She shivered. When he stayed silent, she thought he wouldn't tell her at all.

"Kane," she said quietly, feeling like her heart had dropped to her stomach. "Kane, what did you hear about me?"

"I donna want to trouble ye' with it, love. Just rest. I should no' have brought it up anyway." He pressed a chaste kiss to her lips, then settled into the bed. As they laid in the silence, her mind running wild with her thoughts, she began to notice how tense he was, how...distanced he was.

"What's wrong?" she asked into the darkness.

"Nothing. Sleep." His voice was rougher, pained.

She pushed herself into a sitting position, leaning over him. "Tell me what's wrong," she insisted, gently touching his jaw. This was not how she had wanted the aftermath of their love making to be. Though she had no clue what couples did with themselves after hours of passion, she knew that the sadness in the air wasn't right.

"I canna believe I listened to her," he said quietly.

"Listened to who?"

"Blaine." The word came out as a disgusted sneer. In the dim, moonlit room, she saw his face twist with the force of his hate for her sister. She...understood completely. Saeran dropped her eyes to his neck, unable to look him in the face.

He didn't know who she was.

He had no clue that she was the other sister, the one he could have proposed to if she had revealed herself to him sooner.

"She told me she saw ye' and Saeran...Doing unmentionable things. In the hallway. That he stole yer virginity. I believed—lass, I am so sorry," he said thickly. He wrapped his arms around her once again, crushing her against his chest. His heart was racing. "I'm so, so sorry that I did no' believe ye'. I hurt ye' because o' that, and I—I never wanted to hurt ye' for the world. I felt so betrayed and it turned out..."

Saeran stared up at him, utterly shocked. He had thought she had lost her virginity to herself? Granted, he didn't know that Saeran and Alice were the same people, but it was enough to make her laugh. She hid her face against his neck as the laughter rolled through her. It was so ridiculous! Saeran had lost her virginity to herself. Oh, if Connor could hear this now.

"What are ye' laughing at? Alice, I hurt ye' because of my own ignorance." He tilted her chin up towards him. His gaze softened at her continued laughter.

"I—I am sorry for laughing." She sobered slightly. "But…Kane…You should not believe everything you hear!" Especially from Blaine. Why had she made up the tale instead of revealing Saeran's lie? To hurt her? It had certainly worked. He had nearly kicked her out of the keep because of Blaine's never ending lies. Anger began to build within her. Blaine was no sister of hers. All of her lies, and her deceit… Everything she had said and done to Saeran over the years was beginning to weigh on Saeran's shoulders like a boulder.

"I ken," he said quietly, shamed. "I was blinded by jealousy and betrayal and did not stop to think that mayhap Blaine was speaking out of her own jealousy."

Saeran raised a brow. Blaine? Jealous? What was there to be jealous of if she had everything she wanted? Even if she didn't have something, she eventually achieved it.

"Alice," he said deeply, seriously, gazing into her eyes. "I would have given ye' a gentle first time, had I known. I…I donna know how ye'll forgive me for hurting ye' as I did, and ruining ye' like—" He stopped abruptly, staring down at her with growing horror.

"Alice, I did no' pull out of ye'."

She frowned at him, even though a blush came over her cheeks.

"Is that not the point?" she asked, wringing her hands together. Had she done something wrong? The flush in her cheeks washed away, making her pale. Why was love making so complicated? Shouldn't it be as simple as joining together and then resting? She felt the lull of sleep like a heavy blanket, yet her concern was keeping her awake.

"What if ye' were with child? Alice, I've ruined ye'," he groaned.

Realization dawned. Saeran didn't want to tell him her secret, the one that had caused her to lie to everyone in the first place, but his torment was clear. Her heart felt like lead. There were so many things between them that could potentially drive them apart—she didn't want this to be added to the list.

With a tight throat, she said, "I cannot have children, so it is no concern."

His head snapped to the side, his gaze as sharp as a dirk. "Ye' canno have children?"

She shook her head. "I…I had the fever when I was young. It

nearly took my life from me." Thick arms crushed her against him. Without explaining the rest of the story, he understood—and that meant the world to her.

Blaine had never understood her. She had never been able to confide in her, talk to her about random things, or express the pain she had felt growing up. Kane has been the only one to listen and comfort her, and it made her fall even harder for him.

"It's why—It's why I let this happen…between us. I do not want to trap you in anyway," she said earnestly, meeting his eyes through a watery gaze. He swiped his thumb over her cheeks, clearing away the soft trail of tears. "I have never been with another, but that…that does not mean I will bind you to me."

"I would no' mind it if ye' did, lass," he said quietly. "Because ye' already have."

The meaning behind his words was not lost on her.

Her eyes widened. "But Blaine…"

Maybe there was a chance that she could reveal herself to him. If he accepted her with her flaws, there was a chance. Hope filled her, mingling with the newfound love she held for this man.

"Is leaving the second I return from the MacLeods," he growled. His eyes went dark with stark fury. "I will no' be married to a liar. I detest them more than anything. Liars are too weak to face the thing they hide from, and I'll no' be taking a wife like that. I only misdirected her to protect my clan. Call me a hypocrite, but it is needed for their safety. Ye've seen the way she treats the servants here, or anyone who is not a lady as she is. There is a difference between a conniving liar, and a liar doing so for the sake of his people. I'll never be married to a woman like that."

The hope crashed and burned. Her throat seized, but she nodded, the only consent she could give to hearing him. There *had* been a chance that they could be together, but the moment Blaine had concocted her plan, it died. Of course it had.

He settled into the bed, tugging her flush against him. He did that quite a lot, as if he couldn't bring her close enough.

"But yer the perfect woman," he said into the air. It sounded like he wasn't talking to her, but to himself. "Aye, perfect. Beautiful, pure. Verra strong."

"You've already proposed to Blaine," she said, feeling sick. His hand stroking her back didn't alleviate her sickness. If anything, it made it worse.

"It does no' matter, love. Everyone is aware that when I return, she will be leaving."

Saeran frowned at him. "Why would you propose, just to send her away?"

He chuckled, kissing her temple. "Ye' canna expect me to actually live with a dragon like that, can ye'? Nay, by the time I return, the messenger would have returned, and her dowry will be mine. Then I'm breaking the engagement."

"*What?*"

Kane scowled at her. "Donna shout so, lass."

"*What?*" she repeated, utterly horrified. "Kane! Dowries do not work like that—you have to actually marry the woman to obtain it—wait. You only wanted her for her dowry?" If she had still been the blind little girl who adored her viperous sister, she would have been offended beyond belief. However, all she felt was a tingle of alarm and confusion. "What could she have in her dowry that you do not already have? You're one of the strongest lairds in the Highlands."

"The king and I signed a contract that said as long as I'm betrothed to Blaine, I'll get the dowry. It said nothing about going through with the marriage."

"But it's intended that way—"

"Ah, but it is not written that way, love."

"He's the king. Even if it is not written as such, he'll have his way."

Kane chuckled again. The sound was deep and sensual, making her shiver. Why did he affect her at such times? This was a pressing matter, and he was laughing at her.

"Lass. By the time I return, I will already have the dowry. There's no more to it than that."

"What is so important in the dowry that you have to trick the king? That's treason, Kane. You could become in serious trouble."

"No' if Blaine is the one that breaks the engagement," he said slyly, tapping her on the nose.

"I do not know why she would do that, but tell me why the dowry is important to you?" Had Saeran gotten an important dowry as well? The king had made no mention about dowries to her, or Blaine. At least, that's what she got from the meeting they had held together.

"Amnesty for my family."

"Uhm...pardon?"

"The king added amnesty for my mother and brother if I proposed to Blaine. By the time I return from battle, they will be here, waiting for me."

"I've never known the king to be so…forgiving."

Kane nodded. "Aye. I'm willing to bet he gave Blaine a dowry like that so I would choose her over the other sister—who actually was a boy. Saeran."

"Why do you say that? Surely Blaine is not all that bad," she said, though she almost gagged at the words.

"She's a dragon! Who on earth would want to marry her, let alone live with her? Love, yer as blind as Saeran is when it comes to his sister."

She stiffened. "What is that supposed to mean—"

The door burst open before she could finish her sentence.

Chapter Twenty-Nine

"Kane, I—"

Kane pulled the covers over Saeran's head completely, shielding her from the woman that had barged in on them.

Blaine.

Of course. She always came around at the worst times. Despite the flowing hatred she felt for Blaine in that moment, she didn't want to reveal herself to her. It would only cause more trouble—and Blaine might be angry enough to tell Kane who "Alice" really is.

I will no' be married to a liar. I detest them more than anything. His words from earlier came back to her like a slap. She held her breath, praying that Blaine hadn't noticed her in the darkness.

"Kane," her sister said demurely. "That isn't any way to treat your future wife. I simply wanted to come show you my appreciation for your proposal."

Before, Saeran never would have caught onto the innuendo. Now, however, she did—and she wanted to rip Blaine's hair out. If she hadn't been submerged in darkness, she knew she would be seeing red.

As if Kane knew of her rage, he slid a hand under the plaid, finding her fingers in the darkness. It helped to alleviate the anger, but minimally. She still wanted to show Blaine the skills she'd learned from Brodrick.

"Ye' can show yer appreciation by leaving." He shifted in the bed, a knee raising. Through her anger, a flash of wickedness struck. Keeping their hands together, she used her free hand, feeling along his ribs.

He stiffened.

"Really, my lord. I want you to approve of me…Let me show yousil how thankful I am of you."

Saeran focused on tormenting him more than the anger. The quick beat of his heart, which she could clearly feel and hear with her head on his abs, fueled her determination to ignore her sister. By all accounts, Saeran had won a battle that Blaine would never win—and even though Blaine didn't know it, Saeran was going to enjoy her victory. Her hand slid lower, to his hips.

A sharp warning pat to her bottom made it nearly impossible to hold back her laughter, but she refused to foil her own plan.

The sooner she drove Kane crazy, the sooner he would force Blaine out of his room. Any confrontations her sister had planned—and Saeran knew she had many—could be put off until *after* the battle, when Blaine was on her way out of the door.

Heavy footsteps sounded in the room. Blaine was coming closer to the bed.

"Is there—is there someone else in here?"

Kane grunted. Her hand slid under him, to his butt. This was so improper of her. Never in her wildest dreams could she have seen herself doing this—with her sister in the same room. It was purely for professional purposes, though. When Kane began to crave her in earnest, Blaine would be forced to leave the room—leaving them to their business.

Aye, she thought, smiling wickedly. Leave them to their business. She slid down his body, mindful of the plaid revealing any of her pale skin, and gave his butt a light pinch. Lord, but he had a fantastic butt, even in the darkness.

"You are going to be married to me," Blaine suddenly snapped. Saeran paused, eyes narrowing. Nay, she wasn't. She didn't say it though, and neither did Kane. In a way, his silence hurt, even though she knew he was going to break it off the second they returned. "Not anyone else. I swear, if there is another woman in here, I'll—"

"Do nothing," he growled. "Now get out. I have no need of ye' in here."

"Kane—"

"You will call on me as your lord. Now, get out," he roared. The silence was deafening. Saeran stilled, shocked. When he raised his voice…it was terrifying. Like The Lion he was reputed to be, his voice carried the strength of a thousand men in one word. It felt as if her heart had stuttered—and she was struck by the unbelievable attraction she felt to him.

There were no sounds of Blaine leaving. Saeran waited, and she felt Kane's hand tighten around hers.

"The woman, the blonde one who came to you in the hall. I must tell you something about her. Her name—"

"Ye' mean the one ye' lied about?" He barked a laugh. "All I'll hear out of ye' is lies."

"How—how did you know?"

"Did ye' really think ye' could get away with it? I want ye' to leave me before I show ye' how ruthless a husband I'll really be. I donna like liars, Lady Sinclair, and yer the worst of them."

"What are you saying?" Blaine said. It sounded like the words were ripped out of her throat, as if she were too shocked to believe that he was speaking against her. Saeran wanted to feel bad, wanted to feel a trickle of protective urges for Blaine, but her sister never would have protected Saeran. That was the only reason she stayed silent in the darkness.

Blaine had tried to hurt her. She had known that Kane would react without thinking at the news of "Alice" having intercourse with another man—Saeran knew that as clear as day.

"I'm saying, if ye' donna leave me, I'll put ye' in yer place."

"But there is more!" she said quickly. There were furious footsteps, loud and heavy, like Blaine herself was. "That is not who you—"

"Lady Sinclair," he snarled softly. Saeran had forgotten all about her little game with Kane. Her heart was pounding

"Fine," she said, her voice as stony as a statue. She retreated to the door. Saeran listened closely, waiting for Blaine to exit the room completely. It was silent for so long that she thought she had missed it, until Blaine said something that made her blood go cold. The words were murmured into the room with a chilling knowledge embedded within them. Kane did not react, but with the tensing of her body, she knew that he knew the words were directed to her.

"He'll find out on his own…and when he does, he'll hate you more than even I do."

The door closed softly, leaving her, Kane, and the impending revelations of her secrets the only thing remaining in the room.

"Love," he said with a growl. The covers were removed from

her head, and she was pulled upwards. His lips brushed against her own. "Ye' donna play with a man like that when he canna retaliate."

She laughed, but the sound was empty. The threat Blaine had laid in the open was enough to ruin her mood. The confidence, the triumph, the *happiness* she had felt moments before were now gone. Her mood was so dark that she didn't think they would return.

Kane sighed after a couple moments of silence. "Do ye' want to talk of it?" he asked, smoothing a hand down her hair. She let her cheek rest against his chest, shaking her head. Her heart thumped faster in her chest. The consideration he was giving her, the privacy, meant the world to her.

"Alright, lass. Just let me ask this—it's no' going to hurt ye', is it?"

She raised her eyes to his. "What do you mean?"

"Whatever the dragon was talking about. It's no' going to hurt ye' in the long run, correct?" There was honest concern in his eyes— for her.

"Did you not hear what she said?" Saeran asked, feeling like she had been kicked in the stomach.

"Aye. What about it?"

"I do not understand. She said that what I could be lying about would make you hate me. You should be more concerned about yourself, not me." Her eyes dropped to his neck. She couldn't bear to look him in the eyes.

"Love," he said softly, brushing her hair back from her face. His fingers were tender, his touch feather light. Despite how much she wanted otherwise, he lifted her face to his. "I could never hate ye'. Whatever yer hiding from me…When ye' feel safe to reveal it, I'll do my best to understand. As long as yer no' a MacLeod. Yer no', right?"

She shook her head.

"Good." With a low growl, he bent his head to hers, stealing her breath was a kiss.

~

"I'll miss ye', lass."

Sleep was slow in leaving her. At first, she didn't understand who was speaking or where she was. Saeran was used to waking up in the early hours of the day to a hard, lumpy bed, and a chill that went bone deep.

Right now, she was not cold. Nay, she was quite warm.

Saeran looked up at the man who had spoken. A blush coming

over her face. She was lying in bed with Kane. The morning light poured in through the open window, and his arms were wrapped tightly around her. He was like a living fire under the covers, covering her in a comforting heat. She snuggled into his chest, sighing.

She didn't know what he was talking about, but sleep sounded…amazing. Like the most brilliant plan of the century.

"I do not know what you're talking about, Kane…" She couldn't even finish the sentence before her eyes were closing, a yawn breaking past her lips. How could he expect her to stay awake after the night they had shared? Her body was deliciously sore in all of the right places. Of course she would want to sleep—with him cuddling her right to his chest.

"Alice," he said softly. She felt the light press of his lips on her temple, her cheek, then the corner of her mouth. "I'm leavin' today."

She shook her head, muttering, "No, you're staying, and you're holding me. Quiet, kitty. Sleeping."

"Kitty?" he asked. His chest rumbled under her ear as he chuckled.

"Lion. Kitty. Meow. Please," she whimpered, nuzzling his chest. "Quiet."

"Yer a demanding little thing, aren't ye. For a woman who can hold her own against a man twice her size, yer as cute as a button. I'm sorry, love. I should have left hours ago."

"Then why didn't you," she grumbled, blinking sleep-heavy eyes up at him.

"Because I like the look of my woman sleeping." He pressed his lips to hers in a quick, soft kiss. "I like to know yer safe in my arms."

"I'm always safe." She pursed her lips, eyes closing. He followed her silent request and gave her another kiss. Saeran slumped into his chest, a content sigh escaping her lips.

"Sure ye' are," he said, chuckling. "Now, lass. I really do have to get going. My men are waiting for me."

"They can wait all they want," she snapped sleepily, wrapping her arms around his neck. "I want you to stay here."

"I canna do that, love," he said. A note had entered his voice. It was stern, yet regretful. She flipped her eyes open to meet his.

"Why?"

"The MacLeods—"

That one name had the strength to wipe away her sleep-induced stupidity. Her eyes flew open. They were leaving to fight the

MacLeods. Not just Kane, but Saeran. Today. With everything that had been going on with Kane and herself, she had pushed aside the things she should have been worrying about—Blaine and the MacLeods.

Blaine…Lord. Like the sun clearing the darkness away, she was hit with the full reality of everything that had happened between her and the woman who may or may not be her sister. Her heart felt…empty. All of the joy she'd felt with Kane drained out of her the second the events of the last two days hit her.

She had been so blind. So numb. So enraptured by Kane.

Now…now it was all attacking her like a rabid warrior—and she didn't like it one bit.

Chapter Thirty

"I'll come back for ye, lass."

Right after he had said that, he'd disappeared, shouting for Saeran—the boy version of herself. It had been a madhouse before leaving. She had forgotten to pack, her horse was not ready, and she smelled like Kane and lovemaking. Luckily, the stench of the surrounding men and horses hid that.

She watched as he rode ahead. Gradually, his proud back faded from view as he vanished into the thick forest. The smile he had thrown over his shoulder, the blood-thirsty grin, had killed a piece of her heart. She should not melt for a man who was clearly looking forward to death, but his strength…his masculinity. The way he turned so tender and patient with her, when he was actually a brutal warrior, made her fall harder and deeper for him.

Sadly, he was not as tender and patient with her when she was a lad. Especially when they were in a hurry.

After half-hearted glaring from Kane, giggles from Connor, and helping hands from Brodrick, her horse, sacks, and self were ready for the trip. Actually, nay. Her self was not ready—not physically or mentally. She could barely lift the sword that Brodrick had given her, and the thought of weilding it made her shudder.

She had wielded a sword one too many times. The man she had stabbed in the back was the one time she had ever had to defend herself in earnest…Her hands tightened around the reins. She had done an amazing job of suppressing the thoughts, with all of her distractions. But, now that she was stuck on a horse with numb legs, they were attacking her with a vengeance so fierce, she had no way to stop them.

Would they encounter the men again on this journey?

She tightened her hands on the reins, lifting her face to the cool breeze of the Highlands. The trees and hills were green and sprawling, beautiful. The air was fresh and crisp, the perfect weather for riding. Their horses were trotting at a steady pace, adding a soft clip-clop to the sounds of birds chirping and the low, rumbling voices of the men she was with. They had just crossed the border between the Shaw and MacLeod lands.

The MacLeods had vast, unkempt lands. Yellow-grey boulders dotted the hills, making the journey less than pleasant. It was still a sight for her eyes, though. She found it hard to believe that men so foul could live in a place so serene.

The men they had been accosted by had looked rough—as if they had been roaming around for a while. They had probably hoped to kill the couple on their outing and take their belongings. Rogues, she thought fearfully. Kane hadn't killed them, and she doubted her stab to the back had gotten rid of the one man, so there was a chance they were still around.

Fear slid down her back. If they were, would they recognize her? She had dressed herself in her usual garb—trews, shirt, and dirty face. It was unlikely that they would. Plus, the men around her would dispel of the threat before they could get to her. She was not playing the damsel in distress in this instance, but relying on the cold truth. The warriors had death on their shoulders. Killing is what they did. Any threat that came their way would be taken care of immediately.

"I saw you." Connor's voice jerked her out of her thoughts, and her heart raced. He grinned at her, unaware that he had frightened her enough to give her grey hairs.

"What do you mean?" she asked, shaking the thoughts out of her head. There was no use thinking about it. What was done, was done.

"You know what I mean, my lad—Ow! What was that for?" he asked, rubbing his arm.

"Do not call me a lady," she hissed, smacking him on the arm again.

"Why? The laird is smitten with you. If he found out that you're actually the woman he is lusting after, everything would be perfect!"

Her face flamed. "I don't know what you're talking about."

"Oh, yes you do. I saw that seductive look on your face when you came to take Kane from the hall—Lord, everyone there did. Do not worry, though. Everyone was quite relieved—all except Blaine."

Her stomach cramped. Oh, yes, she knew just how furious Blaine was. Furious enough to tell Kane of their lies in an attempt to make him hate her. She shivered. That was the side of Blaine she hadn't noticed her whole life—and it terrified her.

"Relieved?" she asked, trying to focus on something other than Blaine. She had done well with avoiding all thoughts of her thus far, and she wanted to keep it that way.

"Oh, yes. Seeing you, and the way the laird followed you out of the hall, gave them all hope."

"I don't understand. He was positively a brute before he came with me."

"But," Connor said smartly, nearly bouncing in his seat, "he did all the same—which says something! You have him wrapped around your finger, don't you?" He sighed dreamily, patting his horse on the neck when it huffed as if to tell him to calm down before he was bucked off its back. "That is why you have been so distant lately! Because you're spending all your time with him. Is he as great in the bed chamber as I think he is?"

She sputtered. "Excuse—no! Connor, that is not something I am willing to discuss with you—"

His eyes widened, and a laugh burst from his chest.

"You little harlot." He laughed, shaking his head. "I was bluffing—but thank you for proving me correct."

Saeran groaned, shame burning her chest. She did not regret what they had done—she only regretted that it had been out of wedlock, though it did not matter for her either way. With her barrenness, she was unsuited for marriage. No one wanted a wife who could not bear sons—and neither would Kane.

He needed sons as handsome as he. He needed an heir for his clan, and Saeran could never give him that.

"Do not look so upset," Connor said, reaching over to pat her hand. "I didn't mean anything by it, you know. I'm not like the other boys. To hell with the judge, jury, and executioner. If you want to enjoy the life you have, you can't live it by obeying the standards that society has set for us."

Connor was right, though he had misjudged her sadness over being barren for something completely different.

"If you want to share yourself with Kane, I am——"

A loud, horrible cough came from behind them. She looked behind her, heart falling to her stomach. Of course Brodrick would hear them speaking during a conversation such as this. She gave him a weak smile, but all he did was stare at the two of them.

Connor's demeanor instantly changed from playful bantering to serious squire.

"Saeran," Brodrick said, grunting. "Connor."

"My lord," they murmured together.

"Just so ye' ken, if ye' speak loud enough, no matter how far back in the line ye' are, people are going to hear ye'." He gave them both a nod, then left.

Her heart raced. Had the other men heard the entirety of their conversation? She cast a look at the men, only seeing their backs. No one was looking back at them, not even Brodrick, who rode past them. Everyone was either silent or talking in the form of grunts to one another.

She turned to Connor, eyes wide. "Do you think anyone——"

"No," he said, shaking his head. He was subdue. "No one heard anything. He happened to show up at the right time. It was but a warning."

"Why would he issue a warning without a cause——"

"Saeran," he broke in, narrowing his eyes on her. "Does anyone else know of yer disguise?"

"No! At least—at least, no one should know. Why?" she asked fearfully.

"I'm just curious," he said. Connor reached behind him, pulling a piece of yellow parchment out of his pocket. "I did not know whether to give this to you or not."

He handed it to her. Saeran cautiously took it, studying it. She gathered her horses reins in one hand and flipped the parchment over. It was sealed with black wax, no insignia. She ran her finger over the hard wax, meeting his eyes.

"I saw Blaine giving it to Gwen. A couple hours after you and Kane disappeared, Blaine came into the hall with that. She looked furious—like she could have killed someone."

"Why do you have it?" she asked, gaze returning to the parchment. She bit her lip. Dare she open it? It could just be a list of nothing, something foolish between Gwen and Blaine.

He shrugged, looking ahead. "Someone has to look out for you.

The only person I can think of that can make Blaine that angry is you. Seeing as you and Kane were gone for so long, and Blaine looked...angry, well—I took it when Gwen was not looking. I feel that she was meant to deliver it somewhere. The two of them have become more secretive as of late."

She nodded, swallowing. Saeran knew exactly what he was talking about. She had noticed it as well, as much as she tried not to. When the cold shoulders and rumors had started, Gwen and Blaine had stuck together more and more. Saeran had yet to meet the infamous Gwen who seemed to have a hand in everything, but she sounded like Saeran used to be—Blaine's footman, willing to do anything to please her.

She felt a moment of pity for Gwen, and anger at herself. She had been that weak—Lord, in a way, she still was. Saeran still refused to acknowledge everything her sister had done up to this point. Now, though, with the parchment in her hands and the bad feeling in her stomach, she highly doubted she would be able to put it off now.

"I didn't give it to you sooner because we were all so busy," he said, grimacing. He still didn't look at her, his eyes facing forward, voice sad. She felt the worry coming off him in waves, and had to imagine how hard it must be for him—to not only cater to the laird, but also to her. Saeran reached over, giving his arm a quick squeeze.

"Thank you, Connor," she whispered. He met her eyes.

"You're welcome, my lady." A smirk lit his face, but she didn't reprimand him. With trembling hands, she slid her finger under the edge of the parchment and pulled up. The hardened wax tore, some of it crumbling onto her lap, and then it was open.

The seal had been broken.

Saeran held her breath as she unfolded the yellow letter. Her heart was like dead weight in her chest.

She knows. I'm sorry. I had planned to meet you at the church, but current events have held me back. I've sent a serving woman in my place, as you now know from reading this. In a moon, I may be able to meet you in Birkshire. When time permits, I will be at the boulders. My condition has become critical.

I love you,

Blaine.

Saeran read the letter over again, frowning. She knows? Who knows? Meet who? Blaine was meeting with people? Saeran skimmed the letter once again, then flipped it over. There had to be more. Blaine didn't love anyone—except for Blaine herself.

"What does it say?" Connor asked, peering over her hand. She shoved the letter at him, still scowling.

"I have no clue. She was supposed to meet someone. Read it for yourself."

"Who, though?" Connor murmured, scanning his eyes over the parchment. "'Boulders', 'Birkshire'." He looked at her, eyes narrowed. "That's the village we are camping outside of. There's a ring of boulders behind the whor—" He stopped, clearing his throat. "There's a ring of boulders near the blacksmiths."

"But who was she going to meet?" she asked, picking absently at the wax pieces in her lap. She rolled it around in her fingers.

"A lover?" he asked, raising a brow.

Blaine? A lover? She shuddered. "I'm not so sure."

"She did say 'I love you' at the end, my lady."

"That does not mean she has a lover," Saeran said, wrinkling her nose.

A look of disgust passed over his face as if he realized what he was saying. "Aye. You're right. Not a lover."

The word made the two of them shudder.

She reached for the letter. *What had she meant by condition*? Saeran pushed the thought aside. She was known for lying and exaggerating for attention.

"This is just—when would she have found the time to meet this person before? It seems like she has left the keep to see them," she asked, eyes scanning the parchment. She kept reading it, expecting something new to pop out at her, but nothing did.

"Aye, it does." They rode in silence, their hushed voices quiet for a while. She couldn't stop her mind from thinking, from worrying.

"What I want to know," she said, "is who knows what? And why is she sorry?"

"Do you think she meant you?"

Saeran raised a brow at her. "What could I know? And why would she apologize for it?"

He sighed. She shared the sentiment completely. She wished she could believe that this was a misunderstanding, that maybe Blaine hadn't been the one to send the message, but her name had been signed. Mayhap if she hadn't been furious with Saeran, Saeran could believe that the letter was harmless—but what if it was a lover? She was meant to marry the laird. At least, that's what she thought. Saeran knew it wasn't going to happen, but Blaine didn't know.

It didn't make sense. Why would her sister—

Her sister.

Blaine wasn't her sister—she had told her that.

"I know," she gasped. Saeran could have slapped herself for not realizing it. "She told me we're not sisters—do you think that could be it?"

Connor was silent. He wouldn't even meet her eyes. Her excitement over figuring out who Blaine had meant died down a little, and she knew why he was quiet.

"My lady, I know you and Blaine do not have the best of relationships…"

She dropped her eyes to her lap. A forgotten piece of wax was there.

"That doesn't have anything to do with this."

"Yes, it does. I know—despite how confident and brave you can sometimes appear—that her words have made you worry."

A laugh bubbled up her throat, but it was too tight to break free. They didn't make her worry—her react was the complete opposite. She thought more of Kane than of her sister's words. In a way, she wasn't surprised by them. Her growing annoyance with Blaine had given her a clear view of what was really happening—and had made it apparent that Blaine had never loved her.

Even if they *had* been blood sisters, and Blaine hadn't loved her, Saeran would still consider Blaine as…not her sister. It was that simple. Right now, she had more important things to worry about.

"Connor," she said softly, fighting the truth in his words. "What's meant to be, will be. I'm at the lowest point I can get. The only thing I want to do is make it back home alive, and I doubt even that will happen."

"Why do you say that?"

"Because I'm going to find out who Gwen was supposed to meet."

Chapter Thirty-One

"Camping here for the night. Donna cause problems in the village like last time, aye?" Kane said over his shoulder. He swung himself off his mount, giving the graceful beast a pat on the head.

He began unpacking his bags while his men followed suit, carrying conversation through the dark woods. It was night, with only the light of the moon to guide them, and that's what Kane liked the most.

"Brodrick," he called. "Start the fire. Mayhap we can draw some game to us."

"Yer the only man I know who looks forward to going head to head with a bear," his friend grunted. Nevertheless, he started to make the fire. Kane turned back to unloading his saddle—or he would have. The two figures at the edge of the trees made him pause, however. Kane forgot about the horse.

Saeran and Connor had been talking the whole ride—leaving no one to wonder if their voices were loud enough to carry to their enemies. Though their voices were hushed and blurred together, they hadn't made an effort to stay silent.

His steps were heavy with anger as he drew near them.

"…you are not. I forbid it—I will tell Kane, Saeran. In all that is holy, I will—"

"Tell me what?" he asked, folding his arms over his chest. The two dainty figures froze. Saeran had his back turned to him, but he could see the panic that overcame his squire's face. He had always been a terrible bluffer.

241

"Nothing," Saeran said, quickly turning around. His face was pale, if not whiter than Connor's, but there was a determined gleam to them that made him pause.

Where had he seen that look before?

"It's something, if my squire feels the need to threaten ye'."

A look of frustration entered the lad's eyes. Saeran elbowed Connor, but held Kane's gaze, as if he hadn't done that. Connor grunted, rubbing his side.

"Saeran wants to meet his first whore." Connor gave his companion a snarky smile.

"*What?*" Saeran whirled around, his voice unusually high and squeaky.

"Really." Kane looked between the two of them. They were not arguing over a matter such as that. Whores for young men such as themselves was common—except in Connor's case. Connor was…different.

"Nay, I—"

"Saeran," Connor said, patting him on the shoulder. "You do not need to be embarrassed about your sexual urges."

"But I am not—"

"And I was trying to explain to you that there were two brothels. One of which you may not go to."

Kane knew the one he was speaking of and nodded, grimacing. "Half the men that leave that brothel come down with a sickness near their cocks. I'd strongly advise ye' no' to go there, if ye' want to bed with a woman again."

"Do you have experience with brothels?" Saeran asked, a tone coming to his voice that Kane did not understand. The lad sounded jealous.

Kane grinned. "Oh, aye. What do ye' think I do when I'm away from the keep? Ye' have a lot to learn, lad." He slapped him on the back. The boy was so thin that he nearly fell to the ground. Kane grabbed him, frowning. "Are ye' alright?"

A healthy flush dotted his cheeks as he pulled out of Kane's grip. Connor was standing back, a hand over his mouth, laughing. Kane gave him a look.

"Ye' need to eat more meat," he said, taking Saeran's arm. He wrapped his hand around it, squeezing. Lord, but he was a thin boy—even thinner than his puffy shirt made him appear. Was he malnourished? Kane didn't see him in the hall for dinner often. "Ye'll

242

be taking two servings tonight, after ye' return from the brothel."

He gave Connor a hard glare. "Donna let him go to the brothel near the edge of town. Trust me, lad. No' a good place to be." He gave them both a slap on the back, gentler than before with Saeran, then headed off. Why was there something so familiar about the lad? Kane looked over his shoulder, staring at Saeran.

At that exact moment, Saeran looked over his, and met his eyes. He realized what was so familiar under the dim light of the moon, with the shadows casting over the boy's dirty face.

The eyes.

They were the same, pale, crystalline blue as Alice's.

~

"You are disgusting!" Saeran hissed, smacking Connor on the arm. He winced through a laugh.

"Mayhap if you were not so impulsive, irrational, and a *woman*, I would not have had to put you in that position. You know, if you were actually a man, we would not have that problem." He gave her a suggestive look, making her blush while scowling at him.

"I would like to point out there is nothing wrong with my being a woman—"

"Oh, please. There is and you know it. Only you would be so ready to put your life at risk without means of protecting yourself—"

"Connor, all I am doing is meeting someone. Even if the danger arose, I would be able to protect myself perfectly fine. I'm sorry, but I will not be deterred in this."

He glared at her for so long she became antsy. Then a triumphant smile came over his face.

"How do you expect to meet a man who is expecting a woman? You're not exactly dressed for the occasion, my lady."

Saeran gave him her own smile of triumph, patting the pouch tied to her waste. Her inheritance jingled. "One does not inherit Sinclair assets without a few benefits."

She had kept that hidden from Blaine. At the time, she hadn't understood her own reluctance at showing Blaine the portion she was keeping for herself, but luck had apparently been on her ignorant side. Upon packing for their trip to the Highlands, she had pushed aside her guilt and done what her gut told her—store and hide as much of the money she could. Of course, she told herself that she was doing it as a contingency plan, and that had helped to alleviate the guilt.

Now, she was grateful for her thoughtfulness. Blaine would have never allowed her to leave had she known Saeran had funds.

"What is that look for?"

"Haven't you heard, my dear Connor? Dresses are a girl's best friend—and I plan to buy a few, as well as a room at the inn." She gave him a jaunty nod, turned on her heels, and started away from him. She would not be deterred, and damn anyone who tried to stop her—including Connor.

"The village is this way, my lady," he said in a droll manner, grabbing her by the arm and steering her in what she assumed was the correct direction.

"Thank you, sir." Then she stormed off, hands on her hips, thoughts whirling. When she was only several steps away from him, she began to panic. She couldn't do this alone—she had never done or attempted anything like this!

Yes, she was pretending to, once again, be something she was not in the form of a serving woman for Blaine, but—but this was different! She was in possible danger, no matter how much she wanted to believe otherwise.

Saeran started to tremble, hands sweating.

Connor agreed with that much, or he would be coming with her. Saeran wrapped her arms around her chest, shoulders slumping. Aye, she couldn't do this, but she had made up her mind and would continue on with her decision, as best she could. She felt, deep in her soul, that Blaine was up to more than even Saeran suspected.

The voice that came from behind her moments later made her breathe a sigh of relief.

"Well, you can't be doing this alone now, can you?" Though he was mumbling to himself, she nodded emphatically.

"Aye, I couldn't. Does that mean you'll be helping me?"

"Only because the laird would have my head if he found out I let you do this without protection." They began walking together, Connor twining his arm through hers. To someone else, it would have looked odd. Two men, walking in the forest alone, arm in arm. Saeran didn't care in the least. His presence calmed her enough that she could walk properly.

"The laird does not care for Saeran all that much," she pointed out, remembering the way their eyes had met before he left. There had been conflict, confusion. Speculation. It brought a chill down her back, to think that he might be connecting the pieces. "Alice is a different story, though."

"Yes, which is exactly why I said he'll have my head—because eventually, he will discover who you really are, and, my sweet Saeran, I cannot wait until that day comes!"

"Well I feel terribly sad for you," she said, looking at the ground. "It will not happen."

"My lady—"

"Please," she said, suddenly sick to her stomach. "Can we not just finish our mission? No more talk of that, or of Kane."

He frowned at her. "What are you upset about, my lady?" When she didn't answer, he must have taken it upon himself to think of what could have her upset. He patted her shoulder, nodding knowingly when she looked at him.

"Jealousy is a terrible thing. Do not worry about the other women—"

"What are you talking about?" she asked. Other women? There were other women besides her, and she had not known? Her chest tightened.

"The laird—he was flippant about the brothels. I assumed you were jealous of his past in them. It's why you're upset, no?"

She stared at him, frown growing. "Upset? There is nothing to be upset about that. He is a man, Connor. Men love women in their beds. I might not be married, but I know that much. What he did in his past does not affect our future."

"'Our future'," he echoed. A grin split his lips. "Oh, Saeran, I do believe you are slipping in your effort to be covert."

"You read far too much into things," she growled, quickening her pace. His laughter followed behind her.

~

The grass was shifting in waves over the vast hills. Moonlight accented the journey of the wind as it caressed the green tips of the Highlands. The scene was surreal, cold, and yet welcoming at the same time. A soft, frigid wind blew pale blonde hair back from Saeran's now-clean face. She gripped her newly bought skirts in her hand, waiting in the blue light for her query to reveal himself.

Mayhap she had been late in arriving? Mayhap he had already come and gone? Saeran looked behind her, towards Connor. She could not see him in the shadows, but she knew he was there, waiting. That was the only comfort she allowed herself. She clutched the missive from Blaine in her hand.

It had taken her longer than she had thought to find a fitting dress—bought off of the inn owner's wife, for an unreasonably high price—fresh water to clean her face off with, and black wax to reseal the letter. It had taken so long, in fact, that she was once again wondering if she had missed him.

Mayhap it was for the better that she missed him. This was clearly a terrible idea—Connor had said so himself, and when had Connor ever been wrong? She shifted the weight of her feet, the missive crumpling in her fingers.

Aye, a terrible idea. Saeran resigned herself to a failed plan and, with a not-so-heavy heart, turned on her heels—that is, until a rustling of grass drew her attention to a dark figure just across from her.

"You are not Blaine," the voice whispered. She squinted, trying to see a face. Hidden in the shadows as he was, it was impossible. Saeran held out the missive, bidding him to come forward. Her hand was trembling. She prayed he didn't notice it.

"She sent me here with a letter for you," Saeran said, watching as a bent form came out of the shadows. Inch by inch, a man's face was revealed, and soon enough, his body followed suit. She almost ran screaming for the hills.

He was grotesque, like a demon. His face was pale, fat with skin, and splotched with red, brown, and grey. She retracted her hand slightly, fear settling in her gut. What could happen to a man to make him look so...

She couldn't finish the thought. Saeran felt horrible for her quick judgment of him, but nonetheless kept her space as he came forward. In his gnarled hands, there was a black, velvet sack. She watched him wearily.

"Let me see that," he demanded, his old man's voice weak. She deftly gave him the letter, mentally crossing herself when he met and held her eyes. They were grey, silvery—almost as if he were blind. This was the man Blaine loved?

The thought made her look at the ground. There was more going on than everything appeared.

She listened, watching him out of the corner of her eye, as he opened the paper. She watched as small crumbles of wax fell and bounced on the grass. She had no clue what to do in this situation— she was an imposter, in possible danger, and had no clue what to say to find out answers.

"'Condition has become critical'," he muttered. She jumped when he shot in front of her with much more speed than she would have thought he possessed. "What does this mean, her condition has become critical?"

"I—I am not sure," Saeran said, backing away from him. A ferocious light entered his eyes. "She has appeared healthy to all who have seen her. She just—I was told she could not make the trip, so she gave me the letter to give to you. I will take back any message you have for her, of course," she said soothingly, trying to placate him. With each word out of his mouth, he began to resemble a beast, an animal gone wild.

Thankfully, Connor had stayed out of sight. The man had yet to make a move toward Saeran with actual intent. Even if he did, she was sure she could handle him. He was half her size, and not in the best of shape.

"I—I—woman. Blaine. She should have come. What is wrong with her? What has her so sick that she cannot see her own—I need to speak with her, immediately. Immediately, immediately." He limped backwards, away from her, his own rambling voice trailing off into insanity. Her heart pounded. She couldn't let him go—she had to know what was going on, she had to have some answers!

"Nay!" she said forcefully, taking his arm. She cringed at the feel of pure skin over bone. Not a single ounce of meat graced his flesh. "She does not wish to see anyone."

"I am her—no! Take your hand off of me, I will see her for myself and I—" He stumbled backward, a sharp, airy bark leaving his mouth. She cursed, shooting forward to prevent him from falling. He struggled against her help, but the second he was righted, he seemed to calm. "I cannot make the journey, but I need to see my Blaine. I need to see my Blaine. In so long—so long I haven't. She was…Why didn't she come for me?" he croaked, taking hold of her hands and tightening his grip around them. The velvet sack he had been holding fell to the ground.

She tried to tug herself away from him. In the shadows, just beyond his head, she saw the outline of Connor coming forward. The flash of metal she saw told her he was prepared to defend her. Saeran quickly shook her head, the same time she managed to pull out of his grasp.

With soothing tones, she said, "Give me a message, and I will relay it to her for you. I will make sure she gets it. Alright? Please, sir.

Let me help you."

"Blaine…should be the one to help me."

"And she will," Saeran murmured, patting him on the shoulders. The same grey eyes met hers, though this time they were glazed, confused. It was almost as if he were staring through her, not at her. Saeran tried to keep her fear to a low. It would only send him into a panic if she did otherwise.

"You promise," he said sharply. "Promise to bring me Blaine."

"Yes," she lied. "I promise."

"Tell her—tell her she needs to see him. Him and his companion—and soon, but only after she sees me," he insisted, wild eyes staring up into hers. "She must come see me first. I need to see my Blaine. Need to—need to see her."

"Where and when does she need to meet them?" Saeran asked, trying to make him focus. He was so wrapped up in some inner turmoil that it appeared he did not notice her at all.

"*After me*," he rasped, throwing his hands in the air. The action sent his body balance, and he pitched forward. "After *meeee*."

His wail ended when she caught him, once again righting him. He jerked and growled in her grip, eyes unfocused, hands clenching and unclenching.

This was not what she had expected. At the same time, she was getting more out of it than she had originally thought she would. She pushed the guilt over the ordeal aside, telling herself that this had to happen, that she had to do this for her own good.

"Where and when?" she repeated, praying that she got the information out of him before he was completely lost to insanity. Drool slid out of the side of his mouth, thick and nearly yellow. Saeran backed away from him, shuddering.

There was something wrong with him, and she couldn't begin to think of what. She almost didn't want to.

"Here. Always here. My Blaine knows this—she has to be here in *two days*. Do you understand?" he gasped, gaping at her like a fish out of water. "She has to see *me first.*"

Saeran stared at him with wide eyes. He was honestly foaming at the mouth. His legs gave out, and she was too stunned to catch him for a third time. "Here, two days. Same time?" she asked, kneeling in front of him. He nodded, but it was more of a spasmodic jerking of his body, and his head was caught in the wave.

When his eyes closed and he fell silent, his chest moving with a steadiness that depicted sleep, she looked behind her. Connor was there, watching the man with the same horrified look she wore.

"Do we help him?" she whispered as Connor came up beside her. He was silent for a while.

"I…I am not entirely sure. How bad would we feel if we left him here?" he asked, squinting at the man.

Saeran sighed. "I do not think I would sleep properly."

"Fine. You take his hands, and I'll take his feet. We can take him back to the inn, and mayhap someone can show us where to put him."

"Aye," she said with another sigh, reaching for his hands. Connor picked up the forgotten black sack and tucked it away, then took the man's feet. Upon seeing the grey-yellow nails, she adjusted her hold and took his wrists. They were frail and when they lifted him, it felt as if he'd break.

Thankfully, the village was only a couple paces away. While Connor gingerly took him by the feet, she blessed the Lord that he had come with her. She didn't know what she would do without him.

Chapter Thirty-Two

"Oh, my lady! Tis so good to see you ag—what in all that is holy are you doing with Alan like that?" The inn keeper's wife, a stout old woman named Mabel, gaped at them with wide eyes as they carried the man into the inn. Luckily, it was late enough that all of the towns' people were asleep, so they did not have much to worry about. Even now, the inn was silent besides the crackling fire.

"He…" Connor and Saeran shared a look. How did they say, without looking suspicious, that he had begun foaming at the mouth and they were the only ones there? If she had seen what Mabel had, she would assumed they had tried to kill the man.

"Come, come," Mabel said, waving them into the inn. The fire was hot and warm, taking away the chill of outside almost immediately. She had them set him on a bench. When Saeran released his hands, they flopped to the ground. She quickly stepped away from him, his stench overwhelming her. The entire time she'd been carrying him, she had struggled not to vomit. He smelled…ghastly. "He hasn't died, has he?"

Saeran looked at his bumpy chest, saw the rise and fall, and shook her head.

"Oh, poor thing. We're all waiting for him to take his last breath. He's had a time of it, he has. Come, loves. Tis warmer by the fire." She took Saeran by the elbow, leading her to the hearth. Connor followed, tying the black sack to a loop in his shirt.

"What do you mean, he's had a time of it?" She could clearly see that he had, but the question came nonetheless. For a man to be so sickly that he foamed at the mouth, there had to be something wrong with him, and despite herself, she was curious.

"My lady, I am not so sure that he would appreciate the gossip."

Connor spoke up for the first time since they entered. "Blaine Sinclair sent Alice here to meet with him. While we were in the middle of our conversation, he did…that." He gestured to Alan.

"Blaine?" the woman repeated, eyes widening. Saeran watched her. She sounded as if she knew the name—specifically, the person. "Lady Blaine is such a joy to us. How is she?"

"What?" Connor looked like he couldn't believe his ears— Saeran understood completely. "A joy, you say? The woman is a horror. She—"

"Now, I know she has a rough side that takes some time getting used to, but she really is a sweet girl, so don't go slandering her like so. Alan would be devastated to hear you speak of his daughter like that."

"*What?*" Connor and Saeran gasped at the same time.

Mabel gave them both a look. She was a pretty, thick-boned woman, only a couple years older than Saeran herself, with brunette hair and just as brown eyes.

"She really is, though she hasn't come to see us in a couple days. I do miss her visits. We all understand, though. Her marriage to The Lion must be terrifying. She risks her life coming to see us, but she does, and we admire that of her. Have you heard from her recently? I know Alan was looking forward to seeing her."

Saeran looked at Connor, at a loss for words. What was she talking about? Surely they weren't speaking of the same Blaine, the one who had passive aggressively made Saeran's life a living hell. Surely they were not speaking of the same woman who had made it her point to bring Saeran into a spiraling pit of insecurity and pain?

It did not make sense. The way Mabel spoke of Blaine, it was like she was a saint!

"Is there another Blaine here?" Saeran asked, feeling numb.

"There is only one woman married to The Lion that is named Blaine, you silly girl. Nay, the Blaine I'm speaking of is a joy. Have you heard of Saeran?"

She nodded, her body feeling…empty. Confusion was running rampant, confusion and hurt. So Blaine really wasn't her sister. Saeran had helped drag Blaine's father—a living, breathing man—into the village. She stared at him, at the small drop of drool that was sliding down his chin.

There had to be some kind of explanation to this. Something that would make sense—but there wasn't, not one that she could see.

"Well, that's your proof of who we're talking about. Only Blaine would have someone as evil and atrocious as Saeran as a sister. I've heard that she has boils the size of a foot and eats children for breakfast."

Saeran slowly turned her eyes to meet Mabel's. They were offended on behalf of Blaine, and completely convinced of the falsehoods they had been told. Connor reached over, taking Saeran's arm. She hadn't realized she was reaching for the woman's throat before he took hold of her, stopping her.

She couldn't strangle the woman for believing a lie her sister had spread. Somehow, she had found time to visit the village, and through her father, gain the people's trust and loyalty—while lying to them the whole time. That was all there was to it, and the only thing she could see that would have happened.

Blaine did not have a nice bone in her body. Whatever motive she had to make these people like her was lost to Saeran, but she would find out.

"Where did you hear these rumors from?" Saeran asked, getting the words out through a clogged throat. She was so furious that her vision was turning red. How could Blaine have done that? How could she lie about Saeran, when all she had done was dote on Blaine? How could Blaine paint her as such an evil person to people who should not even matter to her?

"Why, from the laird's leman, Gwen. Blaine is quite grateful to her, despite how ironic it seems. The laird's wife and leman, getting along? Seems strange, but I guess Blaine is grateful for Gwen taking the laird's attention away from her. He's quite dangerous. Have you met him?"

Connor made a low sound from beside her. This time, she was the one stopping him from doing anything rash.

"Kane Shaw and Blaine Sinclair are not yet married," Saeran said, gently correcting the woman through her own confusion. Lord, but what had Gwen and Blaine done?

Mabel gave them a smile. It was full of pity and amusement. "Love, of course they are. Once the laird saw Blaine, he couldn't stop himself from taking her as his own. Tis what a brute of a man does, you know. We were all so afraid for her, our dear Blaine."

"I don't understand," Saeran whispered. The woman was speaking like she worshipped Blaine.

"What is there not to understand?" Mabel asked, cocking her head.

Saeran pushed herself to her feet, shaking her head. She couldn't take anymore of this. Bless Mabel, but she just couldn't sit there and listen to such lies. "I think I will retire for the night."

"Same for myself," Connor said, taking her arm and helping her to stand. Saeran leaned into him, too stunned to focus on holding herself up, and shared a look with him. He didn't have to say it, but she knew he was thinking the same thing she was: *what the hell was Blaine up to?*

Mabel stood, giving them a kind smile. "Have a good night, loves. My daughters will prepare baths for the both of you." Then she waddled off, ringing a bell by the hearth. The muted female voices in the other room were heard. Connor started to lead them to the stairs, but Saeran shook her head, tugging him to the door.

She didn't want Mabel's daughters to overhear them talking, and a fresh breath of air was much needed. The price of the dress she was wearing now had been costly, but it had come with two rooms for the night. Saeran would later pay the full cost of a room for herself, and Connor's if he wanted one, for however long they stayed here. She had lucked out when Mabel had offered to fit dresses to her size, with a discount if she booked two rooms.

"I'm sure you've been thinking this the whole entire time that woman spoke, but something is wrong," he hissed, running a hand through his hair. She leaned against the wall, closing her eyes. He continued. "How can anyone in their right mind even consider liking Blaine? No offense to you, my lady. But honestly! This does not make sense."

Nay, it didn't. And it wouldn't until she could either confront Blaine on the matter, or speak to the two men who Blaine was supposed to meet.

"…and to spread lies about you, no less!" he snapped, throwing his hands up. "If anyone eats children for breakfast, it's the dragon who spread the rumors herself. Lord, but I am furious." To accent his words, he stamped his foot on the ground.

"Do you have the sack that…that her father had? The black one?" She ignored his rambling. It would only make her furious, and she couldn't focus on her feelings. Blaine was planning something, and any clue they had would help her figure what it was.

Connor patted his waist.

"Let me see it, please."

He gave her a dubious look while untying the sack. "What do you think this has to do with anything?"

"What if he had planned to give it to Blaine?"

"Wouldn't he have given it to you?" he asked, handing it to her. "I picked it off the ground, he never handed it over or mentioned it."

She loosened the string.

"He was obviously upset that I wasn't Blaine, and not very coherent. I bet he forgot about it when he realized she wasn't there."

"That's likely, but what do you think that has to do anything?"

She bent her head toward the opened sack, meeting his eyes. "That's what I want to find out." She gave a small sniff, and almost gagged.

Connor took it away from her, doing the same.

He gagged as well. "What in the hell is this?" She held a hand over her nose, trying to forget the rancid, strong smell that had come from it, and touched the bottom. It was too dark for them to see the outline of the sack, and she wasn't prepared to stick her hand into the unknown of a smelly bag.

She clenched the bag in her hand, felt the shifting of cloth and the sound of something grainy. She met his eyes. He took another smell, this time prepared for it. He pulled back with a gasp of air, holding his stomach.

"Hemlock, mixed with something ghastly. I think I might vomit from the scent of it," he said, promptly bending over to do as he had predicted. Saeran turned away, closing her eyes. "Thank you for letting a man vomit in honor."

"Do not go sniffing that again," she said, reaching for the bag. He willingly gave it to her. "What is Hemlock?"

"Very effective poison. It's been ground up and mixed with something horrible. It's best to stay away from that sort of stuff."

"A poison? Why would he have a poison with him—and why would he give it to Blaine?"

"Don't ask me, my lady. I only know what Kane has told me about the plant, not why someone would use it. Though, if I had to guess, I would say Blaine asked her father to obtain some for her so she could kill someone without using any brute force."

Saeran's stomach began to hurt, and not from the stench of the ground hemlock mixture.

"But," he continued to say, rubbing a non-existent beard, "who would she be aiming to kill? From what I know of her stay at the keep, she has made no enemies."

Saeran gave him an arch look.

"What I mean, my lady," he said with a sigh, "is that people are so terrified of her that they generally stay clear of her wrathful dragon eyes. So yes, people may dislike her, but everyone is too terrified to become a friend, causing a betrayal of sorts, then turning her into an enemy. More like, she is angry at someone, and wishes to take care of them so they are no longer a problem. She seems the type to do that, though I can only speak from what I've seen." He coughed, whispering, "Dragon."

"Someone angered her," Saeran repeated, feeling like she was going to reenact Connor's previous dispelling of food. She was too shocked to believe it, but in her heart, she knew it was true. She knew her suspicions were growing, and they were all being pointed in the correct direction.

"Yes, most definitely, though I do not know how because like I said, everyone was too terrified of the dragon. The only person I can think of that has actually stood up to her is…"

She met his eyes, heart jumping to her throat. Tears burned her eyes, tears of frustration, shock, betrayal. She had known that staking a claim on Kane like she had in the hall would come with repercussions. She had known that Blaine would be furious.

Saeran hadn't cared if that hurt her sister. She had felt justified in her actions for all of the times Blaine had put her down and insulted her. She had felt justified in taking Kane from Blaine, when Blaine had taken everything from her.

Now, Blaine was going to make her pay for it.

"Me. I was the one who angered her."

Connor stared at her, the realization dawning just as suddenly as it had on her.

The first tear slid down her cheek, just as the light of the moon cast a shadow when its glare was disturbed. The shadow was in the shape of a man.

"Alice?" Kane asked from behind her.

Chapter Thirty-Three

If anyone could melt on the floor and slip into the cracks, Saeran would gladly sell her soul for that ability. She could not believe what was happening, nor could she escape it. The fact of the matter was, Kane had found her—and she was in the middle of crying.

She stiffened, meeting Connor's eyes. He refused to meet hers.

"Alice," he said again, this time his voice contrite. He turned her around with a hand to his shoulder when she refused to move from her spot. This could not be happening—simply could not be happening.

When she faced him, though, it all became a reality. For whatever reason, he had noticed her—and once again, she had been dumb enough to not change into the garb of a boy. The tears worsened, no matter how hard she tried to stem them.

Kane was here. She had no business crying or appearing weak in front of him. Saeran quickly wiped her eyes, grateful for the darkness. Mayhap he wouldn't see the streams of tears going down her cheeks.

By the angry darkening of his eyes, she knew the ruse was up. He knew she was crying, without her saying a word. He took her hand, pulling her against his chest.

"So help me, Connor, if you..."

"Kane," she said sharply. Her voice was hoarse, low.

Connor backed away from the two of them, casting glances behind her. She became aware of the other men—men she had traveled with, trained with, and gotten beat up by. Saeran looked away from them. Kane might not notice who she was because of his infatuation, but the others…she was not so sure.

"Why were ye' crying, lass? What did he do?" Then a fierce glare settled over his face, and he narrowed his eyes not on Connor, but on her. "You should be home."

"This is her home," Connor said quickly. Saeran tensed.

"Nay, her home is on Shaw lands. Why are you here? This is MacLeod land," he growled. "It's dangerous here. Ye' ken that from the attack."

"Aye." When was Connor going to say something? He was the one who had lied first! Saeran wrung her hands, feeling the heat from inside of her wipe out the chill of the air. This was not good. She shouldn't have stepped outside. Lord, how could she be so foolish!

"Alice," Kane bit out. "Do ye' no' have a brain? Did ye' follow me here?"

"No," Connor said, glaring at him. He reached forward, taking Saeran's hand. "If you must know, Alice is my older sister."

Kane stared at him. Connor tugged her forward, removing her from Kane's arms. "And if you please," he said shortly, "I would appreciate it if you would keep your hands off of her. She is an innocent in this."

"But you donna live here. You live—"

"Father sent her away. There were too many brothers. She came to live with our aunt, Mabel."

"No, she lives—"

"She moved. Before we left, I sent for her to meet me here. Father asked me to tell her. I put it off, since she seemed so happy. The time came for her to leave. There is, of course, no problem with this as she is my sister and my responsibility." Connor gave her a confident smile, but all she could do was stare and think. He was lying for her. When she had first met him, he had been adamant about his loyalty to Kane. What had changed? Did Kane notice his squire's deception?

The hard look on his face told her no. He was too concerned with the fact that she now "lived" on MacLeod lands. "When did you find out?"

Connor, like the dutiful brother he was posing as, filled in for her. "This morning."

Saeran flinched.

"This morning, she was with me."

"Kane—"

"Nay, Alice," he said, cutting her off. She felt like she was being trampled by a stampede of horses, with no way of standing up. Connor had gotten her into this story so quickly that she had no time to prepare the rest of the lie. She had always been a terrible liar. Now, lying to him even more than she already was, had guilt eating her alive. "I want to hear this from yer brother."

He did not sound happy.

~

Why hadn't the two of them said anything to him about their relation? He never would have...Kane grunted. She had said she was visiting someone, but not who. Even after relentless inquiries, he hadn't found out. Now he was left wondering why.

"There is nothing to hear. I was seeing her off to bed, after a tiring travel with Mabel."

"There is no' Mabel on my lands."

"There is. She arrived only moments before we left. My laird, I am sorry, but Alice is exhausted, as you can see."

Aye, he could see. Her eyes were sunken in, face drawn, pale, and nearly sickly looking. Her golden hair was as lifeless as her eyes. His heart clenched. What had happened to her?

"I want to know why she was crying before ye' go."

"Kane," she said softly. He'd never had a woman's voice bring him to his knees, but the weakness there very nearly did. She lacked the normal fire she possessed. What had happened to douse it?

He stepped forward, ready to wring Connor's throat for letting his sister come to such distress, but Brodrick was there, holding him back.

"Yer not like this," his friend said quietly. Brodrick gave an odd, inquisitive look over Alice. Then a look passed over his face, as if he had just realized something. Understanding lit his eyes. "Let the lady leave. She must be most tired from her journey."

"If yer wife were crying, would ye' no' demand to ken why?" he asked, pushing Brodrick away.

"Alice is most definitely not your wife," Brodrick said. Connor nudged Alice toward the entrance of the inn. She went willingly, though he assumed it was more because of her weakness that she could not fight back. She held his eyes, unrecognizable emotion flowing through the crystalline depths.

Kane watched her go, jaw ticking. No better way to put him in his place than to point out what wasn't his. *Nay*, he thought, seeing red. Alice was his—and for whatever reason, she had been crying.

The door closed softly. He wanted to shove everyone aside and go after her. He would. If it was the last thing he did, he'd find out which room she was in and comfort her. No woman, including one as kind and beautiful as Alice, should cry.

It reminded him all too sharply of his sister's tears the night she was sent to Hans Grayham. A cold feeling went down his back at the thought. Just like Alice, his sister had been weak, emotionally destroyed. Nay, a woman should not be allowed to cry if someone can help it.

"Kane," Brodrick said lowly. "We must go. Connor, are you coming along?"

Connor's eyes flickered to a room. One of the open rooms flickered to life as a fire was set. The moving shadows and flickers of light showed them the outline of a slender woman as she moved to the window. The curtains snapped closed.

Alice was there. She was there, and he would return to her.

Jaw clenched, he allowed his men to lead him away in silence. Later, well into the night, he would return for her. Alice would not be settling for rest with a heavy heart. He would clear the weight of whatever was causing her tears, and find out everything that had transpired without him knowing.

Starting with her relation to Connor, why she had kept it a secret, and the real reason she had moved here. It was true that Connor's father had once been a mighty Highlander, who preferred the Lowlands to escape the nagging of his wife. Alice had spoken of that, so he should have connected it.

I am blinded by her, he thought angrily, storming into the pub. The door slammed open on his arrival, and dead silence filled the room. He was too concerned with her welfare, happiness, and bedding her to think of the more important things, like examining the facts that were right in front of him.

Nay, from now on—after he soothed her aching heart—he would pay closer attention to details. He liked the lass, he really did. Did no' a man who cared for a woman pay attention to everything he could about her? Women had tender hearts—mayhap his lack of noticing the things he should have made her upset.

Kane looked over his shoulder, at the closed curtains. Mayhap she was upset because of him. The thought was horrifying enough to make him sick to the stomach. For that reason alone, he didn't enjoy a single frightened whisper as he stalked through the pub like he had death on his shoulders. Perhaps he did. He was angry with himself enough to kill, and God help any man dumb enough to approach him now.

~

Saeran collapsed into the bed, naked and dripping from her bath. She huddled under the thick blankets covering the bed. She was too weak, mentally and physically, to do anything for herself. She wanted to sleep and never wake up.

That would cure all of her problems. All of them. No more Blaine, no more potentially dying, no more lying to Kane, no more fearing for her life… There would be nothing if she simply went to sleep, and never woke up.

It was an easy solution, but she knew she could never go through with it. Nay, perhaps leaving would be the best choice. Leaving and living on her own, in the Lowlands. She had pretended this long to be a boy, so couldn't she continue to do so to protect herself? Mayhap that would be easier. But why, then, did the thought of no longer seeing Kane make her chest ache, her stomach clench, and her hands sweat? It was terrifying, thinking of herself without him. Hearing his deep chuckle whenever she did something amusing, hearing his grunts or growls.

Learning about him.

That, she feared, would hurt her the most. Saeran was a learner—she loved to absorb knowledge, and always had. Kane was like a book to her. A very enticing, intriguing, unexpected book. Every page to Kane was a twist, something she had not expected of him.

His tenderness…kindness…the need he felt to protect. It was overwhelming to see a book that large, but Saeran had always loved the thicker ones, and Kane was…perfect. She smiled a watery smile, and her eyes followed the white outline of the fire as it flickered in the hearth. Nay, no man was perfect—but he was pretty close.

She did not know a single man who would have shown her the honor he had with her so far, despite how he had taken her maidenhood. That hadn't been his fault though; he had assumed she was an experienced woman, and she had done nothing to show him otherwise. What had happened, had for her, in a way, been fate. They were close, happy, and she was learning more than she had ever thought possible from him.

Or she had been, until today. He hadn't looked one bit happy to see her, and the more Connor spoke, the more furious he'd grown. Kane had thought that Saeran and "Alice" had a thing—had he assumed that upon seeing her and Connor together?

She rolled over, bundling herself in the bed. The blankets were becoming damp from her hair and body, but she didn't care. There was a whole other side waiting for her. She stared at it, wondering if Kane would think of coming back for her tonight. He would fill the bed with his size, but she would be comfortable in his arms. She did not think he would come, as sad as that made her. If their roles had been reversed, she would not have left him alone if she stumbled upon him in tears.

The thought was laughable and painful at the same time. Kane would no more cry than she would run through a fire, blazing and naked, to save Blaine. Kane, though, was a man—a man who had apparent issues with tying himself to a woman. It had taken him more than a full moon to propose to Blaine, even knowing that he would not marry her, and with the added stress of Alice in his life... She understood full well that a man needed space, and also understood that a man like Kane, so rough and brutish and head-strong, would not know what to do in the face of a weeping woman.

That was all right, of course. Every man was entitled to his feelings—or lack thereof.

Blaine had told her all of her life that she wasn't worth much. She had told Saeran that she didn't need comfort, that wallowing in her own sorrows when someone else's problems, like Blaine's, were much worse, was horrible and selfish.

"Our parents would be ashamed if they knew you were like this," Blaine would say. Gradually, Saeran had learned to rely on no one but herself. Keep the complaints to her pillow, and turned a blind eye when something began to bother her.

Now, thinking back, she realized that she had let "her sister" destroy her confidence. She had let "her sister" turn her into a slave. She had let her sister abuse her kindness.

There was no one to blame but Saeran for that, and she knew it. Grief and shame had made her weak. She had lived with the consequences, as she deserved to, for allowing Blaine to ruin her life. It was God's way of punishing her, perhaps.

Saeran didn't know. All she knew was that things were changing—for the worse.

Blaine wanted to kill her, Kane was angry with her, Connor had lied for her…and there was something else. Something she had suspected, but now felt with a certainty in her gut.

Knock knock.

The pounding on the door jolted her into action. Heart pounding, she pulled a shift over her head with trembling hands. The knocking was furious and loud, enough to hurt her ears. Kane—Kane was there, and he was furious.

She practically ran to the door, excited yet terrified to see him. Saeran yanked it open and—

"I knew it."

The man standing at the door was not Kane.

Chapter Thirty-Four

Saeran stared into pale green eyes, heart dropping to her stomach. This was not good. She had felt it, but now it was confirmed and she—she was going to faint from the pounding of her heart.

He didn't wait for her to invite him in. She wouldn't have anyways. He pushed past her, took one look at the clothes that were strewn across the floor, and rounded on her with a glare so furious and heart-stopping, she actually felt the fury coming off of him.

"I knew it. I knew ye' were no' just a normal lad. *Why*, Saeran? Why would ye' lie to everyone like that?"

Brodrick slashed a hand through the air angrily. She had never been afraid of him, except for the first time she'd seen him. Saeran was reminded that he wasn't a kind, rough-around-the-edges man. He was a killer, plain and simple. He could play at being amiable, but once it came to the life of his laird, he was deadly.

She swallowed, backing away from him.

"Brodrick—"

"I canna believe I did no' notice it before. I suspected, but—why? I should kill ye' were ye' stand—"

She flinched, reaching for something, anything to defend herself with. She never would have thought that Brodrick would figure it out. She had not prepared herself for this. Saeran had thought Connor was the only one to worry about, but she had been wrong, so foolishly wrong.

"Yer a threat to Kane. To Connor. To everyone—and yer just going to let them put their lives on the line for ye'. Yer disgusting,

Saeran. Disgusting. Kane was beginning to trust ye'—both of yer personalities—and then my worst fears are proved correct. Was this a game?" he demanded. "I donna play games. Neither does Kane. Once he finds out—"

"No," she said sharply, a thick feeling of déjà vu going through her. "No, he cannot know. Brodrick, I swear to you, I am not a threat. He cannot know, not yet." *Not until she was long gone, with no chance of him finding her.*

"Ye' think I'm going to believe a liar like you? I'm disgusted. I thought better of ye' than this." She could see it in his eyes. He was honestly disgusted by her lies, by everything about her. She let out a sharp breath, turning her head away from him. She only saw what she felt reflected in his eyes.

She felt the sting of tears.

"I'm not trying to harm anyone, Brodrick. Please, listen to me. Do you really think Connor would lie to Kane for no reason?"

"If Connor can lie to Kane at all—"

"Damnit, Brodrick," she snapped, a well bursting inside of her. She was tired of all the anger and suspicion. "For once, I would like someone to understand that I'm only trying to protect myself. Connor gave me hell for this. You know him better than I do. He wouldn't lie without reason, and I wouldn't hurt Kane."

He stared at her.

The fire crackled in the dim room, causing dark shadows to move over his face. She stood there, refusing to back down.

"Blaine did this to ye', didn't she?" he finally asked.

That was not what she was expecting to hear. Thinking that it was some sort of trick, she nodded her head. Her best bet was to be completely honest with him.

"The king sent the two of us here for Kane's hand."

"I know this, lass. But I donna understand why you would consent to…that." He gestured to the limp pair of trews on the floor. She crossed her arms over her chest, face flaming. "Ye did no' have to hide from Kane, ye ken."

"If I hadn't, I would be with Hans Grayham right now," she said, meeting him square in the eye. "Blaine was positive that my only choice was to die with Kane or die with Grayham—I chose neither."

"So ye' pretended to be a lad." He frowned, some of the threatening aura disappearing. "Did ye' ken about the dowry?"

Saeran nodded. "I found out the night before."

"Do ye' ken his plan?"

"To make Blaine hate him by the time his family arrives, so that she will break the engagement? Aye."

"Do ye' ken how much the man cares for ye'?"

"Ay—excuse me?"

"Saeran," he said with sigh. "Yer as blind as a bat if ye' canna see that revealing yerself to him is what's best for both of ye'."

"Nay," she insisted. "Brodrick, I must implore you to keep this silent. I've come this far, I can last a little longer." Until she figured out what to do with herself.

"Ye' canna ask me to—my god," he said, glaring at her. "Why did you no' say something before? I put ye' through training. Ye've had to see men's—" He stopped, taking a step backwards, horror entering his eyes. "If my wife found out about this, she would kill me."

She had known Brodrick was weary of his wife, but now she knew the full extent. There was real terror overcoming him when she looked at him.

"I—Saeran, my God, I've ruined ye'."

Funny, Kane had said the same exact thing.

"Brodrick—"

"Nay," he said, shaking his head. He turned his back on her, rigid to the point of looking like a statue. "I came here with the intent of forcing you to tell him, but now—I must go."

"What?" That was it? He was just going to show up, tell her that he knew who she was, then leave? No threats? No forcing? Nothing? Connor had been more adamant than Brodrick was, and Brodrick was Kane's closest friend. He should have been more furious than Connor had been at her deception!

"I—I think I'm going to be sick. Ye' poor lass, I just—my God, Saeran. My God." Then he left, leaving the room as quickly as he had come into it.

She stared after him, wondering what in all that was Holy had just happened.

~

Kane looked around and decided that now was the time to leave. Brodrick had disappeared to God knows where, and that meant he was free to leave without a problem. He would get to the bottom of Alice's pain, and then kill anyone or anything that had caused it.

Aye, killing the problem cured it.

265

He shoved away from the table, threw his payment for the lone ale he'd had on the table, and practically ran to the door. Alice had been left alone for far too long. He would be amazed if she did not hate him for his negligence. He frowned as the cold air blew his hair away from his face. Alice was not a hateful person. She would be upset with him, but her heart was too kind to hold hate.

"Kane." He nearly groaned at the sound of Brodrick's voice from behind him. The one man he did not want to see. Of course. "Kane, ye' canna go."

"How do ye' ken where I'm going?" he asked, raising a brow—then he got a good look at Brodrick. His face was as pale as the moon and his eyes…he looked like he'd seen a ghost. Kane took him by the elbow, drawing him to the side of the pub. "What the hell happened to ye'?"

"I—Kane. Donna go to Alice." He shook his head, avoiding Kane's eyes completely. "She is—"

"Is she hurt?" he demanded, feeling fear rise inside of him. He had known better than to leave her alone. He had known. Shame and fury attacked him like a wolf, digging sharp, angry teeth into his heart and pulling. Alice was too gentle. Too sweet. She should never have been left alone in her misery. He was so furious with himself that he did not think to ask Brodrick how he knew something was wrong with Alice.

"Kane, listen to me. Alice is no'—"

He shot off toward the inn before Brodrick could finish. Time spent talking to Brodrick meant time that Alice could be hurt. Feeling like he was choking for breath by the time he reached the inn, he threw open the doors, racing up the stairs.

She had been in the room with the lone window on the east side of the building. His feet thundered over the wood as he stormed through the hallway. There was a soft sound from inside of the room he suspected was hers, and then a cough and a thump. It was dainty and sweet—completely Alice. With a growl, hating himself more than he ever had before, Kane wasted no time in knocking or waiting for her to answer. He shoved the door open, then froze. Stared. Felt as if his heart had fallen to his stomach.

The delicate figure was bent over the edge of the bed, blonde mop of hair spread over tangled blankets. He surged forward, instinct the only driving force through his fear. There was something wrong with her. No normal person sat like that.

Kane didn't breathe until he had her in his arms.

"Alice," he said raggedly, smoothing back her hair with a trembling hand. "Alice, damnit. What happened? Why are ye'—"

"Wait a moment." The muffled voice was accompanied with a shove to his shoulder. Stupefied, he let her crawl out of his arms so she could resume her position on the floor.

"What are ye' doing?" he said, dazed as he watched her. She did no' move like she was upset, nor had she sounded like it. He recalled the thumping sound. "Did someone attack ye'?"

If someone did, he wouldn't mind taking his confusion out on them by slicing their heads off. His hopes fell when she shook her head, back still turned to him.

"I was trying to walk," she said with a grunt, her voice muffled from her face being pressed into the edge of the bed. He realized that her hands were moving underneath it, searching for something. He frowned. "And I slipped on the corner of a blanket. Then this," she said, pulling out a cup from under the bed triumphantly, "rolled right on under it."

"Ye' were trying to retrieve a cup," he said drolly.

"Aye." Wide, confused eyes lifted to his. "I could not just leave it there. Then Mabel would be missing one! Why, what did you think was wrong?"

"I…" He narrowed his eyes on her, having a hard time coming to terms with the fact that there was no attacker he could kill. "Brodrick came to me."

She stiffened. Like that, all of the innocence and confusion dropped out of her face.

"He did no' say what was wrong, but I figured ye' were hurt. Then I heard the thump, thought you were being attacked…wait. So ye' really just lost yer cup under the bed? There is no one here. At all."

Alice shook her head.

"Is that the only reason why you're here?" she asked, a note tinging her voice that he couldn't stand to hear. He knew she tried so hard to hide her disappointment, but Alice was an open book. The hurt was in her eyes.

Kane reached for her hand. She immediately twined her slender fingers with his, allowing him to pull her to her feet. He sat on the bed, gently tugging at her until she was sitting on his lap, his arms around her waist.

"Nay, lass. I was worried about ye'."

A flush came over her cheeks. *That's what she had wanted to hear,* he thought, smiling. She liked to know that someone was thinking about her. Kane was definitely thinking about her—hell, she was the only thing in his mind as of late! Not even the MacLeods were thought of as much as she was, and to a normal man, they were more pressing an issue than a woman was.

But Alice was not just a woman. She was his woman, and as his woman, she deserved all of the thoughts and attention he had—which was why he wanted to know why she had been in such distress when he'd first come upon her.

"Ye' were crying earlier. I demand to know why."

The shy pleasure on her face turned into dubiousness. "You demand?"

"Aye," he said firmly, taking a stray strand of her hair and tucking it behind her ear. "I donna want ye' to cry again. If I can stop it, I will."

The shy pleasure returned. His heart warmed when she leaned into his touch, like a kitten preening under the caress of her master. "It's nothing," she said lightly, kissing his palm. The action was so surprising that he couldn't stop himself from pulling her closer against him. Kane buried his face in her hair, breathing her in.

He had thought that he would not be seeing her for weeks, months. To be holding her in his arms right now felt like finding an angel in hell.

"It's no' nothing, love. Ye' can tell me. I'll always listen to ye'."

"I…" Indecision warred on her delicate features. As she struggled to speak, he gave her the time she needed while rubbing the creases out of her brows, trying to sooth her aches as best he could when all he wanted was to make her speak. Kane had never been a patient man. Aye, he could play at it for the sake of his clan and his status as chieftain, but the truth of the matter was, he liked things to happen the second they came up—like finding out what had distressed his Alice.

"The move—it was so sudden, and I do not entirely understand it. When Connor sent for me, I did not know this was what he planned."

"I just wish ye' would have said something." His heart physically hurt to think that she could have been harmed on her journey, when she could have easily traveled with him. Connor had known of it.

Why hadn't he said anything to him? Kane growled low in his throat. He would beat Connor into the ground for his carelessness over Alice the next time he saw him.

"Our destination was kept from me until we arrived," she said quietly. He felt her turmoil in the trembling of her body. Kane moved them farther onto the bed, keeping her tight against him, until he was leaning against the headboard with Alice's cheek pressed against his chest.

"I'm sorry, love," he said, and truly, he was. "I ken how it feels to be taken out of yer home and thrust into something different."

She tilted her head up, meeting his eyes. There was such sadness in them, such desolation. He had a feeling that it went deeper than what she had gone through today.

"When my father died, the McGregor took me away from Shaw land. I had to stay in the barracks with his men and learn what it took to be a leader. It was different from the coddling I was used to," he said quietly, tensing when her soft lips brushed against his neck. His hand tightened on her hip.

"I've had a lot of changes recently as well," she murmured. "It's hard. One moment, everything is going perfectly and you have a nice, warm, loving family—and then it's all ripped away from you and you're left wondering 'why'."

Kane tangled his hand in her hair, hating to see the sadness there. She was filled to the brim with it, and he hated himself for only now noticing it. She had entranced him with her beauty and fire, but he hadn't bothered to see the darker things lurking beneath the surface. Now, he couldn't stop himself from seeing it, and all he wanted to do was soothe her.

So he did.

With his hand in her hair, he tilted her head up, leaning down.

His lips covered hers with a groan. When her hands slid up his chest with feather light touches, he knew he had done the right thing. This time, when he took his Alice, it would not be out of anger—but out of the tenderness he felt for her.

She pulled away from the kiss way too soon. Her eyes were lowered, a blush on her cheeks.

"What's wrong, love?"

"I…you do enjoy my kissing, correct?"

The question was so out of the blue that he couldn't stop the laughter that burst from him—until he realized she was serious and

269

looked like she was humiliated. He sobered, taking her face in his hands, and smoothed his thumbs over her warm cheeks.

"I've never enjoyed a kiss as much as I do yers, lass."

"Are you sure?"

He answered her by taking her lips in a hot, passionate kiss. When he was done with her, she would have no doubt in her mind that he enjoyed everything about her.

Chapter Thirty-Five

He undressed her slowly, taking his time with every inch of her body. All she was wearing was a long shift, and when he began pulling it up her body, revealing her skin, he kissed her bare flesh, loving it with his mouth and teeth. Saeran shivered, one hand threading into his hair, the other grasping the bed.

She didn't want him to stop, and he didn't. With painstaking slowness, he finally dragged the shift above her head, throwing it to the side. She laid there in the hot room, breast bared, legs parted around his knees. He knelt in front of her, running his eyes over her. Like fingers made with fire, she felt every glance as if he were caressing her with burning touches, imprinting himself onto her skin, and stealing all of her thoughts for himself.

"God, lass. I've never seen ye' look so enticing as ye' do now." She shivered at the growl in his voice, closing her eyes when he leaned down. His body was braced above hers, his face so close she could feel his breath on her neck. "Yer legs open... Cheeks flushed..." He nuzzled her breast, blowing hot air over the pink tip. "Hard nipples...wet cunt..." Every time he growled a word, he would touch the part he was talking of.

He wasted no time in touching the latest body part. Saeran cried out, shocked from the quick intrusion, as his fingers slammed inside of her. It didn't hurt, as she would have thought—Nay, it felt amazing. Kane slowly worked his fingers inside of her, swirling his thumb over her clit.

"I want to taste ye, love." The sensation of his stubbled jaw against her breast ceased. She opened her eyes in time to see him sliding down her body, his hand and mouth touching every part of her that they could on their descent, until he was taking his fingers from inside of her and holding her thighs open.

"Nay," she cried out, despite the need she felt for him thrumming through her. He scowled at her. "I want…I want you naked as well, Kane. I want…Want to touch you, as you touch me."

His eyes darkened—but not with anger. Desire unlike anything she had ever seen came over his face, and before she could ask him again, he was pulling away from her, shucking everything off his body until he was as bare as she was.

Saeran couldn't help but stare at him. This was her man, standing before her. Despite the claim that she couldn't rationalize or verbalize, Kane was her man, and he was…glorious. His body was perfect, the scars and healing wounds creating a story too painful to believe. The tenderness running through his body was at odds with how strong he was. He was pure masculinity, and his length was proof of that. She crawled onto her knees, taking his member into her hand.

She met his eyes. They were dark and swirling with passion, and it spread across his entire face. It was amazing, the way he reacted to her. Saeran shivered, biting her lip, unsure.

She wanted to taste him, as well, but she did not know how to ask.

The gentle hand smoothing over her head told her that he knew without asking, and her heart pounded with love for this man. He understood her when she couldn't speak, cared for her as no one else had before, and she felt…connected.

Saeran shouldn't be encouraging this, but she knew that she would never find the strength to deny him, not when she craved him so much.

"Move back, love," he commanded. She did as he said, trembling. He laid down beside her, then took her by the hips. Her eyes widened when he moved her.

"Kane, this is—"

"Yer not going to hide yerself from me, are ye', lass?" he growled playfully, biting the inside of her thigh. He had pulled her legs over both sides of his head so that she was straddling him, and she was holding herself up with her hands on his thighs. "I told ye' last time. I donna like that."

"Aye."

He nuzzled the inside of her thigh, groaning, "Damn," then attacked her core with his lips, tongue, and fingers. He pushed two fingers inside of her, taking her clit between his lips and sucking. His tongue licked at her, wringing a cry of shocked pleasure from her lips, and she jerked, her upper body strength giving out.

She caught herself against his legs, shuddering, rocking against his face.

He sucked harder, moved his fingers faster, even added another one, until she was crying out.

Saeran could have sobbed from the pleasure, the sensation of the man she was coming to love making her feel a way she had never felt before. Though they were not face-to-face, she felt closer to him, drawn to him. Nothing in the world could make her regret this, regret him. Kane was perfection. He was her perfection. He was the prayer she had been searching for her whole life.

Fire wrapped around them, binding them together. The connection went deeper than the physical pleasure—it warped her mind, destroyed any resistance she would have had to him. It made her realize that Kane *was* hers, and always would be, no matter what anyone said.

Then, all too soon, she felt the first stirrings of release. He moved his fingers and mouth in a rhythm that drove her to near completion. He tongued her clit hard.

The binding of fire became hot enough to scorch her to her very soul, but before it could completely burn her, he stopped. Stopped and moved her by her hips. Just like that, they were face-to-face, Kane rolling her underneath him, his leg holding hers open.

She shuddered, already feeling the pleasure she knew she would. He leaned forward, taking her nipple into his mouth, then slammed home.

Saeran screamed at the burst of ecstasy that rushed through her, the orgasm never ending as he moved inside of her without mercy. The lovemaking was rough and soul-consuming. There was no breath left in her body that wasn't crying out Kane's name, and that was exactly how it should be.

His lips moved from her breast to her neck, only pausing to give her a breath. She could only shudder in his arms, begging him with her eyes to continue. She would have demanded he did, but the only thing that came from her was, "Kane, Kane, Kane." The reverent chant darkened his eyes until they were dark as night.

Her release finally ended, but Kane wasn't done.

"I'm not letting ye' go until yer screaming my name again," he said, his voice a dark promise in the heated room. "Screaming my name and begging me for more until ye' canna speak."

Saeran turned her head on the bed, shaking it at him.

"Nay, Kane, I cannot handle—" He pulled his hips back, then slowly pushed inside of her. She moaned, unable to finish her sentence. It shouldn't have felt as good as it did with her body coming down from the orgasm, but it did. It felt so good that when he did it again, this time pulling her legs up so he could go further inside of her, tears sprang to her eyes.

He stopped moving.

"Love. Love, why are you crying?" A shaking hand reached to clear away the tear that had fallen. She caught his hand, holding it to her cheek. There was a silence so deafening that it rang in her ears, but she couldn't speak for the life of her.

Kane kissed her. Softly, slowly. Stealing the words right out of her mouth. She was grateful to that, for if he hadn't, she would have admitted her own feelings for him right then and there.

I love you.

The words did not need to be said. The kiss was proof enough. She poured her whole entire soul into that single kiss, begging him to understand, and…he did.

Kane began to slowly thrust himself inside of her, holding her jaw with one hand and continuing their kiss. It was as if he refused to let her go, that by ending the kiss, he would end her, himself, everything. She gasped against his lips as need overcame every sense she had. Saeran wrapped her arms around his neck, hooking her leg around his calf.

"Don't stop," she whimpered against his lips, moaning when he slid his tongue into her mouth immediately after. He tasted like masculinity, like *Kane*. It drove her insane.

"Never," he grated.

And that was that.

Their passion rose like a wave between them, ripping her apart, shattering her into a thousand pieces. The orgasm destroyed her, tore her heart and soul out, and when Kane tenderly took her into his arms, the pieces all came back together. He was there for her, holding her through the shuddering and weeping as his own release wracked him.

He poured himself inside of her, hot jets causing his cock to jerk. It was enough to send her body into oblivion as the final wave to the orgasm hit her like stampede.

But he was still there, grounding her, holding her as if she were glass. Saeran curled herself into his arms, trying to stem the sobs that were ripping from her chest, yet unable to find any control over herself.

"Love," he whispered, tenderly running his hands through her hair.

"Kane," she sobbed. "Kane, it's…it's too much for me. Too much."

"Nay, love. Yer just not used to me loving ye', but it's alright. Ye will be soon."

Saeran didn't have any words to say back to him. Her throat closed up as overwhelming love for him surged through her. He was always understanding, always one step ahead of her.

She closed her eyes, thanking the Lord that he had found her and chosen her. He did not have to say it—she knew without a doubt in her mind that he had chosen her.

He'd chosen her as *his*, and she was going to *stay* his.

Chapter Thirty-Six

"Las—lad, here. Step here." Brodrick didn't give her the time to take the step for herself, instead lifting her by her forearms and setting her over the branch. She pressed her lips, giving him a furious glare.

She never would have thought the big, burly, red-haired man would be this concerned about her. Honestly, she couldn't take a breath without him telling her to hold on, or to move away from the fire. It was becoming ridiculously annoying, and she was at her wit's end.

It was midday, and they had been riding for half the amount of time it had taken her and Kane to part. It had been hard for her, but harder for him. She blushed, turning away from Brodrick without a word. She couldn't speak amidst her heated thoughts.

Their morning had been much like the last one they had had together. No matter how much she insisted that he leave, knowing his men were probably growing anxious, he had refused and driven her to the brink of destruction thousands of time. It wasn't until she was begging for him, much like he had the night before, that he let her reach completion.

"Brodrick," Kane snapped, drawing her attention. "The lad can walk alone, ye' ken. There's no need to treat him like a lass."

The irony was not lost on her—nor Connor. While Brodrick gave her a scathing glare, a look that clearly said he wanted to throttle her, Connor struggled to keep his laughter to a minimum.

The whole ordeal was embarrassing.

She could be riding atop her horse, but Brodrick had made a commotion about her mounting. To save herself the embarrassment of Kane giving them glares, she had decided to walk. Had it slowed them down? Aye. Had it made Kane angry? Aye. Had it made Brodrick leave her be at all? Nay. She would have been better off going through with the embarrassment of Brodrick fussing over her like a mother hen, but pride kept her walking.

"Would ye' just let me put you on the damn horse," Brodrick growled furiously, grabbing her again when she would have stepped over a sharp rock. She shoved him away.

"Would you just go back to acting as if ye'd never found out?" she demanded. Connor had become aware that Brodrick knew shortly after Saeran had joined the warriors. Now, as more and more men cast her glances, some with realization and others with suspicion, she began to come to terms with the fact that mayhap her secret was not such a damn secret—and she had Brodrick to thank for that.

The only time a warrior worried over a person was when that person was a woman—Lord, rarely then, either!

She only prayed that the men that became suspicious or knowing kept their mouths sealed shut. No one made any move to say anything to Kane. For some reason, it infuriated her and made her grateful at the same time.

Furious because the men did not respect their laird well enough to speak their concerns, and grateful that they were silent.

Fergus, one of the men at the front of the line, glanced back at her. His face was fierce, the threat there certain. If she turned out to be a threat, he wouldn't hesitate to end her.

Brodrick was the only reason they were not saying anything to Kane.

For that, her glare towards the mother hen lessened, but it did not completely wipe away her annoyance with him. What was the use of anyone staying quiet and risking Kane's wrath? When they were all making it completely obvious that she was an odd ball?

"I've half a mind to tell him," Brodrick grumbled, though he quickly reached for her when she would have ran into a low-hanging branch. With a huff, she ducked under it—then snorted when Connor met the fate of the branch and stumbled back.

"Sure you do," she hissed, hiking up her pants. It had rained early this morning. It had been short and hard, just enough to make the ground sloppy and the horses slow.

Kane was an insane man who didn't understand the risks of ever-changing weather. This was what he had wanted—the MacLeods too preoccupied with tending to their lands from the fast and furious storm to be prepared to fight. It was a smart idea, but it also put the Shaw warriors at risk as well.

"Oh, believe you me, las—"

"Quiet," Kane snapped. She breathed a sigh of relief, for Brodrick had been just about to slip, when she became aware of the reason he was telling her to be quiet.

Something was wrong. Dangerously wrong.

Instantly, everything changed. She could feel it in the back of her neck by the hairs rising as if chilled. The air was moist and cool, but there was something more to it.

She had felt this before. Ice cold panic slid down her back, and her gut clenched. Kane reared his mount to a stop, and Brodrick didn't give her the option of being on a horse this time. Without a word, he picked her up and effortlessly tossed her onto her mare's back. Connor took hold of her reins as Brodrick went to his own.

She didn't notice any of this, though. She was too busy watching Kane, noticing the tensing of his back, the way his hand went to his claymore. His arms flexed as he wrapped his arm around the hilt, and then he was drawing the blade over his head. The movements were so graceful you wouldn't have thought he was stiff as a rock, ready for danger.

Déjà vu went through her like an icy shroud, covering her in a film of disbelief and fear. They were under attack.

She shouldn't have been surprised. Of course someone would attack them. They were on that very same mission—to attack and terrify. Why shouldn't another clan endeavor to do the same?

As she became aware of the men moving to surround her, she realized that they were not afraid as she was. They were not trembling in their trews like she was, but mayhap that was because they were not wearing trews. They were sitting astride their horses with nothing but their plaids and claymores, which was all they needed to survive really.

"Saeran, I want ye' to ride into the forest. Donna go to the village—they know that we're here now." Brodrick spoke quickly and quietly, but Kane heard them.

He only cast them a glance before biting out the words, "He stays and fights like a man."

"My laird," Brodrick protested. His hand came to her shoulder protectively, as if he could protect her from the battle with just that touch. She felt no comfort in it—only a growing sense of hysteria. Kane was not going to let her leave, not as long as he knew she was a lad.

She should tell him. Now.

Saeran had been foolish to think that this could work, that she could protect herself as a man would. None of it had felt real until now, and in this moment, she saw the full stupidity of her actions. Of her lies. Of her deception.

Tell him, her mind screamed.

But she couldn't.

Memories of the first time they had been attacked assailed her. He had been magnificent in battle, until he realized that she was not safe—his attention had become divided, and that had put them both in danger.

Nay, she couldn't tell him. Even as tears of frustration burned her eyes, she knew that she couldn't put the man she loved at risk for her own safety. Saeran reached for her blade, calling on the weeks of training she had. It wouldn't do her much—she knew that. But at least it would do something.

"What are you doing?" Connor hissed, grabbing her wrist. "If you draw that, they'll take you as a threat. Ride away from here and stay out of sight."

"Connor," Kane snapped. The men became more agitated. She knew they wanted to say something, but they probably held the same thing as herself. Kane couldn't be distracted by a woman and her deception.

It could cost him his life.

The loss of one woman compared to their laird was an easy decision for them. Saeran could only thank the Lord. Nothing terrible would come to Kane so long as he focused on the battle. Nothing.

The riders broke through the forestry, swords raised.

There was no time to speak. No introductions, no threats, no warnings. The Shaws did not give the MacLeod riders a chance to open their mouths before they were charging towards them. The only warriors to hold back were Brodrick and Connor.

They met her eyes. The fear for her safety was clear.

But in that moment, with the sounds of clashing swords, neighing horses, and furious shouts, the fear washed out of her like someone had poured water over her head. She felt no fear. No panic. No horror. The blade in her hand did not feel as if it weighed as much as the moon. The chilling sounds of death did not wring her heart.

Saeran turned away from them, watching.

This was the life of a warrior. Fighting to survive, killing as if they were an animal.

Animals killed to survive.

Highlanders, humans—everyone was an animal in that instant, and the only thing she could see was Kane. Fighting to survive, killing so he could live. The grace with which his body moved, his sword raised as if it were the claw to his lion's paw. His fierce demeanor and the murderous rage she saw in his eyes.

It all came to her like a slap in the face.

"Saeran, go," Brodrick bit out, reaching behind his own back. "We will watch after you. Just go—"

His attention was forced onto the battle when a MacLeod came up behind him. They moved so quickly that she almost missed the flash of his colorful plaid. No, not MacLeod. Campbell.

Campbells were fighting them—and there was no time for her to escape, even if she had felt the need to.

Saeran didn't. She couldn't. She couldn't leave these ferocious men to themselves. Abandoning them was not an option. Her throat closed up, and her body began to react on its own. She wasn't the meek, terrified woman now.

She knew what to do. They might be seasoned warriors, but she at least knew how to defend herself. Connor urged his horse closer to her, but she slid to the ground from hers, using the mare as a way to shield herself from the battle raging around her.

Saeran hid in the shadows of the trees, watching, wincing every time one of her men was struck. That didn't stop them, but she knew it had to have hurt. One of the Campbells came close to her spot in the darkness, his back turned to her.

Instinct was the only thing that could have made her do what she did next. The need to protect and defend rose within her like tidal wave, and with one step closer to her, the wave crashed. Her blade drove into his back, wringing a shout of pain from his throat.

The Campbell fell to the ground

Fergus, a man of Kane's, finished the man off, then stood. He gave her a brief nod before entering the fray. It became a game for him, she realized, watching as he fought with a tenacity that could have rivaled Kane's. He would find a Campbell, wear him out, and then slowly guide him to Saeran.

Her blade and hand were soaked in blood by the time she came to her senses. The wild feelings inside of her only rose. Guilt mingled with insanity. It boiled inside of her like a hot pit—but this was what needed to be done. She had to help them, in any way she could. If she gained the respect of one of Kane's men for aiding them, then that meant another ally, and one less Campbell trying to kill them.

When there were three bodies piled beside her, with her legs, arms, and chest covered in their blood, it hit her.

She hadn't killed them—Fergus had done that—but she had helped.

Saeran sat there, shaking, staring. How long this went on, she didn't know. All she could register was the bodies and that they were now in front of her, with her own dagger wound left in their flesh.

"Saeran!"

She shook her head, unable to tear her eyes away. Animal. She was an animal. She—she had killed to survive. She clutched her stomach and knelt over, vomiting. Still, despite everything she felt, she knew she wouldn't have not done it in order to help Kane, in order to help the men.

"*Saeran.*"

She dug her hands into the ground, hunched. Panting. Weeping. She couldn't move from her spot as the horror of what she had done ran through her mind. The battle was still going on, but for her, it had faded into the distance. The mental agony stole over her senses, robbing her of her sense of reality.

Of course this was going to happen. This was the battle that Kane had been preparing for the past week. This was the battle that she had purposely tried not to think of. This was the battle that she knew would change her, yet had been unprepared for. She had thought that it wasn't going to happen, that it couldn't possibly happen.

It had.

It had, and Saeran had foolishly believed that it was…fake. That everything happening was a façade. It had felt that way—too surreal to be true.

But the men laying beside her were real. Their deaths were true. Their families would be without a father, a brother, a husband…

A sob wracked her. How could she have done this—

Biting pain exploded on the back of her head. Everything went dim.

Her vision swam, but she could feel her body being dragged away from the scene, her head held in a tight grip. The pain was so intense, so sudden, that a choked scream sprung from her lips, one born of pure reaction.

It became so much more—but no one heard it. Whoever had grabbed her was taking her through the forest, one hand holding her by her hair, the other covering her mouth. She couldn't turn her head, couldn't even cry out for help. For the first time since leaving the inn, fear assailed her like hot acid.

This was her punishment for aiding Fergus in those men's death. This was God's way of making her pay for her sins. Saeran struggled against the grip, a strangled, muted whimper escaping her lips when he only tightened his hold, taking her farther away until it became apparent that no one, not even Kane, would come to her aid.

They couldn't help someone they couldn't find.

"What," the speaker snarled, "kind of piece of shit boy kills a warrior? Without honor?"

He threw her into the ground. She didn't understand a word out of his mouth from the ringing in her ears. A shadow fell over her.

The man pushed her back into the ground and grabbed for her neck. He was going to kill her, she realized. Terror slid down her back like cold water. It gave her the strength to sit up, knocking her head into his nose. He cursed, but her hit had been weak.

She finally got a view of her attacker. He was old, with graying hair at his temples. His teeth were bared and a red, long beard fell from his face down his chest. Cruel brown eyes met hers. He was almost as big as Kane, but not quite. Age lined his body, giving her an indication on just how old he really was.

The sun was hot in the early noon, but the breeze whipped his hair around his face. She shivered when it reached her. The clearing was small, with a few spare trees dotting the ground. Tied to one of the trees was a beastly horse. It stared at her with large brown eyes.

He came back for her with a snarl. She tucked her head in, raising her arms to protect her neck. If he was going to strangle her to death, he would have to work for it!

But he didn't reach for her neck. No, he once again reached for her head. His hand grasped her cap and a chunk of her hair, and he pulled viciously. She screamed, forgetting about her neck, and reached for his hands.

They fell away.

Her cap dislodged, and all of the pins holding it there tumbled into the ground.

Blonde locks fell around her face.

The silence was deafening.

"Yer no' a lad at all," he mused lasciviously. "Yer nothing but a wee lass, pretending to be a lad. This...this is quite interesting."

When he reached for her, she didn't move. Didn't flinch. Didn't blink. Didn't even breathe. She couldn't—the panic rising inside of her was too great to bare. He was going to kill her—after he had his way with her.

She met his eyes, slowly, and painfully. Saeran knew what she would see, but to have it confirmed made her gut clench with a terror unlike any she had ever felt before. Not even when the MacLeod had taken her to the ground the day her and Kane had gone for a ride. He had been a foolish, cocky boy.

This was a man who knew how to hurt a woman. She saw it in his eyes, saw it in the tensing of his body as the thought of defiling her crossed his mind.

"Tis a good thing I like a wee lass," he bit out. Fury flashed in his eyes. "I'll no' be killing ye' for killing my boy—but yer sure going to wish ye' were dead."

She tried to shake her head, but his grip prevented it. "No," she said forcefully. "No, I didn't kill anyone."

"Oh, but ye' did," he growled. "Ye' killed him in cold blood—and now yer going to pay for it."

She stared at him, too frightened to speak. Running was pointless. If her hit to his nose, which was now gushing blood, hadn't stopped him, she feared that nothing she did would. He was old and experienced, and full of energy and vengeance.

He reached behind him with one hand, drawing out a dirk the size of her forearm. She stared at the metal blade as he pressed it to her cheek in a soft caress.

"I want ye' to run," he whispered. "I want ye' to run so ye' can feel like the bitch animal ye' are. No one kills the MacLeod's son and survives. Not even ye'."

This was the MacLeod?

Chapter Thirty-Seven

He used his strength to hold her down. One hand on her neck, the other holding the blade to her cheek. She couldn't find it in her to move as she stared up at him. This was the man that had given Kane more grief than he deserved, and this was the man that would kill her.

She felt it in her gut as he smiled down at her. His face was filled with malice. He pressed the blade down and let it dig into her skin. Then he began to pull, slicing her cheek open with a meticulous cut. She felt the warm trickle of blood slide down her face.

A scream broke from her lips, one of pain and fear, but it came out choked. It was more of a muffle, and the fact that it was so quiet, with no chance of reaching anyone else's ears, killed her inside.

The MacLeod grinned as he pulled away, putting the blade to his lips. His gray tongue slid over the sharp edge. Bile rose as she stared at him.

Then the hand that had been holding her down loosened. Her heart hammered in her chest as she watched him remove himself from her.

"Run," he said, laughing. Saeran didn't think about doing otherwise. There was a chance that she could escape. Even though it was clearly a game for him, she knew this was her only chance. Tears trailed down her face as the fervor of her prayers for Brodrick or Connor to notice her absence increased. If they could just search for her…follow the tracks…

She got as far as the edge of the forest, the same spot he had pulled her out of, when she heard him from behind her. He was on a horse. She screamed with frustration around her panting, pushing forward. She was just there. She could literally reach up and touch a low-hanging branch. The trees made for coverage. His horse was too big and burly to maneuver the sharp turns the trees would give her. Thanking the Lord that she was within the perimeter of the forest, she ran forward, pumping her arms.

Connor.

Brodrick.

Kane.

Someone, if they could just notice her missing from the battle. That was all it would take. The MacLeod would be dead within a moment if it were any Shaw warrior that saw her, and this could end.

Something slammed into her heel. She dove for the ground, hands out to catch herself, as an agonized scream ripped from her throat. The shock of the hit didn't hurt, but what happened immediately after did.

The horse didn't stop at her heel, and neither did the MacLeod. He dismounted the horse, arm and sword raised above his head. With a movement so sudden she didn't have time to evade it, he slammed the hilt of his sword into her shoulder, a heavy foot landing on her leg to hold her still. A pulsing pain grew from her shoulder down. The agony was too great for her to bare—and then it all became numb.

Everything. The hoarseness of her voice from screaming. The turning of her stomach from where his foot landed as he dismounted the horse. The searing agony from her broken arm. She turned her head, staring at it as a dark shadow fell over her.

The MacLeod. Going to kill her. Right then. In the corner of her eye, she could see the gleam of metal held high. She could feel the swish of air as he stood over her, pointing the tip of it to her neck.

"Not fast enough, bitch."

Then he swung. She closed her eyes, praying that Kane would be…alright. A tear slid down her cheek. Alright. He would be alright. She stilled her breath, bracing herself for the impact of the sword— and then the most blood-curling, spine-churning cry broke through the field.

Kane.

A sob of relief broke from her lips—just as cold, blood-covered metal sliced through her mid-section. Saeran screamed, eyes rolling into the back of her head as the shadow was jolted away, and replaced by a completely new one. The darkness consumed her, washing away…everything.

~

That sorry piece of shit.

That was all Kane could think of as he charged through the tree line, across the clearing, and straight at Alasdair. In the back of his mind, he knew that Saeran needed help, but Connor and Brodrick were there, right behind him. They would take care of Saeran, as soon as he finished off Alasdair.

His uncle laughed harshly, pointing his sword at Kane. It was coated in a dark sanguine liquid, dripping to the ground. Saeran's blood—the blood of a lad he should have protected. But then, if Alasdair had not been such a sick bastard, he would not have to take revenge for Saeran.

It didn't matter if the lad died or lived.

Alasdair had had this coming for him for the longest time—and now Kane was finally going to show his uncle why Kane Shaw had one of the strongest clans in the Highlands. He rushed forward, swinging his claymore in a giant arch over his head. When Alasdair moved to block him, Kane let the sword fly away from them and dropped low, lunging.

No matter what, Alasdair was family.

One never used their own weapon against family.

Kane drove his fist into his uncle's jaw. He didn't give another thought before he wrapped his hand around Alasdair's wrist, wrenching it up. The sword in his grip followed Kane's, clattering to the ground.

"Yer disgusting," Kane growled, shoving his uncle back. The older man roared, clutching his hand to his chest.

"And yer a sorry son of a bitch. My sister never should have let ye' into the world. Yer nothing but a tainted—"

Kane let his uncle taste his fist again, slamming it into his face repeatedly.

"No," he growled when he finally pulled back. He spat on the ground beside Alasdair's face, sneering when he flinched.

"No? She whored herself out to that bastard Duncan. The clan should have been destroyed, Kane. Yer weak—"

"If ye' want to keep the rest of yer two teeth, I suggest ye' quiet yersef now, uncle." If there was one thing Kane hated the most, it was people saying unjustified things. Alasdair had not seen his sister in nearly twenty-Five years. He had no right to talk of her, to defame her and the name of a great Highland clan, in front of Kane.

"I should kill ye'," he snarled, leaning down so that his face was nose-to-nose with Alasdair's. "Ye've insulted me. Ye've stolen from me. Ye've tried to destroy my lands. Not only that, but ye' attacked a lad who obviously canna defend himself."

Alasdair stared at him with hard eyes. Blood was sliding down the corner of his mouth. His eyes were glazed, dazed from the shock of being hit, and he was clutching his hand. Kane knew without looking that he'd broken Alasdair's hand. It served the bastard right.

Kane had been just on the edge of the trees when he'd seen the blonde haired lad befallen. If he hadn't have shouted and distracted Alasdair, Saeran would be dead.

Kane took too much pleasure in striking his uncle in the face. He fell, unconscious. One of his men would find him soon. There were plenty of bastards riding around the area, waiting for Kane and his warriors to engage in battle with them. The first wave had been the thickest, but most of the men who had dared to go against Kane were dead. For the Campbells to side with a weak clan such as the MacLeod's, it was their own fault.

He shoved himself up, stalking to Saeran.

Connor and Brodrick were moving rapidly. Brodrick was ripping pieces of his own plaid into strips. Connor was holding Saearn's upper back off the ground with one arm, and his other hand was wiping blood, grime, and tears off the unconscious lad's face.

"Kane. We need to get Saeran to the inn. Her arm is broken, and the gash to her abdomen is flowing," Brodrick said, voice cracking.

Kane stilled.

"Mabel will know what to do with her," Connor added quietly. Without another word, the two of them picked the fallen lad up. Kane, without thinking, whistled for his horse. All he could stare at was the blonde locks as they slid over frail shoulders. His arm hung loosely, bent at an odd angle. Brodrick adjusted him in his arms, and that was when the clean, familiar, innocent face turned towards him.

Ash blonde lashes swept over pale cheeks. Her skin looked like wax, and even in her sleep, her breathing was abnormally deep. This was not a lad. This was not the Saeran he had come to know and train. This was not the lad he had sent to battle unprotected.

This was the *woman* he had trained, the *woman* he had sent to battle.

This was Alice.

Chapter Thirty-Eight

"She lied to me." The words were hard and cold. Like the deadweight in his chest that had once beat just for the sound of her laugh, the brightness of her eyes.

No more.

"To protect herself," Brodrick said forcefully.

"She should have known that no matter what, I would have protected her from any—"

"Kane. She was terrified."

"Saeran—Alice, or whoever she is—would have—"

"Kane. Brodrick. Silence, please. You've been doing nothing but arguing for the past hour," Connor snapped from the other side of the bed. Saeran was the only thing separating Kane and Brodrick. The men had been saying the same thing for the last fortnight, ever since they had brought Saeran to the inn.

"I canna believe ye' plan to just—" Brodrick continued, up until Kane slashed an angry hand through the air. The man's jaw ticked.

"Out."

"Kane—"

"I said out."

Brodrick didn't speak as he stormed to the door. Connor stared at Kane, then the unconscious Saeran, then slowly got to his feet. Weary lines of fatigue were etched on all three faces. No one had been able to sleep—including the clansmen that had been in the battle party with him.

Kane understood completely.

"Ye ken," Brodrick said quietly as he paused just on the inside of the door. "I can't help but wonder. If yer planning on leaving her, why are you still here?" He left quietly.

Kane ignored him.

Her face was pale, strained. In the past fortnight, her condition hadn't become better. In fact, the longer he stared at her, the more he began to fear it was worse. Kane knelt down, touching her forehead with a trembling hand. She was so warm. Feverish. It felt no warmer than it had a week ago.

Kane sat next to her, forgoing the chair. This was the last time he would see her. The last time he would let himself gaze at her. After she recovered, he would be gone, and Connor would be left to tell the liar of Kane's departure.

She was not to contact him. Not to come after him. After Connor left her here, she was not to talk to anyone. No one knew of this—he knew how much of a problem it would cause between his men and he. They were all, in a way, attached to the lass who had feigned being a lad.

His lips tightened at the reminder. God, how could he have been so stupid? Saeran had done a terrible job of acting like a lad—she had done literally nothing to convince him she was what she was not. The signs had been there—the fragility, the meekness, how she had shied away from all things unlady-like. The only thing stopping him from noticing her true identity had been the dirt. The damn dirt.

How could she have eluded him for so long? His hands clenched. Her voice had not been overly deep—as he compared the two voices she had used with him, he realized they were almost the same. "Saeran's" voice had been low and quiet, whereas "Alice" spoke with her heart. Her features had been too feminine for a lad—not even Connor had such delicate features.

He should have noticed it sooner, but he had been too busy with his infatuation of Alice, too distracted by her more than anything else.

How ironic, that the woman he loved was the same lad he had ignored, for the very reason that Kane couldn't think of anything except Saeran. He cursed, dragging a hand through his hair.

He loved her. Kane loved her like nothing he had before—and he was leaving her, forcing them apart. Saeran was nothing but a danger to him. She didn't love him. If she had, she wouldn't have lied to him. His love was one-sided, and being alone was better than knowing she would lie to him again.

Nay. Saeran would no' get a chance to lie to him again.

A small whimper drew his gaze to the bed. His heart dropped to his stomach. He hated this part of the fever—the nightmares, the hallucinations. He reached for the bowl of water and cloth, getting the thing wet then pressing it to her forehead. It didn't do anything for her in reality, but by the easing of the lines around her eyes, he knew she took comfort in it.

When her stirring subsided, he called for one of the maids. She knew without asking what to do. A tub and buckets of water were brought up and was placed in front of the fire. Summer was turning into fall, and the Highlands were becoming chilly. He didn't want Saeran uncomfortable, and Mabel said it was best to use heat to draw out the heat.

He would trust the Macleod lass on that only because his Saeran was ill and he had no clue how to take care of her. Whenever Kane became sick, he focused on something else until it had passed. With Saeran and how delicate a woman she was, he was…uncertain. Terrified. She was sick because he had been too blind to notice that she was not what she appeared.

Once the maids had left, he checked the water to make sure it would be comfortable for her, then gently set about undressing her. He made sure to keep his eyes averted. She was sick and weak—he would be a bastard to take advantage of that just to see the perfection of her body.

His hands trembled as he lifted her back off the bed, one hand holding her neck so that it didn't roll, and the other pulling the shift away from her body. She made a small sound in the back of her throat, and he quickly set her down, watching her, waiting for her to start thrashing.

She didn't.

All he heard from her was soft, even breaths. Kane mentally prepared himself to bring her to the bath, like he did every other night that she took one, and stared at her. Not her body, but her. The woman that he didn't know, not truly.

He could think he knew the Saeran laying in front of him, but he didn't. He knew an Alice, and he knew a Saeran—but not the person that was in between them, the true woman he thought he knew.

He had fallen in love with Alice.

Her strength and fire. Her passion. Her kindness. That was what and who he had fallen for. Saeran, the woman laying before him, was not that Alice, as much as he tried to tell himself otherwise. It just…didn't make sense to him. Kane shook his head at his thoughts.

There was no use thinking about it. As soon as she awoke and recovered from her fever, he would be gone. No longer would he make a fool of himself over her. No longer would he watch as she lied to him.

He tried to stay angry. Betrayed. Furious.

All he felt was guilt. Over everything. The lies, her deception, his own stupidity. Kane forced himself to be tender with her as he lifted her from the bed. It didn't take as much effort as he had thought. The anger he felt towards her was…empty.

Saeran turned her head into the crook of his neck. Hot breath washed over his neck and he grunted, moving quickly to get her into the tub. The second her feet touched the water, she made a sound.

Kane ignored it. She had been without a bath for a day. This was needed. It would help her recover and would soothe her pains. But as he lowered her farther into the tub, her distress grew, until he was holding her half out of the water with her arms strangling his neck.

"No," she said, her voice muffled by his neck. "Hot—too hot. Burning."

Kane took a slow breath. He wanted nothing more than to set her on the bed, but she needed the bath. She was giving the tell-tale signs of having another episode. Firmly, heart twisting, he plied her arms from around his neck and let her slide even further into the tub.

"No," she cried. Frail arms reached for him again. Like they always did. Whenever she was distressed, she moved. Not toward Connor, not toward Brodrick, but to him. She was always reaching for him.

"Lass," he said softly, taking her hands. "Lass, listen to me. Ye' need to calm down—"

"No, it's burning me—burning my skin." The mantra was the same as always. The second something hot touched her skin, she began crying, whimpering, that something was burning her alive. He smoothed his hand over her forehead, heart breaking. God, he'd done this to her. This was his fault, and he had no clue how to take care of her.

"It's not, love. It's just warm water. Shh," he murmured, nearly weeping with relief when she seemed to settle down. He took her shoulders, sliding her deeper into the water, until her breasts were completely submerged. The tips of her hair were damp. He waited with baited breath, praying to the Lord that she wouldn't have an episode.

After several moments in silence, he relaxed enough to reach for the same cloth he'd used on her before. The only sound in the room was the softly crackling fire.

Nothing from Saeran. His stomach tightened.

This could have been avoided. He could have chosen to keep Gwen as his mistress. He could have proposed to Blaine with no subterfuge. He could have let his water nymph slip through his fingers the first night he saw her. He could have done the dutiful thing with her, ignored his selfish needs, and let her go.

But no. He'd ruined her, nearly killed her.

Kneeling beside her, he dipped the cloth into the water and began swiping it over her face, wringing it on top of her hair. He lost himself in caring for her, pushing his self-loathing to the darkest part of his heart. It wasn't until she was completely soaked in the water, her blonde hair dark and plastered to her head, that he began rubbing her shoulders. He paid close attention to the wound on her abdomen, careful to look just at that. It was not as deep as they had anticipated, but the sword had been coated with something deadly enough to nearly kill her.

He waited for her to move, to cry.

Still, nothing. Worry began to sit heavily in his gut. She was never this still when she was in the tub. She was never this quiet.

"Al—Saeran?" he murmured, scanning her face. It was oddly...relaxed. No signs of strain or pain, she appeared to be sleeping. Her chest moved in even breaths, the only sign she gave to let him know she was not dying on him.

"It's not burning," she whispered. It was the most lucid sentence she had said in the past fortnight. Nothing was slurred or muffled. It was just the gentle roll of words off the tip of her tongue. "I don't see the fire anymore."

"What fire?" he asked, sliding his hands up the nape of her neck. She leaned into his touch, head tilting like she was drawn to the sound of his voice.

He swallowed thickly.

"The fire in my stomach. It's always there. Guilt. It eats...and burns...my strength. Thoughts."

Kane had no clue what she was talking about, but something in her voice made him tense. There was so much despondency in her voice that he felt it to the center of his soul.

"I'm not human," she whispered. In his hand, her neck muscles tensed.

"Saeran," he said roughly. "Yer as much a human as I am, love. Donna fash yerself with—"

"No. I'm not—I can't be. Humans…would worry. Over family. Life. Aren't I right? I would…worry about Blaine when she said…"

Why was she talking about Blaine at a time like this? he thought, staring down at her.

"Said what, love," he murmured. Talking was good for her, wasn't it? The only thing she had done as of yet was whimper and cry. Talking must be an improvement, he thought, desperate to believe he was correct.

"We're not family. She said…we're not. And I didn't care—humans would care. They would die in the fire." Her legs bent, knees peaking above the surface of the water. She curled forward, arms around her knees. Her eyes remained closed. Her voice stayed quiet.

Kane could only watch her.

"Maybe she made them die…in the fire. Burnt alive."

"Saeran, what are you talking about?" He felt like he should know. It was something the king had told him, warned him of.

"My parents. I'm not human. They…are. Humans burn."

It hit him like a boulder. Her parents had died in a fire. The hallucinations were stemmed from guilt—for not dying with them?

Kane almost vomited. Quicker than he had time to think, he was pulling her out of the tub and wrapping her in a blanket. She didn't fight him, didn't speak. Her eyes stayed closed.

"Saeran," he said firmly, once she was set on the bed and covered in the same shift she'd been in before. He had to ask Mabel for another one soon. "Saeran, open yer damn eyes and look at me."

She did neither. Like a statue, she sat there, head lowered.

His stomach roiled and he could have shaken her. "Saeran, damnit." She wasn't trying to fight the fever. She was letting it overcome her will, her strength. She was letting it kill her—she wanted it to kill her.

Helpless frustration made him angry. How dare she do this to him—how dare she give up and leave him.

His father. His mother. His brother. His sister. Everyone had left him—and she was daring to leave him as well.

He tried everything he could think of to make her eyes open. Threats, warnings, promises, bribes. Anything. It wasn't until he had promised her his eternal life that he let his frustration free and did the only thing he could think of—he kissed her.

Taking her jaw into his hand, he lifted her head and pressed his lips to hers. The plea didn't need to be spoken with the kiss—it was an unspoken appeal for her to come around, for her to wake up and fight.

She was just as unresponsive as before. Cursing and hating himself, he began to pull away from her. He couldn't stay in here—he couldn't watch the woman he loved give up, couldn't watch her do that to herself. It was going to kill him more surely than his enemies would.

Pain and memories stabbed at him. His father had died before his eyes. His mother had been driven to insanity before his eyes. His brother had been stolen from him before his eyes. His sister had been murdered before his eyes.

He refused to watch Saeran die before his eyes. She didn't care—if she had, she would have stayed with him. Would have realized that he needed her to be alive. Out of everyone that had come into his life since his family had been torn apart, she meant the most to him—and that didn't matter to her in the most.

He stormed to the door. His eyes stung, but he ignored it. He refused to acknowledge anything at this point. A brawl—a good, bloody, murderous brawl was what he needed.

Kane was throwing open the door when he heard the soft rustle. "Kane."

Thin, weak arms wrapped around his waist from behind. He felt her cheek against his back.

And then he just…broke down. Great, heaving sobs left his chest before he could do anything to stop them.

Chapter Thirty-Nine

"God damnit," he rasped, swiping a hand over his face. It came away, wet with his own pathetic tears.

"Kane," she said again. Her voice was soft and melodic. Even as weak as she was, he crumbled under the force of her tenderness. How could this woman have lied to him? How could this woman have nearly given up on her own life?

Frustration made the sobs come harder, until he was shaking so much he couldn't stand on his own. He fell against the door, head and arms braced there. The hot sting in his eyes continued.

"Why, Saeran?" He couldn't understand his own voice, or the plea that came through it. What was he questioning? Her lies? Her love? Her…everything about her and him and his life? There was too much to ask "why" about. Too much for him to put into words.

So he did the only thing he could—he stood there, with her arms around him, and wept like a giant, newborn bairn. It lasted until he couldn't breathe, until he was using her as a source of strength. She didn't move away from him, didn't pull or push him from her. She simply stood there, letting him use her.

When he felt the trembling in her arms, he realized how much of a bastard he was. Too weak to bring them to the bed, he unlaced her arms from around him and slid to the floor, back against the wall. She stood there, staring down at him with an uncertainty that wrenched his heart even more.

His head fell back against the wall as he reached blindly for her hand. She threaded their fingers and met him on the floor, her thin, hot body curling into his lap.

Kane kept his face away from her. This was what he needed—to look even more weak and foolish. He had already failed in keeping her safe and unharmed. What was the use of caring about how she felt about him now?

She should hate him. She should be coming at him with a blade in retribution. This was his fault, so there was no reason for her not to. A low sound left his throat, and he slammed his head into the wall, cursing.

"Ka—my lord, I…"

"No," he rasped. "No. I'm Kane to ye', lass. No' yer lord."

She silenced herself, head lowering. He felt choked for words, as if they were stuck in his throat with no way to come out. She wasn't hallucinating anymore. Somehow, she had managed to break through the haze of the fever. There was lucidity in her eyes. "Yer parents…died."

She tensed in his lap, but didn't draw away.

"In a fire."

"Ye'…ye' always cried about burning alive. In a fire. When I put ye' in the bath. Is that…Saeran. God." She had felt so much guilt her whole entire life, and he didn't think she had realized it. The guilt had nearly driven her to her death bed, he thought, physically ill. He knew she had so many more problems, but that was the only one he could think of.

"I don't know where that came from," she whispered. If it was possible, her body became even more stiff, until she was as tense as a statue in his lap. "I…nothing makes sense to me anymore." Crystalline eyes flipped to his. "You know about…"

"Aye. Yer name. Yer lies. All of it."

She inhaled slowly, then pushed herself away from him. His heart jumped in his chest, but he couldn't make himself reach for her. Instead, he watched her. Watched her and fought the craving he felt to hold her, to erase all of her problems.

"You…stayed."

"Aye." He shouldn't have. All he was going to do was leave her.

"You cared for me."

"Aye." No one else had but him. Anyone who came near her had turned into a bloody mess. The only two men who came in here were Connor and Brodrick, but even then, he wouldn't let them touch her.

"What about the Campbells? The men who attacked us?"

"Taken care of."

Remorse and pain entered her face. "By taken care of, you mean…"

"All of them. Except for Alasdair."

"Dead," she said again.

"Aye."

Kane jumped to catch her when she swayed on her feet. Tears glistened in her eyes, ripping his heart in two.

"Lass, be careful. Yer wound has no' fully healed and yer weak from the fever and—"

"I killed."

He paused.

"What?"

Watery eyes met his. "I killed. With Fergus. He…he led the soldiers to me, and I attacked them from the shadows. I—Kane, I killed the MacLeod's son. That's why he wanted to kill me, why he— I'm dead."

"Nay, lass. Yer right—"

"No," she hissed, tears sliding down her cheeks. "I'm dead. I am an animal. I killed to survive, and that means he's going to kill me. It is…God," she whispered, dropping her head to her hands. He didn't understand half of what she was saying, but he chalked that up to the fever. He gently picked her up, carrying her to the bed.

"Lass, ye' did what ye' had to do. I'm the one who told ye' to stay and fight. Ye'll no' be taking the blame for this."

"You're not the one who pushed your dirk into the back of those soldiers," she said. He stood back, staring at her. "You might be used to it, but I am not. I helped them for your safety, and now…now I'm dead. I can't—I can't—" She put a hand over her mouth, turning her head away from him. Not only that, but she rolled onto her side, facing the other way.

It was like she had shut a door in his face.

"Saeran…"

"Don't," she whispered, her voice throaty. He felt bile rise in his throat. If it hadn't been for his own stupidity, she would not be in this position. "I don't want to talk about it anymore. I can't. I just—"

"Why did ye' lie to me?" She didn't want to talk about that— fine. But she was going to keep speaking, if not to keep herself awake. After her two weeks of hallucinations and mumbling, he was terrified of her slipping back into that same state if she became too quiet.

There was more to his wanting to know than that, though. He wanted to know—no, he needed to know. He had told her, point blank, that he hated liars—and she had continued to lie to him. It would have been easy for her to tell him the truth, to tell him that she was actually the lad he had put through training, the lad he had made train the beast—

His stomach revolted. He had made her train a beast of a horse, had put her in danger. The woman he had been so determined to protect could have been killed multiple times.

"Kane, please…"

"No, tell me. That's the *least* ye' can do for lying to me for the past two moons," he rasped, hands clenching at his side. He could have protected her, kept her safe, warm, and loved—but she had lied to him. Anger unlike anything he had ever felt coursed through him.

"I…" She trailed off. He waited, too furious to speak.

"Saeran. Tell me, damnit. I told ye' things about my family that I've told no one else. I've shown ye' a side of me that no one has seen before. The least ye' can do is tell me why you would betray me like this."

"It wasn't intentional," she whispered. The sound of her voice was so quiet and unexpected, he wasn't sure he had heard her. He sat on the edge of the bed, but he didn't touch her. Not until she reached for his hand, that is. The fire crackled in the silence, and he became more convinced that she hadn't answered him. "If you had never seen me in the kitchen that night…none of this would have happened."

"That was no' the first time I saw ye'."

She turned her head. Her eyes were wide when they met his.

"The night we came back from court. I saw ye' in the creek, bathing."

He took pleasure in the soft blush that came over her face, the shock in her eyes.

"I…how? Why did you not say anything sooner?" she asked, taking her hand from his. He frowned, until he saw that she was using it to cover her cheeks. Her adorable, red cheeks. She started to sit up, but winced, that same hand dropping to her abdomen.

Her mouth tightened, face becoming pale. Kane shushed her like he would a bairn, lowering her into the bed with his hand to her shoulder.

"Lass, ye' canna be moving so much. I donna even know how

ye' got out of the bed by yerself before…" Kane paused. Narrowed his eyes on her. He reached for the candle beside the bed, holding it to her abdomen. It was too dark in the room for him to see the dark splotches of red on her shift without the candlelight, but when he did, fury boiled in his gut. "Lass…"

"It's fine," she said thinly, pushing the hand holding the candle away. She turned her face from him, only infuriating him more. He had tasked himself with ensuring she was safe and comfortable, and only moments after she was awake, he was failing. He sought out a clean cloth, one of many that Mabel had left for him, and dipped it in the now cool bath water. He came back to the bed, debating.

"Nay, it's no'. Would ye' be fine if I were movin' about with a wound after being asleep for so long? I think no'." Kane went against everything his head was screaming at him about and slid onto the bed, closer to her. When she only stared, Kane sighed. He was careful not to move her too much as he took her into his arms.

She relaxed into his embrace almost immediately. The pain on her face lessened.

He hated himself for this weakness, his need to touch and hold her. She was in pain, and somehow, he helped to alleviate that…until he lifted up her shift. He felt her panic in the way she tensed.

"What are you doing?" she asked frantically, starting to push at his shoulders. He ignored her. It had to be wiped clean, no matter her objections. He had to grit his teeth to prevent himself from throwing the cloth across the room when she started to cry. Instead, he tenderly wiped away the smeared blood. Hell, he had to grit his teeth against killing himself for causing her pain.

"I donna want it to get infected, lass. I'll ask Mabel to bring up some ale for ye', but we canna let this become worse than it is."

"Ale for me? Kane, I don't drink," she wept mindlessly against his shoulder. When he had cleaned away the last of the blood and checked the stitching Mabel had done to her stomach, he tossed the cloth away. He threaded his fingers into her hair, clutching her tightly.

"It's no' for ye' to drink…though ye' might want to before we pour it on ye'."

"*Kane*," she sobbed. "That's—I can't let you do that. It will hurt me!"

"Aye, but ye' dying will hurt me. Lass," he said patiently, tilting her head back. "Either ye' take the ale or ye' die. The latter is no' an option, love. I'm sorry." The sobbing continued. He knew it was more from the panic and pain than what was to come, and knew he had to distract her. "Ye' never told me why ye' were pretending to be a lad."

"Blaine," she cried against him. Her tiny fists balled up on his chest, hitting him. She had the strength of a kitten. "Blaine made me, to protect myself. What does that have to do with you killing me with ale? Doesn't Mabel have any salve?" Her voice was so watery and distraught he had to decipher what she was saying. But when he understood, he smiled. His woman had always been an adorable little thing.

"I will make sure to ask Mabel about that. How did Blaine bring this about?" he asked, wiping her tears. The more she focused on her thoughts, the more distressed she would become. He would rather find the reason for her deception than have her rip him into shreds with her tears.

She blinked, looking at him, as if realizing there was no way for her to get around this conversation. Saeran lowered her eyes, wet lashes sweeping over her cheeks.

"She convinced me that I would die if any man found out I was barren. Hans, the man I would have had to marry if you chose Blaine. You, if you chose me. Blaine 'offered' herself to save me and keep me by her side."

"Blaine wouldn't save you if you were dangling off a cliff," he growled. "She would no' save anyone." That was the truth. He knew from watching her, listening to her, that she was as deep as a puddle. She held no true love for Saeran.

"I realize that now," she whispered. He flinched. Aye, of course she did.

"Ye ken what's amusing to me," he said softly, wishing he could bring her hopes up. "When Blaine told me that 'Alice' was having an 'affair', she was really saying you were having an affair with yourself."

Her face went scarlet. He laughed, kissing her temple. "Och, lass. Too innocent for yer own good." Then he sobered. As much as he wanted to be lighthearted to ease her mood, this was too pressing, too important.

"Why did ye' no reveal yerself when I told ye' of my plan? I was no' ever going to marry Blaine. All that was needed was the proposal, and she would have taken care of the rest by growing to hate me."

"Oh, I wanted to," she said, raising her eyes to meet his. He was struck by the sincerity in them. "The night before we left…before

Blaine came in…I was thinking of it. I was actually very close to telling you…then you told me how much you detested liars and I realized that I was no better than Blaine for my lies. She always warned me that you would cast me off your lands if you ever found out…"

"Saeran. What have I ever done to make you think I would do that to you, for hiding who you were?"

"You did cast me off when you thought I was having an affair with myself," she pointed out quietly.

"Aye, but ye' have to remember—Alice—ye'—yer all I want. I thought someone else was taking what I thought to be mine, and then yer side of the story seemed like ye' were confirming it. It's two completely different situations, lass. I thought ye'd betrayed me. With this, ye' simply deceived me—and only to protect yerself."

Then it hit him.

She had not *betrayed* him. All it had been was a small deception, something to protect herself with. The woman he saw in front of him right now was terrified and hurt. She must have been like this her whole life with Blaine, even if she did not realize it. Every glance she gave him was a mixture between love and fear. The fear was not of him, but for herself. She was scared of what would happen to herself.

His heart shattered.

Blaine had been terrible to her. Enough to ruin her confidence and securities, enough to destroy the one thing she had an inborn attachment to—her strength. Blaine had cracked her strength, over and over through the years, and Kane could see that as he gazed at her.

"I want an honest answer," she said, drawing his attention. "If I had told you from the second Blaine left the room the last time we…we made love. Would you have been angry with me?"

"Aye."

She dropped her gaze.

"Only because ye' did no' tell me in the beginning. Lass, I'm not a cruel man. Aye, I enjoy bloodshed just as much as the next warrior, but I know that everyone makes the wrong decisions when they think they're protecting themselves. Lord, they make them even when they are not trying to protect themselves. Look at me—I'm a giant oaf of a man who is ruled by his emotions so fiercely, he canna tell when a lass like Blaine is lying to tear us apart."

"Nay," she said strongly. "You're not ruled by your emotions—

at least with everything. I…I understand how you lost sight of things with me, though I know with any other person, what she said wouldn't have gotten to you. She knows how to say things, and who to say them about, to make you furious."

"How do ye' understand, lass?" he asked, massaging her scalp. She looked like she was struggling to keep her eyes open, and he smiled, brushing his lips over her forehead.

"I understand…because if it hadn't been for my attraction to you…I never would have betrayed Blaine's trust as I did when I made love to you." Her eyes drooped, voice becoming soft. "I don't think I would have…enjoyed it so much…with anyone other than you, and normally—normally I have very good self…restraint."

She kept talking until her voice was nothing but a muffled sound against his chest. He was careful of her abdomen as he adjusted her in his arms so that her back was to his chest, their legs tangled.

His plan to leave her became…impossible.

"I have to leave ye', lass. I canna ever see ye' again," he said out loud, trying to make his words the truth. But they felt hollow, empty. Nay. He couldn't leave her. Thinking he had the strength to in the first place showed how weak he was when it came to her. She loved him, even if she had not yet said it to him, and Kane would be a fool to not lay claim to his woman.

He would not allow his guilt to drive him away. Nor would he let his own stupidity get the better of him anymore. The anger he felt towards her could be helped. Aye, they would have to gain each other's trust all over again, but for her…he would wait an eternity. The secrets would all come to light, eventually. Most importantly, Blaine would pay for everything she's done to hurt Saeran.

His water nymph would always remain his, and he would protect her until the day he died.

Chapter Forty

"I have to leave ye', lass. I canna ever see ye' again."

The bed was cold. Saeran sat there, staring around her, the words from last night echoing in her head. She had wanted to say something, anything… But strength had alluded her. She had felt trapped in her own body, unable to speak.

Some part of her had prayed that he would stay, that he would still be there in the morning. Of course he hadn't. Kane was a man set in his ways. He had felt the need to leave her…and he had. She understood. After the lying, the deceiving… It had been the heat of the moment, the relief of her survival, that he had treated her as he had last night. He'd held her like she meant something, talked to her as if he cared for her words. After all of the miscommunication, it had felt…beautiful, wonderful, painful—because she had known then that it wouldn't last. Something always came between them, robbing her of everything she had within her grasp.

A normal life with Kane. Happiness. Hope. Something other than the loneliness she was feeling now. Saeran shoved the thoughts aside—as she had with everything in her life. She always pushed them away. She always locked them away. Never once did she stop to dwell. It hurt too much, made her realize that she wasn't impervious to the things she thought she was.

Her weakness didn't bother her.

She was too numb.

Saeran rose from the bed, wincing at the burning in her abdomen. God, she felt like she had been run over by a stampede.

304

Her muscles trembled as she struggled to hold herself up. She couldn't lay around. There were things she—things she had to—

The first tear fell down her cheek.

"No," she whispered fiercely, swiping them away. "Don't cry over him. He chose to leave you—there is nothing for you to cry over."

The words did the exact opposite of what she had thought they would. Instead of strengthening her, they destroyed her. Kane had really, honestly left her. Just like her parents, just like Blaine. She was alone, with nothing, no one.

No Kane.

Sobs wracked her chest until she was jerking, shuddering. Weeping for things she had only dreamed of. She was always dreaming, wasn't she? Always wishing for something she didn't have within her grasp.

The door opened with a soft swoosh as she cried into her pillow.

"Out," she commanded through her tears, not bothering to lift her eyes. "Please, get out."

"Saeran?" Connor. She clutched the pillow harder, shaking her head into it. "Does it hurt? Do I need to—"

"No! Please, just leave me. I need—I need to be alone. Just let me be alone." Because that's all she was ever going to be. Blaine had isolated her. Kane had left her. Connor's loyalty was to Kane, and she was sure the whole entire Shaw clan had left by now, except for Connor because he was there with her.

"I wouldn't feel at ease if I did that," he said gently, coming farther into the room. His feet carried him over the space of the room, until he was sitting on the edge of the bed, on the spot where Kane had lain while he held her.

A fresh wave of tears coursed down her cheeks as she stared at the spot.

"This is wrong," she said, heartbroken. "He shouldn't…have left. We…"

"I know," he said, reaching out to take her hand. "I know, Sae. If he weren't my laird, I'd be showing him a lesson right about now. If you want some time to yourself, honestly, I will let you be…"

She shook her head.

"Nay, I…Nay. I will not be sitting here, mourning him. I can't." But she wanted to. She desperately wanted to. She had gotten her cry out, however, and it was time to move on. Mayhap he would realize his mistake and come back for her, but she doubted that would happen. Kane was a stubborn man…and he had left for his own happiness. All she wanted for him was to be happy. If he was content without her, she…she didn't need him.

Saeran choked down her tears, giving Connor her hand. "Help me stand, please. Then you can join them."

"Join who?" he asked as he helped her stand. He was watching her as if she were about to explode.

"The others. Brodrick, Fergus…Kane."

He frowned at her. "Everyone except Brodrick and Kane are here. They left earlier and didn't tell us where they were going. But other than that, everyone is here, deep in their cups."

So Kane had been so eager to leave her that he hadn't been able to wait for his men…

Her heart broke. She smiled at him tightly, trying to ignore how much it hurt. There was nothing she could do about it. Running after him would make her look pathetic, and Kane valued strong women. She wouldn't lower her pride for him, after all the times she had recently.

"Is Alan still here? No, he wouldn't be," she mumbled, answering her own question. She pushed aside her pain and forced herself to focus on something else, something just as important. "It's been two weeks. Connor, do you still have the hemlock?"

His eyes widened. "What would you need that for?"

"Why, to take it to him and demand to know why he has it, and if the men who were going to meet with us before are willing to do it again."

"Saeran, you have just woken up from the fever, and I know you are not entirely healed. Do not be stupid—you can't possibly meet them. What if they are enemies of Kane? By now, everyone knows of you. Not only that, but Kane was by your side the whole entire time you were sick. You're a weakness to him, Saeran."

"Not anymore," she said tightly. God, it hurt to talk. Not from the pain radiating from her stomach, but from how hard it was to hear his name, knowing he had left her.

"How are you even standing right now?" he asked, incredulous.

"Pure determination to find out what Blaine's plan for me was," she mumbled, shocked by the truth of it. That, and her determination to forget about Kane. She knew he would always be there, in her heart, but for now…she couldn't wallow in her pain over him. "I won't let Kane abandoning me affect me. I have to be strong."

"Saeran…"

"Do you have the hemlock?"

"…Yes. I do."

"Thank you. If you could bring it to me, I would—"

"I'm not giving it to you. Saeran, you're acting on emotion right now. You're not stopping to think about anything rationally. Mayhap Kane did not leave like you think he did."

"No, I heard him—"

"Did you not notice the way he was looking at you all night long? I obviously didn't get to see it, but he was practically smiling this morning. Something must have happened last night that you misunderstood. Don't shake your head at me, Saeran. You of all people experience more miscommunication than anyone I have ever met."

"That is not the point."

"You're right. Your irrationality is the point, and because of that, I will not let you leave this room. Plus, Kane would murder me if I let you leave!"

He wouldn't care at this point, she wanted to say. But she didn't. Connor was not going to take her side on this. He would force her to stay here, and then she would only think about Kane. The thought made her ill enough to hold her stomach, but that immediately turned into a gasp of pain.

She yanked her trembling hands away, going lightheaded.

"Connor," she said thinly. "Would you help me get dressed?"

He shook his head. "I've already told you I will not let you—"

"I have not been in proper clothing for how long?" she asked, raising a brow. It quickly dropped when her stomach twisted from the agony of her wound. Connor was right—she should be staying here and resting. It hurt so much that she could barely breathe, but she had already lost so much time.

"You're not going to do anything impulsive, are you?"

She sat down on the bed, trying to avoid answering him. Luckily, he turned away the second her arse was on the bed. "Do you want squire clothes or a dress?"

"Squire clothes."

He gave her a look over her shoulder.

"What? I've grown use to them. They're more comfortable to

lay in."

"I don't blame you there," he said, chuckling. "I don't know how you ladies survive in those dresses. The corsets become so tight you can hardly breathe. Reclining in one is almost as bad." He pulled out familiar pieces of clothes, presenting them to her.

"Connor...how would you know what being in a dress is like?"

His face went beet red. Even though she knew it would kill her, she laughed. She couldn't stop it, even when the pained whimpers came.

"I lived with five older sisters," he said, glaring at her.

"I happen to remember you telling me that you took none of their nonsense," she pointed out, enjoying when his face became even more red. *Poor lad*, she thought.

"I also had seven older brothers who thought it would be fun to laugh at me with our sisters' help. Saeran, honestly. Please quiet yourself."

She snickered again, but was dutifully quiet when he helped her to her feet. He had her turn her back to him, and then they set to work with the slow process of getting her dressed. It wasn't embarrassing at all, to be showing him her body. One, she was too weak to be self-conscious, and two, she needed his help no matter what. If she wanted to have any chance at finding Alan, she had to be dressed.

Lord, this was going to be terrible.

Connor stepped away from her, admiring his handiwork, then gently guided her to the bed. "I'm too young to be murdered by Kane, so you're going to lay in bed until he returns. Do you understand?"

She slid into the bed without a fight, holding her breath. God. Everything hurt. It was as if the pain in her abdomen was spreading through her whole body and making her joints ache. She was quiet as Connor walked to the door.

"Saeran?"

"Aye?"

Connor seemed to hesitate. His voice was slow, as if he were planning his words, when he finally spoke. "Kane is...not a perfect man. He tries his hardest to understand and forgive, but just like you, he's ruled by emotions too strong for him to fight. He might have thought of leaving you, but his heart won't let him. Wherever he disappeared to, he's coming back for you."

"Nay, he…"

"Listen to me, Saeran. He hasn't done a great job of being a selfless man with you as of late. There has been so much going on for him lately. He has been trying his hardest to do right by you. Brodrick and I know him better than anyone, so when I say that him planning to leave you was an empty threat, I'm confident in this."

"Leaving me would have done him more good than I," she whispered, staring at her lap.

"Yes, but he doesn't see it that way. He has—albeit indirectly— treated you terribly. He has put you through things no woman has ever had to go through before. Do you know how guilt-ridden he has been these past two weeks? He feels that what happened to you while you lied to him was his fault."

Her eyes flipped up to meet his. "But—"

"Saeran. You know how his sister died. She was brutally raped and murdered by her own husband, a man Kane knew not to give her to. But still he did, and she was the one who paid the price with her life. I think, deep down, he might have known you were actually a woman. Not enough for it to come to the forefront, but he's not a stupid man—he saw the signs. He was simply too blind by his love for you to take note of anything but the stunning woman he craved to see all day."

She blushed, but shook her head. "Kane can't love me, he—"

"I've never seen him more enamored by a woman than he is with you," he said fiercely. "He has lost everyone important to him. He had the weight of a clan on his shoulders when he was a child, and he had to watch his mother and brother be taken away in front of his eyes. His sister was murdered when he could have protected her. He's been too terrified of loving someone and losing them to start a family all his life, and then you come along.

"With one look, he was taken by you. We thought he would never find a wife or love someone. When we brought you to the inn? The guilt and self-hatred was eating him alive. He's never cared so much about someone to stay by their side, without leaving them, for two weeks. He bathed you, cared for you, and calmed you when he should have been home with his clan and preparing a retaliation. So don't you ever say he doesn't love you. I can tolerate any of your silly notions except that one.

"Kane is my laird. He will always have my loyalty. I won't let both of your foolish heads ruin a perfect match, so shut your mouth, lay back, and close your eyes until he returns. Understand?"

She stared at him…then nodded slowly. "Aye. I…understand."

"Good. I'll have Mabel bring you some soup so you can get something in your stomach. Other than that, you're not moving from that spot."

"Yes, sir," she muttered, leaning into the bed. He gave her a warning glare and then exited the room, closing the door firmly behind him. Saeran sat there for a moment, thinking.

Connor had never been wrong before, as much as she hated to admit that, but there was always a time for firsts. She had clearly heard Kane say that he had to leave her, that he was *going* to leave her. Though it had been right before she had fallen asleep, she knew she would never be able to forget those words.

Saeran gingerly rolled onto her side, sighing.

She couldn't sit here, as much as Connor wanted her to. She had to do something, anything, to stop thinking about things better left alone. She had to find Alan, Blaine's "father".

Saeran sat up with a purpose. Aye, she couldn't forget about Alan. Mayhap she could sneak past Connor and find Mabel, ask for his whereabouts, and then leave before the innkeeper's wife tried to stop her.

She sat up—

The door swung open. Three people came rushing in, slamming it closed behind them.

"Pardon," she said, backing away from them. One of them looked vaguely familiar, but the other two were strangers. She reached for her waist, only to realize that she had forgotten to grab the dirk. "I think you have the wrong room."

They stepped farther into the room, until she was scrambling to the other side of the bed. Only one of the three was a woman. Her shoulders were wide, and she had some meat on her bones. There was a feline quality to her face that struck Saeran as beautiful. Dark blonde hair was pulled back from her face and her eyes were dark brown, staring at her as if trying to place her.

A bad feeling went through Saeran. They didn't speak, didn't look around the room. They were all focused on her, waiting for the blonde to come to a decision. Saeran looked around the room, for anything she could use to fend them off with. The door was closed, so she would have to get around them in order to be free…

The blonde seemed to have seen something she liked or

recognized, because she nodded to the two men. They were both tall and broad, with brown hair and brown eyes. They started to come forward.

"Con—" Before she could finish calling out to Connor, the man on the left shot forward, striking her across the face. A shocked gasp left her lips. Everything and nothing happened at once. One minute, Saeran was holding her cheek, opening her mouth to cry out for someone, and the next, black came over her vision.

Chapter Forty-One

"I'm no' sure she'll like it," Kane said for the hundredth time. He held the object in his hands, feeling as if he were going to crush it. His hands were too big and brutish to hold it there, but Brodrick had refused to touch it.

"Of course she will," his friend said. A frown came over his face. "Though she would have liked my idea much more."

Kane gave him a skewed look. "Nay, she would no' have. She prefers trews to dresses—"

"Ye' donna ken that, Kane. Ye' just want her in the trews because ye' like how her arse fills them."

A flush climbed up his neck. Mayhap he had admitted that after recalling Saeran in a pair of trews. He had just noticed her legs looked quite lovely in them, but it was a bad move on Brodrick to mention that.

"Sure," he said, running his fingers over the soft gift. "But I donna ken if she'll have me, so purchasing her a dress for a wedding ceremony—"

"Would have been romantic. My wife would have swooned if I'd done that for her," Brodrick said wistfully. "Kane! Lord, now we can do manly stuff together, what with you and Saeran being together."

"We were already doing manly stuff."

"Aye, but this time it'll be better, because ye'll understand the relief of getting a break," Brodrick said, laughing. "Free time is much different when yer married. Anyone can sit around with a good amount of ale and make jokes, but it's the added relief of having a moment away from the nagging that makes it better."

"I highly doubt that I would want time away from Saeran if she agreed to be my wife," Kane murmured, lifting her present to his face. There wasn't a full ray of light penetrating it, and he smiled. A feather was just as innocent as Saeran.

Even after her deception, he still thought of her as his wee, innocent lass.

Brodrick had suggested they explore the village for something to give to Saeran, something to lighten her mood. Kane had shared only parts of their conversation with his friend, and though Brodrick had been horrified, he had quickly come up with the idea of getting her a gift.

From the type of woman Blaine was, they had both come to the conclusion that Saeran was not accustomed to being treated with gifts and praise. Kane wanted to do at least one thing right by her, and he planned on this being one of many things she would be showered with.

He did not want to earn her trust or love with gifts, and he would make sure to tell her that right when he presented the elegant quill to her. Nay, he only wanted to show her that she could have nice things in life from the people who loved her, that not everyone was out to use and hurt her. Even Brodrick had agreed to get his wife to start baking goods to present to Saeran.

She would never feel unwelcome or fearful again.

"I love my bonny wife more than anything," Brodrick said, slapping him on the back. "But I'd gladly go to war instead of listening to her groan about how dirty I am."

Kane frowned. "She's no' complained about a stench around me."

"Yet," Brodrick added, shaking his head sadly. "Donna worry, my brother. Soon you will know the hardships of having a wife."

"Surely the pros outweigh the cons? I've never heard ye' complain about yer wife before, Brod."

"Of course ye' haven't," Brodrick said, chuckling. "Ye' never complain about a wife to an unmarried man. They donna understand and I, personally, feel that some of the relief is lost to a man who does no' share yer troubles."

"Do ye' fight often? Is it that…awful?" *Mayhap marriage was as terrifying as he had originally thought it to be.* Brodrick had never once said a word against having a wife, and though he was not doing that right now, it still made Kane wonder.

"Donna get that look about yer face. I love my wife, and I would gladly sacrifice anything for her. One day, though, ye'll understand the woes of having a spirited lass as a wife. They donna give up on anything easily."

"What is that supposed to mean?" he asked, staring at Brodrick with a growing sense of unease.

"Nothing, Kane. Nothing." Brodrick looked ahead of them. The inn was just in front of them. They kicked up dirt as they walked, Kane quickening his pace in anticipation to see Saeran. He smiled, holding the quill in his hands tenderly. Aye, she would love this, and no matter Brodrick's revelations of the true horrors of marriage, Kane would pursue her and show her that he could be worthy of her trust.

"She will like this better than a dress, I am sure," he said over his shoulder. Brodrick's laugh carried behind him as Kane burst into a full run, intent on finding Saeran just as she was waking up. It had taken a bit of time to find the right gift, but she had always been a late and deep sleeper.

The closer he came to the inn, details began to jump out at him. The silence was the main one. Normally, he could hear the inn bustling with life. Since it was the morning, there should have been clients readying themselves for breakfast, but there was not even that.

His stomach began to cramp, and a cold draft washed over him. *Saeran.*

His walk turned into a full-fledge charge as he came up to the inn. Throwing the door open, he focused only on finding Saeran, on getting to her room and ensuring she was safe. He stormed up the stairs, taking a sharp turn and then—

Stopped cold.

The quill dropped to the ground.

The door to her room was open. He felt nothing but the beating of his heart as he put his hand to the door, watching it swish open with a silent swing.

His heart rocketed to his feet.

There wasn't a single person in the room except Connor.

The lad was slumped on the floor, his face turned to the ceiling. Blood was dripping down the side of his face from the side of his nose. Both of his eyes were swollen shut and a bloody mix of red and purple flesh, and his lip was split. Kane felt rage boil deep in his gut. As he came farther into the room, closer to Connor, he realized the lad had put up a fight as best he could. There was one dead body in the corner of the room, a burly man with a knife to his chest.

Kane didn't spare him another glance as he knelt beside Connor. With shaking hands, he brushed a dark lock of hair away from the lad's face, taking a closer inventory of injuries. The only thing he'd failed to realize from his spot in the door was the broken arm. It was bent at an ugly angle, with the bone pushing through the skin.

He was close to roaring with his fury, but he couldn't get it through his throat. Connor had been nearly killed—and Saeran was gone.

"What—oh, fucking *bastards*," Brodrick said from behind him. A rushing sound built between Kane's ears, blocking out the sound of Brodrick's heavy footsteps. The rushing turned into a thrumming pulse, until he was vibrating with the force of his rage.

He jerked himself to his feet, pointing a finger to Connor. "Take care of him. Find Mabel or her husband—whoever hasn't died. Someone fix that bastard." Brodrick knelt, sliding his arms under the lad's legs and back. A rough, gargled sound came from his throat.

Kane took one look at the color of the dead man's plaid, and that was all it took. The roar that had been building in his throat broke free. The air seeming to turn into a solid substance as the sound shattered the silence. He threw his head back, letting his wrath crash through him.

~

"I hate her," a low voice sobbed. Saeran turned her head to the voice, eyes heavy with sleep. Lucidity was slow in coming, so she was left questioning who was speaking, and who the speaker hated. "She...stole everything. Ruined everything. I hate them both."

"I'll make the blonde one pay." This one was a male. He sounded bored, uninterested.

"But not the other one? What is their suffering worth if they are not both paying for what they have done to me?"

"She hasn't done a thing—"

"She tried to steal Kane from me!" the feminine voice growled. Saeran heard the sound of a slap, thinking it had to have been on a table. A woman didn't hit a man. It was...unheard of. Saeran lifted her hands to rub her eyes—or tried to. She tugged, making a distressed sound. It was as if her hands had tied down. Trying to lift her head became painful as well. There was a pulsing pain in her stomach, and her head was heavy, like a rock. It thumped back onto the hard surface she had been resting on.

"Tell Blaine she's awake," the male voice said. He sounded more alert. There was rustling in the dim room, and one by one, candles were set. Why candles? It was morning…bright as a light. She tugged at the ropes, holding back a whimper when her abdomen stretched. God, what was *happening*?

"I'm always doing what she—" The blonde was cut off with the sound of a door opened. It came slowly, but Saeran was able to make out three figures. The man, the blonde woman from before, and another one, who was behind them both.

"What who says?" Blaine's voice came from the figure. Saeran tensed, then began struggling in earnest.

"Blaine? Blaine—what's going on? Why am I tied up?"

"I'm not entirely sure," her sister murmured. Saeran locked eyes with her, pleading without words for her to get her out of this. The hope was a dying one, though Blaine did step farther into the room. Why would she help Saeran, after trying to kill her? The hemlock came back to mind and she shuddered, trying to kick out her feet.

Nothing. Tied down just like the rest of her.

"Gwen, get me damn knife. Aurick, please leave. Make sure Gwen stays with you."

"No, I want to see this—"

"Gwen. Do not make me repeat myself." She sounded like the exact same Blaine as before, but there was a sternness to her voice, a firmness that struck Saeran as odd. She was…calm, in way. Like Blaine was not surprised this was happening.

"On second thought, Aurick get the dirk. Hurry."

Once the door was closed, Saeran spoke, "Blaine, what is going on?"

"Well," her sister said, a look of distaste spreading over her face. "I didn't expect Gwen to go through such dramatics over bringing you here, first off. Second, I think you have an idea. I know you've been snooping around—or at least trying to. You've done a poor job of it, really." Her laugh was genuine. No malice, no bitterness. It was as if they were actual sisters again.

A cold ache spread through Saeran.

The door popped open, and Aurick handed Blaine the knife.

"Thank you," she murmured. The door closed, and she came up to Saeran, holding the knife. Her eyes widened, and panic spread through her.

"Blaine, what are you—"

"Saeran, please be quiet until I'm done. Really, I'm not going to cut you into pieces." She proved that to Saeran by slicing through the ropes, both on her hands and feet. She even went as far as to help Saeran sit down. She must have moved too fast, because her abdomen rebelled. "What's wrong? You're pale."

"I hurt…" She recalled the last time she'd told Blaine of her wound from the horse. She wouldn't care, not really. Better to keep silent and keep her unaware of Saeran's weakness.

"You hurt, what?" Blaine's face was a mask as she reached out, taking Saeran by the shoulder. "Tell me. Did Kane hurt you? What— Saeran, God. You're bleeding."

She watched in mute amazement as Blaine ran away from the table she'd been tied to, searching frantically for a cloth. She dipped it into the basin. Saeran became aware of her surroundings as a trickle of blood slid down her stomach. They were in a small wooden room with two windows. There was a chair, table, and a bed. A water basin and a tub. It was like a house, all crammed into one. She glanced at the windows, feeling…odd. Like this was surreal. Her sister came back and forced her to lay back, gently dabbing away the blood.

"What happened to you?" she whispered, glancing up at Saeran. She was too shocked to speak. This was a side she'd never seen of her sister. It was like she actually…cared. Her mouth started moving before she could stop it.

"The battle that Kane dragged me off to—the MacLeod chased me down after he saw I killed his son and—"

"You killed his son?"

"I—yes," she whispered, finding no way around the truth of it.

Blaine's hands turned even more tender, their movements slowing, as she wiped the rest of the blood away. For whatever reason, tears welled in her eyes. She couldn't explain it. Blaine was being more kind to her than she had in all the years of her life.

"But how did this happen?" Blaine asked, a look of pain crossing her face. She looked like she felt the wound on herself from the look in her eyes.

"He tried to kill me. Kane distracted him enough that his sword didn't go through my stomach, just skimmed my abdomen."

"This isn't a 'skim', Saeran," she said tightly. She shoved herself away from the table, cursing. "I warned him. I warned that bastard about hurting you. I should kill him—"

"What are you talking about?"

Blaine looked at her over her shoulder. "The MacLeod. I told him that if a finger was laid on you, I would kill him. He didn't take me seriously. It's his funeral."

"I—I'm having a hard time following this," Saeran said. In truth, she was. Her sister had been trying to kill her with hemlock, and now she was going to kill the man who had harmed her? It was so out of the blue that Saeran was struggling to wrap her head around it.

Blaine sighed, sad and low, and sat down beside Saeran. She looked at Blaine, noticing things she would rather not have. Her hair wasn't powdered, but black and lifeless around her shoulders. Her face was clear of any rouge, terribly pale, and strained. She looked...tired. Beaten. It made it hard to believe this was the woman she had betrayed for Kane. It made it hard to believe that this was the woman who had tried to kill her...who was no longer her sister...

"Fear does a lot of things to people," Blaine murmured, dropping her gaze to her hands. "Makes us crazy. Makes us do things we don't comprehend until it's too late. Fear can turn into anger...jealousy...so many things.

"At first, I never *wanted* you to get hurt. I had made a mistake at court. A huge, terrible mistake and I took advantage of the opportunities it gave me." Her hand caressed her stomach, a look of longing embedded into her eyes.

"Tell me," Saeran whispered. She would no longer hate Blaine after this. As much as she wanted to, for all of the things Saeran had been put through, she couldn't. This was the real Blaine. The scared, lonely Blaine that had hidden behind a mask of hate and spitefulness. Saeran reached out, taking her hand.

Blaine held onto it like a lifeline, like she needed that hand to breathe.

"Hans found me. At court, he found me and...used me. I couldn't process your parents' deaths. I didn't know what to do or how to feel. I knew from the beginning that they weren't my true parents, but I...I loved them. When they died, it hit me hard. I couldn't show you that—I would have looked so weak. I just...Saeran." She put a hand to her face, resting her elbow on her knee. She was hunched over, looking helpless.

Saeran watched her. "What do you mean, he used you? As in...?"

"Like Kane and you, except I...I did not enjoy it. I did it purely for information, for leverage."

"Oh, God. Blaine—"

"I don't want your judgement. It helped me get to where I am now," she said, lifting her eyes to Saeran's. There was a strength in them that took her back. "I found my father through Grayham. He gave me a way to get close to him.

"I am sorry for the pain that I've caused you through my own selfishness and greed, Saeran, but I will never regret it. Not ever. It gave me a chance to learn, to understand who I am. He…helped me. I found out what happened to my mother," she whispered, tears shining in her eyes.

"I…I would like to know," Saeran said, oddly sure of that. She should suspect Blaine of using sympathy to make her defenseless, but she sensed none of that. She knew Blaine, knew her attitudes. She was genuinely opening to Saeran, and for the first time with Blaine, she was…happy. Happy that her sister was telling her all of this, even though she didn't know why.

"Your cousin, King James. My mother was his mistress. She had an affair with my father, James found out, and had her executed. He left my father alone, but…I was sent to live with you when I was six. I was forbidden to ever tell you."

"So we really *aren't* sisters," Saeran said, feeling her heart clench. The signs were there, of course. They did not resemble each other in the least, she had different parents, and their personalities were different to the point of being polar opposites. The signs were all just…there.

"No," Blaine said. She squeezed Saeran's hand. "That doesn't change the fact that I do love you, in my own twisted, terrible way."

Saeran shook her head. "Why now? Why tell me all of this now? Why show me your true self…now?"

"I tried everything I could to make you hate me. Everything I could think of."

"But why?"

"So that when the time came, and I gave you to the MacLeods, you would hate me, not mourn me. I…that is the only excuse I have for you Saeran. I wanted power. I needed it. I still do. When I became pregnant with Grayham's child, I—"

"*Pardon?*"

Pain darkened Blaine's eyes. "King James sent us from court when I came to him with news of my pregnancy. I begged him to make it look as if it were my choice, or everyone would have known.

Grayham knew, but he...wanted more than just an adopted heiress."

"Blaine, my God. Is that why you made me parade around as a lad?"

"To keep you out of my way, yes. Kane and I were going to marry, I was going to poison him, and then Grayham would take me as his wife."

"But you never...showed." There should have been signs to Blaine's pregnancy, right? A swelling in her stomach? Strange cravings?

"I lost it within the first few days of coming here. The ride was too much for my body to handle, and...Gwen helped me through it." A tear fell down her sister's cheek. Like always, though, the strong Blaine wiped it away, taking a deep, steadying breath.

"Why didn't you tell me?" Saeran choked. "I would have...I would have helped you."

"You would have looked upon me differently. You would have doted to my every need, and I was trying to make you hate me. Saeran, I..." A sob wracked her sister's hunched body. Saeran wrapped her arms around Blaine, holding her tightly. She had thought Blaine uncaring, unable to feel for anyone but herself. Now, she was seeing so much more...and she hated it. Hated how Blaine had gone through everything alone, without speaking to her.

"I had to...I had to get the baby back. Grayham would have murdered me without it, so I...I went to the MacLeod. I had to find a way to kill Kane, and as his enemy, he was...the MacLeod was perfect. I...I seduced him."

"Lord... I do not know what to say!" Saeran breathed into her sister's hair. "Were you...were you going to kill me?"

"No," Blaine said sharply, pulling away. "The plan was to kill Kane, give you to the MacLeod to appease him, and then I would marry Grayham. After that, I would kill him and take over the Shaw clan *and* the MacLeods. My father is sick, Sae," she whispered. "He's too sick, and I have to make him well. I'll have enough power in the Highlands, to give him anything he wants."

"I was just a bargaining tool," she said, numb. It made sense. She had always felt that way with Blaine, like she had no worth. Her sister felt justified in her reasoning, but...It still made Saeran sick to her stomach.

"Alasdair would have taken care of you," Blaine said firmly. "See, it's that hurt in your eyes, the betrayal, that I was trying to avoid.

I…everything was for my father. You had everything, Saeran. You had the perfect family, the beauty. Do you think, with the two of us standing side-by-side, that I had a chance to make myself stronger?"

"I was never—"

"Kane fell in love with you with one look, Saeran," she said softly. There was envy in her eyes, but it was softened by reality. "I had no chance of getting him to marry me when I knew he had found you. It was the exact reason I dressed you as a boy. Then you let yourself become involved with him…"

"How did you know?" Saeran asked, feeling guilt stab her heart.

"Many things," Blaine replied, smiling wistfully. "You were happier. Smiling more, blushing whenever you were around Kane. Then people started to notice you, Kane was speaking about you to his men, and…it just fell into place."

"And you told Kane I was having an affair with myself…"

"Yes," she said. She lowered her eyes to her lap. "I was desperate. He was not proposing to me, he was leaving the next day, and I thought…I thought that if he could cast you away, both Saeran and your counterpart, I would be able to finish the plan."

"I was never meant to be happy, was I?" Saeran whispered. Her heart cracked. Blaine had meant to destroy her, and yet…yet it had all been for a good cause. For her father. To give him the life he needed. Surely something could have been done that didn't involve Saeran being discarded like a chess piece. There could have been something else for Blaine to do. She would have found a way if she cared, right? Or had she really been driven by need and jealousy?

She stared at her sister, and found it all hard to believe. There was real guilt, real remorse. Real sadness. Her sister had been pushed into a corner and done the only thing she could.

"Saeran, I swear to you. If I had thought of a way for you and Kane to be happy, I would have left you two alone. I've only made your life hell—I know that, and I'm so sorry for it. But it had to be done. There was no time for me to think of a new plan. I had to act fast. You saw him—you saw my father, didn't you?"

She recalled the foaming man, his tremors, the deranged quality he had about him, and nodded. Blaine had done everything out of love for her father, who needed her more than Saeran did.

"I don't have much time. I just…had to tell you this before I continued. I didn't want you to die thinking that I hated you, because I never did. Ever. I might have been jealous and greedy, but I never once hated you. I tried to convince myself that I did, but it never worked. You were too kind and compassionate. Even my black heart can't hate something as pure as you."

"Die?" she echoed, meeting Blaine's eyes. There were tears in them. "You had me kidnapped so that I would die? Be killed?"

"I will do everything I can to protect you, but I—I'm with child. I am weak, and—I promise, I'll do everything I can. But you…Saeran, you killed his son. He's not going to let you get away. If I could have done something to save you, I would have. I swear. I promise on my unborn child that I would have."

Saeran stood up, hands shaking and heart falling to her stomach.

"Where is he?" she asked, voice hoarse. "Where is Alasdair MacLeod? How long—how long do I have until he's here?"

Blaine stood as well, taking her hands. Her voice was pleading when she spoke. "Saeran, you'll only enrage him if you try leaving. I can try to talk him out of it. Just please, don't try to run."

"You said yourself, he's not going to let me get away. That means I'm going to die. I can—I can find Kane. He'll fix this," she said, hysterical. "I can't—Connor said he was coming back for me. I believe Connor. I have to see Kane, he can do something about this! He can kill Alasdair."

"No," Blaine whispered, shaking her head. "He'll be here by the morrow. It's too dark to find Kane. Saeran, I wish—I had no idea he and Gwen were planning on kidnapping you. I never would have let this happen—"

The door crashed open.

By the tensing of Blaine's body, she knew something was wrong. Very, very wrong.

Chapter Forty-Two

"I'll kill you."

Grayham. Grayham was standing behind her. Slowly, feeling like her world had fallen apart, she turned on her heel. Immediately after seeing the three figures in the doorway, bile rose in her throat. Not just Grayham was standing there, but Alasdair and Gwen. The tall blonde was cowering behind the men, watching the scene with wide, nearly satisfied eyes.

Blaine took her hand, holding it in the folds of her skirts. She gracefully maneuvered herself in front of Saeran, a cool smile coming over her face. As if it had never been there, the remorse and fear cleared from her face. She saw the Blaine she had known her whole life—the haughty, impulsive woman who had too much confidence for her own shoulders.

Now, though, Saeran knew something she hadn't before.

That was not the real Blaine.

"My lords," she greeted. It was as if she didn't notice that they looked as murderous as angry bulls. Saeran tried to move back, but Blaine squeezed her hand, a silent warning. Her heart started to race, mind reeling.

"You're a god damn whore," Grayham shouted. He flew forward, his fist raised. Before she could react, Blaine threw Saeran out of the way. The only thing that saved her face from meeting the swing of his fist was the skirts that tripped her. She stumbled back, throwing her arms out to catch herself.

"There she is," Gwen said to Alasdair, pointing to Saeran. "The bitch who killed your son!'"

Like a dog who had been given a bone, Alasdair came at her.
There was no blade this time. Kane's training came to mind, and she
waited until he was almost to her. It wasn't until the last minute that
she whirled out of his way, and threw her elbow out. It caught him on
the side of his face, knocking his head to the side. That one
movement nearly brought her to her knees. The pain was drowned by
the rush of adrenaline.

She might not be as strong as him, but she did have speed and
surprise as an advantage.

Too bad for her, he recovered quickly, throwing himself at her.
He took her to the ground, his fist raised. It slammed into her jaw.
From beside her, Blaine shrieked with pure outrage. Saeran laid there,
dazed, fighting her mind's dumbfounded reaction to the hit. He came
in again, this time putting his hand on her abdomen to hold her
down, his large hand slamming into the other side of her face.

All of the knowledge she had on self-defense left her. She forgot
about Blaine, about Alasdair. The only thing she could focus on was
the black splotches entering the corners of her vision and the searing
agony rushing to the center of her body. The black dots became
cluttered, until they were completely blocking her vision.

She couldn't...pass out. Not this time. She had to fight, she had
to get them to safety. Pure determination was the only thing that gave
her the mental strength to fight off the unconsciousness. As soon as
her eyes were blinking open, a weight was lifted off of her.

A blur moved over her.

Blaine.

She had managed to throw Grayham away from her, and had
lunged for Alasdair.

"What did I tell you?" she shouted, slamming her hand at an
upward angle at his nose. He roared, falling back. "You don't touch
her. I told you, over and over again, not to touch her."

"She killed my son!" he bellowed. Saeran pushed herself weakly
to her feet, wobbling. Nay. Nay, she couldn't become weak right now.
She had...to help Blaine. A rough cry of pain escaped her lips as her
stomach twisted. He'd done more than put a hand on her, she
realized. He'd dug his fingers into the wound and pulled, worsening it.
All of the stitching that had been done was now pulled apart.

Through her pain, she became aware of the other people. Blaine
seemed to have a hold on Alasdair, but Gwen was creeping along the

way, eyes glued to Saeran. The hate in them was unlike anything she'd ever felt. Gwen darted through the fray, past a waking Grayham, and came at her.

"You stole him from me," she hissed, grabbing Saeran by her hair. "I was going to be his bride. I was going to have his children. You stole him from me."

Saeran wrapped her hands around the woman's wrists, trying to alleviate the pressure, but Gwen wrenched harder. "I don't know how I did that," she gasped.

"I was the one he loved!" she hissed. "The hemlock was for you. I was going to get rid of you and the two of us would have been happy. I heard what you two were talking about. I told Alasdair and Grayham so they would kill you, but you—but you just—"

Her angry rant cut off, and the pressure fell. Blaine stood over her, staring down at the dazed woman she'd hit. "I never liked her much," Blaine said, wiping a hand over her face. "She was always acting like a spoiled harlot."

Gwen slumped to the floor. Blaine reached down, taking Saeran's hand and pulling her to her feet. Like a mother would hold their child, Blaine brought Saeran to her chest and breathed slowly.

"We need to leave," Saeran rasped, pulling back. She thought she had the strength to hold herself up, but as she began tumbling backward, she misjudged. Blaine grabbed for her, steadying her. "Kane will—"

"It's too dark out. I'm not entirely sure where we—*Saeran*." Everything happened so fast. The only thing Saeran could register was being thrown away, into the wall, and Blaine's agonized scream. A sick, cold feeling went through her, just as a hand grabbed her, jerking her down.

Alasdair growled in her ear, "Two Sinclair bitches dead." He wrapped a around her throat, blocking her view of Blaine.

She heard the sobbing. The uncontrollable sobs—the gasps of pain. They rung in the air like a bell…then it all ended.

Nay, it didn't end. It was overcome. The unholy roar that sounded throughout the room was louder than Blaine's sobs and Saeran's gasps for air.

It was Kane.

Before the bellow had finished, Alasdair's weight was lifted, once again, from her body. She sucked in as much air as her lungs would let her, clawing at her throat. The spots were back, and no matter how hard she told herself to get rid of them, they wouldn't leave. Saeran rolled onto her side in time to see Kane throw his sword aside.

Then he lunged for Alasdair. He growled words too low for Saeran to hear, then took his uncle by the head and wrenched it to the side. The man fell lifelessly to the ground.

Kane stormed his way to her, sliding a hand under her neck. "That bastard," he growled. His eyes were trained on her cheeks and neck, and the blood staining her shirt, an even darker red than before.

"Kane," she rasped, pushing him away from her. "Kane—no."

Grayham was standing directly above him, murder in his eyes. Kane didn't react at all, except to give her a swift kiss on the lips. Then he slowly turned away from her.

As the two men stared at each other, she became aware of the silence. The dead, still silence. It wasn't the fact that Kane and Grayham weren't talking, but she couldn't hear Blaine. Hysteria wracked her just as strongly as her sobs attacked her. Using the last of her strength, she crawled her way to Blaine.

She was still. Blood was seeping from her stomach, and her eyes were dead, even though soft breaths still left her lips.

"It's gone," Blaine whispered.

"No," Saeran said, reaching for her sister with a trembling hand. Blaine only stared at it as she lay on her back, hands cover her stomach, tears streaming down her cheeks. "No, it's not. Neither are you. Blaine—"

"Saeran, don't do that. I've always hated the whining." The soft teasing was lost on her. She shook her head, gathering Blaine against her. She pushed her sister's hands aside and frantically looked around, for anything that she could use to stem the floor of blood.

"Saeran..."

"No," she snapped. "No. No this isn't—this isn't happening. I swear to God, Blaine, if you...if you die, I will—"

~

Saeran's sobbing was the only thing on his mind. Not the retribution he should be exacting for his sister's murder, but the sobbing. Grayham, the man who he had been dying to kill for ages, was now in front of him. It would take him hours to go through all the things he wanted to do to the son of a bitch for killing Annalise, but Saeran needed him. He cold-cocked the bastard and watched as he fell next to Alasdair. With a growl, he grabbed him by the head.

Just as he had done with Alasdair, he wrenched his head to the side.

He collapsed to the ground without another sound.

Dreading the sight he was going to see, he turned around—and was right. He hadn't wanted to see it. His heart shattered at the sight of Saeran, kneeling and clutching her sister.

Blaine met his eyes.

"Kane…the king lied. To you."

He froze. Her voice was raspy and weak, but he had heard the words as clear as day. He knelt beside her, wishing he knew what to do with Saeran. She was rocking and sobbing, mumbling incoherently, while Blaine had her eyes locked with his.

"The king lied about your family. They…have been dead, for a very long time." Blood started to seep out of the corner of her mouth.

"Nay, they—"

"Please, listen to me. The Campbells…were the ones who hunted them down and killed them. The King told me all of it. He wanted you to marry me to alleviate his guilt in all the lies he's told you."

"No, no, no," Saeran moaned, clutching her sister.

"And he wanted Saeran to be the one left to Grayham?" He ignored Saeran, furious and hurting. Some part of him had known, in the back of his head, that there was no way his family could still be alive.

"Yes. He…didn't know of my plan to kill you. But Kane…You must protect Saeran. You cannot let her be on her own. She needs…you."

"I need you," Saeran cried, her frail body shuddering. Blaine's glassy eyes roamed over her sister's face.

"Just…take care of my father. That's all I ask. You can hate me all you want, but he's an innocent. He's old…he needs help."

Saeran's sobbing grew louder, until it was ringing in his ears. "Kane, don't let her go—don't let her—she can't. She's not…she…I know the real her. She needs to stay alive. Her bairn—"

"Love…" He took her arm, gently pulling her back. Her tears were ripping him apart, and there was nothing he could do. Her bloodied hands pushed him away. She was inconsolable, and he well understood the loss she was feeling.

"I'm sorry…"

"No," Saeran screamed. The sound ripped through the room as

surely as her heart was tearing in two. "No, please. Blaine—Blaine, I love you. Don't leave me—no, no, no," she moaned. "You can't go. You can't. No."

She took her sister's hand, holding it to her heart. Kane grit his teeth together, turning his head away. Nothing would make this better for Saeran, and he couldn't watch her destroy herself. It wasn't until Blaine's wheezing breath ceased that Saeran collapsed against his chest.

The terrible, gut-wrenching sound that left Saeran's throat killed him…but it was all over. As he stared around him, taking in the bodies of the men who would have killed his woman and he, Kane realized that it was all over.

All. Over.

Chapter Forty-Three

Several moons later

"The MacLeods are starting to move onto your land. Without permission." Brodrick leaned against the cool stone keep, next to Kane. He'd been out here for the last hour, watching the blonde beauty effortlessly lead a black beast in circles.

"Aye," he said absently, distracted by the sight of his woman. God, she had flourished in the past two moons. Ever since she had shared her news with him, the depression had gradually left her. This was the first time in weeks she had laughed and played in the sun, the first time she had actually enjoyed herself, and he didn't want it to end.

"Let them? Kane. They could start a revolt."

"Aye."

"Yer not even paying attention."

"Aye."

"*Kane.*"

"Aye."

"Listen for a moment, would you?" Brodrick elbowed him in the gut, giving Kane no choice but to look at his long-time friend. "Do ye' no' think this could be a problem?"

"Nay. I donna. I heard ye' the first time ye' mentioned it. Can ye' shut yer mouth and let me enjoy my wife?"

"Yer not even the slightest worried."

"Nay, damnit. They have no one to take over the clan that has a backbone. Of course they'd give their fealty to me."

"Aye, but Saeran killed their heir. What if they want revenge? Could ye' stop staring at her for a second to think about the important things?"

Kane turned and gave Brodrick a hard look. "I'm going to say this once, and then the matter is dropped. She's finally enjoying herself, and I'd like to witness it without all this bullshite. From what I understand, the man was horrible. No one liked his son, or Alasdair himself. I told Connor to greet all of them when they come. They are welcome. They donna have a chieftain, Brodrick. Not even a feasible one willing to step up! They're going to go to the next strongest clan. Let them be. Now, let me watch my woman."

He turned back to watching Saeran, who was laughing as brightly as the sun, while Brodrick huffed. "Fine, but when ye' have yer daughters being courted by MacLeods... Some weak grandsons yer going to have."

After another huff, he turned on his heel, stomping away. Kane knew he wasn't that angry over the merging of clans. Nay, he was more upset that Kane had been spending all of his time with Saeran, and not having their manly "my wife is a chit" talk, like he had expected.

Honestly, there was nothing for Kane to complain about when it came to Saeran. Aye, she'd had some problems lately. After their wedding ceremony a fortnight ago, she had retreated into herself. He had rarely seen her lately. She was in mourning over her sister, which was understandable, but she was also beginning to find joy in life again. Her news, and what it had meant for the clan, had brought her back to the realm of the living and he couldn't be more grateful.

"Kane!" she shouted, drawing his attention. He smiled, pushing himself away from the stone wall. "Come, look at what I've taught him to do!"

As he came closer, he noticed that she was...that she was mounting the horse. She was mounting the damn beast that had hurt her those many moons ago, and there wasn't an ounce of fear in her.

"Saeran," he bellowed, fear striking him. "Saeran, donna—"

"Watch!"

Oh, he was watching all right. Watching with his jaw to the floor, fear for her life flooding him. The horse was antsy under her, pawing at the ground with a black hoof. He burst into a dead run as the horse began to rear.

He swore he was going to faint, until he got a look at his wife's face. The pure, radiating joy as she held onto the horse's mane gripped his heart like a vice, wrenching it.

"Saeran, I swear to God—"

"He's not going to hurt me," she said, laughing. "Watch him!"

As if knowing he had an audience now, the horse reared completely, front hooves in the air, the back ones planted firmly in the ground.

Then there was Saeran.

His squealing, laughing, and ecstatic wife, with one arm in the air, the other holding herself to the beast. Black and blonde mixed in silken waves—and then they were racing. Kane's heart seemed to stop in his chest as the beast carried her away from him. It was only the sound of her carefree laughter that kept him on his feet.

She was riding one of the most dangerous animals in the Highlands, when only seven moons ago, she hadn't been able to mount him, and she looked gorgeous while doing it. Pride for his woman soared through his chest, and didn't cease until she was back in front of him, riding astride the beast while moving in perfect harmony.

"You told me to train him, did you not?" She gave him the cheekiest grin he'd ever seen from her. He ruefully shook his head. He reached for her waist, letting her lush body slide against his own as he set her on the ground. The beast pranced in happy circles.

Kane pulled her flush against him, wrapping his arms around her waist. Lord, but to see the brightness of her was like an aphrodisiac. He could get lost in her if he let himself. Kane leaned forward, brushing his cheek against her own.

"Just a warning for ye', lass." He pressed his lips to her temple. A pleased sigh left her lips.

"Aye?"

"If ye' ever do anything as dangerous again as that, I'll be spankin' ye' till morning."

She leaned back, giving him a sultry smile and trailing a finger down his shoulder. He felt his cock harden instantly.

"What if I told you that I've been riding him since last week? Does that mean you'll have me locked up in your room for a week?"

He growled, threading his hand in her hair. She willingly tilted her head back, pressing her breasts into his chest. The arousal worsened.

"For a full moon," he whispered. He took her lips with his own and groaned. Her delicate arms came up, wrapping around his neck, securing herself against him. He growled with approval, dragging her closer.

He swiped his tongue over her lower lip, urging her to open wider, to let him take her mouth completely. She complied with a small, airy moan, and then he lost it, just like he always did whenever he tasted her.

"Kane?"

He ignored the voice of his squire, kissing his wife until she was breathless.

"Kane, honestly?" A hand tugged at his shoulder and he pulled away from Saeran with a snarl. Her lips were swollen, cheeks flushed. Pleased. Aye, he was pleased—or he would be, if he hadn't been interrupted.

He turned and landed a glare on Connor. The lad's cheeks were just as red as Saeran's. "I...ah. The king is here. King James. He...wanted to speak to you."

That stopped him in his tracks.

"Where?" Saeran demanded.

"In the courtyard—"

Saeran breezed past him, running to the courtyard. Kane followed after her without a word, leaving poor Connor trying to catch up to him. By the time he had made it through the throng of people crowding to view the king, he didn't have time to stop her fist from driving into the king's face.

The silence in the courtyard was terrible. As the king's guards began to circle her, swords drawn, Kane became lightheaded. His bonny lass was going to forever get herself into trouble, wasn't she? he thought numbly, watching as the king's head slowly righted itself. That imperial gaze stayed on Saeran, but she didn't fidget or apologize. She met him gaze for gaze, until he finally lowered his.

There was a collective sigh in the courtyard.

"I deserved that," he murmured, lifting a hand to rub his jaw.

"You're lucky you have guards here, or you would have a lot worse done to you than an aching jaw," she said fiercely. *God*, lass, would ye' shut yer mouth before ye' get yerself killed?

The people in the courtyard tensed.

"Lower your weapons," he commanded, giving Saeran a warning glance. They lowered.

"What are you doing here?" There was nothing but hate in her voice. The king's eyes narrowed on her.

"I came to see how my cousins were fairing," he replied smoothly, smiling at her. "I haven't heard from anyone in so long, you know." He gave Kane a glare, one that said this was all his fault. "Where is Blaine? I sent for her, but no one has returned my calling.

"I wonder why?" Saeran snapped, practically spitting the words.

He frowned. Kane came forward, putting an arm around his wife's shoulders, a hand over her mouth. She didn't even fight him over it. Good lass. She didn't have a death wish, then.

King James looked between the two of them, obviously noticing the way Saeran's body curled into his, the way she let him keep his hand on her, his protective stance. A look came over his face.

"Were you not betrothed to Blaine? I received a message."

Saeran trembled against him. She yanked his hand away and spat, "Blaine is dead."

King James froze. "Blaine is…dead?"

"Seven months ago. Grayham killed her and her unborn child."

"I…I had no idea."

Kane pressed his lips, curling his arm around his wife's waist to hold her still. He could feel the rage boiling under her skin and knew that if he didn't do something to hold her back, she'd find herself at the gallows.

"I bet you didn't," she snapped. "If Your Highness is done here, we are too full to allow guests." One of the greatest disrespects to a king and Saeran didn't care. Going by the look on James's face, he understood full well that he was being kicked off the land.

Kane was surprised when none of the guards made a move against her, but even more surprised when the king willingly urged his party out.

"We will need to speak privately about this—"

"There is nothing to speak on. Blaine is dead. Grayham is dead. Alasdair is dead. The MacLeod clan has agreed unanimously to join the Shaw clan and there is finally peace. My *husband* and I are content without your interference."

James looked at Kane as if he couldn't believe he was letting Saeran speak to him like that.

He shrugged. Truthfully, he was as angry with the bastard as she was. Not only had the King ruined his family, but he'd been as deceitful as a rat. The sooner the pompous ass was off his lands, the happier he would be.

Fortunately, he left without another word. Saeran's furious, crystalline eyes met his. "We will never allow anyone of our lineage to be named James. Ever."

"Aye, my love," he murmured.

"And if he ever comes back here, he is to know he is not welcome."

"Aye, my love."

"And if he ever tries to send for us, I want you to send him a pile of horse manure in return. In fact, I want you to send him a large pile of Patrick's manure with a note letting him know that the shite on his lap is that of the prized beast he sent you."

"Aye, my love," he said, chuckling. Saeran tucked her head under his chin, putting her arms around his waist. The people in the courtyard gradually left, disappointed with the loss of drama.

"I just want the day to be over," she whispered.

"Is our little bairn making you hungry?" At the mention of their unborn child, some of the earlier light returned to her eyes, and he couldn't help but smile in response. They had figured out a few months ago that Saeran's infertility had been another one of Blaine's lies. It had become evident when two full moons passed without her monthly bleeding, when the vomiting had woken her up every morning, and when certain smells sent her into a dizzy-spell.

Saeran patted her stomach, letting her fingers caress the soft swelling, and smiled up at him. "Aye, I think he is, but his mother isn't hungry for just food…"

Kane laughed, picking her up in a swift movement, and began walking to the entrance of their home. They had no clue whether it was a girl or boy, and wouldn't until it arrived, but Saeran had told him that calling the bairn an "it" was impersonal and rude.

"My bonny wife, I do love you… But what if we are having a girl?"

"Well, I will be happy with either," she conceded. "Although I would much like a lad to name Alan."

"Aye," he murmured, thinking of the surprisingly kind-hearted man who had passed away several weeks ago. When Saeran had met him that first time, it had been because of a herb the village had him on. In his final months, he had been taken off the medicine and had a chance to be lucid. He really had been an amazing man, for the short amount of time they knew him. "He would have liked that too, love."

"I agree. Do you think Connor will take care of Patrick for me?

334

I don't think I'll be riding him much after that," she said ruefully, smiling up at him innocently.

He stopped in the middle of carrying her. "What's wrong? Are ye' in pain? Where do ye' hurt, lass? Should I call the healer—"

"No, no… Don't do anything of the sort." The innocence in her eyes turned to mischievousness. "I do believe I need a full-body inspection from my husband, though, just to make sure that all is well."

Kane gave her a dubious look.

She leaned up, kissing him on the jaw and whispering, "I just want my highlander's touch all over me."

Kane couldn't get to their room quickly enough.

ABOUT THE AUTHOR

D.K. Combs has been writing since she was fourteen. She first fell in love after reading historical romances, and it turned into a dirty habit. Eventually, she had to write one for herself. Her writing has branched into several other genres, such as paranormal, fantasy, and contemporary. She spends her days with her son and her German Shepherd. Her husband and mother are two of her greatest supporters. When she's not writing, she's either reading, at the dog park, or connecting with her fans. To see more of her works, go to Amazon.com/author/dkcombs.

Printed in Great Britain
by Amazon

70572697R00193